I0819052

Praise for *The Hope Keeper*

"No one writes resourceful women like Heather Webb. Her latest historical heroine is budding jewelry designer Elisabeth Beaumont, reeling from the recent death of her twin brother and desperate to shore up the family jewelry business in post–World War I Washington, DC. Elisabeth courts the patronage of mercurial socialite Evalyn McLean, owner of the famous blue Hope Diamond, and finds herself swept into Evalyn's intoxicating world of parties, jewels, and secrets. But the Hope Diamond is rumored to be cursed, and as bad luck mounts all around Evalyn, Elisabeth is forced to reckon with the possibility that the curse may have deadly implications for her own family. *The Hope Keeper* sparkles, just like the gem at its heart."

—Kate Quinn, *New York Times* bestselling author

"Webb's latest sparkles with intrigue as jewelry designer Elisabeth Beaumont delves into the secrets of the wealthy wives of Washington, DC, desperate to expose the truth behind a family tragedy. Richly imagined and hauntingly beautiful, the story will linger long after you've turned the last page."

—Fiona Davis, *New York Times* bestselling author of *The Stolen Queen*

"Glittering with history, mystery, glamour, and legend, *The Hope Keeper* follows a young jeweler drawn to the allure of the Hope Diamond and its rumored curse. Rich in historical detail and heart, this gripping story of family, courage, and secrets is an absolute must read."

—Madeline Martin, *New York Times* bestselling author of *The Secret Book Society*

"Historical fiction powerhouse Heather Webb plunges readers into the high-stakes world of precious jewels and the rarefied company of those who collect and trade in such treasure. Told through the voice of the young jeweler Elisabeth Beaumont, this is a story of family secrets, second chances, and the fabled curse of the incomparable Hope Diamond. Webb's writing sparkles as her plucky, intrepid heroine cuts through the tangled and toxic world of the rich and the reckless in order to redeem her past and save her family's future."

—Allison Pataki, *New York Times* bestselling author of *It Girl*

"Heather Webb crafts worlds that are so lush and immersive it makes me believe time travel may be possible. Her latest masterpiece, *The Hope Keeper,* is instantly transportive, swiftly tangling readers in the Gatsby-esque world of 1919 Washington, DC, and the mystery, lore, and magnetism surrounding one of history's most celebrated—and feared—gemstones, the Hope Diamond. I read this book in one sitting and know without a doubt that *The Hope Keeper* will be the must-read book of summer."

—Joy Callaway, international bestselling
author of *The Star of Camp Greene*

Praise for *Queens of London*

"Looting, lying, and the letter of the law: *Queens of London* delivers a rollicking ride through the criminal underbelly of post–World War I London. Gritty at times and tender at others, *Queens of London* unmasks the most lawless—and likable—gang of women you've never heard of."

—Sarah Penner, *New York Times* bestselling
author of *The Lost Apothecary*

"Webb lures readers into a page-turning, high-stakes game of cat and mouse in her latest historical novel, *Queens of London.* When Lilian Wyles, one of the first female police officers at Scotland Yard, crosses paths with Alice Diamond, queen of the all-female crime syndicate the Forty Elephants, neither woman will stop until they achieve their own forms of 'justice.' But what neither Lilian nor Alice realizes is that there's more to justice than meets the eye, and in a world disinclined toward women like them, they must redefine loyalty and fairness to prevail. Compelling and suspenseful."

—Marie Benedict, *New York Times* bestselling author

"Heather Webb returns with this compelling glimpse into London's underworld in the 1920s. Readers will cheer for Lilian's straight-arrow ambition, Hira's innocent desperation, and Dorothy's generous spirit. Add in Diamond Annie's criminal intrigue, and Webb is able to weave a rich tapestry of women's lives in the early twentieth century. Webb's storytelling shines, culminating in a fast-paced chase and a deeply gratifying finale."

—Stephanie Dray, *New York Times* bestselling author

"Strong women, ripped-from-the-headlines history, and page-turning suspense in a rich setting, *Queens of London* grabbed me and would not let me go. From the opening salvo, Webb spins an atmospheric and heart-thumping journey into the heart of 1920s London. In these pages, we meet Diamond Annie, the head of an all-girl gang, and Lilian Wyles, one of England's first female detectives, as they each try to outwit the other to survive. With a cast of vibrant and witty wisecracking women and an orphan who might upend it all, this novel will keep you guessing (and holding your breath) until the last satisfying page. Known for her immersive historical fiction, Heather Webb has done it again and better than ever!"

—Patti Callahan Henry, *New York Times* bestselling
author of *The Secret Book of Flora Lea*

"An action-packed story full of glamour and danger, *Queens of London* transports readers into London's criminal world where Diamond Annie rules as queen and Officer Lilian Wyles is the only woman cunning enough to stop her. A gritty, glittering addition to any reader's shelf."

—Julia Kelly, international bestselling author
of *The Last Garden in England*

"Three unique but disparate women and a young orphan are brought together by love, loyalty, and crime in 1920s London. With highly engaging characters and vivid peeks into the secret haunts of history, *Queens of London* is a fascinating and cleverly rendered story of resilience and determination that kept me reading long into the night."

—Shelley Noble, *New York Times* bestselling author of *The Tiffany Girls*

"Diamond Annie is a true original—a heroine who is tough, feisty, and handy with a blade yet also capable of compassion, even if it's against her better judgment. *Queens of London* captures the stench and squalor of Elephant and Castle in the 1920s, in contrast to the glitter and fragrance of the new department stores in the West End. The dialogue is as sharp as Annie's blade, and the plot as fast-paced as her 'Elephants' fleeing after a heist. It's an unforgettable story of vulnerable but resourceful women finding ways to survive and thrive in a world where the odds are heavily stacked against them."

—Gill Paul, *USA Today* bestselling author of *A Beautiful Rival*

"Four fascinating characters whose lives intertwine to create one page-turner of a novel, *Queens of London* is an absorbing tale of three women and a young girl who take charge of their lives and excel at their chosen professions. Still, when those lives collide, you'll never forget Alice, Lilian, Dorothy, or Hira and the choices they make. Set in 1920s London, the novel's action revolves around the infamous Forty Elephants, a gang of female thieves who robbed London's best high-end department stores—led by Diamond Annie, a.k.a. Alice. The tale of a lady detective, an honorable thief, a department store clerk, and an orphan in Webb's skilled hands will keep you reading until the wee hours. A must read."

—Denny S. Bryce, bestselling author of *Wild Women and the Blues*

Praise for *The Next Ship Home*

"*The Next Ship Home* is a wonderfully immersive novel that kept me engrossed from the first page to the last. Through a seamless tale of immigrants, corruption, resilience, and hope, Webb illuminates a dark side of America too often lost to history. An important, timely read featuring a cast I loved to root for."

—Kristina McMorris, *New York Times* bestselling author of *Sold on a Monday*

"With meticulous research and deft prose, Heather Webb crafts an unflinching look at the immigrant experience, an unlikely and unique friendship, and a resonant story of female empowerment. *The Next Ship Home* is truly a beautiful and powerful book."

—Pam Jenoff, *New York Times* bestselling author of *The Woman with the Blue Star*

"Powerful and poignant, *The Next Ship Home* shines a literary light on Ellis Island's dark history, where the prejudices of the past often sit uncomfortably close to the present. Writing with a clear passion for the subject matter, Webb captures the injustices, suffering, hope, and determination of a generation of immigrants. Francesca and Alma roar from the page and leave the reader caring for them deeply. A richly imagined novel and a must read for fans of historical fiction. Brava!"

—Hazel Gaynor, *New York Times* bestselling author of *When We Were Young & Brave*

"A touching and intimate story of two very different young women who join forces in turn-of-the-century New York City to overcome the odds. As a longtime fan of Heather Webb's novels, I found *The Next Ship Home* to be her most accomplished and emotionally compelling book to date. The insightful historical details delving into the Ellis Island immigrations process make this novel essential reading for anyone yearning to understand the roots of the American experience. Highly recommended."

—Kris Waldherr, author of *The Lost History of Dreams*

"Centered around Ellis Island—symbol of America's greatest hopes and scene of some of her greatest travesties—*The Next Ship Home* is the heart-wrenching story of two young women fighting for freedom and independence. In this timely and utterly immersive story, Webb unflinchingly exposes the prejudice, sexism, and corruption rampant within the immigration system of the times while still weaving in hope that we can do and be better."

—Kerry Anne King, bestselling author of *Whisper Me This* and *Everything You Are*

"*The Next Ship Home* is one of the rare stories that will nestle itself in your soul and make a home there. Heather Webb creates two remarkable, endearing heroines that you will root for from beginning to end. Her depiction of Ellis Island and turn-of-the-century New York is lush with meticulously researched detail. But most striking, Webb tackles the thorny and complex issues of immigration and workers' rights with sensitivity and grace. Her message is compassionate and timely, and I was blown away by how deftly Webb weaves it through Alma and Francesca's stories. *The Next Ship Home* deserves a place as one of the great books of the American experience."

—Aimie K. Runyan, international bestselling author of *Across the Winding River* and *Daughters of the Night Sky*

"Reading this story is like stepping back in time to the gut-churning experience of arriving at Ellis Island in 1902 and being willing to do anything for a shot at a fresh start in a new country. The vivid historical details, the fascinating setting, and the tenacity of this book's main characters kept me thoroughly engaged from start to finish. *The Next Ship Home* serves as a powerful and humbling reminder about the courage it takes to start over."

—Elise Hooper, author of *Fast Girls* and *Angels of the Pacific*

Also by Heather Webb

Queens of London
The Next Ship Home
Strangers in the Night
The Phantom's Apprentice
Rodin's Lover
Becoming Josephine
Christmas with the Queen
Three Words for Goodbye
Meet Me in Monaco
Last Christmas in Paris
Ribbons of Scarlet

THE HOPE KEEPER

A NOVEL

HEATHER WEBB

Cover design by Sarah Horgan
Cover images © Ildiko Neer/Trevillion Images, Mrs.Moon/Shutterstock, Elena Zaretskaya/Getty Images, Sittipol sukuna/Shutterstock, createvil/Shutterstock, Calvinda Risky Adiputra/Shutterstock, mouu007/Shutterstock
Internal images © arivana ningsih/Getty Images, Seydoux/Getty Images

Published by Sourcebooks Landmark, an imprint of Sourcebooks
1935 Brookdale RD, Naperville, IL 60563-2773
(630) 961-3900
sourcebooks.com

Library of Congress Cataloging-in-Publication Data

Names: Webb, Heather, author
Title: The hope keeper : a novel / Heather Webb.
Description: Naperville, IL : Sourcebooks Landmark, 2026.
Identifiers: LCCN 2025042728 | trade paperback | epub
Subjects: LCGFT: Novels
Classification: LCC PS3623.E3917 H67 2026 | DDC 813/.54--dc23/eng/20250926
LC record available at https://lccn.loc.gov/2025042728

Printed and bound in the United States of America.
PAH 10 9 8 7 6 5 4 3 2 1

For all the little girls who filled their pockets
with pretty rocks and nature's treasures

"The most precious thing about stones in a jewel box is not always their rarity, their size, or their perfection. It is their stories."

—**Victoria Finlay,**
Jewels: A Secret History

"The wound is the place where the light enters."

—**Coleman Barks,**
The Essential Rumi

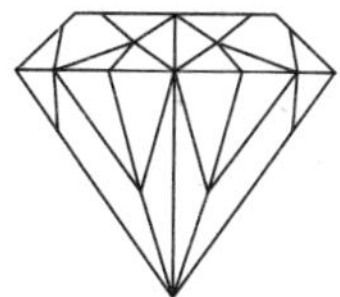

I am born of fire and earth.

Pressed for millions of years, I remain hidden until a single moment when I am swept up by gold-red spirals of heat. I burst forth into the air suddenly, violently, thrust into a world I do not know of light and air. After, I lie in wait for him to find me. I do not count days or years; I do not measure time, for I am immortal.

One day, the trajectory of my existence shifts, and all is set into motion.

A tool chips away layers of rock until I am found, cradled by careful brown hands, and slipped into the soft, muted darkness of a leather pouch. I am thrust again into the light sometime later, passed from one pair of hands to another, prodded and examined, shaved and polished, until it appears I please him. Only, my keeper's countrymen do not want me. They see bad luck in my unusual color, and despite my undeniable beauty, I am traded to the keeper who will carry me to a new land.

Once again, I lie in wait for what is next. For the lives I will forever change, for I am a symbol of power. And what is more seductive than power?

Some say my fate was predetermined. Unusual, special. I am a talisman, a keeper of secrets, my dark-blue depths a well of misfortune, or so it is said. But perhaps you should read on. Perhaps you should decide the truth for yourself.

1

They say the Hope Diamond is cursed.

I didn't believe in curses, or that was what I told myself as I stood on the curb in McPherson Square outside the sprawling McLean mansion in one of the most fashionable neighborhoods in the nation's capital. I shifted from one foot to the other as traffic whizzed around me and stared at the redbrick home spanning a third of a city block. I'd read about homes like these, driven or walked past them, but I'd never seen a marbled vestibule that echoed with each step, sat in a drawing room decorated with a master artist's paintings and chandeliers made of crystal imported from somewhere in eastern Europe. I'd never smelled the mingled scent of Moroccan leather and fine tobacco or felt a velvet-soft Turkish carpet beneath my toes. Such luxuries were reserved for the likes of the women I would not and could not ever be. They were reserved for the likes of Evalyn McLean.

A passing car honked, startling me from my thoughts. It was now or never. My pulse thrummed in my ears as I crossed the street and strode along the front walk to the door. I didn't have time to consider whether I should stay or flee, back to the safety of my workshop and cozy redbrick home across town in the neighborhood where I'd lived my whole life.

The door whisked open in an instant.

•

A rather short, stout butler with eyebrows raised in a question stood before me in pristine black-and-white livery. "Good afternoon. How may I help you?"

"I'm Elisabeth Beaumont," I said, clasping my handbag a little more tightly. "With Beaumont Jewelers. I believe I am expected." I wasn't expected, but showing up unannounced didn't open doors on this side of town.

"Wait here a moment, won't you please." He closed the door, leaving me on a narrow stoop.

I rehearsed the lines I'd practiced in my head a thousand times already. Gérard Beaumont, my father and my boss, was unwell and had sent me in his stead.

The door opened again. "Mrs. McLean will see you in the drawing room. Follow me."

As I stepped over the threshold, someone shouted, "Careful!"

I leapt out of the way as two servants hefted an enormous rug rolled into a tight tube over their shoulders and staggered under its weight across the foyer. An equally harried maid pushed a shiny new Hoover vacuum cleaner after them.

"Look out below!" a young boy shouted from the top of a staircase before barreling down the stairs with all the manners of a baboon.

A woman dressed like the butler, who was likely the nanny, clambered after him. "Vinnie!" she shrieked. "You come back here right now!"

The little boy had to be Mrs. McLean's son. He raced through the hall and a nearby doorway without so much as pausing, his laughter and whoops of glee echoing in the vast cavern of the seemingly endless rooms. The sensation of stepping into the middle of a play—an actor without lines and without direction—swept over me, and suddenly I wished I hadn't come.

The butler noticed my awkwardness. "You'll have to forgive us, ma'am. We're hosting a party this evening, so we're attending to some last-minute chores."

I imagined the diplomats, politicians, and tycoons who'd likely been invited to the party. Perhaps even the president and his wife would be in attendance. Evalyn McLean knew everyone who mattered, and her parties were legendary. I'd heard she hosted thousands of guests every year and spent tens of thousands of dollars on making each experience unforgettable. It helped that both her maiden name and married name were known all over town and beyond.

We passed a handful of guards and wound through a series of immaculate rooms and finally stopped in a drawing room decorated with an array of luxurious wooden and silk furnishings. Antique lamps stood prettily on end tables that flanked the sofa, and a large potted palm tree posed as a centerpiece beneath a magnificent skylight made of stained glass. I was shown to a chair and offered a refreshment that I refused. I wasn't interested in food or drink. My appetite had shriveled since the accident months before and had yet to return. My usually voluptuous frame had grown thin, my face wan, the shine of my pin-straight hair dull. All color and sensation had drained from my world that horrible, fateful day.

"Mrs. McLean will be with you in a moment."

I sat on the edge of the sofa cushion, restraining my natural inclination to fidget, forcing myself to appear as if I were confident.

I shouldn't be here.

A woman dressed in the now-familiar uniform appeared, pushing a tea cart. "Would you care for tea and cake, ma'am? Or lemonade?"

Again, I refused. I wanted to meet Mrs. McLean briefly, to introduce myself, to appeal to her to rehire Beaumont Jewelers and be on my way. It was getting on in the day. I'd nearly lost my nerve and had let the hours slip from morning to late afternoon as I'd listlessly cleaned the workshop, sweeping, stowing tools, and organizing our book of receipts. By three o'clock, I'd finally accepted that I couldn't put off the house call any longer. With Father unable to work, our bills had begun to pile up with nary a commission in sight. Beaumont Jewelers was near to closing for good, and everything we'd worked for would be lost, our home included. At least this was the lie I'd told myself, but I knew the truth. I could approach a number of wealthy women who would entertain my request for work or clamor after a new beautiful piece from my father's workshop, but there was only one place I could go for answers. Answers to the searing questions I could no longer ignore. I squeezed my eyes closed against the rush of instant emotion and the desperation that had suffocated my days and dominated my nights.

When minutes turned to half an hour, my unease propelled me upright onto my feet to walk around the large room. I pretended to admire the tapestries and porcelain trinkets and the exquisite carvings in the wood paneling, but the truth was my eyes roamed over the beautiful things without really seeing them. Movement in the doorway drew my gaze; one of the guards I'd seen in the front hall was watching me. What was this world of valets and butlers, maids and hired guards?

When I was certain I'd been forgotten, the stout butler from earlier returned, followed—at last—by his mistress.

"Mrs. McLean, may I introduce Miss Elisabeth Beaumont of Beaumont Jewelers," he announced.

Forgetting my manners, I didn't offer a polite greeting but simply stared at the most renowned socialite in Washington. Evalyn McLean was stunning in long white gloves and a navy, floor-length gown with a drop waist, covered in glittering beads. I took in her ivory skin and bee-stung lips, her dark curls pinned in an elegant chignon. Though not beautiful, there was something attractive about her presence and demeanor. More distinctly, she was wealthy as sin, so her assets were enhanced to their fullest potential with creams and powders and fine clothing. Her most striking feature was her clear, curious blue eyes framed by a quizzical brow as black as coal. My gaze dropped lower, to a pair of perfect collarbones and another of the reasons I'd dared to pay her a visit: the Hope Diamond.

If legend was to be believed, the most notorious gem in the world brought bad luck to those who owned it. Perhaps even to those who merely looked upon it. Father had forbidden our family from working for the McLeans for that very reason—to steer clear of the diamond and all within its orbit. Though I'd always teased Father about his silly superstitions and the "feelings" he had about potential clients, his intuitive notions had proved correct more than once, the most terrible among them that night six months ago.

I shouldn't be here.

And yet I couldn't tear my gaze from the diamond. The awe-inspiring blue gemstone was nestled in a cradle of bright, cushion-cut diamonds of the finest clarity and dangled from a necklace composed of equally perfect diamonds. Mesmerized, I stared at the piece with wolfish intensity. The stone was darker than I'd imagined, a deep-sea blue tinged with steel. It didn't seem evil—it was exquisite—and I longed to touch it. To feel its heft in the palm of my hand, to slide it beneath my magnifier and turn it this way and that while I counted its facets and searched for flashes of red hidden within its depths.

I wanted to search it for answers. Was everything they said about the stone true? Perhaps this object of desire, beauty, and bad luck truly was responsible, at least in part, for the incessant ache in my chest as I lay awake in bed each night.

"Why, you're a woman," Evalyn said, surprise lifting her voice into a question. "I was expecting someone else. A man in fact. Was it Pierre? Or Julien maybe. Something French."

I froze at the mention of his name. Felt myself hurtling back in time to when all had been good and right in the world, and it seemed as if I'd had my whole life before me. Now, I hovered somewhere between waking and oblivion, a mere shadow without solid form behind it.

When Evalyn's expression turned to one of impatience, I blinked. "Yes, ma'am." I cleared my throat. "That is to say, my father is Gérard Beaumont. Your jeweler, ma'am." I left out the part about Julien accompanying him and his short-lived time as her employee. I couldn't bear to say his name aloud.

She frowned. "Your father never returned my call. That was months ago now."

I nodded. "Yes, I apologize for that and for the surprise visit here today. My father has taken ill. I hope you won't mind working with a woman in his stead. I know it's untraditional—"

She held up her gloved hand. "I'll stop you there. This world is modernizing after all, and it's high time women do as they wish. Isn't that right?"

I warmed to her words. If she only knew how often I'd been denied or pushed aside at festivals and showrooms. Women were to wear jewelry, not design it or—God forbid—make it. They simply didn't have the skills or the strength to hammer metals or solder or use heavy tools. Thankfully my immigrant father wasn't so traditional in that sense; he'd never believed a person's sex determined their abilities. He'd always been my champion. But he would never champion this—a reunion with the McLeans. For once, though, my dear father didn't have a say in the matter.

"Yes, ma'am," I replied. "I design jewelry as well as maintain collections. Should we work together, I'd clean and polish each piece in your collection. Examine the prongs to make sure the stones are secure. If you had questions or needed advice about purchasing a new piece, I would also be on retainer for your needs."

Evalyn peered at me, taking in my clothes, my hair, my features before speaking. "I don't keep my collection here. We only use this house for serious entertaining. Speaking of which, I really should get back to it. I'll have guests arriving soon. It was nice to meet you, Miss Beaumont."

I gripped my handbag more tightly. She was already sending me on my way. We'd lost our chance to remain her designated jeweler when Father didn't show to his appointment or reply to Evalyn's inquiries months ago. But I had to try again—even if the curse was real, even if the Hope Diamond had everything to do with our sorrow. I needed to know what happened the night of the accident and the weeks leading up to it. In my gut, I knew my brother's death had something to do with this family and their friends with whom he'd done business for months. I only hoped learning the truth would silence the nightmares, the resentment, the fathomless well of loss.

First, I had to convince Evalyn that my services were indispensable.

"We could set a schedule to meet as often as you'd like," I said, my desperation bubbling to the surface. "I'd be available to you at a moment's notice. We're also working on a new collection that I'd be delighted to share with you in an exclusive showing before it is open to the public." A lie of sorts, but I knew the wealthy expected to be treated differently, special, as if their money placed them above everyone else.

Her smile had edges. "I'll be in touch should the need arise." Without hesitation, she swished away in a sparkling blur.

As I met the butler's gaze, I felt my face fall. His eyes were contrite. I guessed he knew all too well what it was to be at the mercy of the McLeans' whims.

"Right this way, Miss Beaumont," he said.

A pit formed in my stomach as I left. Nothing awaited me at home but an evening of vast emptiness.

The early part of the evening I spent stewing, wishing for a different outcome to my visit to the McLeans' home. I stared up at the fat orange moon beckoning me as if I were under a spell, the tapping of the oak branch at my window interrupting the slurry of my thoughts and the muted color of my evening. I pictured the diamond and the curse itself, its slippery tendrils wrapping around my wrists and tugging me toward the great rare stone I so longed to touch. I wondered if it was too late for me as well, if I, too, would face some unexpected dark fate. I didn't know, couldn't see the future. I only knew one thing: My beloved twin brother had once worked for Evalyn McLean, and he was dead. I had no choice but to put myself directly into the stone's dark orbit and risk everything I had left in this world.

As a new plan sparked to life, I pushed aside my dinner of congealed potatoes and cold fish, collected my father's sketchbook from the workshop, and pulled on my coat. Soon, I'd made my way through town across the grassy square to the very spot where I'd stood only hours before, as if some inner engine had fueled my movement. I paused as I faced the McLean house. Nearly every window glowed, and a steady parade of people floated across the front walk or stepped out of their Model Ts and streamed to the door. The guests were glamorous in their smoking jackets and cravats, their shimmering silk gowns and glittering hair barrettes, laughing politely, gripping their cigarettes with long, lean fingers.

I hesitated, unsure of how to proceed, once again standing on the edge of a world as foreign as the moon. My gaze flicked to the moisture pearled on the tender grass of the narrow lawn, reflecting moonlight like a thousand tiny gems. Time unspooled in the shadows beneath the canopy of trees where I stood unseen, unmoving, unfeeling, until a cool breeze nipped at my cheeks and pulled me back into my body where unwelcome sensations awaited me. A persistent awareness that something, or rather someone, was missing.

As a peal of laughter drifted toward me, I ran my fingers through my hair. Did I dare disrupt their evening, attend an exclusive formal event without invitation when Evalyn had already turned me away? As an older gentleman with a crown of snow-white hair was escorted to a waiting car, an image of my father came to mind: him bent over a gold brooch, pliers in hand, followed by one of him in bed, listless, unable to face the day, and I crossed the street without pause. I was here for him, for us.

Like before, I was greeted politely at the door, but my name wasn't on the guest list, and I was asked to wait. When the butler had gone, I ignored his order and rushed inside, heart pounding. I darted through a set of French doors and followed the music and din of voices to a ballroom with burnished oak floors and candlelight, a stretch of windows on the east wall, and clusters of terrifyingly elegant men and women who were enjoying the party. An enchanting scene, I had the feeling of being somewhere far from Washington, DC, far, even, from America.

As I filtered through the crowd, some of the guests threw curious glances my way. Who was this woman in plain dress and coat, nose pink with exertion, and dark windswept hair? I was so very unlike them all. And I was a fool for returning during a party when I'd already been turned away. I chided myself as I realized I could have waited a day or two. And yet my instincts had told me otherwise. To return that night, to catch Evalyn off guard, to tempt her with something beautiful, this was the key. For there was one thing I knew about her already in my short time inside the mansion among her extravagant things: Her love of beauty and the desire to possess it trumped all.

"Care for a glass, ma'am?" A waiter held a tray of crystal glasses filled with effervescent liquid. Champagne. I'd never tasted it before and was suddenly tempted to try it, to pretend I was made for such elegance.

I shook my head. "No, thank you."

I retreated to the farthest corner of the room to search for Evalyn—and to hide from the butler who would escort me out if he found me. I only needed a few moments to speak to Evalyn again and show her my father's sketches. Perhaps I might persuade her to give me a chance.

For some time, I watched the elite in their finery float across the floor, mingling as the staff attended to everyone like a flurry of worker bees. I caught sight of Evalyn several times in the midst of what appeared to be impassioned conversations, her face changing only when a staff member approached and skittered away quickly, as if doing their best not to impede their mistress in her fun. Or perhaps they fled for other reasons I didn't yet understand.

As murmurings came from a quiet alcove on my right, I turned to see two figures in a heated discussion. Without warning, the man took the woman in his arms and kissed her. She gasped and pulled away, and they both laughed softly. I wondered who they were. They didn't behave like husband and wife, long married. Not that I'd had much experience with men outside of friendship. I was far too busy working, too devoted to the family business and to my stone collection and books, to consider men of any import. Except for one.

I shuttered the thought of Henry Cooper and the piercing stab of regret immediately. What was once between us was over now.

"Here all alone?" I jumped and turned toward the sound of the voice.

A man of average height and build with dark hair and mustache held a highball glass with a generous pour. His elegant tuxedo made me aware, once again, of my modest appearance.

"I don't know anyone. I–I wasn't invited," I admitted. "To the party, I mean."

He smiled, a crooked thing that I supposed could be charming. Perhaps it was. "You look like the kind of girl we need more of around here. Come, let's get you a glass of something. A side car, perhaps? Gin and tonic? And there's always champagne."

"Ned?" A voice I vaguely recognized drifted toward us. "Where did you get off to?" Evalyn McLean walked toward him with a staccato rhythm.

I hadn't noticed her limp before and wondered if she'd been born with it or if she'd injured herself. I'd been too in awe of her elegance that afternoon—and the Hope Diamond around her neck—to notice it earlier. Instantly, my eyes sought the stone as if drawn by a magnet. And there it was again. This time, the diamond looked midnight blue in the candlelight.

"What is it?" the man named Ned replied. "I was just offering our guest a drink."

"John Whitehall is looking for you." Evalyn glanced at me. "Wait a minute, aren't you that jeweler?" Her tone was gay, and she held one of the beautiful coupe glasses of champagne that I'd rejected. She jerked her hand to her lips too quickly, splashing the sparkling wine on her glove. Her eyelids were heavy, her pupils dilated, leaving little room for doubt that she was enjoying the party. "Elisabeth, was it?"

"Yes, ma'am."

"What are you doing here, young lady?" she said and giggled at the faux-stern tone she'd taken with me. "Lord, I sound like my mother."

She hiccuped and giggled again. "We'll call you Lizzie, and you will call me Evie. And this is Ned, my husband."

Ned was actually Edward McLean, owner of the *Washington Post*, the *Cincinnati Enquirer*, and the *New York Morning Journal*. I remembered reading about him when his father had passed away. Ned had inherited the family businesses. If rumor was to be believed, he ran them rather poorly.

"Hello, sir. Mrs. McLean, if I may show you something? I've brought a sketch to share with you of a stunning necklace I think you'll love. I—"

"Ned, John's waiting." Evalyn interrupted me without preamble.

"It's nice to meet you, Lizzie." He smiled again. "I'd better see what John wants. If you'll excuse me." He snaked through the guests until he disappeared from sight.

A servant approached, consternation stamped on his brow. "Ma'am, the champagne has gotten warm. Should we refresh the ice bath, or did you have something else in mind?"

His southern drawl was thicker than most of those who lived in the DC area. He'd likely come from the hills of Virginia. I wasn't certain where I'd come from—I'd never known my mother or the small town in northern France where I was born. All I knew was that my father had immigrated to America, carrying his children through Ellis Island and onward to Washington, to go as far from the memory of his lost wife as possible and, I learned later, to put as much distance as possible between him and the Cartiers, the family who dominated the jewelry market, in Paris and New York City.

"The Moët?" Evalyn asked.

"Yes, ma'am, and the Dom Pérignon," the servant said. "There are eight opened bottles left."

"Pour it down the drain," she replied. I didn't realize my eyes had widened until she laughed. "Appalling, isn't it? All that liquid gold ruined. But that's the beauty of champagne. When it's first opened, it sparkles over the tongue like fireworks, but the fizz doesn't last so you can't hesitate, or the moment is lost."

I thought of all the moments I'd lost these past months and the hundreds of future moments I would never have with Julien. And yet I couldn't accept that my twin brother was gone for good.

"Goodness, here," Evalyn said. "Have a sip of mine. You look like you could use a drink." Her tone was jaunty, her eyes bright. She didn't seem to mind that I was a virtual stranger, and her snub from earlier seemed entirely forgotten. She'd also said nothing about the sketch.

"Ma'am, I'd really like to show you a one-of-a-kind piece my father designed. It's so unique, I thought only one woman should own such a necklace." I watched as she fingered the Hope Diamond at her neck. She didn't need a unique necklace; she had one. Inwardly, I berated myself for the blunder but continued anyway. "Ma'am, I know that my father didn't return your call, but he's ill and we'd value your business tremendously." I held out the sketch of a masterful rendering of an opal and diamond necklace.

"Don't call me ma'am," she corrected me. "Call me Evie. And let's not speak of business tonight. We're at a party!" She sipped from her glass and grinned. "Ah, that is better."

"Why don't I leave the sketch with you so you may look at it another time?" Offering my father's designs was a gamble. He would have my head if he knew I offered to leave his precious compilation of drawings, especially should the book go missing by accident or be discarded. But it was a risk I was willing to take.

"You're awfully persistent, aren't you? Maybe your father should have sent you to do the work in the first place." She read my expression and laughed. "Don't look so forlorn, darling! How about I call you tomorrow. Leave your first and last name and your address with Jerry on your way out. We'll talk then." She flagged down a member of her staff. "Jerry, bring Lizzie a pen and paper and a drink. She looks parched. Now, no more talk of business tonight. Enjoy the party," she said, sauntering away.

Relief crashed over me. She was giving me an opening at least, and I wouldn't have to leave Father's drawings behind.

"I see you've found your way to the party after all," Jerry said curtly.

"I'm sorry, sir. Really I am, but I am desperate for the work."

His round face softened into an almost smile. "It's wise you returned during a party. She's always in good spirits when her house is full of people. And persistence with the mistress often pays off."

"Thank you," I said with sincerity.

"Now that you're a guest, what may I bring you, ma'am?"

"It's kind of you to offer, but I'll leave my information with you and be on my way," I said, my eyes following Evalyn's form as she stopped briefly to speak to a guest. She clinked her glass against the woman's and they both laughed.

"All right, ma'am," Jerry said. "In that case, let me show you out."

As he escorted me to the door, something stirred in my chest. A sensation I thought I'd never feel again. One treacherous autumn night six months ago, I'd fallen into a chasm so deep, the light in my world had diffused until I could no longer see. But as I walked away from the McLean mansion for the second time that day, a tiny fleck of hope glimmered in the darkness.

2

Evalyn McLean didn't call the next day or the next week. I made excuses for her at first, assumed she'd had too much champagne the night of her party or had talked with so many guests that she didn't remember our conversation or me. In the end, I decided she'd made a promise she'd never planned to keep. Why should she go out of her way for a woman far below her station and a stranger at that? And who could say what inspired the whims of the wealthy? They lived by their own set of rules, and the rest of us were made to pay for them. And yet I had to find a way in, if not to work for Evalyn, perhaps for one of her friends. I might still learn the truth of what Julien had been doing all those weeks. But who to approach and how? I didn't know Evalyn's friends personally. I'd have to do some research, inquire about them through existing Beaumont clients.

I looked out at the quiet rain pattering softly against the windowpane and beyond where rivers of bright-yellow pollen streamed into the street drains. First a Christmas without Julien, and now a colorful, rain-soaked spring. Sighing, I rose from my dressing table and extinguished the lamp. Though the rain suited my mood and the lethargy that came with it, I had to work. With a very real need for new commissions to satisfy the bank and ward off foreclosure of our three-story home and storefront in Logan Circle, I'd need to put in long hours to finish my father's abandoned pieces. I'd also need to attend jewelry shows and house parties, reach out to some other socialites in the city to solicit business.

In the workshop, I switched on a series of lamps and reached for my father's ledger. Rifling through the pages, I cross-referenced delivery dates with the progress of various pieces he'd either begun or had planned to do but had never finished. I flipped open his sketchbook and studied his creations that scrawled across the pages. They were beautiful, intricate, and always unique. I turned to the last sketch, still unfinished. Father hadn't touched a single project in months, not even to fix a clasp on a necklace or replace a diamond stud in a lorgnette. Only in recent weeks had I managed to shake the weight of my own lethargy.

I'd done my best to fill the outstanding orders for the company, delivering repaired necklace chains and polished stones with newly tightened prongs, and finishing outstanding commissions. We'd worked too hard on the Beaumont name, building our client list and our reputation, to allow it to languish now, despite all that had happened. But nearly all had been finished and delivered, and the remaining pieces were already paid for, in full. We needed to design new jewelry, to advertise, to sell. The enormity of the undertaking—which I must do alone—left me sagging in my chair.

I forced myself up to the telephone, prepared to call each of our previous clients to "check in on their satisfaction with a piece" as a guise to offer appointments for future visits to the Beaumont boutique. Few answered their telephones, and not a single client booked an appointment, so I set about writing greeting cards with our logo and posting them to everyone on our roster. Someone would come through—they had to, or...I didn't want to think about the alternative.

A knock at the workshop door startled me from my thoughts. I drew the drapes aside from the window and watched Henry Cooper fidget with a bouquet of scarlet tulips in his hands. I took in his pinstriped suit, auburn hair combed neatly away from his forehead, and gray-green eyes trained on the door. The desire to stroke the soft mound of his cheek hit me with a violence I didn't expect, and I leaned against the doorframe for support. What was he doing here? I hadn't seen him in months, and it was better that way. He could move on with his life, and I could try to make it through each day without reminding myself to breathe.

When I let the drapes sweep back over the window, he knocked again. What could I possibly say to him? The familiar self-loathing I'd grappled with these past six months rose to the surface with a vengeance. If he'd treated me the way I had treated him since Julien's death… A pang of guilt prompted me to open the door.

"Henry, what are you doing here?"

"Can I come in?"

"I don't think that's a good idea."

When he sighed heavily, I stepped aside, allowing him to push past me.

"Did you work today?" he asked softly. "On your sketches."

I shook my head. "I don't have the energy." The truth was I'd abandoned my own designs completely. I knew my brother wouldn't want that for me, but I couldn't seem to muster the strength to care about the collection I'd told myself I'd always wanted to create.

"I miss him, too," Henry said.

"I know." I looked down at the pearled skin of a long, thin scar I'd inflicted on myself with a jeweler's awl on the nights when I felt I couldn't go on. I tugged my sleeve over it, too late.

Henry reached for my hand, cradled it in his as he pushed the cotton cuff of my blouse aside. He gently traced the row of flesh that had once been a wound, opened over and over again. "Oh, Elisabeth," he breathed.

I met his eyes. Pain swam in their gray depths, and I quickly glanced away. Guilt rushed to the surface again. Every time I looked at him, I remembered that night, how it was our fault that Julien was killed. If we'd only been with him when we said we'd be, we could have saved him. I'd wished for a million things since that night that could never be, and I didn't know how to move on with Henry or with anyone. I'd simply disappeared after Julien's funeral, retreated from the world, Henry included. I couldn't do anything, be anything, for anyone, not even for myself. Henry might have been Julien's best friend, but Julien was my twin brother, a missing organ, a part of me in a way that few could understand.

"Why don't we go to the Tidal Basin," Henry said. "See the cherry blossoms. They're nearly at their peak, and you look as if you could use a break."

It was one of our favorite places to walk in the city. Seven years before, the mayor of Tokyo had donated three thousand Japanese cherry trees to the American people as a sign of friendship. The First Lady, Mrs. Taft, had listened to the advice of Eliza Scidmore, famed travel writer and admirer of the magnificent trees, and ordered the first saplings be planted in a show of gratitude and solidarity with the Japanese. Now the trees thrived, and a riot of pink blossoms joyfully erupted every spring in Potomac Park, drawing visitors from all over for a week or two. They'd inspired me to sketch a pretty little choker, a diadem, and a bracelet that I'd always hoped would become a part of the Elisabeth Beaumont collection. Now I wasn't certain I liked them, or my talents, or anything at all.

"Come, it will be good for you to see something beautiful," Henry insisted. "Maybe it will inspire you."

I hesitated. I'd declined every invitation that had come my way for months, Henry's included, unable to face the dizzying questions, the condolences, and most of all the eyes that shone with pity that meant nothing and everything. I couldn't face Henry or the need in his eyes. All the words never spoken and the feelings never fully realized between us hovered like a specter.

"I can't, Henry."

His face crumpled. "Why won't you let me console you? We can find solace in each other. We both lost him, and I feel like I'm losing you, too. I miss you, Elisabeth."

I didn't know what to say, how to feel, who to be. I didn't know who I was without Julien, and I wasn't convinced Henry knew who I was without him either. So I stared back at him blankly, a face so familiar and so dear, and said the only thing that came to mind.

"I have to go. Goodbye, Henry."

His eyes glinted with disappointment and frustration, but he didn't plead again; he simply left.

Heart heavy, I closed the door behind him and turned the lock.

After Henry's visit, I couldn't focus on the work that needed to be done. At last I gave up and warmed a bowl of clear soup, fresh bread, and a cup of coffee, arranged it on a tray, and carried it to my father's room.

I knocked on his bedroom door. "It's me."

"Come in." He was sitting up in bed, staring blankly at the wall. His rotund middle had deflated entirely, my robust father withered to a ghost of himself. I'd brought in the doctor on multiple occasions, only to be reassured that he wasn't physically ill in any way, and there was nothing to be done but wait. To hope and pray my father would awaken from his reverie of grief and be himself again. I knew the truth: Neither of us would ever be the same again. But I also knew we had to try, to pretend until the motions became less forced.

"Here we are," I said, setting the tray down on his bedside table. "You need to eat, at least a little."

His gaze remained fixed on an indistinct point of the powder-blue wallpaper. "The commission that Julien sold to Rosalee Smith...you know the one?" he said. "The design I made? Have you finished it yet?"

I stiffened at Julien's name, as I'd come to do every time someone said it aloud. What was more, I was surprised by Father's interest in the business. He hadn't mentioned a word about it in all these months, and suddenly he wanted to discuss one of our client's commissions? Mrs. Smith had commissioned the earrings last fall, and she'd been waiting for them ever since. I was doing my best to finish the delicate gold filigree webbing my father had started, but gold of that nature was so soft, it was easier to snap the pieces than it was to bend them. Though logically I knew my skills were nearly as good as my father's, it was his confidence and his creativity, his ingenuity, that I lacked. Perhaps it was something a person grew into, or perhaps my deficiency came from years of being excluded by a society not interested in women's work. Maybe I wasn't as good at jewelry-making as I'd always been told. Maybe I didn't care.

I looked at my father, a diminutive figure of the larger-than-life man I'd always known, and tried to find a way to respond to his request, to reassure him that everything would be all right with the commission and his business, even without his only son and heir. That our home wasn't about to be seized by the bank and everything we'd worked for reduced to nothing. That eventually, I'd finish the Rosalee commission, but it wouldn't help us with our bills because she'd already paid for them.

Words failed me.

"You didn't answer me," he said. "Is Rosalee still waiting for her commission?"

Thankfully, the brassy sound of the telephone drowned out my feeble reply. I thumped down the stairs to the old sewing table and picked up the receiver.

"Hello, Beaumont Jewelers. How may I help you?"

"Hello, is this Lizzie? I believe I promised you a call."

My grip on the receiver tightened. It was the distinctive drawl of Evalyn McLean. She'd fulfilled her promise after all. "Hello, ma'am. How nice to hear from you."

"Why don't you come for a visit, to my main house. We call it Friendship, and it's on Tenleytown Road, north of Georgetown. I have a little time this afternoon if you're free." Though presented as a suggestion, I had the distinct impression it was an order.

"I... Well, yes, ma'am. Would three o'clock suit you?"

"See you then."

Hands shaking, I scratched her address on a notepad by the telephone. I could hardly believe it. She wanted to see me, had called me to the house. A flare of hope nearly blinded me as I took the stairs by twos and returned to my father's bedroom. I immediately noticed he'd made a dent in his soup, and I said a silent prayer of thanks. He couldn't afford to lose much more weight. In fact, neither could I. I made a mental note to make myself some lunch, too.

"Who called?" he asked, resting the spoon in his bowl with a clatter.

I sidestepped his question. "I need to go out today, but the Smith earrings are nearly done. I'll be able to deliver them next week."

"Out?" His pale-blue eyes sparked with uncharacteristic interest. "Where to? Is it a new client?"

I paused, weighing what the truth might do to my fragile father. I could never be certain what his reaction might be. Since Julien's death, he was as unstable as a ship on stormy seas. At times, I'd catch glimpses of the loving, warmhearted man who'd raised me, but the smallest trigger could send him into a fit of rage. He'd curse the universe and its cruelty for taking not only his wife years ago but his son, too. Other times, he would curl into himself, not speaking for days, and I was once again left alone without him, without Julien, without anyone.

To avoid his eyes, I busied myself, tucking the blankets in around his feet. "I'm meeting with a new potential customer in Georgetown."

"Good girl. Be sure to let them know I'll be working as soon as I'm able."

I knew the subtle meaning behind his words: He wanted to assure potential customers who would not purchase a woman's work that it was, in fact, a man at the helm, and I was merely the messenger, an assistant standing in for him while he was ill. I didn't tell him it was his absence—ignoring the calls from Evalyn McLean months ago—that might have ruined our relationship with this potential customer.

"Yes, Father, I know," I said wearily.

"Who is it?" he persisted.

I couldn't tell him it was the McLeans. Their story was inexorably twined with ours in a way that would forever haunt us both, my father and me. And I wouldn't concern him with the risks I was taking by returning there.

As I fabricated a surname for an imaginary client, I headed to the bedroom door and called over my shoulder, "Please finish your lunch, Father. I'll be home this evening to look in on you."

Before he could needle me further, I closed the door behind me. And the determination I'd felt earlier returned in a welcome rush.

3

I traveled up the slippery sidewalk to the second McLean home I'd visited in the past two weeks. A wide porch ran the length of the building's facade, and window boxes burst with an assortment of happy flowers. Peeking out from the edges of their "country" home, I could see the start of an emerald lawn and magnificent garden. Though the house was large enough to call it a mansion, the energy of the McLeans' second home felt less formal, more inviting, than the monstrosity on McPherson Square. Even in the soggy weather, I saw precisely why the McLeans had named their large Georgetown estate Friendship and why they planned to spend most of their time here on Tenleytown Road.

I mounted the stairs to the porch, closed my umbrella with icy fingers, and glanced down at my stockinged feet. They were drenched from the steady rain. Given our financial status of late, I'd decided to save the taxi fare and took the tram to its farthest point instead and walked the rest of the way. Now I regretted it. I wasn't a fashionable woman by any stretch, but I knew not to arrive for an important meeting at the home of an elegant socialite looking like a drowned rat. And yet here I was at the McLeans' doorstep, having made another poor decision.

Trepidation tingled in my hands as I knocked at the door. I didn't know if I'd be cleaning Evalyn McLean's collection that day or not. I also didn't know how to handle the matter of fees and scheduling, or whether I should discuss the Hope Diamond with her. Julien had never recorded his time in the ledgers as he ought to, and I was left to piece a plan together on my own. Most of all, I was uncertain how I should speak to Evalyn. I'd made something of a mess of it before, showing up not once but twice, uninvited and unprepared, at her home on the night of one of her parties. I was lucky she would see me again at all.

I was invited inside by the same butler from before.

"I'm Jerry, ma'am, should you need anything. It's nice to see you again." His demeanor toward me had relaxed.

"And you as well," I replied, wondering why he'd changed toward me. Perhaps it was because I didn't look as if I belonged in the McLeans' world but rather more like I belonged to his. Or maybe it was because I hadn't shown up unannounced. Either way, he might make a great ally one day, should the need arise.

"Please ignore the smell of paint," he said as we threaded through the rooms. "Friendship was used as a convalescence for soldiers this past year. We've reopened the house only yesterday."

"How kind of the McLeans to open their home," I replied.

"They're a generous family," he said.

But it wasn't the odor of paint that I noticed right away; it was the squawk and chatter of birds. "Does Evalyn have birds?" I asked in surprise.

"Parrots, ma'am. Care to meet them?"

"I... Sure. Why not? I've never seen a parrot before."

He led me to a sunroom populated with beautiful wicker furniture, several potted green plants and brightly colored tropical blooms, and a large gold birdcage. "Here they are."

"Pretty girl," one of the birds said. "Pretty girl."

"Hello," I said to the pair of birds with grass-green bellies and plumes of red, black, and white feathers. As I reached toward the cage, Jerry held out his hand.

"Better not, ma'am. They bite."

"Oh!" I yanked my hand back.

"They can say ten words and a few full phrases. They're very intelligent."

"So I see," I said, marveling at yet another outcome of having too much money. One could buy anything, exotic animals included. "Thank you for showing them to me."

"Of course. Mrs. McLean is partial to animals. She has a dog named Mike, a llama, and several others. I'm sure you'll meet them in time. For now, we'd better show you to the parlor. Mrs. McLean will be waiting for you. She would have you join the others."

The others? Though I hadn't the slightest idea what he was talking about, I nodded to be agreeable and followed him as he showed me to a smaller private parlor in the farthest part of the house.

Several women were already strewn across the furniture like flower petals blown by the wind, their figures prone as if their day had been taxing. I wondered what I was interrupting and why Evalyn had invited me to join her while in the midst of a gathering. As I glanced at the impossibly stylish women, I felt myself shrink in their presence.

"May I present Miss Elisabeth Beaumont," Jerry said.

"Beaumont?" one of the women said. "As in the jewelers? I bought my favorite bracelet from Beaumont Jewelers."

"Yes, ma'am, that's us," I said with a nod, pleased our name had been recognized and that she liked our pieces.

Several of the others murmured among themselves. I tried to relax, to present a professional front.

"Jerry," Evalyn said, "do be a dear and tell George to bring the ladies our afternoon sherry. In fact, he may as well leave the bottle. Beatrice will be joining us, too, and you know how she is."

I wondered what Evalyn meant by her comment. Did Beatrice drink twice as much as everyone else, or was she insufferable and the others drank more to dull their senses around her? If Jerry knew something about his mistress's reference, he didn't show it. He was the consummate polite professional.

"Of course, ma'am." He nodded and left the room as quietly and swiftly as a ghost.

"Lizzie, darling..." Evalyn waved me forward. "Come in and have a seat." I must have looked as uncomfortable as I felt because she added, "Really, we don't bite."

The ladies tittered at her comment. I blushed and inwardly chastised myself for being so easily embarrassed.

"Ladies, this is Lizzie," Evalyn said. The ladies greeted me with a nod or polite hello but didn't rise from their chaises longues. "Lizzie, this is Rita, Sharon, Gwen, and Carrie."

Two of the women looked familiar, and I was certain I'd seen them before, perhaps at one of the jewelry shows or the bazaars. One of the two in particular caught my eye: the woman named Carrie. I racked my brain for some memory of her as I stared at the beautiful redhead, her ruby lips, the white silk that poured over her willowy frame. She held a cigarette between two fingers, and a thread of smoke snaked above her head. Boredom stamped her perfect features and vacant eyes. I came up blank, yet I couldn't ignore the echo of recognition.

Carrie noticed my stare and looked at me properly then, and I suddenly felt uneasy in her direct gaze. She was a part of the crowd, and yet she clearly stood apart from the others. Something about her expression was vulnerable: her large doe-like eyes, her soft mouth. As

I met her eyes, she looked away to the window opposite her as if she were searching for something, or someone, that wasn't there.

"Why don't you sit down and join us," Evalyn said.

Though I wanted to flee instead of making conversation with the women, I did what I was told. Remembering my posture, I sat rigidly on a chair. I couldn't imagine why Evalyn would be so open to my joining their party. We weren't friends, and I certainly wasn't of their social standing or breeding. I silenced the nagging questions in my mind; I was too glad to have been invited and more than ready to learn about the world my brother had inhabited before his death.

Everyone prattled on about the weather, a charity luncheon, and inane details about some holiday bazaar their ladies' club would be putting on in the fall. All the while, I sat quietly, hands folded in my lap, wondering if Julien had met these women, if he had sold them any of our pieces. I also wondered if Evalyn had opened her doors to him as readily and easily as she had to me. My eyes were drawn to the gregarious hostess, and I watched her as she smiled brighter than the rest, her peals of laughter inviting the others to laugh in kind. A single diamond-studded barrette held the dark hair at her temples out of her eyes, and the rest fell in soft waves to her shoulders. Her lips were shell pink, her skin luminescent against the cream silk of her day dress. Around her neck, she wore two necklaces draped in concentric loops, one a long gold chain with a locket and the other, the Hope Diamond. I watched the diamond and the locket and the way they shifted as she moved. The Hope dazzled in comparison to the lesser necklace and to every other piece of jewelry in the room. It was almost impossible to tear my gaze away.

Jerry suddenly reappeared. "Excuse me, ma'am. Ladies, may I present Mrs. Beatrice Cauldwell."

"Bea!" Evalyn exclaimed. "There you are."

Bea strode into the room confidently, wearing a printed floral skirt and oversize hat. After the sherry was poured, it wasn't long before the small party erupted into giddy laughter with Evalyn leading the charge. I didn't dare interrupt them after my antics the first time I'd met her, and yet I wondered if I'd been forgotten as I sat quiet as a cat, watching the women and their mannerisms, their tongues becoming looser as Jerry refilled the sherry. I found I didn't mind that I was invisible to them—I'd never liked being the center of attention—but I also yearned to speak with Evalyn about my services.

"Who might you be?" Bea asked at last. Her eyes raked my form, taking in my not-quite-dry stockings, the worn hem of my navy dress, and my limp hair.

"I'm Elisabeth Beaumont," I said, extending a hand, but the woman peered down at it as if I'd insulted her. I jerked it back, realizing that women of her class probably didn't shake hands. I'd been raised by a tradesman and surrounded by my brother and his male friends most of my life. What I knew about femininity and gentility was embarrassingly limited. Given that I'd always worked behind the scenes of our business as well, I hadn't had much time interacting with our nearly always affluent customers. I blushed deeply, but Bea didn't seem to notice.

She gulped down her sherry. "How did you and Evie meet? Are you a member of the ladies' club?"

Inwardly, I squirmed beneath her shrewd gaze and her pointed questions. "I'm not a member of the club. I'm a jeweler."

"A jeweler?" Her brow arched in surprise. "I didn't know women did such a thing."

"Most don't. I'm something of an anomaly."

"Has anyone offered you a sherry?" she asked. "Here." And before I could reply, she reached for a glass from a nearby tray that was filled to the brim. She grabbed another for herself while she was at it.

My eyes found Evalyn, who watched our exchange with interest.

Not in the habit of drinking in the afternoon, or ever really, I hesitated before I accepted the glass. "Thank you," I said, at least appearing to play along. I didn't care for sherry or much for alcohol in general.

"Why are you here?" Bea asked, her brown eyes filled with curiosity. "Are you going to show us some of your jewelry?"

Even I knew such direct questions were impolite. I was beginning to see why Evalyn had made the comment about Beatrice. This woman was boorish and clearly liked her drink.

"Bea, what was the name of that fellow at the yacht club?" the woman named Sharon asked, interrupting our conversation.

After another fifteen minutes of trying to catch Evalyn's eye, I finally gave up and took a sip of my sherry. Heat uncurled in my chest and crawled up my neck. I lost track of the mindless conversation and stared past the French doors at the series of enormous windows framing a lawn so beautiful, it could be a watercolor painting. Despite the rain, the garden was vibrant with pastel-pink dogwood blooms, cheerful yellow tulips, and flaming purple blooms of carefully pruned azalea bushes. My hometown put on its best show in the spring. I wished, more than anything, that I was outdoors with my umbrella, strolling through the hedgerows and around the trees lush with new leaves, rather than facing what, or rather whom, sat around me.

By the time Bea returned her attention to me, I'd emptied half of my glass. She topped me off and poured a third glass for herself.

"How did you come to work for Evie?" she said.

"I don't work for her at the moment," I said, realizing a little too late how odd that might sound.

"Well, new friends are always welcome," she replied sweetly, but her smile didn't reach her eyes.

There was something about Southern gentility that I'd never quite taken to, always felt outside of, and as I studied her expression, I knew she meant the very opposite of her alleged welcome and her feigned friendliness. I preferred her frank delivery from before.

"Lizzie, are you eager to be on your way?" Evalyn interrupted us. "I'm sure you're a busy woman and don't have time for our nonsense."

I shifted uncomfortably and set down the sherry. How could I broach the topic of business in front of everyone?

"Nonsense?" Bea said. "Speak for yourself, Evie."

Evalyn laughed.

The others laughed politely, too, but I didn't miss their thinly veiled unease at making small talk with a working woman who was clearly unlike them in every way. I was a duck in a room full of swans.

As Evalyn walked me to the door, I racked my brain for the right thing to say. To plead with her for work again might put her off me for good.

She slipped her arm through mine as if to draw me into her confidence. My gaze fell to the Hope, its glittering facets mere inches from me. How I longed to touch it, to peer into its depths, and yet the thought also did strange things to my stomach.

"Thank you for joining me today," she said, "but I feel I must be fair to you. I have met with two other jewelers, Ralph Stein and the Druskovich family."

"Of course, I understand," I replied, swallowing my disappointment. Her patronage wasn't a sure thing, and worse, Ralph was our biggest competitor. He'd called to the house many times since Julien's death to offer his assistance to Father, but I knew he was also capitalizing on our loss of visibility in the jewelry world.

"I had to speak with other jewelers, of course," Evalyn continued. "Your brother missed three appointments. Julien, was it? And your father did not return my calls. And now here we are, some months later, and they've sent sweet little Lizzie in their stead. What's this about?"

I took a deep breath and pushed out the difficult words. "I apologize for the inconvenience." I stopped, unable to continue, to say the words I was trying so desperately to avoid.

"I only employ those who are reliable," she said. "Surely you can understand that. Why, I nearly didn't call, but I'm a woman of my word."

"Julien died," I blurted. "He's my twin brother. Was. Was my twin brother. He died tragically, hit by a car. That's why he broke the appointments. And since Julien's death, my father has been bedridden."

I felt a fissure split my careful countenance, a monumental shift of something inside me. It was the first time I'd said the words aloud: Julien died. Julien *was* my twin brother. *Was.* My mouth went dry as a pulse of hot pain left me breathless. And for an instant, I relished the searing sensation. The pain was a reminder that my brother had once been here beside me and very much alive.

I squeezed my eyes closed, and the pain passed, the gray expanse of emptiness returning, echoing inside me like the lonely cry of a loon in a winter fog. It had become an all-too-familiar feeling: sleepwalking through my days as they cycled one after another, each less remarkable than the one before it. Each another day without him.

The range of emotions that played across the woman's face was painfully clear: surprise, curiosity, and worse, pity. "Oh dear," she said. "I'm so terribly sorry to hear that. He was your twin?" She gathered my hands in hers. "How tragic."

Shocked by her easy familiarity with me—and fearful a tremor would creep into my voice—my eyes fell upon the Hope Diamond once more as if it were a lodestone, a steadying point. I focused on it, drew in a breath to calm myself. As a girl, I'd learned blue diamonds were one of the rarest materials on earth: a stone made of coal pressed for millions of years, more deeply buried than the others. All blue diamonds were rare, but the Hope Diamond was the rarest among the rare. And now I was so near it, I could touch it. How often had Julien held it? I thought of the stories I'd read about the tragic deaths, the bankruptcy, and even the end of a kingdom that had come to the stone's previous owners and I shivered.

"Lizzie? Are you all right?" Evalyn asked. "Why don't you sit down a moment." She led me to a chair.

As I sat, my eyes glazed over, the room growing fuzzy, and a memory surfaced like a wrecking ball from the past.

Julien had finished his toast-and-jam breakfast in a hurry and pulled on his coat. "I've got to run. I have a meeting this morning."

"Who's the client?"

He lowered his voice. "You'll never believe this, but it's the McLeans."

My brow arched in surprise. "I thought Father didn't want us working for them."

It wasn't the McLeans our father disapproved of, though any resident of Washington, DC, had heard the stories about Mrs. McLean's wild parties and eccentric nature. It was her necklace.

He shrugged. "He's old-fashioned and superstitious. Besides, they know everyone worth knowing. It could be our big break. Might even bring us national recognition. Who knows?"

Julien had always been as ambitious as our father, so I knew there was nothing I could say to dissuade him.

"What about the curse?"

He rolled his eyes. "Do you really believe in curses?"

I shrugged. "Maybe?"

I'd never given it much thought. Curses seemed like a relic of the past. Something that outcast women from dark fairy tales inflicted upon others when things didn't go their way. I wondered briefly why the stories about curses and their origins often featured women instead of men.

"Will you work on the Hope Diamond?" I felt my eagerness ooze into my words. "I want to know everything! About her, about the necklace, about her home. Everything!"

He laughed. "You're more excited than I am."

I reveled in his warm laugh and the happy gleam in his eye. My twin brother was the sun to my moon, the charismatic, joyful half of the Beaumont siblings, while I was introspective, serious, and studious. We both knew it, and that was precisely the reason Julien had sold far more pieces than me. I could never be a salesman.

"How could I not be!" I said. "It's the Hope Diamond! But I'm sure her entire collection is incredible."

"I'm sure it is. Listen, for now, don't tell Father, all right?" he said. "He'll make me end our acquaintance, and I really do think this could be a boon for us."

"Don't worry, I won't. It'll only make him obsess about bad luck," I replied.

Gérard Beaumont was precise, neat, and clean, nearly to the point of madness, or so I secretly thought as I watched him wash and rewash his hands or use a ruler again and again to ensure he had correct measurements. If he could obsess about something, he would. It was his nature. The other larger issue was that he believed losing his wife was a stroke of bad luck, a repayment from the fates for some imagined sin he'd committed in his past. The loss of his wife had made him a more protective father than most. Should we work with a stone that was allegedly cursed, perhaps it would evoke that terrible luck again, or that was his fear. We all knew it, even without him putting his fears into words.

Julien squeezed my shoulder. "I don't want you worrying over nothing. There's no curse, so put it out of your mind."

"Of course not," I said a little defensively as I watched him disappear through the front door.

As my eyes refocused, a decorative table with an expensive ceramic vase from the Orient came sharply into view. Evalyn was studying my face. I startled at her nearness. After all the sherry she'd drunk, she didn't seem to notice.

"You must be devastated, you poor thing," she said.

I realized I hadn't heard the last few things she'd said. Numbly, I repeated, "Devastated, yes."

Some cerebral part of me knew I was devastated, but I couldn't pinpoint it, couldn't reach the recessed depths of what that meant. We were still connected, Julien and I, tethered forever, even if the thread had grown thinner, harder to see in the opaque existence that had become my life.

"Look at my manners. How atrocious!" she replied. "Let's say nothing more about it. Unless you'd like to talk about it? Sometimes it helps."

It seemed it was she who wanted to talk about it and was a little too eager at that. I shook my head. "Thank you, I'm all right."

"Why don't I ring for a refreshment. You're as pale as a ghost."

Within moments, I held a snifter of brandy in my hands.

"Drink up," she said.

As the liquor burned my throat, one of Evalyn's friends stepped into the hallway. "Everything all right?" It was the beautiful redhead, Carrie Wellington.

In no mood to pretend I felt at ease, I gulped the rest of the brandy. I needed to leave immediately. I wasn't as ready as I'd thought I was to talk about this or to be here at the place that had marked the beginning of the end for my brother. I'd have to talk business later. For now, I had to go. I stood abruptly and clutched the top of the chair as a wave of dizziness gripped me.

"Oh goodness," Evalyn said. "Let's get you home so you can rest."

"Thank you, Mrs. McLean," I replied, though I knew rest would not come. I didn't remember the last time I'd been able to quiet the tangled thoughts and memories plaguing me the moment I closed my eyes.

"It's Evie," she insisted. "And not to worry. I'll have my chauffeur drive you."

Moments later, I was pushed into a car. My head swam with confusion from the alcohol, from the memories that had resurfaced, from the awkward exchanges with Evalyn—a conversation far too personal to have with someone I'd just met, let alone a potential employer. Most of all from the weight of all those eyes upon me and their beautiful, lively smiles while my brother lay in the ground.

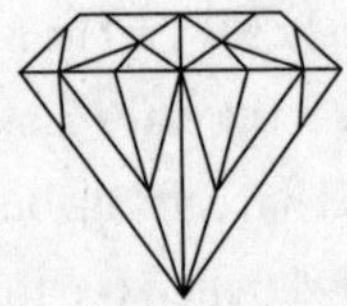

We cover ground as we travel thousands of miles from my birthplace. My keeper crosses desert and rocky terrain, tumultuous seas, watching as the skies shift and the hot winds transition to something wild and damp and green. Soon, buildings and streets made of stone arise on the horizon.

Eventually, our coach brings us through the gates of the most important man in this new land. It is here where I resurface.

"What have you?" the man demands.

"The Tavernier Blue, Your Majesty," my keeper replies.

As I am presented, there is a gasp of pleasure, or is it one of surprise?

"Let me see it!" The king takes me into his hands.

I am a mirror, reflecting a long face and nose, intelligent eyes, and dark waving hair.

"It will be the Tavernier Blue no longer," he says. "It is now the French Blue."

"The great violet diamond of His Majesty, King Louis," my keeper, Monsieur Tavernier, agrees.

I am pleased to be held in high esteem, shaped into the rough outline of a heart, set in gold and worn on a blue ribbon around the neck, or mounted on a stick. Sunrays beam into my depths, and I enchant

His Majesty and His Majesty's subjects—for a time. They do not know that which I carry; they only feel the heady spell I cast.

Though I am not living and I cannot feel or see or breathe, I can witness, and witness I do. The rise of a great château, of a remarkable king and a remarkable kingdom, and admiration for reason and power and beauty so vast, I become valued above all.

But there is a cost for such multitudes.

News of my first keeper's demise reaches the palace. His Majesty's most trusted gem merchant has died a gruesome death. And there is more. I witness misfortune passed down from His Majesty to grandson and great-grandson. I witness need so pervasive, its violence brings down a kingdom.

Mankind always forgets one very important thing, you see. To possess is to be possessed. And power is an illusion.

As the country burns, whispers arise again of the darkness I carry, and I am buried once more, hidden away until I shall show my lustrous face again.

4

I buried my face in my hands as I rode home from Evalyn's, mortified I'd behaved as I had. It seemed my father wasn't the only one who was fragile. I hadn't managed to secure another meeting with Evalyn or talk about a schedule of any kind. I also hadn't discovered a single thing about Julien's time at the McLeans' save the fact that he'd sold several of our pieces to Evalyn's friends, and they all recognized our name.

Once the chauffeur dropped me at home, I slipped out of my still-damp clothes. Stomach churning from the alcohol I wasn't used to drinking, I took some bicarbonate of soda and wandered into the workshop barefoot, my nightgown billowing around my legs. The rain brought chilly spring temperatures, and had I been a child, my father would have scolded me for walking through the workshop without shoes. But I wasn't a child, and my father wasn't here beside me. He was gone, retreated into the corners of his mind, and I was alone. More alone than I ever thought possible.

I drifted from workstation to station like a ghost, floating aimlessly, the day replaying through my mind. The women draped over the furniture in their jewels and dresses, more beautiful than anything I'd ever seen, cheeks flushed from the sherry. I could still feel their stares upon me as they evaluated me, weighing my worth and excluding me from their conversations. I cringed at the humiliation of nearly fainting and the shock of speaking so openly about Julien. Unsettled, I scoured the floors and windows and tidied the two workstations, each fit with a floor lamp and table, a jewelry saw, pliers of various sizes, a file and buffing rags, as well as an open-flame jeweler's lamp and a mounted magnifying glass for peering carefully at our works in progress. I did a sweep over the station with a metal roller comprised of a crank and a system of gears, used to compress and flatten molten metal. After, I cleaned the area around the soldering station and organized the rolltop desk and its dozens of locked wooden drawers where ring mounts, gemstone dust, webbed gold, necklace chains, and lockets were categorized and stored.

When I was satisfied my mind had quieted, I sat in the worn armchair and leaned my head against the cushion. In an instant, I saw Julien's crooked smile, the mischief that danced in his eyes—and then flashes of that terrible night. The car screeching away in the dark. An image of his broken body. The blood and the confusion of what came next. And the small crack in my composure that had opened for the first time that day widened another inch. My heart beat raggedly in my chest, my eyes burned, and I jumped to my feet, shoving down the dark that roared inside me. I paced, stroking the scar on my hand until my heartbeat ebbed into a steady, softer rhythm.

Perhaps I shouldn't be pursuing work with Evalyn after all. Perhaps I shouldn't be seeking the truth about the hit-and-run that killed my brother. It had been ruled an accident after all, even if the coward who'd hit him had left him there without stopping, without making sure Julien was all right. I shook my head. It didn't matter if his death was an accident. I had to understand what he was doing all those weeks he was mostly absent from the workshop. Why he'd spent so much time at the McLeans and, most of all, why he'd become so agitated and erratic those final weeks before his death. My instincts told me there was more to understand, that the moment he'd begun work for the McLeans, his fate had been sealed. If I was wrong and my time at the McLeans' was a waste of time—an unnecessary risk to my own safety—at least I'd know the truth.

I inhaled a deep breath and opened the sketchbook I'd abandoned months ago. I sifted through the my drawings, some fully formed and others too ambitious so they'd been forgotten. When I neared the end, a large, well-shaded sketch of the Hope Diamond filled the page. The diamond looked more oblong on the page than it was in person, but the necklace itself was surprisingly accurate. As a girl, Father had taken me on his knee nightly, told me many stories from his home in France and stories about famous gemstones. The Hope Diamond had captured my imagination. What could a curse mean after all, and who would be brave enough to wear the stone? I'd longed to meet such a person. I'd never seen myself as brave, but I wanted to be that kind of woman.

I reread my notes about the diamond in the margins. The stone had belonged to a French gem merchant named Tavernier in the seventeenth century and was originally 112 carats. At the time, its cobalt hue was considered bad luck in India, so the merchant easily acquired the diamond for a bargain and carried it back to France where it was sold to King Louis XIV, forever famous for his love of power and beauty.

I turned the page, reading on, realizing I'd forgotten how much of an interest I'd taken in the stone before Julien had met the McLeans. I knew a bit about King Louis XIV; he was something of a favorite of Father's. The Sun King had been ahead of his time, using collected tax money to distribute an allotment of food for all in his kingdom, including the poor. He also loved gemstones and art and his beloved Versailles with its vast gardens. He valued reason and knowledge in a way that had never been seen in a French monarch. The classical period, they'd called it. Though Father was an ardent citizen of the Republic, he admired those qualities in the long-deceased king. I remembered Father remarking on the fervor the stone had created when it had arrived in the kingdom, showcasing some of the first brilliant cuts ever made to a gemstone.

It was a story that Father had loved and had retold many times, his voice hushed.

"A jeweler is a storyteller, *chérie*," he'd say. "This is what gives the stone its true value. The wearer becomes a part of that story and sees a reflection of the person they long to be in a gem's facets."

It was my father's love of story that had sparked his interest and his superstition around many famous gemstones from the Koh-i-Noor to the Black Prince's Ruby. But his heritage as an ardent Frenchman put the Hope Diamond at the center of his fascination and imagination, as did its legendary curse.

I wondered what secrets the Hope held and where it had disappeared to during those two decades after it was stolen from France during the Revolution. I traced the sketch with my fingertip, picturing the diamond at Evalyn's neck, and wondered if she believed in the curse. My disquiet returning, I flipped to a clean page and chronicled all that had happened that day: the names of the women I'd met, their appearance, their jewelry, and anything I remembered from their snippets of conversation, Evalyn included. One day soon, the information might be useful.

One day soon, I'd find a way to see Evalyn McLean and the Hope Diamond again.

5

I dreamed about dark things coming for me: things I couldn't see, shapes shifting around me in a swirl of forest green and midnight blue until I was plunged into a dark body of water. I awoke in my bed, the back of my nightgown soaked with sweat, my hair wild around my face. Julien's broken body flashed again before my eyes. So often I had seen it, so omnipresent was the vision of my beloved twin, that it was startling when it was gone. And yet the next day dawned crisp and bright, as if my dreams had never been.

After a scalding cup of coffee and a hot bath, I pulled on my coat, ready for some fresh air to clear my head. I was restless, needed space to think, but as I reached for the door handle, the telephone rang.

"Is this Miss Elisabeth Beaumont?" A man's voice came over the line.

"Speaking," I replied.

"Hello, I'm Bradford Jones with Planters Bank and Trust. I'd like to speak to you about your outstanding balance here at the bank. Do you have a moment?"

My heart leapt into my throat. "I… No, I was just on my way out. Another time, perhaps."

"I'm afraid it can't wait, ma'am."

I slammed down the telephone.

I ripped open the front door and dashed outside, as if Bradford Jones hadn't been on the telephone but was standing in my front hall and I must flee. What were we going to do? I had to pressure Evalyn to commit somehow. At the moment, she and her friends were my best hope of making some initial payments on our debt. Flustered and anxious, I walked swiftly to the streetcar line and rode it through various neighborhoods and parks as I racked my brain about what to do next, how to entice Evalyn to choose us over the other two jewelers.

Eventually I found myself in front of one of my favorite places in Washington, the National Museum, the main branch of the fast-growing Smithsonian Institution. The museum had been closed to the public the past two years and used for a makeshift office for the Bureau of War Risk Insurance during the Great War. It had only recently reopened. Wandering through the museum's magnificent halls had always put things into perspective for me. As I read about evolution of the natural world and peered at a huge range of specimens, my problems shrank, and I was reminded that I was but one organism in a vast and complex harmony of life, struggle, and death.

I headed inside and inhaled the smell of clean, cool marble. My neck craned to take in the vaulted dome ceiling that echoed with every footstep, every hushed comment or titter of laughter. It was early, the museum was nearly empty, and I roamed among the variety of exhibits in solitude.

Was he here, I wondered, working in one of the many private workshop rooms where the incoming specimens were cleaned and positioned according to a meticulous plan? Henry had begun law school like his father before him, only to eschew the plan entirely for his passion: historian and museum curator for the Smithsonian Institution. I'd admired that in Henry. His courage and the quiet, steady way he moved toward what he wanted. We'd always seen eye to eye in our passion for the museum, in the way it preserved and displayed the world's wonders so others might learn about them, too. Our discussions of history and science were the only time we'd left Julien on the outside of our tightly knit trio. While my brother was busy helping Father charm potential buyers, Henry and I lost ourselves talking about his latest collection of artifacts and discussing the details of the coming exhibits. We pontificated about nature's many miracles and what it must be like as a mineralogist roaming the globe for the next spectacular, undiscovered stone. Something I'd only been able to dream about from the corner of our little workshop. Henry had a brilliant mind that was thrilling to watch in action, and at one time, I knew he saw me in the same light. I wondered what he thought of me now, after shutting him out completely.

A docent spotted me and walked in my direction. It was Ronnie, a congenial gentleman close to my father's age who knew the museum's exhibits as well as the archivists, historians, and scientists. We'd had a few conversations on the quieter days when I'd found myself in the museum seeking comfort and inspiration, or while I was waiting for Henry.

"How are you, Elisabeth?" Ronnie said. "I read about Julien in the paper. I was sorry to hear it. He was a good man."

I hated this part, crossing paths with those who'd known my brother and felt it necessary to offer their condolences. And what did those condolences truly mean anyway? What could they change? I didn't want them, couldn't stomach the mostly sincere but insufficient words and gestures. Still, I knew Ronnie meant to be kind, so I forced words around the instant lump in my throat. "Thanks, Ronnie. I was just going to visit the Hall of Gems."

"Ah yes, of course." He offered a faint smile. "If you need company, I'll be at my post on the first floor by the front booth." His astute ability to gauge when to come to someone's aid and when to let them be was my favorite thing about Ronnie.

"Thank you." I hesitated. "Is he here?"

"Mr. Cooper?"

"Henry, yes."

He shook his head. "Not today. He's probably in the field."

In the field was code for assessing a recent donation or acquisition. Henry spent a good deal of his time assessing new potential exhibits. The Smithsonian's Board of Regents and its patrons were encouraging an expansion in their collection, and it seemed there were more specimens and materials arriving all the time. Though I'd avoided Henry for months, I felt oddly disappointed he wasn't there. Silly, really, when I could stop by his house at any time. Silly, too, when I'd turned him away only days before.

"Would you like me to leave a message for you?" Ronnie asked.

I shook my head. "No, thank you. I'll see him another time."

As I made my way through the Hall of Gems, I browsed crystal formations that looked as if they were from alien planets, stones with layer upon layer of ancient sands, mud, and compressed animal remains, shattuckite formed from secondary minerals in the vast rocky soils of Arizona, and magnificent Australian black opals. I imagined the adventure in searching for the minerals, the challenges with bringing them to display, and felt a surge of envy. I moved on, perusing the emerald and ruby diadems that had once belonged to monarchs, the garnet and sapphire brooches and rings, and the range of other jewelry pieces that had once graced the collections of the world's wealthiest people.

I thought of Evalyn and her collection and wondered what she would do with it when she eventually passed. I assumed her children would inherit it, Hope Diamond included. My mind turned to Father, to the business he'd planned to leave to his son, who would, in turn, take care of his sister. But that was all gone now, and Father was in free fall. So, too, was my future. Suddenly, I felt the urge to have a hand in what came next for me.

I left the museum at once and returned home. The moment I arrived, I dialed the operator to connect me to the McLeans' residence, and within moments, Evalyn's voice came over the line.

"Mrs. Mc—Evalyn, hello," I corrected myself, knowing I might irritate her if I were too formal. "This is Elisabeth Beaumont. I wanted to thank you for your kindness yesterday, for looking after me and sending me home in your car. I'm feeling much better."

"Think nothing of it. Carrie and I were just talking about how you must feel."

I didn't like the idea of them speaking about me without me there, but at least they were being kind.

Evalyn continued. "Lizzie, I'm afraid you've caught me at a bad time. I was just leaving, and I really must be going."

Panic rippled through me. I couldn't squander the last opportunity to encourage her to hire me. "Of course. I'll come right to the point. I called because I have a gift for you," I said. "It's small, but I made it myself as a thank-you for being so understanding about my father and"—I forced out the words—"my brother."

"Well, that isn't necessary, but who can resist a gift?"

"May I drop by tomorrow to deliver it?"

"Come at eleven."

I hung up the telephone, lightheaded with relief. I'd guessed right. Evalyn was precisely the kind of woman who could never own or experience too much of a good thing, gifts included. And this time, I'd make sure she knew my services were a good thing, too. The kind of service she couldn't live without.

After I'd worked for several hours on a set of hair combs for Evalyn, my eyes began to fatigue and my legs grew stiff. As I stood to stretch, I decided I could use another walk. It was a lovely late afternoon, the perfect time to stroll along the mall or through one of the parks that were cropping up all over Washington. I thought of Father, how he'd always made time for an afternoon walk—to give his creations breathing room, he'd say, and to get the blood flowing in his limbs. But that was during happier times, when he still took care of himself. Perhaps he might again, should I invite him? To spend proper time together outside the house might be precisely what he needed. What we both needed.

I bounded up the stairs, intent on rousing him from bed. After rapping on his bedroom door, I pushed it open to peek inside. He was propped up against his pillows, reading a book. It was the first time I'd seen him read since he'd taken to bed. Something resembling relief flickered in my chest.

"It's beautiful outside," I said, opening the door wide. "Warm and sunny, breezy. Would you like to go for a walk with me?" He gazed at me vacantly, and my brief moment of levity began to deflate. I wouldn't be able to convince him if he didn't want to go, but I had to try. I decided to take a different tack with a much firmer hand, something I'd never done before with him. "Father, you're becoming a frail old man, and that will affect your mind, too, if you don't take care of yourself. Besides, this will be a nice distraction. You haven't left the house in months. Come, I'll put out some clothes for you. And why don't you comb your hair and clean your teeth while you're at it. We're leaving in fifteen minutes."

His brow shot up in surprise. "Are you telling me what to do, young lady? The world must be upside down."

Surprised by his attempt at humor, I felt my shoulders relax. "Someone has to, or you'll rot away in here." I sorted through his wardrobe, pulled out a pair of clean, pressed trousers and a shirt, and laid them across the foot of the bed. "Fifteen minutes, all right? I'll see you downstairs."

I retrieved my jacket and handbag and waited for him in the front hall. When I didn't hear the creak of his old mattress or his footsteps on the floor, my heart sank. Even with a direct, stern approach, he'd ignore me, ignore what he needed most? I didn't know what else to do.

I sighed heavily as I watched the clock, more and more convinced he wouldn't be joining me. When twenty minutes had passed, I reached for the door—just as I heard his footfall on the stairs.

My heart skipped a beat. "Father? Are you coming?"

As he rounded the corner and descended the final flight of stairs, he called back, "I am, you stubborn girl."

My relief left me lightheaded and a little giddy. I hadn't spent any real time with him in far too long.

Rather than walk our neighborhood streets, we took the tram to downtown and strolled along the National Mall, past the east-west canal that was so still, it reflected puffs of cheerful clouds that scudded across the sky with the breeze. We walked slowly and silently for a while, lost in our own thoughts, but I knew the best thing to draw him out of his shell would be for us to talk, about anything. Perhaps it might help him—help me—feel a little more normal again.

"What was your favorite museum in Paris?" I said as we walked around a pond where a family of ducks skimmed across the surface toward the cover of a large weeping willow tree at the water's edge. In the distance, the redbrick turret of the original Smithsonian Castle soared toward the sky.

"The Louvre, of course," he said, patting the seat of a bench beside him so he might rest a while. "It's magnificent. Over a mile of art in one place. Did you know it was once the palace of medieval kings?" He went on without waiting for me to answer. "And I also like the Musée d'Ethnographie for its tribal art, which I've always found fascinating. There weren't as many museums back then as there are now. If you wanted to see art, you attended the art salons, where the best and the brightest artists had to apply to have their work shown." He regaled me with tale after tale of his childhood in Paris, and I knew I'd asked precisely the right question, giving him the chance to revisit his happy past.

When the edges of the clouds were tipped in pink and gold, he said, "*Chérie,* I think it's time we returned home. It was a short walk, but my feet are aching, and I need a nap. I can't believe how much work all this walking has become for me." He shook his head. "It has been too long."

"It has," I agreed. "But it won't be work for long if you do your daily walks again."

"Perhaps." He gazed off into the distance.

I slipped my hand into the crook of his arm and squeezed affectionately. "I'll make us something to eat, and you can rest."

He didn't argue, and we headed home. I was grateful for the time with him, even if we avoided the topics we most needed to discuss: our loss, our future. But those could wait for now. I'd missed my father, had needed him more than I realized. I prayed this was the beginning of bringing him back to life.

6

The following day, I fussed over what to wear for the first time in my life. Everything in my closet seemed too boyish or too plain next to the beautiful clothing Evalyn and her friends wore. And yet I felt I must make some effort to fit into her world. At last, I settled on one of the few skirts I owned and paired it with a blouse with a lacy collar. I spent extra time brushing and pinning my hair and applying what little makeup I had. As I reached for my plain and likely out-of-fashion handbag, I caught sight of my reflection in the mirror and realized what was missing: jewelry. Of course I should wear our pieces! It was the perfect way to advertise. I tried on several pieces before I finally settled on a pair of teardrop pearl earrings, a brooch made of shiny platinum shaped into a seal balancing a pearl on the tip of its nose, and a bracelet of four strings of pearls held together by a large platinum clasp dotted with tiny, brilliant white diamonds. The jewelry, as beautiful as it was, didn't suit my personal style, but I hoped the others would admire it. As a finishing touch, I spritzed on a dash of French perfume reserved for special occasions, slipped Evalyn's gift into my handbag, and reluctantly headed across town.

When I arrived at Friendship, Evalyn swept into the room in a tulip-pink dress as fresh as spring that cinched at the waist and flowed to her calves. She wore a long double strand of pearls and, suspended from it, another legendary gemstone I recognized on sight: the Star of the East. The nearly ninety-five-carat, pear-shaped diamond was set with an enormous hexagonal emerald of at least thirty carats or more and a coin-size pearl that hovered above the Star like points in a constellation. Despite the necklace's stunning beauty and size, my gaze flicked to Evalyn's neck, drawn to the irresistible blue of the Hope Diamond. Somehow, it overshadowed the other stones, despite its smaller size.

"Stunning, isn't it? I thought you'd like it," Evalyn said, noticing my bold stare. "The Star of the East once belonged to a sultan of the Ottoman Empire. How could I resist it? I bought it on my honeymoon from Pierre Cartier." She reached for my hand. "Anyway, darling, I'm glad you stopped by today. I was just telling Jerry that I needed some air. What do you say we go for a drive?"

A drive? She didn't seem to care that I wasn't a part of her regular circle, and I found myself wondering if she was lonely. Given how she was surrounded by people every time I saw her, that didn't seem likely, and yet here she was, inviting a virtual stranger on a drive with her.

Ned bounced down the staircase, dressed in a pin-striped suit, whistling as he went.

"Have you met my husband, Ned, yet?" Evalyn asked, reaching for her purse. "Ned, this is Lizzie Beaumont."

I hid my surprise. I'd met him the night of their party, but it was clearly an unmemorable event for either of them. Perhaps the champagne had had something to do with it. "How do you do, sir."

"Sir!" he said. "The only sir is my father and he's gone. Call me Ned." He reached for my hand and brought it to his lips.

My cheeks grew hot at the unexpected show of gallantry.

"Always the charmer," Evalyn said, her voice tinged with sarcasm. "You'll have to excuse my husband. He can't seem to help himself."

He smiled broadly at the quip, as if he'd enjoyed it. "Where are you two ladies off to?"

"We're going for a drive."

"The last time you drove, we ended up with a bent fender and a hefty repair bill," he said. "Why don't you let Johnny drive? I'd take you myself, but I have a meeting."

"Don't be ridiculous, darling. I'm a better driver than you are, by far."

"Not a chance," he said, laughing. "I'll meet you for dinner later?"

"I'll have Cook make the steak you like." She kissed him lightly. "Perhaps even Lizzie will join us, too."

He winked at me before he continued on his way.

"He's the worst flirt," she said, turning to me. "Mama always warned me, but he's the love of my life, so what can I say? He charmed me, too, all those years ago when we were children. Let's go, shall we?"

I hesitated, deciding if I should mention her hiring me. Something told me I shouldn't, especially given how aggressive I'd already been with her and the gaffe, too, where I'd all but bolted from the house when Julien's name was mentioned. I capitulated to her request, at least partially. "Mrs. McLean—Evalyn—I'm not sure I can get away from the boutique for long."

"I suppose I'll have to settle for Evalyn rather that Evie," she said, ignoring my concern. With an amused smile, she added, "But anything is better than Mrs. McLean."

"I'm sorry. I didn't want to overstep," I said, blushing to my hairline.

"Not at all. Say, what's the package sticking out of your handbag? Is that the gift you promised me?" Her tone was playful.

"Oh! I nearly forgot. Yes, here you are."

She took it, all smiles, unwrapped the butcher paper monogrammed with the Beaumont seal, and untied the red ribbon. "They're lovely!" She held up the ornate pair of hair combs to examine the scalloped edges I'd designed to look like seashells. I'd painted them silver and affixed three small aquamarines on each for added sparkle. It had taken me most of the afternoon and evening to finish them, but I was pleased with how they'd turned out.

She slipped the hair combs into her handbag. "Now, how about that drive?"

Given her easy dismissal of the combs, I doubted she truly liked them, but I forced a polite smile and pretended not to notice. This wasn't the time for me to worry about my skills or ruminate on my shortcomings. "I'm delighted you like them," I replied. "And a drive sounds nice."

We met the chauffeur outside as he pulled up in a creamy-yellow car with red wheel spokes and a roof that opened and closed in folds like an accordion. As he slipped out of the driver's side, he held open the door for Evalyn and then the passenger side for me.

"Are you sure I can't take you somewhere, Mrs. McLean?" he said.

"Have I ever been unsure of anything, Johnny?" Evalyn said with a smile. "I'm in the mood for a drive."

I was surprised to see the smallest flicker of relief pass over the chauffeur's face before his expression changed back to one of stoic servitude. Before I had time to consider the strange behavior, she shooed him away.

"I've never seen such a beautiful car," I said.

"It's a convertible. Isn't it gorgeous?" Evalyn bubbled like the champagne she loved.

"Is it safe?"

She grinned like a schoolgirl and shifted the car into drive. "Must everything be safe to enjoy it? I hope you pinned your hat well, because the wind's going to be fierce."

She laughed at my expression, and we shot off with a jolt. Perfectly manicured lawns and impressive homes streaked by as we trundled over the roads. Cloudless blue skies stretched overhead, and a soft warm wind blew around us, tossing loose tendrils of hair into my eyes. We drove for well over an hour, Evalyn prattling on about all manner of things, pointing out landmarks, homes of people she knew, and I got the distinct impression she didn't mind that I was mostly silent. It gave her the opportunity to fill the space with her own musings, her own voice, and she carried on without restraint.

She laughed as she took a corner too fast, and the tires screeched against the pavement. I didn't complain, but I clutched the dashboard with a death grip to steady myself.

"Oh, don't be such a prude, Lizzie. Enjoy yourself. This is fun!"

"It is fun!" I shouted back, trying to play along. I hadn't known fun in months, could hardly grasp the meaning of the word, but I wouldn't ruin her good time. Not if it bought more time with her.

Evalyn zoomed through an intersection, passing a traffic policeman and a red electric traffic light. The policeman blew his whistle, but she didn't so much as brake. Instead, she threw back her head and laughed.

"As if his little old whistle is going to slow me down!"

There was talk of installing a fully automated system of traffic lights in Ohio as had been done in Los Angeles, as well as in the busier intersections in Washington, but they were still being tested. Julien loved inventions and progress—and argued with our father about whether they helped humanity or caused more nuanced problems—and I'd been subjected to far too many discussions about it. As Evalyn mashed her foot on the gas and we roared through another intersection without a traffic light, veering to miss another car in the midst of turning, I couldn't help but wish the city had more traffic lights already in place.

"Tell me more about yourself," she said, interrupting my thoughts.

"There isn't much to tell. I was born in France but raised here. I've never been much of anywhere else." I didn't mention the way I'd yearned to explore new places and go on expeditions in the wild to search for stones, or the many times my father had planned to take us to New York, center of the country's jewelry trade, or to Paris, only to be derailed by his latest obsession over a project.

"We'll have to remedy that," she said with a wink.

I blinked. I couldn't imagine where Evalyn might possibly take me and, more importantly, why. I certainly couldn't afford such an extravagance. "I imagine you've traveled the world," I replied at last.

"Oh, not everywhere, but I've been to some of the prettiest countries in Europe and the places that matter in America."

The places that mattered? I suspected Evalyn required designer boutiques and reputable restaurants and expansive homes for partymaking in her "places that mattered." Expectations I couldn't relate to in the slightest.

"How wonderful," I replied, forcing a wistful tone. "My father has traveled some, for gemstones, of course."

"Something he is passionate about, I imagine. Has he started a new collection recently? Anything of note that I should know about?"

I realized then she was more than a spendthrift and an admirer of beautiful things. She was competitive about her status and the things she owned, and she probably liked to outshine her friends in that way, too. I shouldn't be surprised, given the way she flaunted her wealth.

"Yes, he's working on the pearl and diamond necklace design that I showed you at your party," I said. Afraid that wasn't impressive enough for her, I added, "One of our regular clients from Paris requested an original. It'll be quite beautiful when finished." A lie but I wanted to make us appear as in demand as possible.

"How interesting. Do you work on originals?"

"I've worked on many of the Beaumont designs, including my own when there's time. I'm in the process of designing my own collection." I didn't add that I hadn't had the heart or the will to work on them lately.

"Will you show them to me?" she said.

"I'd be honored to," I said, enthusiasm pouring into my voice for the first time since I'd met her. She noticed.

"Well now, it seems you should have told me that first."

A ghost of a smile played on my lips. "You've been so generous with your time after being left in the lurch by Beaumont Jewelers. I'm still so embarrassed. I didn't feel I should—"

"You're not like your brother, are you? Where he was boisterous and congenial, you're quiet and clever." She turned the car onto Sycamore Lane.

I froze at the mention of Julien but forced myself to breathe normally. I had to become accustomed to this somehow, to people mentioning him in casual conversation as if he'd simply gone on holiday. I trained my eyes on the road in front of us. "Yes, we were different but complementary."

She flicked a glance my way. "I apologize. I shouldn't have mentioned him."

Though she'd said the right thing, I had the distinct feeling she'd meant to bring him up, had watched my expression to see how comparing me to him would affect me. I'd caught a whiff of emotional manipulation, perhaps, or maybe I was being overly sensitive, thinking too much of it. Evalyn had been kind and more than accommodating by entertaining my request to consider Beaumont Jewelers again. And now this, inviting me on a drive...

She patted my knee kindly. "Are you hungry? I could eat a horse."

Grateful for the change in subject, I agreed.

We rolled to a stop in front of a redbrick, two-story home with black shutters. Rocking chairs and potted ferns dotted a narrow porch. I hoped Evalyn hadn't decided we'd dine at another of her friend's houses. It took most of my energy to put on airs with her, and I didn't think I could face yet another afternoon with a handful of silly women who did nothing but gossip the day away.

To my chagrin, she put the car in park and honked her horn until the front door opened. The woman named Carrie glided down the walk. As I watched the uncannily beautiful woman climb into the car, the flicker of recognition came again. Where had I seen her before? I was certain I had... When she noticed I was staring at her, my eyes darted away, past her, and I pretended to focus on something behind her.

"Hello, ladies," she said. "Where are we off to for lunch?"

"Oh, the usual," Evalyn replied. "Lizzie, you remember Carrie, don't you? She's my closest friend." She threw Carrie a wide smile.

Carrie returned her smile. Though her expression seemed genuine, I noticed she didn't make the point of agreeing with Evalyn's comment.

We drove to the Monaco, a swanky little hotel and restaurant where a valet parked the car. Inside, we were shown to "Evalyn's table" near the window overlooking a garden. Bea and Sharon already waited for us there, along with a third woman, a beautiful, elegant blond. She wore her hair in short waves around her face and a spring-green dress that dipped in a deep V in the front with mesh-style lace covering the would-be-bare areas of skin. Ropes of pearls encircled her neck, and an enormous yellow diamond sparkled on her right hand. Everything about her exuded confidence, wealth, and self-possession. I wondered what that must be like, to be looked upon with constant admiration and envy.

As we took seats, everyone exchanged pleasantries.

Evalyn tucked her hand into the crook of my arm. "This is my new friend, Lizzie Beaumont. Lizzie, this is Gwen Chaney."

"How do you do," I said, offering a polite smile to the blond, more than a little surprised by Evalyn's introduction.

"Charmed, I'm sure," Gwen said as she took in my attire. "Who designed your dress? It must be..."

A couple of the others exchanged sharp smiles, and I realized I had stumbled not only into one of the most elite circles in the country but a den of barracudas.

"Oh, Gwen, don't be so dreadful," Evalyn retorted. "Not everyone has your sense of style. Lizzie is my guest, and I may be hiring her."

I didn't miss the slight, even from Evalyn. I refrained from looking down at my faded sage-green dress and instead reminded myself of my posture. I wondered when—and if—Evalyn was going to hire me officially or if she would ultimately turn me away. Perhaps enduring these women would be for nothing, and I was as close to the truth about Julien as I'd ever be. The thought left me cold.

Understanding lit Gwen's eyes. "Oh, I see. Lizzie is the help." She forced a smile. "Well, I'm sure Evie will make you feel right at home. She's awful good at that."

The help.

It didn't take a genius to glean what she meant: The help didn't belong among them, drinking their champagne and smiling their smiles, and my clothing only underscored it.

Bea covered her mouth to hide a smile.

And I realized something in that instant. They enjoyed this, shooting arrows at one another, besting each other in the art of conversation and in the game of who was better in deed, appearance, and breeding. It seemed here, among the wealthy, friendship took on a different definition from the one I'd been taught. I squirmed inwardly as the others watched me with a hint of curiosity and the glint of challenge in their eyes. Did I have what it took to be counted among them, they said with every gesture, every flutter of lashes, every mannerism that seemed rehearsed.

I forced myself to smile brightly, as if Gwen hadn't insulted me. "Thank you for the welcome. I'm delighted to be counted among Evalyn's retinue."

"You'll have to fill me in on your little jewelry shop," Gwen replied. "Perhaps I could tell my nanny about it. She has quite the collection of trinkets and paste jewelry."

My father's heart would seize in his chest should he hear such an insult. He despised the newly popular industrialized jewelry, the fake stones and poorly constructed pieces. He'd spoken of the department stores who sold them as if they were his mortal enemy. I'd grown to despise the factory-made colored glass and banal designs as well. They threatened the very nature of what jewelers had done for centuries: created art. It was no secret every jeweler despaired at the increasing popularity of costume jewelry. Making luxury items readily available to everyone rendered our business of refined beauty, of aspirations and dreams, obsolete. If costume jewelry took the place of true craftsmanship, Beaumont Jewelers' doors would be permanently shuttered. Where we'd go from there, I couldn't imagine. My father had ranted about it often enough. Craftsmanship and artistry took a lifetime of practice and skill. Starting over in another field wasn't an option.

Suddenly I felt compelled to defend his honor, if not my own. "I assure you, Gwen, nothing we make is paste jewelry. The pearls I'm wearing are from the South Seas off the coast of Australia. They're of the finest variety in the world."

"Let us see those!" Bea said, leaning across the table to reach for my bracelet.

I slid the bracelet off and gave it to her. She oohed and aahed over the piece before passing it around the table. When it came back to me, I fastened it on my wrist with satisfaction.

"Are the earrings and brooch yours, too?" Sharon asked.

I nodded. "Yes, of course."

"Your family's jewelry is divine," Evalyn said before ordering a round of martinis for the table, two dozen oysters, pâté, and canapés.

"Thank you," I said, genuinely delighted and surprised by her compliment. "My father apprenticed with the best in Paris and taught me everything he knows." I didn't go into how successful our company had been before Julien's death. My father had hummed along with new designs at quite a pace, especially since he'd had me and Julien to help with much of the labor. We were able to expand quickly. Though our name was well established and respected, our industry required we create new pieces regularly to compete with other jewelers and with the costume jewelry market. All in a bid to stay relevant and to keep revenue flowing.

As the food arrived, I filled my plate. I'd never tasted anything so fine—had been unable to taste anything for months—and found my reluctance receding as my hunger flared. I ate without reserve as the others picked at a bite here and there.

Evalyn watched me with delighted amusement. "Isn't the food divine? Eat up, darling. You're as thin as a ghost." Next, she ordered an array of amuse-bouches, fruit and vegetable salads, and two bottles of champagne.

"My, you have quite the appetite." Bea's brown eyes were hooded and her freckled complexion flushed from the wine, but her tone was unmistakable.

With an unfamiliar courage that came with drink, words I didn't expect sprang to my lips. I glanced meaningfully at her thrice-emptied glass and said, "I've heard you do as well."

Her neck turned blotchy with embarrassment.

Shocked by my easy cruelty, my fingers flew to my lips. I couldn't believe I'd said such a thing, the implications I'd made.

Evalyn snickered and laid her hand on my arm. "What a sly thing you are. You do surprise me, Lizzie."

I reached for my water glass, feeling triumphant at her praise but slightly ill at ease. I didn't usually take pleasure in another person's embarrassment, but it appeared it was what I must do to be a part of Evalyn's crowd. And for now, that was what I wanted—and needed—most. To gain their trust.

After lunch, Carrie squeezed into the front seat beside me in Evalyn's sleek, beautiful car. As we eased the car into traffic, Carrie leaned toward me, her breath thick with alcohol.

"You can't imagine how sorry I am to hear about your brother," she said. "I've urged Evie to hire you. I thought it might help."

I stared at her blankly a moment. Why should she help me…unless she'd met Julien when he'd spent time at the McLeans' home? Evalyn liked collecting people, bringing them into her fold and holding court. That was now clear to me, and given how handsome and utterly charming Julien could be, I knew that must have been the case. I pictured Evalyn inviting him to her parties, to meet her friends, just as she had with me. Perhaps he'd wiled away many an afternoon in the presence of all these women. It wasn't the most proper behavior, but then again, he'd always seemed to get away with many things he shouldn't, proper or not. And I knew for certain he'd at least been commissioned as Evalyn's jeweler, that he'd serviced the Hope Diamond several times. He'd said as much.

"I–I don't know what to say," I replied, still stunned by the comment.

"'Thank you' is tradition, I think," she said, flashing her brilliant smile to soften the light sarcasm of her response.

I felt my neck heat. "Right, thank you."

"What are you two whispering about?" Evalyn said as she narrowly missed a pedestrian waiting on the curb to cross the street.

"How generous you were at lunch," Carrie lied. "And, darling, keep your eyes on the road, will you? We'd like to get home in one piece."

As they laughed and continued to prattle on about this and that, I sank deeper into my seat, watching them, studying them as they lobbed one comment after another at each other. The way they laughed, the phrases they used, the sly insults. After one particularly intense volley about a diplomat's wife followed by an exchange of meaningful looks, Evalyn glanced at me with her quizzical brow, and I knew I was onto something.

I must play their game or be played.

With nightfall and our return to Friendship, the liquor haze began to wear off, and a headache followed. I didn't know how society ladies drank alcohol the way they did or even if it was normal practice for others outside of Evalyn's friends. As enjoyable as it was while in the midst of it, the sobering side of things was anything but.

"I really must get home to look in on my father," I said. "Thank you for the drive and the lovely lunch."

"You simply can't go yet," Evalyn purred. "I need to show you something." A mischievous grin played across her lips. She looked like a child then, her pupils dilated, her lids heavy. She was as drunk as an Irish prizefighter. She stumbled as she leaned to my ear, her lips brushing the tender skin of my earlobe, and whispered, "I'd like to show you my collection."

"Your jewelry collection?" I perked up.

Blue eyes sparkling, she laughed like I'd said the funniest thing she'd ever heard. "Of course. What other collection is there?"

I bit my tongue. Her dishes and silverware, her gowns, her beautifully polished furniture, the Limoges, the original breathtaking art that graced the walls of her homes. There were many collections, and she likely considered none of them of particular value beyond the status they represented. They'd come too easily, without much thought or care, just as everything had for her.

"I'd be delighted to see it," I replied with far too much eagerness. "I've been wanting to ask you about it, but I wasn't sure... I didn't want to—"

"You didn't think I'd show you the crown jewels all at once, did you? Why, I didn't know you from a bump on a log at first." She looped her arm through mine. "You had to earn my trust, silly Lizzie. Now I'm absolutely certain you're the man for the job. Or the woman." She giggled at herself as she led me to the dining table.

When Jerry hefted a large box onto the table, my heart skipped a beat. As he unlocked the jewelry box, Evalyn covered my hand with hers.

"I'd like to hire you," she said. "I'd need the collection cleaned and serviced every two weeks, but I really wish you'd come around more often. I hope you will."

My shoulders sagged as relief surged through me. "I thought you'd never ask."

She laughed. "I do like to keep a person guessing. What's life without a little excitement and tension? Now, go on, open it."

I opened the lid of the jewelry box, marveling at the sheer number of items from pearls to onyx to rare Burmese rubies of the finest clarity and color. She'd collected far more than her grand pieces like the Hope Diamond and the Star of India. I ran my hand over the gold bracelets lined with diamond baguettes, platinum rings featuring a variety of stones, magnificent opals, a pair of teardrop pearl earrings, and several necklaces fashioned in the whimsical art nouveau style.

"Most of these are locked in the safe on a regular basis," she said, "but a few of the things I wear daily I leave in the drawers of my vanity."

"You really should keep all of them in a safe," I scolded her gently. "It isn't the premeditated thieves you should fear as much as the casual ones. Something my father has always said."

"I know, I know. It's silly of me to leave them out where anyone can take them, but opening the safe every day is a chore. I do wear the Hope Diamond nearly all day, every day."

I glanced longingly at the gleaming blue diamond.

She grinned. "Would you like to hold it?"

I fell silent a moment. This was why I was here, to take care of *all* of her jewelry collection. And I didn't believe in curses. Did I? Yet if I were honest with myself... My real answer was this: I didn't know if curses were real. The Hope Diamond had certainly been in the presence of more than its fair share of tragedies, a tragedy like my own. To be near the diamond, to be a part of Evalyn's circle as Julien had been could be very dangerous indeed. I was playing with fire. But I'd already crossed that line the moment I'd knocked at Evalyn's front door two weeks ago. And I'd already lost the most precious thing of all. Now I only stood to gain. Clients, reputation, and, most important of all, the truth.

When I didn't reply, Evalyn grew impatient. "Well?" she said, her voice testy.

"Yes," I whispered at last, as if we were in a sacred place and the diamond a holy relic. I didn't know if I believed in the holy, but I believed in beauty in all its forms, that which inspired and intrigued and outlasted us all. I also believed in the ephemeral, poignant moments in our lives that could change the course of everything, and this felt like one of them.

With a wicked smile, Evalyn unfastened the clasp and placed the Hope Diamond in my outstretched hand.

7

I dreamed of the Hope that night.

The diamond rested on a dais in the center of a dark room. The air was velvet around me as an invisible pull lured me closer, closer. I grasped it, closed my fingers around the diamond's solid middle, and a shiver ran over my skin. At once, a solitary beam of light poured over its dazzling facets, making the stone sparkle like ice in sunlight.

"Gemstones are creatures of the light," I whispered aloud.

Father's words. How true his statement was. When light illuminated a stone, it awakened, came alive. Its mineral veins and many faces became a map of its creation.

Something stirred in the dark room around me. I couldn't see what else—or who else—lurked there, I knew only to run. I clutched the stone to my chest and raced through blurred rooms from something unseen behind me until a strong hand clapped my shoulder and wrenched me backward.

I bolted upright in bed, out of breath, sweat staining my nightgown.

As the remnants of the dream hovered in the air like a fog, a heaviness pressed against my lungs. I slipped from bed, eager to escape the confines of my room. Flinging open my bedroom door, I padded barefoot to the workshop, the cool air against my damp nightgown sending a shiver down my spine. Reaching blindly for the lights, I turned the switches quickly, exhaling deeply as the room flooded with light. No one waited for me there; no phantom stalked me in the dark.

Exhaling, I reached for my notebook, fumbling as I turned to my notes about the Hope Diamond. Now I knew precisely what it looked like. What it felt like. Its inexorable pull.

Evalyn had laughed gleefully at my discomfort, the way I'd taken her necklace into my hands gingerly, holding it by the diamond-studded chain at first to avoid touching the Hope itself.

"Darling, it won't hurt you," she said with a smile.

I looked up, startled that she read my mind. "Oh, I know," I said, biting my lip nervously. "I don't believe in curses." I'd repeated the mantra to myself since I'd first set foot in the McLean household. And yet as Evalyn presented me with the gemstone, I faltered, touched only the outer rim of cushion diamonds.

"Neither do I," Evalyn said, pouring us each a sizable finger of whiskey. "Here, whiskey always helps."

I accepted the drink. I found myself warming to the numbness the whiskey brought as it spread through my limbs.

Evalyn sipped from her highball glass. "I say I don't believe in bad luck"—her voice dropped—"but if I'm honest, maybe I do, a little. I've always tried to see the Hope as more of a good-luck charm, and I enjoy the way people are as taken with it as I am. But since we're sharing secrets"—she met my eyes—"if I look back at the events of the last few years and think about the ways people around me have met with a series of disagreeable incidents, not to mention losing my dear brother, Vinnie, and my poor father to a dreadful illness, I can't help but allow a tiny sliver of doubt to eke through."

She'd lost her brother, too? And her father. I shivered at the coincidence of what we'd both lost. Three deceased and my father as lost as he could be…though I hoped that was going to change. I looked down at the necklace. The Hope shimmered in my hands like a blue eye, watching me with some preternatural sense. I hesitated an instant, the stories swirling through my mind, but in the end, I was here to do a job. I dragged my thumb across the surface of the stone. As another shiver traveled up my spine, I fought the conflicted impulse to both fasten it around my neck and the opposite—to put as much distance between me and the stone as possible.

"I suppose it would be difficult not to doubt occasionally," I said quietly. I wondered if Evalyn considered my brother's death worthy of her list of mishaps, or if she'd considered it at all. I dared to insert him into the conversation, to steer her in the direction I needed. "Did my… did my brother clean your necklace regularly?"

"Of course, darling. That was the whole point of hiring him, though he was wonderful to have around, too. He spent time with the girls and with Ned and his friends. Everyone adored him."

I perked up at the new information. "He spent time with the men, too?"

"Oh, sure. He was a charmer, but he was also great fun. I was sure Julien had become a permanent fixture around here until… Well, you know."

"The accident."

She sipped from her glass, but her eyes never left my face. "Well, yes, until that."

So she'd known about the accident all along, though she'd pretended otherwise. I flushed at the realization. There was something else she wasn't telling me, but I also keenly felt the boundary line between us. I shifted my approach. "So how did you come to own the Hope Diamond?" I asked. Though I knew who'd sold her the diamond, I wondered if there were details about the gemstone's provenance—and the curse—that she knew and I didn't.

I pulled out the jeweler's loupe, a strong magnifier, that I always kept in my handbag to examine the diamond more closely. If there were inclusions, they were small enough to be undetectable without a more invasive process. "Its water is astounding!"

"Water?" Evalyn said, distracted by my comment. "What does that mean?"

"Clarity or purity of the stone."

She rolled her eyes. "Well, of course. It's the most perfect blue diamond in the world. We bought it from Pierre Cartier. Ned and I already knew him because he'd sold us the Star of the East while we were on our honeymoon in Paris, and then a few years later, Pierre opened his store in Manhattan, and we brokered the deal for the Hope Diamond." She leaned forward, her eyes glassy from drinking champagne and whiskey all afternoon. "Mama and my sister pressured me to sell it back, given the rumors. I haven't told anyone this, but I tried to. Pierre wouldn't take it back."

I arched my brow at her. So she believed far more in the curse and bad luck than she was willing to admit, at least publicly.

"Originally Pierre wanted us to buy the Hope Diamond the first time we met, but the setting was old-fashioned at the time, and I didn't care for it. Pierre pushed me in his persuasive way, telling me a long, fancy story that's ludicrous, really, but I'll admit, it has stayed with me." She laughed. "By the looks of it, you're positively dying to hear it."

"How could I resist?"

She smiled. "First, the diamond was stolen from the eye of a statue of a god in India. It was sold to a French gem trader who carried it with him all the way back to France." She leaned forward again. "After the gem merchant sold it to the king, he traveled to Russia where he was torn apart by wild dogs."

Though I'd known the gemstone had come from France, I'd never heard the bit about the wild dogs. A shiver raced over my arms. Evalyn noticed my flinch.

"I know!" she said, gleeful she could unsettle me. "Gruesome, isn't it? Louis XIV wore it around his neck, suspended by a ribbon or as a brooch, and eventually his grandson used it as a ceremonial piece for the Order of the Golden Fleece. Marie Antoinette is also said to have worn it, and we all know what happened to her. Unfortunately for them, the stone was cursed from the beginning. A Turkish gem merchant who owned it briefly drowned at sea, and the Hope family went bankrupt. May Yohé, the actress, doomed her career the moment she clasped the necklace around her neck. She hasn't booked a leading role of any importance again, and from what I hear, her theater named the Hope is struggling. The diamond brought bad luck to France and to everyone else ever since. Except for me."

I gazed at her in disbelief. Some of the story was as silly and the facts as convoluted as she'd said, but more importantly, how could she be so blind to the events in her own life that had been less than lucky the past several years? Evalyn's own brother and father passed away unexpectedly. Perhaps she saw only what she wanted to, only believed what she could face. I was beginning to learn that wasn't always the truth.

She yawned and stood. "It's getting late. Why don't you come by tomorrow, and we'll set up a proper schedule. Besides, there's somewhere else I'd like to take you first."

I agreed to her request, relieved to, at last, put a schedule in place. She kissed my cheek good night, and I left on a high.

As the memory of the night before receded, the comforting scent of sandalwood candles rushed my senses, and the drawing of the Hope leapt from the page, I picked up my fountain pen. I recorded what Evalyn had told me the night before and tried to put the curse out of my mind. I'd never believed in them anyway.

And yet I'd touched the Hope only once, and now it invaded my dreams.

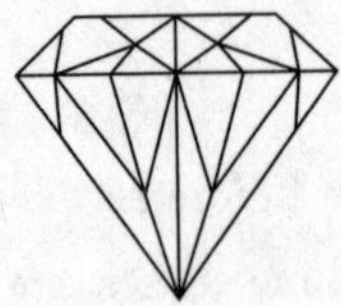

A whisper breaks the silence.

Two voices arise, four, many. I hear the clamor of footsteps and shattering windows, the splintering of wood, crashes and shouts and laughter as precious items are stolen from the king's crown jewels. The stash he'd hoped would remain locked away and hidden from the mobs has been discovered.

Suddenly I am lifted from a once-locked drawer.

"Ain't this the diamond from the Golden Fleece?" one man says to another.

A grunt and a shrug, a cacophony of voices swirl around me. I am quickly wrapped in a handkerchief and shoved into a pouch. Once more, I travel a long distance, across lush fields to the edge of the ocean where I embark on a journey to yet another kingdom. A kingdom of sea cliffs and foggy moors, of moody skies and a grand, ancient city at its heart.

I disappear from view and from human thought for years. They believe I am gone for good, but I am lying in wait.

At last, my keeper presents me to an expert in a shop filled with curiosities and dark corners.

The jeweler gasps upon first sight of my dazzling facets. "You have the French Blue! How did you get it?"

My keeper shakes his head. "That doesn't concern you. All that matters is what I will do with it."

"You are a fool. It will be recognized," the jeweler rasps. "The French government will demand its return. Napoleon will wage war on us."

My keeper nods. "That's why I'm here. Do with it what you must but make it new again."

The jeweler's eyes fill with uncertainty, with a tinge of disgust. To change something already perfect feels sacrilegious, but there are men who do not understand such matters. Men who are ruled by greed. "Do you know where you will sell it?"

"It's better if I do not say," my keeper says and departs with the promise to return.

The jeweler speaks to me as he works, admonishing my keeper for being so reckless. For I am a diamond known not only for my size and my starkly unique color. It is the story I carry with me: a story grown of bad luck, of death, of a kingdom's destruction that has lent more value to my glittering facets than ever imagined.

But the jeweler cannot turn away from a challenge. He understands what must be done, and in one swift moment, I am cleaved in two.

My other half is gone.

8

Some days, I still couldn't believe my brother was gone. As I stood in the doorway of his bedroom, I wondered if I would ever accept his passing, ever be able to see past the monolith of loss that divided my life into the before and after. Julien's scent had faded, but traces of his energy emanated from the dented pillow on his bed, the forgotten socks on his floor, the assortment of his toiletries, comb, and shaving blades scattered across his dresser top. Dust coated its surface, and the window was grimy after months without cleaning it. I couldn't bring myself to sort through his things and give them away, to erase the final proof that my other half had once been here, vibrant and more alive than anyone I'd ever known. I wondered, as I gazed at the photograph of us on his wall, if he walked in the space between death and afterlife or if there was no such thing as life beyond the grave. And yet I felt his presence in every breath, every corner of my mind, every cell of my being.

Mist clouded my vision, and I quickly closed his door. I crossed the hall to look in on my father. He was dozing, but he'd left only a single bread crust and the last dredges of porridge in his bowl. I was heartened by his returning appetite, though I still hadn't fully regained my own. As I crept into his room to retrieve the tray, my gaze fell upon the small porcelain dish on his dresser filled with four ticket stubs. Curious, I read the small print. They were admittance to Barnum & Bailey's Circus, "The Greatest Show on Earth."

I was transported instantly to that day seven years before when Father, Julien, Henry, and I had spent the morning watching the circus parade. Colorful chariots, camels, dozens of elephants and gilded cages filled with wild jungle animals and those from the safari, and streams of glittering performers had marched through our city down Pennsylvania Avenue past the White House and to the circus grounds on First Street. At two o'clock, we'd attended the variety of shows beneath the ten-acre tent along with tens of thousands of men, women, and children. It had been a perfect day. When the acrobats had entered the ring nearest us, we'd thundered with applause.

"Can you imagine swinging from a hoop that high above the ground?" I'd said.

Henry had bumped my shoulder. "I could see you doing that. You're braver than you think you are."

"You really think so?" I asked, surprised by his comment.

"You don't remember the way you climbed the trellis up the side of my house without batting an eye? Or the tree behind your house?" He shook his head. "One day, you will surprise us all."

I blushed with pleasure. I liked the way Henry saw me, the way he encouraged me to be myself without apology.

"She could definitely be an acrobat, but you couldn't," Julien said. "You'd be crying your eyes out at that height!"

Henry tossed a handful of hot corn at my brother, and we dissolved into laughter. Julien loved to tease Henry about his fear of heights, and Henry in turn teased him about snakes. He'd even made a fake snake once and hid it under Julien's pillow.

After the flying trapeze, leopard tamers, and men diving through flaming hoops, we'd headed home where Father had regaled us with stories of the first circus he'd attended as a boy in Paris. We'd laughed at the mischief he'd made with his brothers and the boys from his neighborhood.

I returned the tickets to the porcelain dish, the comforting image of that perfect day fading as quickly as it had come. In its stead, a persistent ache spread through my chest. I'd never thought of my life as perfect, but I'd give anything to go back in time, to savor every moment when we were all together and the world was right again. To marvel at every instance I'd had with the four of us together, easy in our laughter, easy in the knowledge that we had each other and always would.

My eyes misted over for a second time that day, and I quickly shoved the thoughts away. As I reached for Father's tray, he stirred in his bed and sat up.

"Where were you yesterday?" he said. "You've been gone a lot these days."

He'd noticed? I assumed he wouldn't, given that he so rarely left his bedroom. I scrambled for something to say, some lie I could offer to hide where I'd really been. I decided on some version of the truth.

"I've been conferring with potential clients."

His graying brow raised in a question. "How so? Are you going door-to-door?"

A lie tumbled from my lips. "I was invited to dinner by one of Julien's old friends, Sam Jacobs. Remember him, from Julien's dinner party last summer? Sam introduced me to a few people while I was there, and I've been able to set up several appointments."

He nodded. "Good. Keep me abreast of what's happening."

"Of course," I said, smothering my relief that he'd bought the story. "Can I bring you anything else?"

"I'll get the newspapers in a while. You don't need to bring them up."

Both glad to escape more questions and that he seemed to be moving about the house a bit more lately, I nodded. "I'll be in the shop if you need me."

I headed downstairs just as a sharp rap sounded at the boutique door. I opened it to find a stranger on my doorstep.

"Hello, are you Miss Beaumont?" he said.

I frowned, trying to place the man's face. He had angular features, gaunt cheeks, and a dark suit that looked as if it had seen its better days. I was fairly certain I didn't know him. "I am," I answered cautiously.

"Might I come in?"

"Are you here to see our collection?" I pressed. He certainly didn't look the sort who would spend much on jewelry, but then again, most people liked to celebrate special occasions in some way. Perhaps it was his wife's birthday.

He pressed his lips together before speaking, and I decided I didn't like the edge to his voice and the set of his shoulders or the permanent groove between his eyes from years of frowning. "I am not, but I'd like to speak with you. It's important."

"I'm not in the habit of entertaining strangers without an appointment, sir."

"Of course. My apologies. My name is Bradford Jones. I work for Planters Bank and Trust."

All the blood drained from my face. The very same collector who had called the house and sent the notices I'd shoved into a drawer in my desk. My face must have reflected my panic, because before I could think of how to respond, he rushed on.

"Your mortgage is seven months past due. Shall we discuss how you might begin to pay for it? I'm afraid ignoring our notices isn't an option, Miss Beaumont. We'd hate to expel you from your home."

"Oh, I..." My heart raced. We didn't have the money, not quite yet. And I hadn't the slightest idea how I could come up with it any faster. I'd spent far too many days at silly events lately, playing at being a socialite, hoping it would bring in new clients, but nothing had come of it yet, save cleaning Evalyn's collection, and we hadn't yet set a date for when I'd begin or the payment schedule. What was more, I hadn't heard a peep from our long list of previous clients to whom I'd sent handwritten invitations to drop by the boutique. There were a few outstanding items I could finish that were already sold, and then there was my collection... But I didn't want to waste time on it when I wasn't certain it would sell anyway. I needed my father to return to work as soon as possible. I needed to impress upon him how difficult things had become for us.

"If I might come inside, we could talk about a repayment schedule," he pressed.

But rather than invite him inside, I slammed the door in his face, locked it, and raced through the boutique into the workshop to distance myself from the inevitable, persistent knock that came next at the front door. Heart pounding, I squeezed my eyes closed. Being the official jeweler for the McLeans would be helpful in a few weeks' time, but it wasn't enough, I knew. I'd have to woo Evalyn's friends, too.

I listened to the gentleman's pounding at the door for some time before he finally gave up, and I was able to breathe again. As I returned to my worktable, mind racing, my eyes fell upon the Rosalee Smith commission. It was nearly finished, and though she'd already paid for it in full, an idea shimmered in my mind. She was a long-term customer who, like Evalyn, never seemed to have enough jewelry. If I finished her earrings quickly, I could deliver them personally and perhaps talk her into purchasing another piece. I had to try at least.

I didn't waste any time. I pulled on my smock and jeweler's goggles and dove into my work, losing myself, losing sense of time and place, my mind emptying of all but the exquisite earrings in front of me. For the first time in months, it felt like a refuge as every other thought dissolved but my attention on the weight of the pliers in my hands and the sparkle of the diamond. By noon, I'd finished the earrings.

When I arrived at the Smith residence and the butler showed me inside, Rosalee's surprise registered on her pretty features.

"Hello, Miss Beaumont. How nice it is to see you."

"I'm sorry to disturb you, but I've finished your earrings and thought I'd deliver them in person as a courtesy," I said. "Thank you for your patience. It's been…a difficult year."

"Not at all," she said with a kind smile. "I know you've been through a lot. You've grown very thin, my dear. I hope you're eating."

I avoided her eyes and the pity I was sure to see in them. "I—yes," was all I could manage.

She seemed to understand and changed the subject. "Can I see the earrings?"

"Of course!" I said, relieved she'd let the topic drop. I gave her the velvet bag with a small jewelry box nestled inside it.

As she opened it, she smiled. "They're so beautiful! They're prettier even than the sketch your father showed me. Let's have a look in the mirror, here at the end of the hallway." She removed the pearls she was wearing and replaced them with my father's creation. A sizable diamond rested in the middle of a nest of gold that looped around the stone. "Incredible."

I nodded. "He is a master, isn't he?"

"You made these, though, didn't you?"

"My father started them, and I finished them. It was a team effort." As Rosalee peered into the mirror, admiring the way they sparkled, I knew this was my chance. "There's an exquisite necklace that pairs with the earrings. I don't know if my father…or Julien showed it to you?"

"A matching necklace?" Her hand touched the hollow of her throat as if the necklace were already there. "No, he didn't. Now I must see it."

"It hasn't been made yet, but it is in the works. This is the design." I held out the sketch I'd brought with me. "You see, here's the nest and a series of diamonds. I've begun work on it and could likely finish it within two to three weeks should you be interested. I'm finally back at work in earnest."

"You're a temptress, Elisabeth!" she said with a smile. "My husband wouldn't notice the new jewelry. He never does… Nor does he need to. I'd love to have the necklace, too."

I nearly collapsed with relief. "Wonderful. Would you like to make a deposit or pay in full?"

"Why don't I pay in full?" she said. "I know you're good for the jewelry, and since it's only going to take a few weeks, we'll see each other again soon. Let me just get the banknotes for you."

We were in a good position to fulfill this commission. We had all the stones and the gold in stock, so the sum collected could immediately cover two of the seven outstanding months of the mortgage. I could also pay several of the utility and supply bills. It wouldn't relieve us for long, but it was a start until I managed to find other clients. At the very least, it would silence Bradford Jones for a while.

"Here we are," Rosalee said as she returned. She'd placed the banknotes in an envelope. "I look forward to wearing the set to my in-laws' gala this summer."

"Thank you, Mrs. Smith. I'm thrilled to make this for you and will do my best to finish it quickly."

She smiled. "I know you will." As I turned to go, she stopped me.

"Elisabeth, I'm so sorry about your brother, but I'm happy to see you on your feet again."

A lump formed in my throat, and not trusting myself to speak, I forced a weak smile and headed for the door.

9

Morning dawned, and with it, my exhaustion. I'd spent the rest of the day and the better part of the evening working on Rosalee's necklace and had made excellent headway. It would be done in a week rather than three at this pace, which was precisely what I was aiming to do. The more I thought about the exchange with Rosalee, the more I realized her purchase had been an act of kindness. She'd sensed my desperation, seen how I had changed since Julien's death, and she had the kind of wealth that could buy a hundred necklaces without feeling a strain on her budget.

I was still in the midst of shaking off my fatigue as I made my way to Evalyn's. Though I wanted to set a proper schedule for cleaning her collection, I'd also settle for connecting with more of her friends. I only hoped she wouldn't notice my red eyes and my disquiet. I needed to be fresh, bright, ready to charm everyone and ingratiate myself to anyone who might be at Evalyn's that day. Though she included me in her gatherings with her friends, I knew gaining their trust—and their willingness to confide in me about Julien—wouldn't be easy. And now that I was more desperate than ever for income, I really needed to secure them as clients, too. A task that was never as simple as an introduction or a glass of champagne over lunch. I had to woo them, make them feel special wearing Beaumont jewelry, and assure them the purchase was worth it. I might also have to use the Beaumont Jewelers' strongest tactic that rarely failed: create a story about a particular piece to make it more alluring, its beauty more tempting—a skill I lacked entirely. It was always Julien who'd crafted fanciful tales that charmed our buyers, but I would have to learn how, too, should I truly want to keep the business afloat and, more importantly, a roof over our heads.

Jerry greeted me with a smile. "Miss Beaumont, how nice to see you. You'll join the others in the drawing room."

I followed him inside, a spring breeze rushing in behind me as strains of music from the piano floated through the hall. In the parlor, a musician sat rigidly at the beautiful Steinway, lush sounds pouring from the instrument. Several women were scattered throughout the room upon the various sofas and chairs as usual. I couldn't help but search for her face—for Carrie Wellington—and was instantly disappointed to find her absent from the day's party. Now that I knew she'd put in a good word for me with Evalyn and that her husband had hoped to go into business with Julien, I felt indebted to her, which left me unsettled. And there was also the gnawing sensation that I knew her somehow, from somewhere else.

The others regarded me as I was announced, their thinly veiled surprise I should again return to their company reflected in their eyes. I didn't belong there, they said with their gazes that raked my form from head to toe. I was nothing but a temporary distraction, a pet project for their friend. I tried not to let it bother me; they would never understand me—what it meant to work for a living, or, God forbid, wish to—but I would come to understand them in time. It was an important part of the job. Luckily, they didn't appear to be the most complicated of subjects.

"Oh good, you're here," Evalyn said, waving me over to her and a woman I didn't recognize. "Come, Lizzie, meet Florence Harding. Flo, this is my new friend, Lizzie. She's also my jeweler."

At once my tongue tied into knots. Florence "Flo" Harding was the wife of a former United States senator serving for Ohio. Warren G. Harding was a popular Republican running for president in the next election. I had never given politics much thought until recently. I'd been following the coverage of the Nineteenth Amendment—the women's right to vote—which was rumored to be going to the House of Representatives the following month for review and a vote. If it passed, it would go on to the Senate, and finally, individual states would be able to ratify the amendment. Suddenly I had a big reason to pay attention to politics, and I couldn't help but be curious as to what Flo Harding's stance would be—or Evalyn's for that matter. Would they vote, given the chance, or were their lives far too busy with other things? I couldn't imagine what other things could be more important. Still, I didn't bother to pose the question; I had a feeling it wasn't the right time and that Evalyn would scold me for being too serious.

"How do you do, ma'am," I said, taking a seat in the chair opposite them.

Flo greeted me politely but made no effort to speak with me after the introduction. While they continued their conversation, I studied her; she wore tiny spectacles and a plain dress, and her frizzy hair was pinned tightly to her head. She was stalwart, passionate, but generous with her smiles for Evalyn. For the others, she wore a pinched expression, her lips pressed together and her forehead drawn as if in constant pain. Like me, she clearly didn't fit well with the other women, who were as tidy and beautiful as the pages of a fashion review. As I took in Flo's mannerisms, her appearance, I felt less conspicuous in my plain skirt and blouse, despite the fact that my skirt was several inches longer than those of the other ladies. No one else was bothered by their lower calves showing. I was critically out of fashion—that much was clear—and I knew better than to assume this crowd wouldn't notice.

As I listened to the women catch up with one another, I noticed Evalyn's voice sounded strained, her laughter bordered on shrill, and her shoulders were set too high. I wondered what had put her on the edge. Despite her obvious disquiet, she chattered on as if nothing were wrong, inserting little details about each of her friends as she introduced them to me, how she came to know them, and where they lived in the city. I nodded politely, trying to file their names away for later by pairing them with their most prominent piece of jewelry. Pearl brooch: Jane. Ruby ring: Marjorie. Teardrop diamond necklace: Marcie. Spectacles and absolutely no other adornment: Flo.

"Let's start our game, shall we?" Evalyn said, eliciting a smattering of claps. "We have one extra player we can rotate in as needed."

"Which game are we to play?" I asked. It seemed there was little chance Evalyn would discuss business with me, so I might as well play along.

"Bridge, of course," Evalyn said, as if I'd asked the most absurd question in the world. "Do you know the rules?"

I shook my head. "I've always played poker."

She laughed. "For such a quiet little thing, you do surprise me. Don't you worry. We'll play poker one night after we've gotten into the whiskey. It would be horribly uncouth at this hour." She dropped her voice. "Or ever, really, but we don't have to tell anyone, now do we?"

The others joined in her laughter. Clearly poker wasn't considered a ladies' game, but how was I to know? The men in my life had always treated me as their equal, and I was beginning to realize how much that set me apart from other women. My lack of fashion sense, my complete ignorance of town gossip, and the fact that I'd prefer traipsing along a riverbank in muddy boots collecting rocks than doing just about anything else made me alien to these women in nearly every way. With each additional day I spent with Evalyn, the more I realized how much I had to learn about her society and the rules applying to upper-crust women. I wasn't certain I cared for any of it, and yet I knew how important it was to mimic them as best I could to garner their business—and hopefully to mine their secrets.

"Pardon me, Mrs. McLean, but you have another guest." Jerry swept into the room, escorting a woman who looked to be around thirty-five years of age. "Mrs. Alice Roosevelt Longworth."

"Alice! Why, I didn't think you were coming today," Evalyn cooed. She kissed Alice on her left cheek and motioned to an open chair. "I'm glad you're here. We were just about to play bridge."

I felt my mouth fall open and quickly closed it again, hoping no one had noticed. *The* Alice Roosevelt had quite a reputation in Washington. She was unconventional, known to be overly bold in her directness, and even a bit raucous as my father would say. She'd smoked in the White House, created a new fashion trend with her "Alice Blue" gowns, and served as an adviser to her president father. She'd also remained in the political sphere after her father had left it. Most scandalous of all, it was rumored she had a string of lovers despite her marriage to Representative Longworth. I had never cared about such matters much, but Julien had followed all the goings-on in Washington. He'd always tried to be close to the powerful, or at the very least, be in the know, which was a large part of why Beaumont Jewelers had done so well. While he followed the tabloids and gossip columns, I'd been too busy with my nose in a book or talking with Henry about some fascinating new artifact from a burial site somewhere in the world I'd always longed to visit.

I couldn't help but stare at the infamous Alice. Her dark hair was pinned to make it appear quite short. Her countenance was pretty enough, but her piercing blue eyes were striking. She scanned the room quickly, her sharp gaze taking in every detail. I had the distinct impression she was far more "woman" than many in the room. I liked her on sight.

"Well, what a surprise," Alice said, turning to Flo Harding. "You made it to the party. Not feeling under the weather after all, I see?"

"Alice, hello," Flo replied stiffly. She looked down and busily rearranged her pale skirt over her legs.

"I should have expected to see you, but I suppose I was hoping otherwise," Alice replied.

Pearl Brooch Jane giggled at Alice's overt rudeness. Ruby Ring Marjorie exchanged looks with Diamond Necklace Marcie. Stunned, I looked to Flo and waited for a rebuttal.

"I often wonder what you'd be like if you'd had a mother at home," Flo quipped. "Perhaps then your manners would be better."

I smothered my surprise. Who knew Flo had it in her. It seemed she belonged to this crowd after all. Evalyn looked positively delighted by the exchange. It seemed the only thing better than good gossip was witnessing a tête-à-tête in person. Fascinated, I looked from one woman to the next, once again mentally recording their exchanges. And back to Evalyn again, whose shoulders hadn't yet relaxed. Despite her valiant show of happy hostess, I sensed something was wrong.

"Come now, ladies, we're here to have a good time." Evalyn waved a hand dismissively. "Jerry, be a dear and set up the table for bridge. We'll need refreshments, too. The full cart and a round of mint juleps, 'tout de suite,' as the French would say."

I knew what the full cart meant. The game would likely devolve as the drinks flowed—this was something I was coming to understand about Evalyn and her friends—and it would be a long day of either becoming the topic of conversation or choosing to participate.

"Darling, you know I'm not drinking right now," Flo said. "I've just recovered from that terrible kidney attack."

Evalyn patted her hand. "You poor dear. We'll bring you as much tea and lemonade as you can drink."

Flo threw her hands in the air. "Oh all right, I'll have one."

Evalyn's blue eyes glittered. "That's the spirit."

The rest of the ladies chattered while choosing their places around the table. A young maid flitted about after them, rearranging cushions and setting up our playing table. As Evalyn dismissed the pianist, Jerry rolled out a cart of fresh glasses and the makings for mint juleps. While the glasses were distributed, I noticed the worry lines in Evalyn's forehead had deepened and her hands were trembling as she reached for her mint julep. I'd never seen her in less than a jovial spirit. I watched her over the rim of my glass, deciding if it was my place to ask her what had shaken her. She was attempting to hide whatever it was but doing so poorly. As she dealt the cards, Alice noticed Evalyn's hands, too.

"What's got you so rattled, Evie?" Alice set down her drink. "And don't bother denying it. You're shaking like a leaf."

"It's nothing to worry about," Evalyn said.

"It isn't nothing," Alice insisted.

"What is it?" Concern etched Flo's face as she touched Evalyn's forearm.

Evalyn set down her cards, crossed the room, and returned with an envelope. "This arrived today."

Flo skimmed it, her brow arching in surprise. "Do you know this person?"

Evalyn shook her head. "Can you imagine? The gall! I don't even remember crossing paths with her, let alone recall giving her the chance to touch my necklace."

"Don't leave us in suspense," Alice said. "Read it aloud."

"Be my guest," Evalyn replied, handing Alice the letter.

Alice smoothed the letter, cleared her throat, and began.

April 18, 1919

Dear Mrs. Edward McLean,

You may not remember our encounter, but we met at Gloria Harris's charity auction. We spoke at length and at one point, you let me touch the Hope Diamond necklace. Since, I've lost my beloved husband. My assets have also been seized. I will never forgive myself for being lured in by the beauty of that evil talisman. I shudder to think of what ill may befall you. I urge you to rid yourself of the necklace as soon as possible.

May God have mercy on your soul.

Yours sincerely,
Maude Hughes

I looked from one stricken face to the next as the women shifted uncomfortably in their chairs. My eyes were drawn irresistibly to the Hope twinkling brightly at Evalyn's neck.

Evalyn's strained laughter broke the silence. "What utter nonsense. The Hope Diamond is my good-luck charm. Everyone knows that. It has never brought me an ounce of bad luck."

Given our private conversation about the curse and now her trembling hands, I didn't buy her act. She could insist she didn't believe in such nonsense, but the truth showed in her wrinkled brow and the lines around her mouth.

In the marked silence that followed, several of the women

exchanged weighty looks. I, too, wanted to deny the stone's power and deny something as foolish as a curse, but tragedy had touched my own home only weeks after Julien had begun work for the McLeans. And the more I learned about the misfortunes that had befallen those who came within the stone's orbit, the larger the seeds of doubt grew. Nausea rolled over me in a hot wave.

"Lizzie," Evalyn said. "You work on legendary gemstones all the time. I'm sure you find this as foolish as I do."

I hesitated until the silence grew too heavy to bear. "Of course," I said. Evalyn's expression was almost pleading, and I rambled on to try to make her feel better—to try to distract myself from the encroaching dread and the realization that a curse may not be so ridiculous after all. "I can't believe that woman had the nerve to write such silliness."

"What utter nonsense!" Flo agreed.

"Maude is nothing but a superstitious ninny," Alice said. "Imagine, a stone being cursed. We aren't living in a novel, for God's sake."

"If you aren't worried, why did you hire guards for the children?" Rita asked.

"Why would you ask such a thing," Evalyn replied. "Anyone with our wealth can't be too careful. Besides, we've been receiving kidnapping threats since Vinnie was born."

My eyes bulged, but the others merely nodded. I'd seen the guards and had considered them superfluous. The sign of an overanxious and spendthrift mother. But kidnapping threats were truly horrifying.

"That's more bad luck, Evie," Jane chimed in and then added, "Your brother also died in a car accident, and it left you lame. And you'd seen the diamond by then already. By the time of your father's death, you'd held it."

My eyes darted to Evalyn's face, looking for some sign of pain or fear, of grief. Instead, it was Marjorie's face that paled. Evalyn merely shrugged.

"Maybe it's too late for me, too," Marjorie said, voice strained. "I've tried the necklace on. I may be cursed already."

Evalyn rolled her eyes. "Please, this is all ridiculous! There's no such thing as a curse." Though her words were brave, I didn't miss the way she gulped down the rest of her mint julep and signaled for Jerry to pour another, all the while her hands still trembled.

The conversation fractured into many. I overheard Marjorie confide in the woman on her right.

"That's the fifth note she's received this week, and they're each from different people," Marjorie said. "She's told to save the letters, too, should the police need to investigate. Can you imagine being threatened or blackmailed every day? I don't know how she can stand it."

"She drinks herself to sleep," the other woman replied in a hushed tone. "Or takes Veronal."

With effort, I hid my surprise. Veronal was a powerful sleeping aid that could easily become addictive. Between the pills and alcohol, Evalyn was sedating her nerves. Given the fact that she received so many threatening notes every week, I was no longer surprised she threw herself into life with such reckless abandon. If she stood still for long, she'd be too terrified to leave her house. I glanced at Jerry, who perched in a corner beside a Chinese vase on an exquisite oak table near the door. He tried to appear politely detached, but his eyes were bright, and if he leaned forward any farther to better hear the conversation, he would topple over.

"But what about that young man who used to work for you?" Flo insisted. "Wasn't he a jeweler? What was his name?"

I froze. Flo clearly didn't know "that jeweler" had a twin sister, sitting in the very room, close enough to touch her.

Everyone started talking at once, the volume increasing as they carried on, until someone began to laugh. Suddenly the room felt stuffy, the collar of my dress too tight, the insufferable laughter a condemnation. I stood abruptly and excused myself to the ladies' room, nearly tripping as I bolted for the door.

As I stepped into the hallway, I heard Evalyn's voice ring out through the commotion. "You all know Lizzie is the jeweler's twin, don't you!"

"No!" someone replied. "She looks nothing like him."

"I assure you, she is his sister."

Another voice. "Goodness, how tragic."

"Isn't it?" Evalyn replied. "How could I turn her away?"

I veered left, narrowly missing another vase. Footsteps clacked over the polished hardwood floor behind me, but I picked up my pace. I couldn't face them—couldn't face the conversation inevitably waiting for me. And yet wasn't that the very reason I was here? To find out more about what was happening with Julien, or had I been lying to myself? Perhaps the truth was too painful. Perhaps I should leave well enough alone. As panic bore down on me, I took in a sharp breath and suppressed my urge to flee.

"Ma'am? Ma'am, can I help you with something?" Jerry called after me.

I halted in my tracks, face flushed, and turned to the kindly butler, who had quickly shed his haughty and gruff demeanor once Evalyn had accepted me into her fold. Eager not to appear ill at ease or fleeing Evalyn's *again*, I scrambled for an excuse. "I've just remembered I have another appointment today, and I'm on the verge of being late."

"Of course, ma'am." He led me to the door to open it for me, and we nearly collided with Ned, who laughed heartily at the near mishap.

"Hello, Lizzie. How are you today?" Ned asked. He noticed my expression and frowned. "Are you all right? I know Evie's friends can be intimidating at times, but they're mostly a bunch of bored, silly women."

I forced a polite smile. "I lost track of time is all. I forgot an appointment that I'll be late for if I don't make a run for it. The mint julep did me in, I'm afraid. If you'll excuse me, I need to go."

"Let me escort you."

"Oh," I said, surprised by his offer. "Thank you, but that won't be necessary. I can walk to the tram."

"I insist," he said. "I'm going into town anyway. It's no trouble. Let me pull the car around. I'll meet you out front."

Heart racing from the turn Evalyn's conversation had taken, I strode outside onto the porch. I couldn't stand it, listening to them discuss my brother so flippantly, as if he were an insignificant stranger. Besides, I wouldn't have time alone with Evalyn to talk about schedules with her party of friends, their manners and their attention span rapidly dissolving as the mint juleps continued to flow.

Jerry followed me out of doors. "Shall I give Mrs. McLean a message for you?"

"Please apologize for me, and tell her about my other appointment?" I said. "I'll return tomorrow to work out the schedule and to do the first cleaning."

"Of course, ma'am," he replied, concern reflected in his kind eyes.

I wondered how much he knew about Julien or if Jerry believed the accidents were connected to the shadow of bad luck the Hope Diamond seemed to cast on all who were near it. Scenes from the night of Julien's death pushed at the wall I'd carefully constructed in my mind. The squeal of tires, the screams, the blood. I exhaled slowly, willing myself to remain calm, to focus on the front walk where I waited for Ned. Moments later, he pulled up to the house in the same yellow car I'd ridden in once before. As I slid inside it, the scent of his cologne rushed my senses: sandalwood and some floral note I didn't recognize.

"You're from Washington?" Ned asked as he steered us down the drive and into traffic.

"More or less," I said. "My father is French, and I was originally born in a small town just north of Paris, but I've spent my entire life here."

"Ah, now the jewelry makes sense. The French do admire beauty. I learned that while visiting Paris myself. Americans don't really see things the same way, do they? It's all bigger and more and faster rather than an appreciation of the small, fine details of life. I must admit, I do like that about being an American." He chuckled to himself.

I wasn't sure how to answer so I didn't. Instead, I said, "It's kind of you to drive me. Thank you."

"Any friend of Evie's is a friend of mine." He smiled and I could see how Evalyn had fallen for him. He had a gallant air about him but a deep intensity, too. I wondered briefly how they had met. Their mutual fortunes, I assumed, put them directly into each other's orbit: Ned, son of a self-made riverboat manufacturer as well as a newspaper mogul, and Evalyn, daughter of the most successful miner and owner of the largest gold mine in the United States. Together, they made quite the pair. Though their fortune was vast, I'd heard they were big spenders—big enough to inspire a string of gossip that followed them in the newspapers and tabloids about their lavish parties, multiple homes, and extravagances from furniture to cars to racehorses. After spending a little time in two of their homes, I could confirm the gossip to be true.

"Thank you," I said simply.

"You're Julien's sister, right? I almost would have missed it. You two look nothing alike."

A pang hit me, but I tried to remain calm, to not become too emotional. It was bad enough I'd fled Evalyn's gathering for a second time. "Yes, I am. We've heard that a lot over the years."

"He was a good man. Enjoyed the hell out of our time together. John Whitehall, Jet Wellington, Peter Willougby, and I, along with your brother, had become quite the band of compadres."

I sat rigidly in my seat, surprised he'd shared the information so readily. "Really?"

"Sure, sure. He spent some time with the women, too, but that was usually to encourage them to part with their money." He grinned.

I searched my memory for some recollection of Julien talking about Ned and the others. I could only recall one thing about Ned, something about his love of gambling. I glanced at him, studied the side of his face a moment before returning my eyes to the road. If Julien had become friends with both the men and the women in Evalyn's circles and everything was running along smoothly between them all, why had he become increasingly preoccupied and distant? The circles under his eyes, the haunted look in his eyes. There had to be more to the story. I watched as the trees receded in the distance and the buildings of downtown Washington took their place. We took Connecticut to Rhode Island Avenue and continued eastbound until the redbrick homes of my neighborhood in Logan Circle came into view.

As we pulled up to my house, Ned said, "If you ever need anything, don't hesitate to ask. Evie is an accomplished hostess, but she can become rather caught up in the party sometimes. I'm always happy to rescue you."

Uncertain of what he meant by a rescue, I replied with an honest thanks. "Thanks again for the ride home."

He jumped out of the car, scooted around the side to open the door for me, and bowed. When he straightened, he said, "Have a good day, Miss Elisabeth Beaumont of Logan Circle."

I flushed at his attention.

He grinned as he saw the deep blush color my cheeks. "Pretty in pink, I see. Well, until next time."

I managed a polite smile.

Inside, I peeked through a slit in the curtain at the front window, watched him pull away from the curb and disappear into traffic. Was he always so kind and attentive? And the compliment he'd made... Did he truly find me attractive?

As I let the drapes sweep across the window and back into place, I shuttered the ridiculous thoughts of Ned McLean. That was a dangerous road upon which I didn't want to travel.

10

The next morning, I climbed the steps of the tram, paid the fare, and took a seat on an empty bench. As the conductor rang the warning bell and we began to move, my mind circled back to the events of the previous day and Ned's comment. I'd been too stunned by the new information to react quickly, to probe him with more questions about his friendship with Julien. I silently berated myself for not being quick enough on my feet.

I also worried I'd embarrassed Evalyn by departing so quickly. She'd given me a chance, brought me into the fold of her home and friends, and I might very well have ruined it. If I wanted to remain a part of her circle, I needed to tread a careful path between "friend" and "the help," appear amiable and clever and not sensitive or too sharp-tongued. I had to be infinitely useful or at the very least be entertaining, something I was learning to do a little more each day. But the thought of such careful calculation exhausted me. It wasn't in my nature to put on airs or to attempt to mimic the kind of society that made me uncomfortable. And yet here I was, trying to be someone of whom Evalyn and her friends might approve.

I pressed my forehead against the cool, smooth glass of the

windowpane. I thought again of the ladies' reaction to Julien's death and their whispered concerns about the curse. The idea of a curse was a silly notion made for novels and treasure hunts, and yet I could not seem to dismiss it. Despite my skepticism and my logical need to explain the why and the how through concrete evidence, I found my mind opening to the possibility. There were simply too many coincidences: Evalyn's own family tragedies and the stories she'd shared, the outrageous number of letters she'd received in the mail, and then there was my brother… I wondered if there were other mishaps that had taken place in her household or among her friends. There had to be at least some grain of truth in the notions of bad luck. I'd felt the pull of the diamond myself from the first moment I'd seen it.

Instantly, my logical brain attempted to find reason, a rational explanation for dark omens and the draw of an object. Perhaps the owner of a relic shared a magnetic field with the item, and as the person passed on, they left behind a trace of their energy. This made sense to me; particles and energy and electricity, the tiniest components of all things living and inanimate objects, interacted with one another. This was a concept Albert Einstein had discovered a decade and a half before. Since then, his work had become an essential aspect of scientific study, and I had read everything I could about it. I mulled these thoughts for the rest of the journey. Possibilities and impossibilities and Julien's time in that house with all those people.

When I reached my stop, I joined other pedestrians in the street. As I walked down Maryland Avenue to a cluster of homes and small offices, a warm breeze carried with it the promise of summer ahead. As motor cars, bicycles, and taxi cabs whizzed past me, I admired the small plots of greenery dotting the homes and boutiques featuring trees and shrubs that flowered in a brilliant riot of color.

At last, I reached the home of scientist and friend Ken Davis. I needed a distraction and a little inspiration, and the Davis home was just the place to find it.

"Elisabeth, great to see you," Ken said, running a hand over his hair. His mop of silver curls was unruly as usual, his shirt and trousers rumpled. He'd never put much stock in his appearance; he was far too busy with his work. His wife, Maye, was similar in mannerisms and appearance. They were almost comical in how well they resembled each other. "It's been quite a while since I saw you last. I hope you've been well?"

"I've been busy with new clients," I said. If Ken had learned of Julien's death, he didn't let on, and I had no intention of mentioning it. I appreciated that about Ken. He didn't pry.

"Lovely to see you, Elisabeth," Maye said while reaching for her umbrella in case the predicted afternoon rains came. "I was just on my way to work." Maye worked as a lab assistant with a chemist in the north end of the city.

"Next time we'll have tea," I said, kissing her cheek before she disappeared through the door to join the rush of pedestrians outside.

"I've got some new specimens in," Ken said as he closed the door behind his wife. "If you'd like to see them?"

"That's why I've come," I said eagerly. "I could use some inspiration."

He showed me to his half-study, half-laboratory room in the back of his home.

I'd met Ken two years before while reading up on the historical and geological origins of the gemstone peridot. I'd ventured first to the Capitol building downtown, where the Smithsonian library stored its vast collection of records in a fireproof vault. There, the librarians had directed me to Ken, one of the Smithsonian's premier mineralogists. When I'd asked about the Capitol and why the Institution didn't store records on-site, he'd told me about the original Smithsonian Institution building, nicknamed the Castle, where two massive fires had destroyed far too many precious items and files. Those that could be salvaged were quickly transferred to the only location large enough that was also fire resistant. Despite the library at the Capitol, many curators like Ken housed most of their own records due to the library's limited capacity. Since the Smithsonian Institution was rapidly expanding into an extensive network of museums, record centers, and laboratory spaces, there was talk of building a much larger central archive center and library.

Ken pulled out a tray of stones, each carefully labeled. "They've found a large pocket of lepidolite at the Harding Pegmatite mine in New Mexico. See its deep purple color? It comes from the lithium inside the stone." He went on to explain several of the other stones found recently, how the veins of color within the stones were a result of their mineral composition, as well as their various other properties, including hardness, porosity, strength, and optical qualities.

I listened intently while furiously writing notes. As he described the expedition where they were discovered, I felt the familiar sense of wistfulness I hadn't felt since Julien's death. I'd always dreamed about what it would be like to trek over unfamiliar landscapes, meeting with miners and collectors who knew the earth better than anyone, toting samples to examine in my lab just as Ken did. My imagination swept me away as I wrote the last of my notes.

After he showed me all his new items, we enjoyed a cup of coffee.

"I have a question for you," I said. "I've taken a new job with Evalyn Walsh McLean. She owns the Hope Diamond."

He removed his spectacles. "She has quite the collection from what I've heard."

I nodded. "She does. It's impressive. What do you know about the Hope Diamond?"

He shook his head. "I'm afraid I don't know much. My focus is more on mineralogy rather than gemstones, though of course I've heard it's said to be cursed."

I nodded. "Evalyn insists otherwise, but there are a lot of rumors and many stories of things going awry... I don't know. Do you believe in such things?" I asked, hoping he didn't find the question foolish.

He shrugged. "I would say it's a ridiculous idea, but as soon as I call anything nonsense, I uncover some reason why it isn't nonsense after all. That's the way of science, isn't it?" He leaned forward. "Science isn't only a tool used to prove a hypothesis. It is a pathway to infinite possibility."

As I internalized his words, I thought about the rumors I'd heard and of Evalyn's losses. He was right. If there was one thing people like Ken and people like me tried to do, it was to keep an open mind and to look for possibilities until a hypothesis could be disproven.

"I'll be right back." He left the room and reappeared a moment later. "Take this." He placed a smooth stone in my palm.

I peered at the dark-green stone dotted with irregular red dots. "Heliotrope?"

He nodded. "Bloodstone. Keep it. You might find you need it."

It was a stone known in the ancient East as a way to increase higher consciousness and clarity, but it was also used for something else entirely: as a protector against evil.

At home, I sorted through my own collection of stones stored in the desk drawer of my worktable. I'd found most of them on my walks, during trips to the quarry with Father, during the handful of vacations we'd taken in Maryland along the Chesapeake Bay, or in Virginia, in the Shenandoah Valley that stretched between the Blue Ridge Mountains to the east and the Ridge-and-Valley Appalachians to the west. Many of the stones were smooth, worn by time and the elements. Granite, limestone, quartz, a piece of amethyst, several seashells with pink and cream whorls, and many others. I'd even found a nearly perfect flint arrowhead in the quarry. I ran my thumb along the arrowhead's sharp edges, picturing the man who'd made it in his leather clothing with long black hair and intelligent eyes. I added the piece of purple lepidolite Ken had given me to my collection. As for the bloodstone, if it did bring good luck, I could use plenty of it, so I tucked it into my handbag.

After a satisfying lunch of omelet, greens, and a hunk of buttered bread, the sting of the embarrassment from the previous day at Evalyn's had faded, and I knew there was only one thing to do. I had to call her and pressure her to set a firm date for my services. With a party of friends ever at her side, I'd learned quickly the talk of business was nearly impossible. A telephone call might be easier.

I dialed the operator, and Evalyn's voice came over the line. "Hello, McLean residence."

Surprised she'd answered rather than Jerry, I paused. "Yes, hello. This is Elisabeth Beaumont."

"Oh, Lizzie, I was just waiting for another call. How are you? I was sorry to see you leave yesterday, but Jerry and Ned told me you had some other engagement."

"I—yes, I was so taken with meeting your friends and enjoying the conversation that I'd nearly forgotten about it," I said. "I apologize for leaving in a rush."

"Not at all. And here I thought it was because the conversation had turned toward your poor brother."

My cheeks burned. She'd seen right through me. "Oh, yes, well, that was a little uncomfortable. I'm not used to talking about my brother so openly."

"Of course, darling. Don't worry one bit about it. I let everyone know the situation yesterday. They all offer their condolences."

I felt my throat tighten. I didn't know Evalyn or her friends well, but I'd spent enough time in their presence to grasp they'd likely enjoyed the fact that I'd inadvertently provided them with fresh gossip.

"I meant to speak with you yesterday about setting a schedule," I said, gripping the telephone receiver a little too tightly. "Do you have a preference of date and time? I wanted to give you the first choice before I schedule my other appointments." Another little white lie—there were no others at the moment outside of Rosalee's necklace, but if there was one thing I already understood about Evalyn, it was her need to feel as if she had some special privilege others didn't.

"Why don't you start tomorrow?" she replied. "Ned and I won't be here in the morning, so you won't be disturbing anyone. Jerry will let you in."

I felt a prick of disappointment. Without Evalyn at home, the Hope Diamond might not be there either, and after my discussion with Ken, I could hardly wait to examine it again more closely. I was also hoping to entice her and her friends to talk about Julien and the friendships he'd developed with them and the men. I closed my fist around my bloodstone and rubbed a thumb over its smooth surface.

"Does ten o'clock suit?" I asked.

"Fine. And I'll expect you every two weeks."

"Wonderful," I said, relieved we'd finally set a schedule. It was extravagant of her to request my services so regularly, but everything about Evalyn was proving to be extravagant, right down to her generosity.

"Lizzie, I wanted to tell you something," she continued, her tone suddenly somber. "When I lost members of my family... Well, the grief never leaves us, but it does become easier to manage."

Surprised by the admission, I paused before replying. She'd seemed the sort who'd rarely suffered despite her losses, who sought pleasure and excitement as if it were a lifeline to happiness, but perhaps I'd had her all wrong. Perhaps there was more to her than I knew, more than the spoiled but friendly woman with whom I'd spent a few afternoons. And it was generous of her to offer the kind words.

"I can't imagine it ever being easy," I said softly. "But thank you."

"It's best not to spend too much time thinking about things we can't change," she said. "Ruminating hasn't ever helped me with anything, and it certainly hasn't lessened my grief."

"I suppose not," I replied, though I couldn't imagine putting Julien out of my mind the way she seemed able to do with her deceased loved ones, nor did I wish to.

"One last thing." She paused. "Don't you worry about what the others said about Julien or the way he conducted his business. I adored him. We all did."

"Thank you," was all I could manage.

I frowned as I hung the receiver on its cradle. I wondered what she'd meant by "the way your brother conducted his business." I pressed my lips into a thin line. Evalyn couldn't offer a kindness without a thorn. She also seemed to like playing games with her friends' affections, pitting one against the other so she could retain the upper hand. And I would do as she wished for now. I would do whatever it took to remain in her employ to uncover the truth—even if I had to play her games to win.

11

The next morning, I arrived early for my first official scheduled day to work on Evalyn's collection. Tool case in hand, I was promptly shown to the dining table while Jerry collected the jewelry from the safe. Friendship was oddly quiet for a change. Not even the children scampered about with their nanny. I moved to the window overlooking the flower gardens that bordered the rolling green lawn of the golf course beyond it. The McLeans' country residence was a peaceful, beautiful spot, far enough away from the center of Washington to feel like another world. I wondered if Evalyn knew how kind fate had to been to her: She was born into the right family, married into another well-connected family, and had everything her heart desired. Her home was a kind of paradise, her lifestyle beyond imagination. Had I not seen it in person, I would have never believed it could be true, that people lived the way the McLeans lived.

But then there was the excess and showmanship, which disgusted me on some level. Still, I couldn't lie—I was also a little envious. Who wouldn't want everything they'd ever desired at their fingertips? It was the expectation of always having what they desired at a moment's notice that irked me, and the way Evalyn never expressed true gratitude, never talked about anything of substance. And given that she was the center of a very powerful crowd, she set the tone for the others, whether it be in thought or taste or the direction of the conversation. She demanded without thought or care about what others wanted, and her circle of friends accepted her whims.

I wandered back to the table just as Jerry whisked into the room, carrying the tray of Evalyn's jewelry. "Here we are, ma'am."

As he set the collection down before me, a rush of excitement, trepidation, and curiosity coursed through me. I'd seen her entire collection once before, but I was still impressed by the sight of it all in one place and thrilled to be the person chosen to care for it. I opened the box in reverent silence. There were two diamond-crusted diadems, at least a dozen wide-set gold or platinum bracelets featuring a range of stones, and at least three necklaces beyond the spectacular diamond collar with large oval links that held the Star of the East. The Hope Diamond was notably absent. Though I'd suspected Evalyn would be wearing it, I still felt the sting of disappointment. I was hoping she'd have considered it too important not to have it evaluated to ensure the prongs were secure.

"Thank you, Jerry," I said.

He nodded. "Of course, ma'am." He strode to the corner of the room to give me space, but he watched me intently as I handled each piece.

I withdrew a cleaning rag, polish, and a tool kit from my satchel and placed them on the table. Untying the leather strap of my kit, I rolled open the soft pouch lined with miniature loops that held a pair of jeweler's pliers, an awl, a magnifying glass, and several tiny brushes.

Feeling Jerry's eyes on me, I said, "How are you today?"

"I'm doing fine, ma'am. Thank you for asking."

His drawl was charming. I liked him, could see why Evalyn did as well. He was a hard worker, obedient, and obviously trustworthy, or she wouldn't have given him access to her safe. He possessed the perfect qualities for a butler/footman, but these weren't the reasons I liked him. He seemed kind and stalwart, the sort of fellow you could rely on no matter what the scenario. I hoped Evalyn paid him handsomely.

"The house is so quiet today," I said. "It's almost alarming."

The usual clatter of footsteps, the hum of voices, and the strains of music were absent, leaving a vacuum of deep silence in their wake.

He chuckled. "Yes, ma'am," he said.

"The rest of the staff must be off today?"

"Some of the staff are here, ma'am. They're busy in the kitchen, but most of us have the afternoon off today."

The sound of rapid footsteps surprised us both, and we glanced at the door. In a flash, Evalyn's son Vinnie shot across the room, looking over his shoulder to see if anyone was behind him. When he noticed me with his mother's collection, he stopped, his flight forgotten, and sidled up next to me.

"What are you doing?" he asked, eyes wide with curiosity.

I smiled at the boy. "I'm cleaning your mother's collection. I also make sure the fasteners work. She would be very sad if she lost one of her pretty stones, wouldn't she?" I showed him the prongs and fastener on the Star of the East pendant.

He nodded. "How do you clean it?"

I showed him the solution I used for the stones and the polish for the metals along with the cloths and tiny brushes. He listened attentively, eyes wide with curiosity. He was such a darling little boy with dark hair and freckles sprayed across his nose.

"What do those do?" He pointed at the tools in my leather pouch. "There are so many!"

Jerry smiled as he watched us.

"These are jeweler's tools," I said, taking out each one and explaining what they did.

"Can I clean that one?" Vinnie said, pointing to the Star of the East for a second time.

"You sure can," I replied. "Here." I demonstrated how to scrub and polish the stone.

With pink tongue poking out between his lips, he concentrated on the task for several minutes and then presented the piece. "It's really sparkly."

"You did a great job," I agreed. "Would you like to learn about new stones? There are some you can find in your backyard."

His face lit up. "Yes!"

"Vinnie!" his nanny called him from the other room. "Your tutors will be here any minute. You need to get your things together!"

He shrugged and smiled, revealing a missing tooth, and shot off through the room, disappearing quickly from sight.

"He seems like a sweet boy," I said.

"He's boisterous at times, but he's a gentle soul," Jerry agreed. "I shouldn't say this, but he's the favorite. Mr. and Mrs. McLean dote on him, as do his nanny and younger brother. He's a good-natured little fellow."

I moved on to the next piece, an exquisite emerald ring with nearly perfect clarity. As I checked the prongs to ensure they were tight against the gemstone, I couldn't help but wish again that I could also work on the Hope Diamond. Despite my growing apprehension about the gem, I wanted to touch it, to study it. Most of all, to slip it around my neck.

"Jerry?" I said.

"Yes, ma'am?"

"Did my brother polish the Hope Diamond?"

"Yes, ma'am, many times. I believe Mrs. McLean had him polish it every week."

Somewhere in the back of my mind, an alarm bell sounded. He'd spent a lot of time with the diamond—and in the path of the curse. I also couldn't help but wonder why Evalyn had only deigned to let me hold it one time.

"Do you believe in curses?"

His thick dark eyebrows shot up. "Do you mean the Hope Diamond, ma'am?"

I nodded. "I've heard a lot of stories about it."

His face changed, and he glanced around as if looking for anyone potentially lurking around a corner. "I shouldn't say this but yes, ma'am. It's definitely cursed."

Despite myself, goose bumps ran over my arms. "Why do you think so?"

"I really shouldn't say, ma'am."

"Of course, I understand." I'd returned to my work for only a few minutes when Jerry approached the table and lowered his voice to a near whisper.

"If I tell you this, ma'am, please don't say anything." His brows were drawn together in a frown, but there was a light in his dark eyes. He positively couldn't wait to tell me his secret.

"I wouldn't dream of it," I said. "You have my word."

"Mrs. McLean hired an Italian immigrant named Josephina as a scullery maid, but she quit after only two weeks. She claimed she had nightmares from the first day she began working here. She also said small things had started going wrong for her. Truthfully, Josephina seemed at odds with Mrs. McLean's demands. One night after dinner service, Josephina disappeared and didn't come back to work the next day. Several days later, we heard from one of the others through the grapevine that she had fallen down a flight of stairs and broken both of her legs."

I was surprised by his blunt honesty. I'd expected him to skirt around the topic or dismiss the curse entirely as a silly legend without merit. But I could see the idea of a curse was all too alluring to him, and sharing it with someone interested in hearing the gossip made it all the better.

"Goodness, is she all right?" I said. And then I remembered the way Evalyn's staff had behaved the first time I'd set foot in her home, at that first party a few weeks ago. How they'd tended to her guests but took a wide berth around her, answering her only when she called on them directly, and after, darting away quickly as if frightened. I recalled, too, the chauffeur's face the day he'd seemed relieved when Evalyn had wanted to take the car out for our luncheon on her own, without him. Perhaps it wasn't fear of being chastised or dislike of Evalyn and her demands. Perhaps it was fear of the diamond's bad luck.

He shrugged. "One of the maids looked in on her, but she no longer lived in the apartment she was sharing with her family. I suppose we'll never know."

"Did she touch the diamond?"

He shrugged. "I never saw her touch it, but I suppose anything is possible." He leaned closer now. "But there are others in this house who have had bad luck, too."

"Who are the others?"

"Minnie, Mrs. McLean's lady's maid, contracted smallpox and nearly died. She recovered, but her face is so scarred that Evalyn had to change her position to a kitchen maid so her guests wouldn't be frightened by her face. Then there was Harriet. The first month Harriet worked here, her dog was stolen and her fiancé *died*."

"Oh my goodness. How did the fiancé—"

"Freak accident. His house was struck by lightning in a storm and caught fire. The whole thing burned to the ground before the fire department could put it out."

I looked up from the pair of ruby earrings I was cradling in the palm of my hand. "You're kidding!"

He shook his head. "If only I were."

He seemed encouraged by my surprise, and his stories continued to pour out of him. All the while, my mind raged like the Potomac River swollen after a summer storm. So many had been pulled into the Hope Diamond's path only to be faced with ruin or worse. And yet here I was, tempting fate. I reached for the bloodstone tucked inside my handbag and rubbed its smooth surface. As much as I wanted to dismiss Jerry's concerns as silly, I couldn't let go of the idea that the curse—even if only appearing to be true through coincidence—could have been part of why Julien had died so unexpectedly and tragically. My stomach clenched at the thought.

"Has anything happened to you, Jerry?"

He shook his head. "Nothing of note, thankfully. But I must admit, I second-guess everything. Sometimes I think I should have taken a job elsewhere, with another of Mrs. McLean's friends. As much as Mrs. McLean would like to proclaim otherwise, I believe she, too, has bad luck. Things have...happened."

I remembered the brief conversation I'd had with Evalyn about losing her brother and father. I wondered if there had been more unsettling events than she was willing to admit to, at least publicly. My curiosity got the better of me. "What else has happened?"

Jerry suddenly realized his error, and his face colored a deep red. "I really shouldn't have said that. You won't tell Mrs. McLean? I'm so grateful to have such a generous mistress, and I would hate to upset her for any reason."

"It's all right," I said. "I have no intention of telling her or anyone, Jerry. I wouldn't dream of putting your job in jeopardy. You have my word. Besides, I know how much you mean to Evalyn. And despite the mishaps, a curse is merely conjecture, isn't it? We'll pretend as if we never spoke of it."

His shoulders relaxed, and a grateful smile crossed his round face. "Thank you, ma'am."

It suddenly occurred to me that Jerry might know about Julien's time in the McLeans' home, too. Perhaps even his death. "Do you remember my brother?"

He nodded. "Of course, ma'am. He was a friendly young man."

I hesitated a moment, considering what to say and how to say it. "Yes...it seems he made friends with Ned and the other men. Ned said as much to me."

"Yes, he spent a lot of time with them at first. Less so toward the end."

I frowned. "Did they have a falling-out of sorts?"

"I believe there was some conflict, yes. Something about a business deal?" He shook his head. "I'm not certain of what, but a couple of weeks before he died, he wasn't coming by the house at all."

"A business deal? How odd." But what struck me most was the second part of what Jerry had said—Julien hadn't been going to the McLeans'. Where had he been going?

Jerry shrugged, but I got the distinct feeling he was keeping something from me. But why? And what in the world could Julien have gotten himself into with some of the wealthiest and most connected families in the country?

"I'm afraid that's all I know, Miss Beaumont," he said.

"Thank you for sharing that," I said agreeably.

But as he moved back to his post a few paces away, silence fell between us again, and my mind was a cyclone of questions, all without answers.

12

That night, I dreamed of dark things coming for me. They shifted like smoke, morphing around me in a swirl of green-black and midnight blue until I was plunged into a dark body of water. I swam with all my strength against a current that dragged upon my limbs until the current won and swept me toward an outcropping of rocks. Just as I was to be smashed upon their sharp edges, the location shifted, and I found myself no longer in the sea but in a room where the dark things returned, pressing around me, against me, forcing me to face them. I squeezed my eyes closed, balled my hands into fists to will them away, and as I did, liquid heat pooled in my chest. Somehow I'd summoned something buried beneath my skin that I didn't understand. My body shook so intensely with the power of it that I awoke with a start.

I bolted upright in bed, heaving, my hands trembling. I couldn't make sense of the dream. It had felt as if I were being chased by something evil. Had my imagination run away with me, or was I truly sensing an energy beyond my understanding? Either way, the dreams had intensified lately, and I couldn't seem to shake them.

When morning dawned, I slid out of bed, padded into the washroom, and peered into the mirror at my pale face. I hardly recognized the haunted eyes, the deep creases around my mouth. I bent over the porcelain bowl and splashed my cheeks with cold water. In an instant, an image of Julien's broken body flashed before my eyes. I gasped, clutching the sink. I had seen the horrible vision so often, and still, each time it returned, it was as if I were seeing it for the first time. The way the car had raced around the corner, skidded as it hit a puddle from the afternoon rain. How I'd screamed as the car crashed into my brother, felling him instantly. Henry and I racing down the park slope toward him. The swarm of police and bystanders.

I winced and slumped against the wall, grappling with my emotions, trying to collect myself, to push it all away.

"Elisabeth?"

My father's strained but clear voice cut through the cloud of emotion bearing down on me. Father needed me. I pushed up from the floor and wiped the moisture from my face. Some days, he seemed better, as if emerging from the fog that had enveloped him since Julien's death, and others, he was lost in another world, lost in his mind. I could see a change in him for the better, though, and I'd begun to have faith he would return to himself in time. I pulled a housecoat over my cotton nightgown. By the time I'd knocked at his bedroom door, he was waiting for me.

"Come in!" he called impatiently.

I pushed open the door to find him sitting up in bed. Though his hair was wild, his cheeks were flushed as if he'd exerted himself.

I perched on the edge of his bed. "How are you feeling?"

"I'm hungry," he replied, laying a hand on his deflated abdomen. "Have you eaten?"

I covered his free hand with mine. "How about some ham and eggs? I'm going to make a plate for myself. I can bring up a tray."

"No need to bring a tray up. I'll come down to the kitchen. Perhaps I'll go for a short walk afterward. I think it's time I built my strength again, don't you?"

Feeling optimistic at his reply, I allowed the smallest smile. I had never admitted my real fear aloud, that I had worried that I'd lose him forever, too, and I would be left without my twin and my father, without anyone. But times were changing yet again, and I was relieved.

"I'm glad to hear it," I said.

In the kitchen, I heated a pan, fried two thick slices of ham, and slid them onto plates. After, I melted a pat of butter, whipped eggs vigorously in a bowl, and poured them into the hot pan, pushing the mixture with a spatula until a thick, fluffy cloud of eggs formed. As I spooned the eggs onto the plates, the sound of Father's foot on the stair came behind me.

"You're just in time," I said as he took a seat at the table. "Everything is nice and hot." I set the two plates down on the table and poured us each a cup of coffee.

When our forks scraped against empty plates, he broke the silence.

"We received an invitation to a bazaar tomorrow," he said. "You remember the spring bazaar?"

"Of course, yes."

"You should go," he said. "See what others are selling. Perhaps it will motivate you with your own collection."

"Perhaps," I said, not enthused with the idea of going to the bazaar alone. In years past, it had been great fun going with Julien and my father and occasionally with Henry. And yet I knew my father was right. At the very least, I should speak with the organizers so I might set up a booth for the bazaar in the fall.

Preparing himself another cup of coffee on the stovetop, he added,

"I forgot to tell you. There was a call from a woman named Evie while you were out yesterday. She asked you to stop by her house on Saturday morning. Is she a new client?"

I froze. He hadn't put two and two together, realized that Evie was Evalyn McLean. He'd assumed it was a different woman—trusted I wouldn't go back to the woman who wore a cursed gemstone, to the house where Julien had met the beginning of the end. As I searched for what to say, I glanced at the pink in his cheeks that had at last returned. He was finally up and about the house, finally making his way through a full plate of food, finally planning to go out on his own after seven months in bed. I couldn't risk how he'd react to the news of my working for the McLeans. He wouldn't agree to it, wouldn't allow it. And it very well might send him back to the precarious edge from which he finally seemed to be retreating.

I forced a light tone. "Yes, she's one of several new socialites who would like to hire me. To hire us," I amended. "I might even be able to work with Alice Roosevelt Longworth! Father, she's as colorful as they say."

His brow arched in surprise. "Are these Sam's friends?"

In that moment, I realized I shouldn't have linked my new clients to Julien's friend Sam, because Father was good friends with Sam's parents. It would be easy enough for him to trap me in the lie. I still couldn't bring myself to tell him about Evalyn, so yet another lie sprang to my lips. "I met them through Rosalee Smith."

"Ah, Rosalee. How is she?"

"Oh, fine. Lovely as always. How's your coffee?" I asked, eager to change the subject. My dear old papa had no idea what I was up to, how much I was risking for our home—or how close I was to the Hope Diamond and the people with whom Julien had entangled himself before he died.

"That's great news," he said, cradling his mug. "I always knew you had it in you, no matter how much you've protested against being a salesman. You should invite them to the shop, show them our entire collection."

It was a good idea to invite Evalyn and her friends to the shop, as long as it was during a time Father typically napped or went for a walk. I didn't want to risk him seeing Evalyn. Perhaps instead, the next time I visited Friendship, I'd bring our showcase box to her.

"I plan to," I lied. I didn't like lying to him, but given the circumstances lately, I didn't see any way around it.

He pushed his empty plate forward and tossed his napkin over it. "When they come, be sure you show them your own collection as well."

I knew this was his way of saying he was proud of me. Part of me warmed to the clear but unspoken praise, and the other felt the shame of wishing I didn't have my unfinished collection hanging over my head.

All I said was, "I will," and squeezed my father's hand.

The following morning arrived bright and clear, and as I arrived at the bazaar, everyone appeared to be cheerful. Vendors were ready to sell, sell, sell, and customers delighted in the array of goods. I sauntered through the dozens of booths featuring fuchsia, orange, and cobalt blue silks of glittering saris from India, paintings from scenes of the purple Virginia mountains or the jagged Maryland coastline, knit shawls and caps and gloves, and a hundred other items. The jewelry section bled into the wholesale stones, and I found myself sorting through bins of tiger's-eye and rose quartz and shiny chunks of pyrite, fool's gold.

As I wandered back to the jewelry booths, featuring a range of semiprecious stones from smoky quartz to jade, I thought of Julien, his involvement with Ned and his friends, and their possible business venture. What had he been up to? If he'd sunk money into their schemes and lost it, I could see why he'd become so agitated those final weeks before his death. Or perhaps he'd overstepped, inserted himself with the big boys too quickly, too soon. Evalyn had made a quip about how he did business... I knew I was closer to the truth, but something still didn't add up.

I stood over a display of hammered gold bracelets and thought back to the last jewelry show I'd attended with my brother. He'd been in great spirits, and I'd been desperate to sell something from my collection, though it wasn't yet complete. All I'd wanted was to prove to Father—to myself—that I could do the work he so longed for me to do. The colorful bazaar before me blurred as I retreated into the memory.

The show had filled quickly, patrons pouring in with smiles of delight, accepting a glass of champagne from a tray as a waiter circulated through the room. It was a great strategy on the organizer's part, to fill patrons with fizzy warmth so they were more likely to buy.

"How are things, Beaumonts?" A familiar voice caught me by surprise.

"Henry! What are you doing here?" I asked. He was handsome as always with his boyish smile, neatly combed auburn hair, and lawyer's suit.

Julien shook his hand. "Come to buy something for Marjorie?"

Henry grimaced. "I broke it off with her. We had nothing in common in the end."

The spark of pleasure his words inspired was unexpected. I wanted to add that Marjorie was impossible to talk to, even if she was one of the prettiest women I'd ever seen. She didn't care for reading, didn't play games or instruments, and wasn't creative, and as far as I could tell, she had no hobbies outside of shopping. I'd found it baffling Henry should date her for months. It was clear she wasn't his type—at least it had been clear to me.

"She doesn't deserve you," I said emphatically.

A fleeting emotion passed over his features, and then he grinned. "You think so?"

"I know so." I grinned back at him, and he blushed. I was about to tease him the way I'd done my whole life when he changed the subject.

"Say, let me have a look at your rings." He skirted the edge of the table and bent over the tray. He picked up each one, studying them intently. Though he wasn't a jeweler, we'd taught him well over the years. He knew to look for the four C's of gemstone grading: cut, color, clarity, and carat weight. He also knew he needed a magnifying glass to see inclusions, or impurities, in the stones.

"What do you think?" I asked, suddenly shy.

He rotated the globe ring to watch the stones catch the light. "I like this one in particular. It looks like Earth. I've never seen anything like it."

I warmed to his praise. I liked it best, too, because it was a globe made of stones, as our world was. "Thank you."

"Have you sold any today?"

"Not yet," Julien cut in, "but she will. Someone is going to fall in love with her style one day. You'll see," he said, putting his hand on my shoulder.

"They will," Henry agreed. "I already am! If I had someone to buy them for..."

I knew the three men in my life—the people I cared about most in the world—supported me, and I was grateful for it, but it wasn't enough. They couldn't exactly force others to see the merit in my work. I needed the impeccably groomed, handbag-clutching, nose-in-the-air types that circled the room to take notice, too. Or I needed to do something else entirely with my time and set aside the dream my father and I had so carefully guarded.

As the hours passed, we sold several pieces, thanks to Julien and his sunny good looks and bright smile. I, meanwhile, hadn't sold a single thing. Worse yet, no one had so much as paused to look at my collection.

As a new group of women arrived, a buzz of excitement rippled through the crowd of attendees. They wore smart dresses and gloves and Merry Widow hats with wide brims and layers of chiffon that resembled the layers of a cake adorned with flowers and feathers or taxidermy birds. These women were the elite of the city, and every jeweler in attendance pinned their hopes on securing a sizable sale or, at the very least, serious interest in their work.

Eventually a pair of them arrived at our table.

"Aren't these just gorgeous," the woman with red hair said. She was so beautiful it almost hurt to look at her. She wore a comely yellow gown with a sailor collar and a triple string of pearls with an oval clasp studded with diamonds.

Julien flashed his perfect row of pearly whites. "Good morning, miss—"

"Mrs.," she corrected him. "Mrs. Wellington. How do you do."

"I'm doing just fine. Very happy to meet you, Mrs. Wellington," Julien replied, his eyes twinkling, his dimples on full display. He was flirting, something he did well with the socialites to encourage them to open their purses. "I see you have exquisite taste."

Amusement danced over Mrs. Wellington's pretty features. "I like to think so."

"Is there something in particular that you're looking for?"

She met his eye. "I thought so at one time, but now I'm not so sure. What I'm looking for has changed, Mr.—"

"Beaumont. Julien Beaumont."

"Oh? Are you French?"

"In a manner of speaking, yes. I was born in a small town outside of Paris, but I've lived my whole life here in the DC area."

"Aren't we lucky for that."

I gaped at her openly flirtatious manner. A woman of her breeding was rarely so forward.

"I've always heard you make your own luck." Julien smiled his most charming smile, and I expected to see the woman melt on the spot, given the way she was looking at him.

"I couldn't agree more." She diverted her gaze to our trays of jewelry. "These are beautiful." She fingered a pair of gold earrings shaped like a fan. "I can't imagine how you made them."

"I'm an expert at making beautiful things. And caring for them, too."

"Is that so." A gleam shone in her crystal blue eyes, and for a moment, it appeared they'd both forgotten they were in the company of others.

I nearly shoved my brother for being so forward. The whole exchange was nauseating. But she was undeniably attractive, and I knew Julien could never resist something or someone beautiful. He was like a magpie in that way.

As two other women joined her, she leaned closer to Julien. "There's a party at the McLeans' house next week." She returned the exquisite platinum brooch shaped like a fly with sapphire and diamond wings trapped in a spider's web. "Why don't you drop by? Bring a sample case of your favorite pieces. I know a lot of women would like your collection very much."

"Mrs. McLean won't mind if I stop by unannounced and uninvited?" He smiled at her again.

"Not at all. She's one of my dearest friends. I already know she'd be delighted to have you. In fact, you may steal the show." She fluttered her lashes at him.

"I doubt that, given present company."

It took every effort not to roll my eyes.

A smile spread across the perfect contours of her beautiful face. "I'll forward the address to your shop."

When the women had moved on to another table and were safely out of earshot, I said, "You sure poured that on thick."

He shrugged. "She bought one of our pieces, and I booked a showing at a private residence—and not just any private residence. The McLeans' house."

"Doesn't she own—"

"The Hope Diamond," we said in unison.

We exchanged a look that said more than we could aloud: This was the chance of a lifetime.

I gasped as the bazaar came sharply into focus once more. That was the day we'd first connected with the McLeans. I'd forgotten, assumed Julien had approached Evalyn on his own by calling to her house directly in hopes of gaining a new high-profile client. He'd done such things in the past. But no—it was because of Carrie Wellington! I knew I'd recognized her that first day in Evalyn's parlor. My mind raced as I remembered that she'd encouraged Evalyn to hire me. Was she the reason Julien had been so busy, so absent those few weeks before his death? My stomach swam with unease.

"Excuse me, ma'am." A woman of solid stature pushed around me where I stood in the middle of the walkway.

"I'm…I'm sorry," I stammered, the daydream that had paralyzed me for a moment dissipating like smoke. I moved out of the way and joined the circulation of people at the jewelry booths. But I didn't see the jewelers' artistry in the dozens of well-crafted pieces. All I could see was the scene from months ago—of Carrie and the beginnings of my brother's dark future among the McLeans—replaying behind my eyes.

13

As I arrived at Evalyn's the next day like she'd requested, for once I hoped she'd also invited her friends. I was eager for a chance to talk to Carrie about my brother. They'd flirted, something real had sparked between them, but given her emphasis on her married name when they'd met and the fact that Julien had spent a lot of time with her husband, I suspected it had been a harmless meeting one afternoon at the bazaar and nothing more. The thought was followed by instant doubt. I couldn't discount the fact that Julien had become mixed up with a married woman before. Still, the affair had been short-lived. Once a woman became too infatuated with him, the thrill of the chase would end, and he would stop courting her almost immediately. More than once, I'd had to take over his client account after explaining away his terrible behavior. My brother's most prominent character flaw was his short attention span. Paradoxically, his lust for life that made him so attractive and such great fun also made him flighty at times.

Jerry smiled in greeting as he opened the door. "It's nice to see you again so soon."

"I've brought something for you." I held out a small wrapped package. Perhaps it was too much, but I was grateful for his candor and his kindness, and should I work for the McLeans for the foreseeable future, it would be good to have an ally.

"For me? Whatever for, ma'am. That wasn't at all necessary," he said coyly while tearing open the paper as if his life depended on it.

I stifled my amusement and said, "Gifts are always a good idea."

He turned over the money clip to peer at the long, narrow pewter strip etched with a lion's head. "It's a handsome piece, ma'am. Thank you! You really shouldn't have gone to so much trouble."

"It's a thank-you for being so welcoming and looking after me while I was having a rough time of things."

Though half of his face was covered in a thick, dark beard, I didn't miss the glimmer in his eyes. "Anytime you need anything at all, you come to me, ma'am."

"I'm glad you like it."

"I do." He smiled, revealing a row of crooked teeth. "Now, Mrs. McLean is having her breakfast. Right this way."

Evalyn was seated at the dining table, cradling a cup of coffee in her hands. "Would you like some coffee?" She blew at the steam rising from the hot liquid. "I couldn't get out of bed this morning. I'm such a lazybones! I've just now sat down to breakfast. How luxurious is that?"

I recalled the conversation I'd overheard about Evalyn's use of Veronal to sleep. Combined with booze, the medication was enough to put a whale to sleep. I watched her as she set her cup on the table and tapped the shell of her two-minute egg. It cracked obediently, and she dipped a spoon into the creamy mixture to scoop out the insides. Her hands shook slightly as she spread the goo on a point of toasted bread. A leftover from the drug and alcohol combination, I'd be willing to bet.

I found two-minute eggs repulsive—runny and undercooked—but I hadn't eaten since lunch the previous day, so the sight of a runny egg still made my stomach grumble.

"Goodness, was that you?" Evalyn asked with a smile.

"I forgot to eat breakfast," I said sheepishly.

"That's easy to remedy. Tillie!" she called.

"Yes, ma'am," the young woman said as she whisked into the room promptly. Now, after my conversation with Jerry about the curse, I noticed Tillie's subtle but obvious distance from Evalyn. The way her eyes darted to her mistress and quickly darted away. She wanted to be anywhere but here, in the presence of the diamond. Her bills and the need for a job likely dictated otherwise.

"Bring Miss Beaumont a plate of breakfast. She's famished. How do you like your eggs?" Evalyn looked at me for confirmation.

"Scrambled, thank you." When a pile of warm sourdough toast and fluffy eggs arrived, I didn't hesitate and dug into the mound of food.

"There now, that's better," Evalyn said with a smile. "Eat up. You'll need your strength today. We're going shopping."

"Shopping?" I said, holding my toast slathered in melted butter and strawberry jam an inch from my mouth. To spend an entire day shopping would be an egregious waste of time, precisely when I didn't have time to lose. Though I envied the simplicity of Evalyn's days, her easy come-and-go, I did not envy the endless hours of meaningless tasks like shopping.

"We're going to pick up a few new dresses for you."

"Do I need new clothes?" I looked down at the carefully chosen gray skirt and white blouse and felt a pang of embarrassment.

As her eyes dipped to my shirt and skirt, she smiled brightly. "I think we can do much better than that, don't you? With your dark hair and eyes, a little color would go a long way. Red, perhaps, or royal blue."

I set down my toast and wiped my mouth with my napkin, deciding if I should tell her that I didn't wear what most women did, who were still confined to skirts and dresses. "I wear trousers nearly every day. It would be a waste to buy beautiful clothes when I so rarely need them. They would be ruined in the workshop."

"Nonsense," she said dismissively. She pushed her plate away and lit a cigarette. "If you attend events at my house, you'll need a new wardrobe." She blew out a stream of smoke. "I know just the place. You'll be stunning after I'm finished with you."

I hesitated a moment before replying. I wanted to keep Evalyn close, to remain a part of her circle, but I didn't have the funds to spend on something I ultimately didn't need. It was an unnecessary extravagance I couldn't afford.

She exhaled again as if growing annoyed and continued, "Come now. It'll be fun! Besides, we have a lunch date afterward at the Café St. Marks by McPherson Square. We simply *must* dress to impress while dining there, and impress them we shall." She winked.

"I couldn't possibly… It isn't in the budget this month and—"

"This is my treat, Lizzie." Her voice was firm. "I can't have a young woman who works for me wearing worn and dreary clothing from five years ago. Anyway, I dress all my employees, so think nothing of it, darling." When she saw my expression, she added, "I insist."

I knew without looking in a mirror that my face had gone blotchy with embarrassment. I wasn't going to get out of this, no matter how much I protested. When Evalyn insisted, everyone obeyed, and I had learned this the first day I'd met her. "That's very kind of you," I said. "Thank you."

At that moment, Ned and Vinnie crashed into the room, each carrying a wooden sword painted black and red. They both wore an eye patch and a makeshift cape that tangled around their limbs as they tried to move like fencers.

"Take that, you villain!" Vinnie cried as he hit his father's sword with a thwack.

"You'll never get me this time, Black Beard!" Ned shouted back.

Vinnie noticed me and flashed his toothless smile. "Are you cleaning the diamonds again?"

"Not today," I said with a smile.

"En garde!" Ned shouted as he jumped over a footstool.

"Oh, that's enough, Ned!" Evalyn shouted. "Go outside if you're going to play like that."

"But, Moooom," Vinnie whined.

"You heard your mother," Ned said with a grin. "Let's go outside. And hello, Lizzie." He gave me a short wave and led his son out of the room.

"Hello," I called after him as they were pushing through the French doors onto the patio. It was so nice to see a man playing with his children, and Vinnie was such a charming little boy.

Evalyn threw her napkin on the dining table. "While you finish eating, I'll get dressed."

I didn't argue, but I was glad I had a quiet few minutes to myself. As I watched Ned and Vinnie sparring on the lawn, nostalgia bloomed inside my chest, warm and comforting as a vision of playing in the spring sunshine with my brother flickered in my mind's eye.

A few minutes later, Evalyn blazed into the room again, handbag and coat in hand. "Are we ready?"

This time, the chauffeur drove us to the fashionable Georgetown neighborhood at the intersection of M Street and Wisconsin. I looked warily at the row of boutiques, showcasing beautiful window displays filled with the kind of clothing I'd never considered wearing. Silk dresses with drop waists, beaded and feathered headbands, evening gloves and day gloves in every color and length, and an endless array of shoes, hats, and handbags. The dizzying selection overwhelmed me on sight. I hoped Evalyn would lead the way; I hadn't the faintest idea where to begin.

She saw my face and shrieked in glee. "Oh, don't be such a bore. This is going to be so much fun!"

We browsed first, stopping at several boutiques where Evalyn greeted the salesclerks whom she clearly seemed to know. After a first sweep of her favorite places, we circled back to where we began.

"Now that we've seen everything, we're ready to buy," she said. "I think blue looks particularly well on you."

Chattering as happily as a bird the whole way, she directed the shop clerks and selected my wardrobe as if I were her doll. She didn't allow me to pay for a single item or to broach the subject of anything owed. After we'd purchased four new dresses, three for daytime and one for evening, along with shoes and handbags, we made our way to a hairdresser.

"Are you sure you're all right with this?" she asked, reaching for a lock of my hair. "I do think a little trim will do it wonders."

I'd always worn my hair long and loose, and no one had ever said a thing about it. I supposed I was uncouth in the eyes of Evalyn's friends, whose hair was always either rolled and pinned elegantly or worn in soft short waves that cupped their chins.

"Do you think it's necessary?" I replied.

"I do," she insisted.

After a substantial cut and half an hour of hot irons and hair oil, the hairdresser was finished. He held out a hand mirror. "Here we are. What do you think?"

"Gorgeous." Evalyn clapped in glee. "She's just gorgeous, Randy. Thank you."

I gaped at the person in the mirror. I hardly looked like myself. In fact, I looked a little like—

"You two almost look alike with her hair like this," Randy said. "And her dress, too."

Evalyn laughed. "We do, don't we! And isn't that great fun? You should wear your hair like this all the time, Lizzie."

Stunned by my reflection, I didn't reply. Who was this pretty and elegant woman, out about town? I was utterly transformed. I was no longer a plain-faced young woman with flyaway hair, wearing plain dresses or trousers and a smock. My dark hair waved softly around my face. The makeup Randy had applied accentuated my large dark eyes that turned down at the corners, a feature Henry had admired. I wondered what he would say now. Surprised he should still come to mind so easily, I quickly looked away.

"Well?" Randy said. "What do you think?"

"I don't recognize myself."

Evalyn giggled. "Isn't it marvelous! Let's go to lunch with your new 'do. What do you say? I'm famished."

I pictured the kind of restaurant Evalyn would like, the enormous bill I couldn't afford and also couldn't allow her to pick up, yet again, as well as the time I'd lose in my workshop and shook my head. "As lovely as the morning has been, I'm afraid I need to get back to work."

"Oh, pooh," she said, waving a hand dismissively. "We need to celebrate your new look! Besides, I have a reservation. They're already expecting us at the Café St. Marks."

We gathered the many packages and gave them to the chauffeur, who swept them up and stored them in the car.

"This has been so generous of you, Evalyn. I can't thank you enough."

"My little Lizzie, let's get something straight. For the rest of our time together, you won't be paying for a thing. You're my employee, and my employees have certain perks. This is one of them. Now, let's go."

I didn't know what to say, so I simply reached for her hand and squeezed. "Thank you."

She flashed me her big pearly smile. "There now. Is that so hard? We'd better move along, or we'll be late for our reservation."

At the restaurant, she treated me to an elegant lunch, including enough champagne to drown a horse.

"May as well finish this up," she said, tipping the rest of the second champagne bottle into each of our glasses.

Despite my initial reticence to drink alcohol like Evalyn and her friends, I was beginning to like it, especially champagne. It calmed my nerves, and with more than one glass, the room became soft around the edges, my vision fuzzy and the light golden. A welcome respite from my thoughts. Through the haze of my inebriated state, I watched Evalyn: how beautiful and full of life she was, how easy her manner. She was perfectly self-possessed, as if she had all the confidence in the world and not a single doubt about herself. I also marveled at her nonchalance as the large bill was added to her tab. How did she live like this, day to day? How did I not? As the thought came quickly, I realized there were aspects I liked about this world of beauty, of fine clothes and food and champagne lunches. It was easy to be swept up in the fantasy of Evalyn's world and forget the real reasons I was here.

"Can you believe they're talking about banning alcohol?" Evalyn said, her cheeks rosy and her tone gay. We climbed into the back seat of her car, and the driver pulled away from the curb into traffic. "Those barbarians. What would we do without champagne or a stiff whiskey? Sometimes a girl needs a drink."

"Do you think they'll be able to pass it?" I asked. "I don't know how they'd stop people from making their own liquor."

"They couldn't," she agreed, her tone pensive. "I can't imagine where Ned would be without his whiskey. He'd probably behave better. Or perhaps he'd drive himself right off a cliff."

I cocked an eyebrow at her but didn't ask her what she'd meant by her comment. It seemed like a sore topic between husband and wife, and I didn't want to intrude, even if I was curious. My eyes wandered back to the focal point, the lodestone that I couldn't stop thinking about. All the misfortunes the staff had suffered and the intimidating letters Evalyn received almost daily.

Eager to encourage her to talk about the diamond, I blurted, "Your necklace is so spectacular with your blue dress." The magnificent Hope twinkled in the late-afternoon sunlight that filtered through the car windows.

"This old thing?"

We laughed as she fingered the Hope Diamond, and I realized I liked this uninhibited version of Evalyn, without the others around. Even if she never asked me anything about my interests or my work. I supposed that was only natural, given she was my employer. I also realized I'd laughed—for the first time in seven months.

She grinned. "Well now, I think we've done enough damage for one day. Shall we go home?"

"Let's."

Though the day had been pleasant, I was relieved when we pulled into the drive of Friendship.

"Before you go," she said, "I have something else for you, but you'll have to come inside."

"But you've already been far too generous," I said.

She rolled her eyes. "I don't know a single woman alive except you who wouldn't jump at the chance for some of my clothes." She took my hand and led me inside to her bedroom.

I followed willingly, secretly pleased by her touch and at the fact that she seemed to be so comfortable with me.

"I asked Tillie to pull out some of my older things for you," she said, motioning to a pile of dresses on her bed. "I know we've just bought you a few dresses, but that simply isn't enough. Besides, I'd planned to donate these. I'd rather you have them than give them away to strangers." She held up a mint-green dress to my body. "This will be darling on you. Do you like it?"

I fingered the chiffon and lace, intricate and light as air, and like before was stunned by her generosity. "It's beautiful."

"Try it on," she commanded.

I didn't argue, and for the first time, it occurred to me that was probably why she enjoyed my company—my easy acquiescence to all her suggestions. I slipped out of my dress, baring my very plain and ratty chemise beneath it.

"Oh goodness, that won't do at all," she said, touching the faded cotton fabric at my waist. She sifted through her dresser drawers and returned with a cream-colored silk undergarment. "Try this instead."

I removed my slip and pulled Evalyn's luxurious silk over my head. I ran my hands over the slippery fabric, enjoying the way it felt against my skin. "It's so soft."

"Isn't it? Now let's see the dress on you."

As I reached for the green dress, the bedroom door swung open.

"Evie, are you in here?" Ned poked his head inside the room.

I scrambled to pull the garment over my head.

"Ned!" Evalyn shrieked. "Knock before you come barging in here! Poor Lizzie isn't decent."

"I apologize, Poor Lizzie," he said with a grin, and before withdrawing from the room, he said, "That dress is beautiful on you."

I burned with embarrassment. I couldn't be certain about what he'd seen, but judging by the smile, he'd seen more than he should. I'd never been half-naked in front of a man except in bathing clothes with Julien and Henry, and though I was a little drunk and mostly covered, I blushed deeply. "Thank you, sir."

"Stop calling me 'sir,'" he insisted. "We're friends now, aren't we?"

"We *are* friends," Evalyn agreed as she straightened the collar on the dress.

"Ned it is," I replied, my cheeks still hot.

"I'm meeting John, so I'll be out late," Ned said. "Don't wait up."

Evalyn pressed her lips into a line, and I wondered what it was about John that displeased her. She was normally so agreeable, so the sudden shift in her demeanor unsettled me.

After she'd firmly closed the door in his face and locked it, she turned to me with a strained smile. "The dress looks wonderful. What do you think?" She led me to a full-length mirror.

The pale-green silk transformed me as the others had. "It's lovely." What I didn't say aloud was the dress might complement my complexion and figure, but I felt strangely foreign, as if I were trying to be someone else, and perhaps I was. Perhaps that was precisely what I needed to be.

"That's settled then," she said. "I'd like for you to keep all these dresses, if you like them." She motioned to the small pile on the end of her bed.

"Evalyn"—I shook my head—"I couldn't. It's too much, especially after today. I could never repay you for your generosity."

"You do repay me, silly girl," she said. "You repay me by coming when I need you. I've already told you I dress my staff." She took my hand in hers. "Besides, you're also my new friend, and there's nothing I wouldn't do for my friends."

I felt the smallest thrill that she wanted my company. I didn't know why she'd taken me into her fold with open arms so easily and comfortably—perhaps she felt some guilt about Julien's death—but I wasn't certain I cared to know the answer. I liked spending time with the McLeans. The sense of belonging was like air in my lungs, a newness that felt good, better than anything I'd felt in a long time. For the first time in months, the urge to touch someone and to be touched overwhelmed me. I threw my arms around her.

"Thank you. Thank you so much, for everything." I swallowed hard against the lump of emotion in my throat.

She laughed and patted my back, assured me it wasn't anything to get worked up over, and continued to prattle on happily. I lost track of time, barely heard her, but as I stood to leave and embraced her again, I felt the reminder of why I was here—the real reason.

The sharp prongs of the Hope Diamond necklace scraped against my skin.

14

I blinked, rubbed my eyes, as the trill of birdsong drifted through my window. I surveyed the room around me, confused even by the sunny yellow wallpaper I'd known my whole life. The world seemed too bright, its color and song assaulting. An ache thudded dully in my chest, and I felt...different. Being a part of Evalyn's world, however small, had teased something open inside me, and it was as if I were stepping back into my body after a long slumber. I winced at the squeak of the faucet and the boom of the grandfather clock, and I squinted at the shards of sunlight knifing through the curtains at the window. My teeth ached from the searing heat of the coffee I made for breakfast. And I found myself wishing for the numbness I'd grown accustomed to these last months. Somehow I knew the Elisabeth who had blindly moved through her days was gone for good, and a raw version of myself and an uncertain path lay ahead of me.

I carried my coffee to the workshop and reached for the box holding my collection. The set of rings I'd pored over for countless hours gleamed against the velvet lining of the case. I ran my fingers over their grooves: one with a silver setting of four tiered lines dotted with glittering rose quartz and diamond chips, another featuring a vivid, green peridot paired with rectangular diamond baguettes, and still another ring of gold that I'd stretched into a filigree net studded with sapphire chips, giving the appearance of a globe, the ring Henry liked. There were three others, too, all studded with semiprecious stones. Father had only allowed me to use the smaller stones until I'd garnered the attention of a few of my own patrons. At that point, I'd have earned the use of the larger, more precious gems. I'd never reached that goal, and so far, the nearly flawless gems and the rarest varieties had been saved for Father's creations or the occasional piece Julien had designed.

Had been saved.

Had designed.

Now it was I who must make the decisions about each piece, I who reviewed the budget and wrote in the ledgers and kept careful records of the stones in the vault, I who secured not one or two but several new clients. And yet I didn't relish the responsibilities or the opportunities. I felt as lost as ever about what came next for me. Frustrated, I flipped open my sketchbook, my eyes raking over every page, over all the half-completed sketches. I looked through Father's and Julien's sketchbooks, too, studying every design, impressed by some of my brother's drawings, though they weren't as intricate and astounding as Father's. My father was nothing short of a brilliant artist. I'd always thought this about him as a devoted daughter, but after time and with perspective, I could see his genius within the pages of his sketchbook with true clarity.

I bent over the set of rings, slipping them onto my fingers, shifting them to catch the light. I'd been so certain my jewelry would be unique, eye-catching, and could set me apart from the rest of the Beaumont collection. But after the time away from working on my collection over the months—and the time I'd spent with Evalyn and her wealthy friends who wore as much jewelry between them as our entire inventory—I could be truly honest with myself for the first time. I knew with absolute certainty they were lovely, but they weren't anything special. They wouldn't stand out next to pieces of a true designer. They wouldn't even stand out in a jewelry box.

Bristling with irritation, I closed the collection box and stored the sketchbooks. Why hadn't I realized this before? Why hadn't Father told me? He'd led me to believe I had a special gift, like him. Now I could see it had only been the encouraging words of a doting father and perhaps his hope that I should flourish, but it wasn't the truth. My pieces were pretty and competent but pedestrian rather than the awe-inspiring collection I'd hoped to create. Worse still, I didn't feel the tug to finish it or the yearning to better my skills.

Suddenly I couldn't see my way forward from here. I only knew I couldn't continue to work for my father for the rest of my life, creating mediocre designs and managing the books as I always had. Perhaps stepping into Julien's shoes as salesman for the business would be the right path. But again, as I pictured the endless hours of trying to charm people I didn't know, a wave of trepidation and exhaustion rolled through me.

"What are you doing?"

I startled at the sound of his voice. "Oh! You're up again."

"I am," my father said, pulling on a smock. "I have a few things I'd like to work on today." He laid a scrap of paper covered in ink on the workshop table.

My brow arched in surprise. "What's that?"

"A new design."

I nearly wept with relief. Father was sketching again, which meant he was ready to work again, even if on a limited basis. "Can I take a look?"

"Not yet. I'm struggling with it a little."

This wasn't new for him, to be private about his drawings until he was ready to show them. I respected his process, as he'd taught me to do.

"I'll take a look when you're ready."

"Did you see the note I left for you?" he asked.

"I did, thank you." Henry had called and he'd left a small bouquet of tulips on the doorstep.

"Did you return his call?"

"I will," I lied. I had nothing to say to him, no way to parse out what had happened the night of the accident or my feelings for him, so I did nothing and would continue to avoid him until I could meet his eyes and not hate myself, not despair over our mistake.

My father kissed my head as if I were his little girl instead of twenty-eight years old. "Don't turn away from a good thing."

Surprised by his comment, I set down my now-tepid coffee. "What do you mean?"

"*Chérie*, you may be difficult for some to read, but I know you and I know your heart. I'm your father, remember? Henry is a good man. Dependable, intelligent." He pointed to his chest. "He's also big-hearted. He will take good care of you. Whatever happened between the two of you can be resolved."

"I can take care of myself," I said reflexively. Father would never force me to marry. I'd never had to worry about that, even as I flirted with the label of spinster. All the other young women I'd known from the neighborhood or attended school with had married ages ago, and most were already saddled with children. I'd always seen myself moving toward that path eventually—and Henry had been at the center of my imaginings—but since Julien's death, I couldn't see, not anything.

"I know you can take care of yourself," my father replied. "Just don't let time get away from you. We don't know how much we'll have on this earth, and what little time we do have is not to be wasted. I don't want you to have regrets."

I looked at my beloved father, his silvery beard and pale-blue eyes that didn't see as well as they used to but were still as warm as ever. If there was one thing I'd learned these past months, it was how short our time could be. Henry's dear face rushed into my mind again, and I squeezed my eyes closed against the flood of emotion held back by some invisible dam.

"Speaking of time, let's get to work," he said. "I'd like to start this new piece."

"Right," I said, relieved to change the subject.

I turned to Rosalee's necklace, working diligently for several hours until I'd finished it.

I packaged the jewelry and made the journey across town to Rosalee's home to deliver it in person. I wasn't in the habit of doing such things, but I owed her more than I cared to admit.

Her doorman showed me inside to the sitting room.

"Why, Miss Beaumont," Rosalee said with her thick Southern drawl. "I didn't recognize you!" She was originally from a small town in the Virginia hills, and despite the polish that came with marrying wealthy, there was no mistaking her origins. "Have you changed your hair?"

My hand flew to my hair, brushed into shorter, soft waves. "Yes, thank you. I think."

She laughed sweetly. "It's a compliment. The last time I saw you, you were wearing a dirty old pair of men's trousers, and you looked as if you hadn't eaten in ages. But now, my goodness. Your haircut suits you. It makes your keen dark eyes stand out, and that dress! I'd wear it myself."

I'd worn one of my new dresses, a pale-pink silk with ruffled skirt and elbow-length sleeves tied with ribbons. I offered a small smile. I'd never cared about clothes, but it was nice to be seen for a change as someone besides "the other twin" or the awkward daughter behind the scenes who never really acted like a lady.

"Think nothing of it, truly. Well, I was just about to have some lunch. Care to join me?"

I glanced at the time. Evalyn had asked me to stop by Friendship later that day, but the thought of facing all those women again so soon left me cold. I promptly felt the sting of guilt for having such an ungracious thought after the generosity Evalyn had bestowed upon me the day before.

"That would be nice," I replied at last.

While we ate ham salad sandwiches and cold potato salad with iced tea, we talked about the possibility of a new commission, her piano tutor, and then a topic I hadn't expected: Rosalee's lack of friends.

"What would you say about dinner next week?" she said.

Surprised by the invitation, I hesitated before answering. "Dinner? That sounds nice." She was a kind woman, and though I wasn't sure we had much in common, I decided that might not be a bad thing. Perhaps we'd really enjoy each other's company.

"It's so lovely having you here," she said. "I hate to admit it, but I've been awfully lonely lately. My husband is always working or golfing, and I haven't found the other women traveling in our circles very welcoming."

Surprised by her directness and her honesty, I was speechless.

When she saw my face, she laughed nervously. "Now I've gone and said too much."

"No, not at all," I replied, composing my face so as not to belie my surprise. "Good friends are hard to come by. I've only ever had a few myself."

Her lips curved into an appreciative smile. "How right you are. Well..." She held up her glass of iced tea. "To new friends."

I gave her a genuine smile in return, wondering why a woman who should be in Evalyn's circle, given her status and fortune, didn't seem to belong there any more than I did. She wore her wealth and status with grace, almost as if it embarrassed her to flaunt what she owned. It was endearing and so different from the other socialites I'd met thus far. I liked that about her.

I clinked my glass against hers. "To new friends."

15

Good gracious, is that you, Lizzie?" Bea exclaimed as I joined the others in the sunroom at Evalyn's. "Why, you've changed into a butterfly!"

Bea sat in a circle beside Evalyn and Alice Roosevelt Longworth and several others, who all sorted through a pile of invitations for one of Evalyn's charities. After the unexpected afternoon with Rosalee, I'd made my way to Friendship, as I'd promised, to help stuff envelopes, and though I'd prefer to be doing nearly anything else, I couldn't say no. By the looks of things, they'd been at it a while already. I'd taken my time at Rosalee's, enjoying myself more than I had in a very long time, completely surprised by how much I liked her.

"Shocking, isn't it?" Evalyn cooed. "Lizzie is positively adorable."

"And her hair!" Bea continued.

"Thank you," I said, taking a seat in an empty chair. Given Bea's response to my appearance, I must have looked like a troll before the makeover Evalyn had given me.

They continued to talk about me as if I weren't in the room, my new wardrobe, which colors complemented my skin, and the similarities in my facial features to Evalyn's. All the while, I perched on the edge of my chair awkwardly, attempting to look as if I felt at home among them. I hated to admit I felt a sort of pride in being allowed to be a part of their circle, and I found myself wanting to please Evalyn. I sneaked glances at her, studying the way she held her glass, the way her head tilted when she laughed, the phrases she used in conversation to be polite. Her manners were practiced, learned many years ago as a young girl when her world had shifted from being the daughter of a working-class Irish immigrant to the exalted position of one of the most successful gold miners in history.

I noticed Carrie wasn't among the crowd and felt a wave of disappointment. I'd hoped to talk to her about Julien.

"Are you going to Gwen's luncheon on Friday?" Bea said as she licked an envelope and sealed it closed.

I hadn't been invited, nor did I expect to be, but I didn't want to look left out so I tilted my head the same way I'd seen Evalyn do as if assessing whether the question warranted attention. "I wish I could, but I have several client meetings that day."

"That's a shame," Bea replied.

Evalyn reached for a stack of envelopes and handed them to me. "Well, I can't imagine why Gwen would invite Lizzie anyway, given the way Gwen had spoken to her."

I looked down to hide the surprise I knew must show on my face. Was the slight aimed at me or Gwen? Both perhaps. Gwen had mocked my appearance and the fact that I was "the help," something Evalyn clearly alluded to, but she also hinted at the fact that I would never be accepted among them. Her double-edged comments still took me off guard, and I didn't know when I'd grow accustomed to having a "friend" who spoke to me that way, but some instinct told me I should never show my unease. "It's all right," I replied. "I don't have time for someone who is jealous of my clothing anyway."

Evalyn responded with a sharp smile. Several of the others giggled. Bea winked.

I'd chosen correctly—deftly hitting back at Gwen behind her back. It seemed this was the constant dance in Evalyn's circle, to be overtly generous and follow it with a series of clever, if sometimes hurtful, rebukes. It didn't matter that Gwen would never be jealous of my clothes. All that mattered was I'd taken part in their game of cat and mouse, tit for tat.

In that moment, I was as proud of my quick tongue as I was vaguely sick to my stomach.

The faint sounds of a baby crying interrupted our conversation.

"How is little Eddie?" Alice asked. "He's such a beautiful baby, Evie."

"Can you believe he's a year old already?" Evalyn said.

The nanny popped into the room. "Mrs. McLean, Eddie is up from his nap. I'd like to take the children outside for some fresh air."

"Of course. And see that Vinnie doesn't ruin his shoes again." To us, she said, "That child is somehow always in the mud."

It was easy to forget Evalyn was the mother of three boys: a one-year-old, three-year-old John, and Vinnie at nine. She didn't spend much time with them. It seemed that children, for the wealthy set, were another possession to be owned and enjoyed from a relative distance, or when there was time. Though it looked to me as if they had all the time in the world, they'd say otherwise as they filled their days with parties and luncheons and charity events.

A maid rolled a cart of refreshments into the room, and within moments, she'd poured mint juleps for each of us, despite the early hour. I didn't care for the sickly sweet, thick drink, but I gulped mine down to ease the nerves. Regardless of how much time I'd spent in the company of these women, I couldn't seem to relax. Soon after I'd finished, another round was poured. I demurred initially, only to give in to Evalyn's persuasive plea I should keep pace with the others.

Jerry reappeared briefly to announce another guest.

"I'm sorry I'm late." Carrie whisked into the room, fluffing her already perfect red hair.

I stiffened at the sight of her. I studied her as she chose a seat and began talking animatedly with the woman next to her. I longed to speak to her alone, to ask her about Julien. When she caught me staring, I tore my gaze away, managing to exchange a few pleasantries with the fascinating Alice.

"Washington really is so boring," Evalyn complained. "If we didn't have our parties, what would we possibly do?"

"Move to Paris," Alice replied.

"Or Rome," Sharon added.

Carrie reached for a mint julep. "I'd move to New York City."

"Precisely!" Evalyn said. "Anywhere but here."

"It's a good thing you're here for us, Evie," Alice said. "We'd be lost without you."

"And we'd be lost without your commentary," she replied.

Alice winked and slugged the rest of her second mint julep.

A raucous sound came from the hall, and the children crashed through the door chasing their dog, Mike the Great Dane, their nanny hot on their heels. By the looks of it, several of the neighborhood boys had joined in the fun. And none had decided to remain outdoors as the nanny had planned.

A burst of laughter erupted from my lips. The others laughed, too, Evalyn included.

"Stop running in the house!" the nanny called. "Go outside!"

They all ignored the nanny. Vinnie continued to chase his little brother, John, hands outstretched like he would tickle him should he catch him. John giggled as his chubby legs moved surprisingly fast around the edges of the furniture. The other boys ran after the dog.

I couldn't help but delight in the juxtaposition of perfectly coiffed and refined ladies in the midst of all things proper and the raucous children and dog romping through the room.

"Children, give your mother a kiss," Evalyn called to them, but they zoomed past her.

After she called to them a second and third time, they circled back to their mother, Vinnie planting a hurried peck on her cheek and three-year-old John copying his brother's every action.

"When are we going to the park, Mom?" Vinnie said, grabbing Evalyn's hands, pulling her up from her chair, and spinning her around in a circle.

Evalyn laughed delightedly. "Another day, sweetie. Nanny is going to see to your dinner and baths tonight."

I felt a pang of regret that came from wishing for one's mother. I'd never known mine, never had her spin me around or soothe my fears. I'd pictured her a thousand times; I was her duplicate with dark hair and dark eyes and a lean and tall build. Father had always said she looked like me, but her temperament was just as Julien's had been: vivacious, charming, full of life and laughter. I ached at the loss of having never known her—and at losing the only other person like her.

My chest tightened as Evie patted the children on the head and shooed them away.

"Your children are darling, but I've never wanted any of my own," Carrie said. "My husband disagrees, of course."

"I'm sure he does," Bea said under her breath, helping herself to a third mint julep. I wondered what that meant, so I shot Bea a questioning look. She winked, and while the others kept prattling on, she leaned toward me and lowered her voice. "Every man who crosses Carrie's path falls in love with her. And my, is she a flirt in return. Her husband, Jet, probably wants to have babies to lock her down indefinitely. He seems the type."

I regarded the mirth in her eyes after imparting a morsel of gossip, and I realized she might be the perfect person to ask about Julien and Carrie. "Do you think...was my brother one of those men?"

Her smile wavered. "Oh, I doubt it. Your brother flirted with all of us. He was such a charmer. And he spent most of his time in the study or playing billiards with Ned and the husbands."

I watched her face carefully, noting the quick slip of her smile for a fraction of a second. Was she surprised by my question, or was she hiding something? I decided it best to continue with her line of thinking, see if she'd reveal anything more. "He was a flirt, that's for sure, and amiable in general. I'm not at all surprised he enjoyed his time with the husbands. In fact, I heard he was in the process of working on some business venture..." I let my words trail off in hopes Bea may fill the silence.

She shifted her attention abruptly and held up her glass. "These drinks are sweet as candy, Evie," she called. "Where are you hiding the vodka?"

Whether Bea was avoiding the topic or simply done with it, I sensed I shouldn't broach it again, at least for now.

"Goodness, Bea, is it that time already?" Evalyn replied.

"Of course it is. It's afternoon. Not that time ever matters when it comes to a good drink."

Bea winked at me. She wasn't a drunk exactly, but she flirted with the limits of propriety. Still, she was the friend of Evalyn's I liked best. She didn't put on any pretenses, and she said what she meant, even if what she meant was a little rude. I supposed Alice was somewhat similar, but I didn't feel comfortable in her presence. I wasn't certain the others did either; the tenor and easy flow of conversation always changed when she joined the party.

Evalyn rang for Jerry, who promptly returned with a brand-new bottle of vodka. Within the hour, Evalyn's eyes were glazed over with drink, and her cheeks were rosy. "Have you ever been to the races, Lizzie?" she asked, taking a seat beside me on the sofa covered in floral silk.

I frowned. "Are there races in this area?"

"No, silly. The Kentucky Derby."

I shook my head. "Never."

"You really must come this year. You can sit in my box and stay with me. The others will come, too. Bea and Carrie, Sharon, and perhaps Gwen and Rita, too. Speaking of Gwen! You handled her nicely."

The alcohol had loosened my tongue, too, and before I could stop them, the words sprang from my tongue. "Gwen doesn't like me much." As soon as I'd said it, I wished I could take it back.

Evalyn's face positively beamed at my abrupt omission. "Don't worry about Gwen. She can be a little nasty at times, but she means well. Though..." She shook her head. "I really shouldn't tell you this." Evalyn leaned in closer. "Would you like to hear a secret?"

"If it's private, you don't have to tell me."

"You talked me into it," she said with a laugh. "The rest of us already know, though Gwen doesn't realize it."

I thought again of the barbs the women exchanged about each other and those in their extended circles and realized Evalyn wanted me to know, was positively dying to share her gossip, and hoped I'd be dying to gossip, too.

I quickly backtracked, and forcing false eagerness, I said, "I was hoping you'd tell me."

Her smile widened. "Well! Gwen's father was a tobacco farmer, and he lost everything in one bad hand of poker. Can you imagine, betting your entire estate on a hand of poker?"

"I can't imagine betting a single cent of hard-earned money on a game," I replied. "When my brother and I used to play, we'd play for penny candy from Woolworth's. Tootsie Rolls and Necco wafers or even Hershey Kisses. But never money."

"What a sweet memory," she replied, pursing her lips. She wasn't pleased I'd interrupted her with an anecdote of my own.

I blushed hotly at the dressed-up rebuke.

"As I was saying, Gwen's father gambled away every cent he could get his hands on. She and her mother had to scrape by, hiding money from her father all over the house. They even buried some in the garden! Imagine!"

I could imagine it. I'd heard rumors from Julien that Ned was also a serious gambler. Evalyn must struggle with his recklessness, too, which made it all the odder she should condemn Gwen's family for it. But pointing out her hypocrisy wouldn't endear me to her.

"That's horrible!" I mimicked her enthusiasm, despite the dreadful story.

"When Gwen was of the marrying age," Evalyn continued, "she set her sights set on a wealthy man, and boy, did she get one. She's married to a banker who owns half the real estate in Maryland and Virginia."

"How fortunate for her," I said. "Things worked out for her in the end."

Evalyn quirked an eyebrow at me. "There was nothing fortunate about it. It was planned. In fact, there's more." She dropped her voice to a near whisper. "She slept with her husband before she was married and before they were even an item. That was her first mistake. She had no commitment from him. Tom had already started chasing someone else. And that's when she took matters into her own hands." She paused dramatically, clearly waiting for me to beg for more.

I humored her, though I honestly felt compassion for Gwen more than glee at her difficult situation. She'd struggled through a poor childhood with an unreliable father and then felt she had to sell herself to a willing man so she wouldn't be destitute. I couldn't imagine much worse. "What did Gwen do?"

Evalyn's eyes gleamed. "She lied, told him she was pregnant with his baby."

My eyes widened. "And he believed her?"

Evalyn shrugged. "He couldn't see why she'd lie about such a thing."

"Did she?" I asked. "Did she lie about it?"

"She confessed the truth to me one night after the others had left and we'd had one too many drinks. Tom had threatened to leave her anyway at first and denied the child was his, but she blackmailed him. He proposed shortly thereafter."

This time, I really was stunned. "She blackmailed him into marrying her?"

"Can you imagine doing such a thing? But Gwen is ruthless when she wants something. You should see her speak to her staff. She acts as if she wasn't just like them at one time, scrambling to make ends meet. It's a good thing you stood up to her the way you did. Now she won't underestimate you."

I'd hardly call what I'd said standing up to her. I'd simply ignored her slights and gone on about my business for the remainder of the time spent in her presence. I didn't understand this world of secrets and thinly veiled barbs aimed at so-called friends or joy in another person's struggle, but I knew one thing was for sure. I wouldn't let Gwen Chaney talk to me the way she had again without consequence. And I clearly needed to watch myself around the others, too, Evalyn included. As malaise spread through me, I shifted uncomfortably in my chair, wishing I could make my excuses and leave. But I couldn't, not now. I'd have to play along until the day's activities wound down naturally, or I'd appear rude, especially after having left Evalyn's last gathering early.

At that moment, I looked up to meet Carrie's eyes. She was watching me, her lips pressed together, a deep wrinkle prominent on her forehead. For the first time since I'd met her, I held her gaze boldly until she looked away. And then I noticed it for the first time. She wore a small silver pendant shaped like a rose with a single ruby at its center. A rush of adrenaline surged through my veins. I'd recognize the pendant anywhere. Julien had made it. And he'd either sold it to Carrie—or he'd made it for her.

I watched her chatter happily and laugh at Bea's jokes or Evalyn's comments until I couldn't sit still any longer. I had to ask her about the necklace, about my brother.

When there was a break in the conversation, I stood and started toward her.

She caught my eye for the second time and stood, too, announcing to the others, "I'm afraid I need to be on my way."

"Why, darling?" Evalyn said, sticking out her lip in a put-on pout. "We're only getting started."

"I'm meeting with my caterer to discuss the dinner menu for the party next week."

I watched Carrie curiously as she blew air kisses and made a beeline for the door. Had she been trying to avoid me, or did she truly have an appointment with her caterer? I glanced at Bea and then Evalyn. They weren't watching Carrie leave. Their eyes were fixed on me.

The rest of the afternoon flew by as the alcohol haze enveloped us. My mind was a flurry of questions, and I longed to have Evalyn to myself, to probe for information about Carrie and the pendant.

Fortunately, she asked me to stay for dinner and to keep her company as the others trickled home. I was beginning to understand she not only liked being the center of the party but also didn't like to be alone.

"I'm starved," she said. "Supper must be ready by now. Come on, darling. Let's eat at the table tonight. I make a frightful mess when I attempt to eat anywhere else."

The cook served oysters and lump crab cakes, filet of sole with sorrel cream, and a magnificent strawberry and vanilla confection. I felt guilty at first, leaving Father to his plain chops and potatoes, but he'd lost any real interest in food the day Julien died. He'd lost interest in everything until very recently. And only now, away from him day after day, did I realize how his desperate loss had compounded my own. I'd never felt more alone than I had these past seven months. But here, at the McLean mansion, at the extravagant parties and on our drives through the city or during the long luncheons and late nights, I felt the blood move through my veins again, heard my own heartbeat in my ears, felt air seep back into my lungs. I dared not hope before, but now it seemed perhaps there was a future beyond the home that had become a tomb, especially now that my father was back on his feet.

As we finished eating, Evalyn reached for my hands. "Say you'll stay the night. We'll tell stories in our pajamas and eat bonbons until we're sick."

The thought of sleeping in a luxurious bed at the McLeans' home as if I were a member of the family gave me a thrill. And yet, I knew I couldn't possibly leave my father alone. How would I explain should he go looking for me in the middle of the night?

I shook my head. "I really couldn't leave my father. He's on the mend, but he's still not quite himself."

"Nonsense," she said. "I'll send Tillie to the house. She can bring him a covered dish and make sure he's comfortable for the night."

I pictured his face as he discovered I'd sent a maid and stranger—employed by the very woman he'd forbidden me to see—to look in on him. Sooner or later, he'd find out the truth, and though he wouldn't condone it, in the end, I would see the job through with the McLeans, no matter what he said, both to continue to repair the Beaumont reputation among the social elite of Washington, DC, and to ensure our income. But that time wasn't now, especially at such a late hour.

"How about I stay until midnight," I said, aiming for a compromise. I was already full of delicious food and longed for bed, but I'd humor her until then.

"Oh, pooh, all right," she said with a laugh.

Thoughts of my father brought to mind the conversation we'd had about our showcase boxes, how I should bring the collections to Evalyn's house. I might make a few more sales that way.

I cleared my throat. "There's something I've been meaning to ask you. Would you care to see more of the Beaumont collection? I could bring a case with a sampling of our pieces to your house one afternoon. I'd be honored to show you my own collection."

She looked confused a moment by my abrupt change in topic.

"I apologize for the abruptness," I continued. "I've been meaning to ask you for a few days, but as soon as Jerry rolls out the drink cart, I forget everything."

She laughed. "I have the same problem. But I'll do you one better. I'll stop by your boutique. I'd like to see where my little Lizzie lives anyway." She pinched my cheek as if I were a child. We both laughed this time, though mine felt put-on and overly bubbly. Or perhaps that was because I felt as if I were faking it, faking this entire charade of belonging and seeking the approval of a woman who could not and would not ever understand me. Faking the need to share my own collection with her when in fact, all I wanted to do was store it away in the back of a closet and never think of it again. Surprised by the direction my thoughts had gone, I frowned and set my half-empty drink on the table.

Evalyn didn't seem to notice my change in demeanor. "What time should I arrive tomorrow?" she persisted.

Despite the haze of a full stomach and too much alcohol, it hit me. If she came by the house, Father might see her. But I couldn't turn her away. The possibility of a confrontation with Father was a risk I'd have to take and a truth I'd have to confront eventually. I quickly decided the best time for Evalyn to come would be after lunch, when he usually took a rest or went for the walks he'd finally begun again.

"How about two o'clock? Does that suit your schedule?"

"Wonderful," she said. She motioned to Jerry to pour us another cocktail.

When he'd gone, I ran my finger around the rim of my glass, avoiding Evalyn's eye, and at last brought up the question I'd been burning to ask her since Carrie had left that afternoon. Forcing a light tone, I said, "I heard the others say Carrie is a flirt. Is that true?"

Evalyn shrugged. I relaxed a little as she followed the shrug with a smile. "She can be a bit saucy when she wants to be. Can't we all?"

No, I thought. I couldn't be saucy with a man if someone paid me a million dollars. Rather than admit the truth, I conceded, "I suppose you're right." I paused for a beat before adding, "My brother was such a flirt. We used to tease him because he'd bat those golden eyelashes and women would fall at his feet. I imagine you saw him in action?"

"Your brother was a beautiful man, I must say. And he certainly did win us over." She reached for the wine bottle on ice that Jerry had left for us and refilled her glass.

"I...noticed Carrie was wearing a pendant that he made," I continued.

Though Evalyn looked right at me, her expression was carefully blank, her tone measured. "Many of us bought jewelry from him. That was why he worked for me."

"Of course, and what a kindness it was for you to hire him. And me," I said hastily, not wanting to offend her while I was fishing for information. I'd have to be more careful.

"Julien spent very little time with us women, though," Evalyn went on. "He and my husband and their friends wandered off regularly to the gentlemen's club or the cigar bar in town. They played a lot of cards and billiards, too, from what I gather. I had the impression they got themselves into trouble a little too often. Boys will be boys, right?"

Beyond the gambling and the loose women to which she was alluding, I wondered if Julien had found himself in some other kind of trouble. Maybe Jerry had it wrong, and Julien hadn't been in business with the husbands but with someone else? The wrong kind of people. Those with money and power often crossed lines regular people did not. Julien was a regular person, without access to a vast fortune that could shield him from his mistakes. Perhaps my brother had become too daring, had acted out of turn with one of the most powerful groups of people in Washington. My stomach roiled at the thought, of someone retaliating for some perceived slight he'd made.

As Evalyn rose from her chair, I realized I'd been lost in thought.

"I'm going to look in on the children for a moment," she said. "You make yourself at home."

Before I could reply, she stalked off in the direction of the suite of children's rooms.

I watched her go, my mind circling our conversation. Something didn't feel right, but I couldn't quite pinpoint what it was. While I considered what it might be, Ned slinked into the room, lit cigar in hand. My stomach dipped as I remembered the way he'd looked at me the afternoon he'd driven me home after an evening out. Tonight, he was especially handsome. His cheeks and nose were tinged pink as if he'd been outdoors much of the day, his hair was pleasantly disheveled, and he had a gleam in his eyes.

"Did I hear we're having a slumber party?" he said.

"I'm afraid not," I replied with a weak smile. I thought back to the slumber party I'd had with my childhood friend Amy Thompson. When she'd moved away, we were both devastated. I hadn't really had many female friends since. I'd been too busy reading my books and maps, working with my father, or spending time with Henry and Julien and his other friends.

I didn't realize I was staring at Ned until he winked. Heat spread across my chest and up my neck.

"You're awfully pretty with that haircut and your new dress," he said, a smile stretching his mustache.

He was flirting with me so openly? Though I'd spent a lot of time with men, I'd mostly been treated like the kid sister I was.

Except with Henry, the night neither of us would ever forget.

I shook my head to dispel the image. I needed to be here in the moment rather than live in the past. Ned misread the gesture.

"But you are pretty," he insisted. "You would turn heads at any party."

I blushed more deeply and hated myself for the embarrassing reaction with which I'd always struggled.

"Say, why don't you join me for a drink while we wait for Evie? She doesn't do anything fast, so we may as well kick up our feet."

I practiced one of Evalyn's smiles. "All right."

He winked and a small thrill zipped through me. To have an effect on men—a man of Ned's caliber—made me feel powerful. Something I'd never felt before.

He grabbed a set of crystal glasses and led me to the patio. We sat in lawn chairs facing the expansive, verdant landscape stretching out behind the house. The chairs' headrests tilted toward the sky. Without so much as a sliver of moon in sight, stars took center stage, glittering overhead.

"How beautiful," I said, making my voice breathy like Evalyn's when she was talking to a man. She didn't know she'd given me more than a haircut and new dresses—she was teaching me all I needed to know about behaving like a society woman.

"Very," Ned replied, his eyes not leaving my face.

I shifted my gaze back to the stars, uneasy with the intensity of his expression. "Evalyn said you like horses."

"I'm a betting man," he said agreeably and filled me in on the horses he'd bought for his farm and the Kentucky Derby coming up in a couple of weeks.

Julien had been correct about Ned and his gambling. Yet Ned acted as if his habit wasn't a negative one but rather some laudable hobby. Regardless, he was charming if intense but funny, too. He regaled me with stories of his trips abroad, some anecdotes about his adventures in golfing, and I couldn't stop laughing. Truly laughing. My sides ached with it. Something tightly wound inside me was unspooling. I noticed, too, how much more at ease I was in his presence versus when I was in Evalyn's.

When Evalyn finally reappeared, it felt like an age had passed. I glanced at the time. Ned was right; she'd taken more than an hour looking in on the children.

"Did you save a glass for me?" She was smiling, but there was a flicker of something in her eyes I couldn't pinpoint.

"Of course, darling." Ned poured her a glass. "I was keeping your friend company while you were busy. I told Lizzie here all about my pathetic attempt at golfing."

She rolled her eyes. “He hit someone with a ball once. I thought we were going to be sued.”

We all laughed this time.

Evalyn began a litany of stories about their mishaps. Two hours later, as I set down my nearly empty glass, Ned caught my eye and held my gaze for a beat, then two, and longer still until my breath caught in my throat and my cheeks burned.

Something flickered between us. Something I knew I needed to let lie.

Forcing myself to look away, I stood to go. “It’s getting late.”

“My driver will take you home,” Evalyn said.

“Thank you. And thank you for the wonderful evening.” I focused on Evalyn’s face—not on her husband’s lovely eyes—and made my way to the door.

16

I threw open my bedroom window, and a cleansing spring breeze poured inside, whisking away the oppressive air that had stifled me for months. I watched a pair of robins hopping about on the grass below, pecking at the ground and singing their distinctive song. Dappled sunlight formed a pattern of golden light around them. I couldn't believe I'd slept half the morning away. After the long day and late evening at Evalyn's, I supposed I'd needed it. I hadn't settled into bed easily once home either, my mind churning with thoughts of my brother.

I dressed for work and prepared to clean the boutique for Evalyn's visit later that day. Though we were open by appointment only, it had been weeks since I'd cleaned the space, much less scheduled a meeting with a client, and every surface was coated in a thick layer of dust. After I'd shined both the large front window and the glass counter where we showcased our designs, I cleaned the honey-colored wood floors and claw-footed lamps stationed at each corner of the room. After, I dusted the watercolor paintings, one of a scene in Paris along the Seine and the other of the wild marshes of the Chesapeake Bay. The boutique was an inviting, light-filled space, designed to complement our jewelry in every possible way.

By the time I'd finished, a sheen of sweat dampened my forehead. As I put away the cleaning supplies, I realized that for the first time in months, I hadn't awakened with a start or with the vision of my beloved twin, broken and bloodied, pinned behind my eyes.

As I considered what that meant—the forgetting, the ebb of pain—grief slammed into me. Was he fading from my memory? I closed my eyes, and his scent filled my nose, his laughter my ears, and his hand found mine. My breath steadied as my heart knew what my head did not: He would not and could not leave me, not ever. Evalyn and her glittering world, her friends and parties and beautiful things, her husband with his piercing blue eyes, distracted me, diverted the darkness roaring inside me, like river stones directing the water's path. But it didn't mean my brother had left me. I swiped at my eyes and the tears collecting there.

Outside, the sound of the lid on the letter box clinked shut.

Grateful for the interruption to my thoughts, I stepped outside to retrieve the mail, glancing momentarily at the retreating back of the postman. Richard used to say hello when he delivered the mail, but Father and I had avoided nearly all human contact long enough that Richard no longer took a moment out of his day to be friendly. Suddenly I felt the urge to call out to him, to say hello.

I cupped my hands around my mouth. "Richard! I hope you're well!"

He paused at the end of the sidewalk and raised his hat above his head. "Hello, Elisabeth. Nice to see you up and about."

I appreciated his sensitivity in not mentioning the obvious. "I'll see you tomorrow. Have a nice day."

"You, too, miss."

Satisfied, I stepped inside and sorted through the envelopes. There were three more bills and one envelope of what looked to be expensive stationery. My address was marked on the front, but there wasn't a return address, and the postage stamp came from a town in Virginia. I frowned as I closed the door behind me and slit open the letter. A small card was stuffed inside.

Beware. Trouble will find you as long as you are the caretaker of the Hope Diamond.

I reread the card three times. Frowning, I turned it over, looking for some clue as to who the sender might be, but the back was blank. Was it the same woman who'd warned Evalyn? It couldn't be—I'd never met Maude Hughes and apparently neither had Evalyn. I wondered if Evalyn's other friends had received notes as well. Surely they would have mentioned it if they had?

"I don't believe in curses," I whispered. Yet even as I spoke the words aloud, some sense, some knowing filled me with dread. I couldn't imagine who would send the note and what they'd have to gain by warning me away. Why go to the trouble when I was a jeweler, and it was my very job to tend to the necklace?

The doorbell chimed, and I jumped like a frightened cat. I peered out the window to see several people clustered near the door. It was... Evalyn and a few of her friends? I glanced at the clock. She was two hours earlier than we'd agreed upon, and she'd brought others. I paused before opening the door. Father could come downstairs at any moment. I chewed the inside of my cheek, wondering what in the world I would say to him if he did. Or worse, what he'd say to Evalyn. I'd have to take that chance.

The doorbell chimed again, and I opened the door. "Evalyn! Hello, you're here."

"Hello, darling." She pushed past me inside the shop, a cloud of jasmine perfume swirling around her. Bea, Gwen, Sharon, and two other women I didn't recognize followed her. "What a day it is. I'm already perspiring."

"And I'm sweating like a hog," Bea said crassly, making everyone laugh.

Gwen lightly touched her coiffure to make sure every hair was in place. I felt my own hair then, my fingertips brushing damp clumps that had escaped my once-tight bun. As I glanced down at my work trousers and the scuffed tips of my boots, I wished fervently I was wearing anything else. I hadn't had enough time to clean up like I'd planned. I cringed inwardly at the sight I must be. I knew someone would make a comment about my attire before they left, so I braced myself for it.

"How nice it is to see you all," I said, sliding the menacing letter into the pocket of my smock.

One of the women I didn't know stared at me, her eyes skimming my body. When she met my gaze, I noticed she wore a tight smile. "How do you do. I'm Peggy, and this is Frances." She waved a hand in the direction of the woman beside her.

"We'd like to see your pieces, darling," Evalyn cut in. "Where are they?" She frowned as she peered at the empty case.

"We keep them locked in the safe until we have an appointment with a client. Let me gather them." I pushed through the door connecting the workshop with the boutique and fetched the trays and my collection as well.

As I carried the trays to the boutique, snippets of the women's conversation drifted toward me.

"Shhh, don't be so rude." Evalyn's voice.

"Come now, Evie. Really, she's dressed like a man," Sharon said.

Snickers followed, and I felt my stomach sink. What did they expect me to wear while I worked? Silk and lace? And they'd arrived two hours early!

As I pushed through the door and set down the trays, my irritation bubbled over. "I'm afraid my silk robes and sapphire diadem are being cleaned at the moment. They get rather dirty while I'm cleaning or creating new masterpieces."

Evalyn laughed heartily at my sarcasm. Sharon looked stung by Evalyn's laughter and my reply.

Served her right.

"Oh, you do make me laugh, Lizzie," Evalyn said. "Now let's have a look at your jewelry, shall we?"

As I lay out the trays in an artful display, the ladies made sounds of delight.

Sharon, despite her snideness, bought a pair of gold earrings with pearl inlay and a matching necklace. Two of the others bought brooches, and Evalyn bought the largest and most expensive piece: a stunning diamond collar with a pear-shaped ruby pendant my father had designed several years ago. He'd hoped to sell it many times, but the price had ultimately spooked the few women who had considered it. He would be thrilled to see it finally had a home.

To my surprise, the others, Sharon and Gwen included, set up a schedule for me to clean their jewelry collections. I was thrilled to have secured them as clients at last. The hours of spending time with these women had paid off. I didn't know how things would develop from here, but it was a good start.

Before leaving, Evalyn put her hand on my arm. "Stop by tomorrow, will you? Five o'clock. Dress for a dinner party." She flashed her white teeth.

"I'll see you then."

"Good." She turned to go but stopped when I called her name. "What is it?"

"Have any of the others—your friends, I mean—have they received warnings or threatening letters like you have?"

"No," she said, frowning. "Why do you ask?"

I hesitated a moment and finally decided it would be best to keep the note I'd received to myself for now. I wasn't in the habit of confiding in Evalyn, and I didn't know what good it would do to share the information with her. It might upset her. I opted for flattery instead. "I wondered if it might be a hazard of being part of such a sought-after crowd."

"I'm the only lucky one," she said facetiously.

And so was I, apparently. Something I would think more about later.

"I really must be going. Toodle-oo." She waggled her fingers at me and disappeared through the front door.

When I'd locked the door behind them, I breathed a sigh of relief. Pretending to be someone else was exhausting, but as I flipped through the stack of receipts, tabulating the money I'd made, I couldn't help but feel a glimmer of satisfaction. Their business had effectively paid off the worst of our stack of bills, buying me time to decide on my next move as well as what to do about my designs. How could I regret succumbing to Evalyn's demands and wasting many hours and days on her whims with such rewards? She and her circle were keeping Beaumont Jewelers afloat until my father returned to work in earnest. And yet...

My fingertips brushed the letter in my pocket. The same spike of dread I'd felt earlier returned in force. I didn't know who could have sent the letter or what their agenda might be, but it was an obvious warning to stay away from the Hope Diamond or face the consequences.

As I glanced down at the pile of receipts, I knew I'd ignore the warning. I'd already worked too hard, was in too deep, and depended on their income. Never mind the questions that I still needed to be answered. I was getting closer to the truth about Julien. I could feel it.

"Are you going to tell me what that was all about?"

I jumped at the sound of Father's voice. "You scared me!" I collected the trays and locked away the unsold jewelry, racking my brain for something to say. Had he noticed the Hope Diamond? I bit my lip as I turned to face him.

"What was she doing here?" he said, crossing his arms over his chest.

"It's the new group of society ladies I was telling you about," I said, trying to redirect him. "Look at everything we sold today." I held out the sales ledger.

He made no move to look at it, and my stomach dropped. "Elisabeth Marie Beaumont, you'd better tell me right now why that woman was here."

"She's the one who helped us," I said, avoiding his eyes. "She's introduced me to all her friends. She's invited me to her gatherings... I've been wearing our jewelry as an advertisement. You should see how many things they bought today! Look!"

"I don't care how much she's bought! I forbade you from going to that house!" he thundered. "Have you forgotten what happened to your brother?"

"She feels terrible about Julien," I pleaded.

"Oh, she feels terrible?" he shouted. "She feels terrible as she spends thousands of dollars on clothes and cars and a million other insignificant things and gets on with her life? And now you, my only daughter, are at risk, just as your brother was. Dallying in a world where he didn't belong. Toying with that woman's affections. Look where that got him. You will not go back there. Do you hear me!"

"I'm not a child!" I shouted back. "I'm twenty-eight years old, for

Christ's sake. And I'm the only adult holding this business together. If you don't like who our clients are, then perhaps you should rise from your chair and help me. If I'm to do this alone, we'll do it my way. I don't want to forfeit everything we've worked so hard for, including our home!" My chest heaved with the force of my anger.

Stunned by my vehemence, my father's eyes widened, and he took a step back. He opened his mouth to speak, but before he could say another word, I stormed from the room.

17

The next few days, I fussed over my collection, my frustration growing before I finally gave up. Evalyn and her friends hadn't bought a single piece of mine, and only one person had so much as admired them. It was my father's designs that had truly captured their attention and his pieces they had bought. Their lack of interest solidified the fear I'd harbored for longer than I wanted to admit but now couldn't avoid: I wasn't as talented a jewelry designer as my father and never would be. I didn't have the knack for predicting what others would like or discerning tastes and unique styles. I catered to my own tastes, and given how little jewelry I wore on a daily basis, my taste didn't amount to much. I'd tried telling myself that it was about timing. I needed more time to practice my skills and more access to the larger stones—and perhaps there was a shred of truth in that. Or perhaps I should no longer waste my time or our supplies designing a collection that no one would want to buy.

I turned my attention to an easier project: another gift for Evalyn. It was a thank-you for her generosity and for bringing her friends to the boutique. Though she wasn't perfect and being in her presence was something of a minefield I had to navigate, she still didn't have to include me in her excursions and events, and she didn't have to hire Beaumont

Jewelers, but she'd been generous anyway. Father would say otherwise, but I would do what I must, and for now, that included working with Evalyn. I'd only spoken to him the bare minimum since our argument. I knew he was wounded by what I'd said about his abandonment of our business and home, but I couldn't bring myself to care. He'd all but disappeared and left me to fend for myself for months.

I sifted through our smaller gemstones and a set of feathers and added a piece of gold fabric to the pile of things for Evalyn's gift to make a headband. I hoped she'd like the headband more than the hair combs, which she'd yet to wear. Headbands had recently become more popular, and feathers never went out of fashion, or at least that was what I'd heard one of the society ladies say one afternoon. I carefully sewed a band of elastic to the shimmery gold fabric. At one end, I attached a long, dramatic ostrich feather. After, I slipped on the headband and checked my reflection in the mirror. I looked silly in such an extravagant thing, but I couldn't deny that it was beautiful. Once I'd affixed the gemstones, it would glitter brilliantly.

When a knock came at the door, I hesitated, deciding if I should pretend no one was home. It had been a long few days of more socializing than I could usually stomach, and all I wanted to do was hide.

Someone pounded again, more insistently this time.

"Elisabeth? It's Henry. I know you're in there!"

My stomach clenched. What was he doing here? When would he accept that I didn't want to see him?

"Elisabeth!" My father called from the kitchen. "Why aren't you answering the door?" He bounded down the stairs and pushed past me to the boutique door with a huff, clearly still angry with me. "Hello, Henry," he said. "Come in, my boy."

"Hello, Mr. Beaumont." Henry stepped inside. "Is Elisabeth—" He caught sight of me and stopped, his mouth slightly ajar. "Your hair!"

In a self-conscious gesture, I touched my newly shorn hair. Bea had said I looked like a movie star, but I wasn't so sure about that. Her compliment had made me feel good just the same. "Is it that bad?" I asked. "You look appalled."

"No!" he said quickly. "I mean, of course not. It's just so short."

"Evalyn had it done."

"Who is Evalyn?"

"A client."

His brows shot up, but he didn't reply.

"And a friend," I added. It was certainly out of the norm for me to fashion my appearance based on the advice of a client and entirely unlike me to care.

"I see," he said, looking around. He removed his hat, held it in his hands. "Am I interrupting something?"

"Not at all," my father replied. "Elisabeth, get your coat."

I glared at my father. Why did he believe he could still tell me what to do? I supposed I'd always let him, but things were different now. I was different. "I'm sorry, Henry, but I have work to do—"

"Not today, you don't," Father said. "Off you go with Henry. I've already promised him you were free to do as you please today."

Henry cleared his throat. "I wanted to take you to the museum, but if you're busy, I can call another time."

Suddenly the idea of an afternoon at the museum felt like much-needed air in my lungs. If Henry broached a subject I didn't want to discuss, I could always tell him I wasn't interested in rehashing the past. He'd respect my wishes. He always had.

"Fine," I said at last. "Let me change." I quickly changed out of my work trousers and pulled on a lavender dress with a handkerchief hem. In minutes, I met him at the door.

"Goodness," Henry said. "That's quite a dress."

"Evalyn bought it for me," I said. "She pays for all her employees' uniforms, so she insisted she buy her jeweler some new things."

"So I see," he said.

"What do you see?"

"Nothing. You look lovely."

"For a change."

He shook his head. "You've always been attractive but..."

"I look like a woman for once."

He rolled his eyes, clearly becoming exasperated with me. "You're as beautiful as ever. Can you stop putting words in my mouth? The changes surprised me, that's all. Are you ready to go?"

We walked silently in step to the nearest tram stop. It was another perfect spring day with sunny skies and the scent of lilacs infusing the air. Everyone on the streets appeared light on their feet, in a good mood.

"You seem...different," he said. "You've been spending an awful lot of time with the people who got Julien into trouble—" He stopped abruptly, shook his head. "I'm sorry. I didn't mean to bring him up. And it's your business, not mine. I just want to make sure you're all right."

I stiffened at what felt like a criticism. I didn't need this, not right now.

"You're right, it isn't your business," I said, my tone biting, angry. "I need to make a living until my father is back to full-time work, and if this is what it takes, I'll do what I have to do. We almost lost the house, Henry." I climbed into the tram car warily, wishing I had decided not to go with him after all. If we were going to argue or I was going to field criticisms from him, it would be a long afternoon.

He raised his hands. "You're right. I'm sorry. You're doing what you can. Which is one reason I wanted to bring you to the museum," he added. "You deserve a break and time doing something that makes you happy."

I glanced at him long enough to catch the sincerity in his eyes and felt guilty for being testy with him. "Thank you," I said at last.

As he settled in the seat next to me, his familiar spiced cologne laced the air. A scent I knew intimately and had loved for so long that I fell back in time, the present day fading like the colors of a quilt bleached by too much sunlight.

One afternoon, I'd opened the door to see Henry on my doorstep, as I had so many hundreds of times before, but that day, my heart skipped a beat. He was smiling broadly, and a special gleam shone in his eyes.

"Julien isn't home," I said as Henry bounded into my living room. "He's out with Father, on business."

The smile on Henry's face didn't wane. "I know. I didn't come here to see him. I came to see you, to rescue you from working too hard. Julien said you needed someone to force you to take a break."

"Oh," I said, oddly disappointed by the omission. It was Julien who'd sent him, of course. Henry hadn't come of his own volition. I removed my protective goggles from atop my head and set them on my workbench.

"How about lunch?" he continued. "I have an hour before I have to go back to the office, and I'd like to talk you about something."

I glanced down at my filthy clothes and knew I must look a fright. "You want to take me to lunch looking like this?"

He chuckled. "Somehow, you look most like yourself with dirty trousers. Even filthy, head to toe, you're the prettiest of the Beaumonts."

I blushed hotly, as was my way. What he said simply wasn't true. Julien looked as if he were the offspring of a Greek god and a mortal. Though I resembled my brother in bone structure, my features were more exaggerated somehow. My nose was more pronounced, my high cheekbones almost sharp, and the solitary dimple in my right cheek formed a deep-set groove. Along with the differences in features, Julien's fair hair and light eyes to my dark tones made us look more like cousins than brother and sister. Luckily, I wasn't the jealous type. I was proud of my beautiful, ebullient brother—as proud of him as he was of me.

"Come on, don't act as if you've never heard a compliment before." Henry's lips quirked up at the corners into an amused smile. "You've got a strand of hair sticking straight up." He reached out to brush away the hair, but assuming he'd make a mess of it the way he and Julien always had done to be funny, I stepped out of the way. As his hand fell to his side, his eyes dimmed.

Was he...disappointed I didn't let him touch me? It couldn't be... We were friends. In fact, I'd known Henry all my life. We'd made mud pies on the banks of the Potomac River, shared flavored ice in the summer, and invented games with rocks and sticks the way that children do. He'd been my constant companion, second only to Julien. And yet somehow, I'd always known he was Julien's friend and mine only by proxy. Nearly everything had been that way with my brother. He was the leader and I was the sidekick, the second in line.

After I changed my clothes, Henry took me to the Hungry Tiger for lunch. Over barbecue sandwiches and coleslaw, we talked about Henry's frustration at the continued closure of the museum since the war and about the fieldwork he'd need to do for his research in the spring. He'd studied history and more recently had become a curator for the Smithsonian Institution at the National Museum.

"I'm worried about Julien," I said, nudging the last dregs of coleslaw on my plate with my fork. "He's been acting strange. He rarely spends time in the workshop or with Father for their sales outings. He's out until dawn all the time. When I ask him where he's been, he insists that he's working for the McLeans. Has he said anything to you?"

Henry laid his hand over mine. He'd touched me in such a way a hundred times, perhaps even a thousand, but for the first time in my life, I felt a flicker of something different. A heat, an eagerness.

Embarrassed, I yanked my hand away.

"I'm sorry. I didn't mean to..." Light pink dusted the curve of Henry's cheeks, and I realized he was either offended or as embarrassed as I was.

"I... No, I'm sorry," I said. "It's fine, really. I'm not myself today." The truth was I'd dreamed about Henry a few times since I'd last seen him. I'd awoken discombobulated on those days, as confused as I was filled with pleasure. Just that morning, I'd realized something I hadn't wanted to admit to myself for quite some time: My feelings for Henry were changing, deepening in a way I couldn't have predicted. But I would never jeopardize our friendship, and I'd never come between my brother and his best friend, not ever. Besides, come what may, I knew Henry thought of me as his best friend's sister. His touch was merely perfunctory, or so I told myself.

"That makes two of us," he said, his eyes on mine.

My stomach did a slow turn. When he looked at me like that...I didn't know what to say, what to do. All I knew was I hoped he would never stop.

"As for Julien, I'm worried, too," he said, his expression changing. "At first I thought he might have a crush on someone new, but when I asked him, he denied it. Said he was consumed with trying to court this new influential group of people. Apparently, they have ties to the president and an impressive list of powerful people in Washington. He said he's trying to play his cards right and all that."

Hurt that my brother had kept the truth from me, I avoided Henry's eyes, played with the edge of my napkin. "Whatever he's doing, I hope he's being cautious. The McLeans are known all over town. One wrong step and he could hurt the business's reputation. Father would be livid—and devastated." I groaned as I thought of Julien being pulled in way over his head and pushed my plate away. He might be highly competent and capable, but he was also a little too confident for his own good sometimes.

Henry shook his head. "I know. I've warned him, too. But he insisted he's fine and that he's being careful. He said I was acting like his dad."

"His attention span never lasts for long, and in this case, I think that's a good thing. Do you think…" I shook my head.

"What?" he said, covering his glass with his hand as a waiter offered more sweetened iced tea. "No, thank you."

"I keep thinking about the Hope Diamond."

"Why? The curse?"

I shrugged. "He has been acting erratic lately. He's gone a lot, has circles under his eyes. I don't know. I'm sure I'm being ridiculous. I've always thought curses were dumb." But whether it was the curse or something else entirely, a pit lodged in my stomach along with a sense of foreboding I couldn't shake.

He nodded. "No, you're showing your sisterly concern. I suspect we're both worrying far too much about nothing. But keep an eye on him, and if he continues running himself ragged for these people, we'll talk to him. Convince him to find work elsewhere."

I nodded, but what I didn't say was I'd never been able to convince my brother of anything once he put his mind to it, and I was pretty certain Henry had the same experience. Julien might follow flights of fancy, but he was also as stubborn as a mule. The only thing we could do was say our piece and wait for the fallout.

We couldn't have known that day how dangerous Julien's pandering to Evalyn's circle would become.

"Elisabeth?" Henry nudged me, pulling me back to the present.

At the memory of that day, my hands began to shake. Our worry about Julien had turned out to be right on the nose—and my fault. *Our fault.*

"Yes," I said, clutching my handbag to steady myself. "I'm sorry. I was...lost in thought."

"We're here. Are you ready?"

"Good. Let's go."

We walked from our stop to the National Museum, its gleaming white dome and pearly facade bright in the sunlight. The lengthy stretch in front of the building would become a park soon, but for now, it was a puzzle of crisscrossed dirt paths and patches of greenery where construction had flourished for nearly a decade. To the west, an enormous monument dedicated to Lincoln was nearly finished. The original Lincoln statue had been deemed far too small for the massive classical style temple that would house it, so the statue was recommissioned at twice its original size. Soon, it would be installed for posterity.

"I'm looking forward to seeing it when it's finished," Henry said, following my gaze.

"How big do you think the statue will be?" I asked, thinking of how much marble they used for such a magnificent monument.

"I've read it'll be somewhere between eighteen and twenty feet tall."

I pictured Abraham Lincoln in gleaming Georgia white marble.

How regal he would be. It was befitting of one of America's greatest leaders.

When we arrived at the National Museum, we bounded up the steps and headed inside. As the smell of cool marble rushed around me, my shoulders relaxed and the tight knot of anxiety in my stomach eased.

"It's this way," Henry said.

"What is?"

"You'll see," he said.

We crossed the rotunda in front of the building and took the stairs to the ground floor. In the easternmost wing, there was a series of offices for research. As we wound through the halls, I tried to picture rows of desks and typewriters and stacks of documents from the war organization that had marred the beautiful space for the past two years, but I couldn't. To me, museums were as sacred as a church, not to be desecrated by the mundane.

Henry steered me to a back room closed to the public where new exhibits were being constructed. "We're building another whale exhibit, but this time, they'll be using its entire body."

I gasped at the massive cradle of would-be bones and plaster, the stacks of tools and blueprints, the expansive scaffolding, and the three men lifting what looked like an enormous puzzle piece mimicking the whale's skin. "How in the world did they manage to make this mold so accurate?"

He grinned. "Do you remember when we talked about the death masks from the French Revolution? How they poured wax over the face of the dead to create a mold?"

I cringed. "How could I forget."

He chuckled. "Our scientists didn't use wax, but they worked in much the same way. They left the deceased whale suspended in the water near the beach where they found it to accurately capture how its fins would float and covered the entire form with burlap, fine curled wood shavings used for packing, and plaster of paris. They worked in sections from the tail to the head. Apparently the head deteriorates more slowly than the rest of the body."

I couldn't imagine such an undertaking, sitting in a dinghy on the water for hours upon hours, rocking over the tide as I attempted to wrap the world's largest animal in plaster. "It's incredible."

"Mmm, isn't it," he said, staring up at the framework. "Think about how many people will see a blue whale for the first time. It may change the way they see the world. Perhaps they'll better appreciate nature and science. That's always my hope anyway."

I nodded, eyes wide, considering the incredible lengths scientists went to in order to understand our world and to bring that understanding to others. I felt a pang of jealousy at missing out on such important work.

I glanced at Henry. He was watching me, and he'd read my face, just as he had since we were children. I wondered how I must look to him, how the woman and the girl he'd always known was morphing before his eyes. I'd felt the seismic shift inside me with Julien's death, and since I'd taken over the business, I'd felt it again—the grinding of one version of myself against the other. I only feared that part of me would disappear in time, and I wanted to hold on to both somehow.

"One of the scientists is in the process of cataloging a set of stones," he said. "Would you like to see them?"

"Would I like to see them?" I rolled my eyes, eliciting a laugh from him. "Of course I would. Isn't that why you brought me here?"

He laughed.

In the hallway leading to Henry's office, a woman walked toward us and almost passed without a greeting.

"Hello to you, too, Julia," Henry said.

The woman turned, laughing. "I'm sorry, I didn't see you there. I was lost in thought." Julia looked to be in her mid- to late thirties. Her braided hair was pinned neatly, and her navy dress was modest, though the cut was in fashion.

"Lizards again?" Henry asked playfully.

"It's always the lizards," she replied with a smile.

"This is my friend, Elisabeth Beaumont. I've brought her in to show her the new specimens. Liz, this is Julia Wane. She's a lab assistant for a couple of the herpetologists."

"Hello, how do you do," she said, shaking my hand.

I was surprised by the gesture. Evalyn and her circle would be appalled by such a masculine display of manners, but I liked Julia and her manners instantly. We exchanged a few pleasantries, and when she excused herself to return to her work, I was disappointed she had to leave so quickly. I'd never met a female scientist or lab assistant other than Ken Davis's wife, Maye, and I found myself wanting to ask Julia a dozen questions.

"She's great, isn't she?" His gaze lingered on her retreating form. In only one meeting, I could see that Julia Wane was intelligent and passionate about her work, something I knew he found appealing.

I watched him watch her, my stomach clenched, and yet I had no claim on him, and he had every right to seek the affections of another woman. Even if I couldn't stand the thought of it, I also couldn't deny Henry happiness. He meant too much to me, despite everything.

When he realized I hadn't answered him, he arched his brow at me in expectation. "Well?"

"She is great," I said. And what I didn't say was that I envied Julia in other ways, too. How lucky she was to be doing the kind of work she loved in such a magnificent space.

He eyed me curiously for an instant and then said, "I have something else to show you. Come on, this way."

I swallowed my unexpected jealousy and followed him to the back offices. I was making too much of things. Probably. Maybe. I glanced at him. He was thankfully oblivious to my line of thinking and fully focused on his task.

"Here we are," he said, showing me inside an office where a massive collection of stones was spread across a long table next to an assortment of tools, microscopes, and various other instruments. The scientists were clearly in the process of identifying and labeling the stones. I looked around, admiring the space, wishing fervently that I were a part of the team. Sketches of the stones were mounted on the wall, and a special case displayed hundreds of labeled specimens. Others were so large they occupied floor space.

"Look at these," he said. "Jack has been studying meteorites found in Missouri, Texas, and Florida. This is—"

"Peridot," I said, bending over the table to peer at it more closely. It was a gorgeous darker green, which meant its iron content was quite high. Peridot was one of my favorite stones, though its value was lesser in the eyes of the market. What made it so unique was that it was either formed by lava in the mantle of the earth, rather than the earth's crust like almost all other stones, or formed inside a certain kind of meteorite. In other words, it could be a stone from outer space. Something about its otherworldliness appealed to me.

I looked past Henry at a magnificent amethyst geode that was nearly as tall as me. The crystals were a deep purple in the middle, while its outer fringes were lavender and violet as the traces of iron within the crystals' structure lessened and became a crust of sparkling, clear quartz.

"Magnificent," I breathed. "I've never seen such a large geode intact before."

"I've missed you," he said. "I've missed this, spending time with you, especially here."

My eyes darted to his face. Pain etched lines around his mouth and made grooves in his forehead. *He missed me.* What could I say to that? I didn't want to think about how he felt, how I felt or didn't feel, or what came next.

"Aren't you going to say something?" he asked softly.

I met his gray-green eyes. "What do you want me to say?"

"That you miss me, too?"

"Henry—"

A cloud passed over his features. "You don't have to say anything." Anger tinged his voice. "I thought there was something special between us, but maybe I was mistaken."

Didn't he feel the guilt I did? How could he move on as if nothing had happened, as if we weren't partly responsible for Julien's death? As if we had a right to keep living when my brother—his dearest friend—was gone.

"Don't you feel guilty about what happened?" I asked, brushing off his anger.

"Of course I do," he said. "He was like a brother to me. I would give anything to go back to that night, but I can't." He ran a hand through his hair. "And I don't regret how I feel about you. I wouldn't change that, no matter what. How could I? And yet it seems you would."

I shook my head. I didn't know how I felt about Henry in this moment, but how could I not regret that night? We were too late to save Julien. *We were too late.* I looked away, and when I didn't reply, Henry blew out a steadying breath.

"Let's not talk about this now," he said. "Let's enjoy the afternoon. Come on, I want to show you the dinosaur skeletons. They're almost finished assembling them."

"Can we tour the anthropology exhibits, too?" I asked, relieved he respected my limits. Despite how things had evolved between us,

I'd always be grateful for his friendship. I only wished I could bring myself to say it.

"Of course." He held out his arm so I might take it.

Hesitating, I bit my lip and looked up at him.

As he read my expression, his smile faltered, and without a word, he withdrew his arm and ushered us down another long hallway.

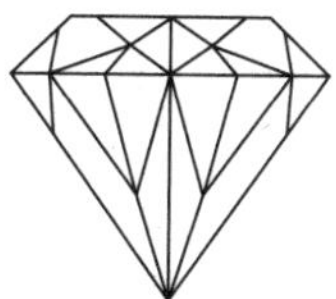

I am ushered through time and circumstance and location. I am lighter, a lesser version of myself, separated from my other half. Still, I am very large and beautiful. My value is as great as ever, perhaps greater as my legend grows, and I am sold quickly to a collector. Mr. Hope is from a greedy family, one that must own as much art and property and jewels as they can acquire. He does not love, he does not cherish; he possesses, and I am promptly renamed after my new possessor. But as with the others who have kept me for a time, misery and misfortune haunt him and those he will bequeath me to. And their lives become a tangle of bankruptcy and desperation.

Soon, I am once again sold and passed on from one gem collector to another.

A remarkable beauty, a symbol of wealth, a marvel!

This is how they tempt the willing to purchase such a stone. This is how I find a new home with a Turkish diamond merchant. But he does not pay his debts, and I am once again unbound and dispossessed.

Ruin streams behind me. Despair infuses the air around me. For I am not a diamond of hope. I am, in fact, hope's thief. To such a fate, it seems I must be resigned and so must my keepers.

As I embark upon the next leg of my journey across the Atlantic and back again, I arrive at last on the doorstep of an expert jeweler. A man who understands the power of legacy.

"Sir, it is not only one of a kind," my keeper says as he presents me. "It was once a prized French possession."

Pierre Cartier gasps, takes me into his capable hands. "It is the French Blue!"

My keeper smiles. "It is. *It was.* But now it is the Hope."

"And now," Pierre says with his own broad smile, "it is mine."

18

I bent down to retrieve a Pierre Cartier leaflet from the carpet in the entryway to my home. Either the postman had stuffed it through the mail slot in the front door, or my father had dropped it. I turned it over, reading the advertisement for the recently opened Cartier Mansion on Fifth Avenue in New York City. Though Beaumont Jewelers would likely never reach the same heights, I knew my father's designs easily competed with the Cartiers'. I'd always thought as much when I'd seen pages of Cartier designs. I wondered what my father thought of the advertisement. Likely not much, given it had been left in the doorway where feet would surely tread upon it.

I trudged upstairs and changed into my smock and trousers after the trip to the museum. Rather than work on the collection I was beginning to loathe, I retrieved the unfinished headband I'd been making for Evalyn. I hadn't seen her wear anything like it, but given her propensity for flash and glamour, I guessed she'd like it. Despite the unease I felt in her presence—and despite the unease I felt working near the Hope Diamond—I was grateful for her patronage.

I carefully affixed tiny diamond and sapphire chips to the headband fabric. Concentrating intently on the detail-oriented nature of the work, I lost track of time. When a knock came at the boutique door, I nearly leapt out of my skin. I peered at the clock. It was almost suppertime. I wondered who could be calling so late on a Saturday afternoon, especially unannounced.

I swung open the door—and stepped back in surprise. Carrie Wellington perched on my doorstep in pale green, her torch-like hair tucked under an enormous white hat.

"Hello, Lizzie, I was hoping you were home," she said. "May I come in?"

"I… Hello, yes, of course," I said, though my stomach lurched wildly at the sight of her. Perhaps we could finally talk about Julien.

"I saw Sharon's pair of earrings and the lovely brooch you sold to Bea and thought I might pop by to see if you had any other pieces for sale. It's my mother's birthday next week. She's been so blue since Daddy died, so I thought something pretty might cheer her up a little."

Naturally she assumed buying her mother's affections was the key to making her feel better. I clamped down on my tongue. I was in the business of selling luxury items, and the Wellingtons and others of her ilk were the kind of people I had to do business with, whether I liked it or not. More importantly, she was a close friend of Evalyn's, and not serving her could potentially raise questions.

"Come in," I said, forcing a smile.

As I led her inside, I thought of the pendant she'd worn that Julien had made, and then the way she'd encouraged Evalyn to hire me, and I couldn't help but think something more was going on between her and my brother. A harmless flirtation was likely all, given how the others had all said so, but something about her set me on edge. I retrieved the jewelry trays from the safe and laid my father's latest collection—now thoroughly picked over after the others' visit—as well as my own collection and a handful of other pieces on the counter for her perusal.

"If you're looking for a fresh design, I could show you some of our loose gemstones and our sketchbook. I can also design something new for you if there is a particular style or stone you like, but it would take some time."

She flashed a winning smile that probably charmed most people. I saw only feigned interest and the same competitiveness the others displayed when trying to outdo each other.

"This is fine," she said. "There are so many beautiful pieces. I'm sure I'll find something my mother would like."

I watched her as she picked through the choices and half listened to her prattle on about her mother and Evalyn's party the next evening, all the while trying to discern if she and Julien had been involved in any way. After the third mention of Evalyn's name, a memory from the past emerged, hovering like a specter in my mind's eye.

It had been a sticky southern October day, the lingering heat of summer at last fading into a balmy night with a cooling wind lovely enough to open the windows. Julien had been frustrated, concerned. His emotions were always as evident as the weather, sketched clearly on his features. He'd come home uncharacteristically disheveled. His jacket and shirt were wrinkled, his usually combed blond hair sticking up in the back.

"Are you all right? Where have you been?" I demanded as he breezed into my bedroom and closed the door behind him. I was already in my nightgown, reading in bed—and trying not to worry about him. "It's late."

He sat down on the edge of the bed, causing the mattress to dip. I scooted to my left to make more room for him. "I lost my wallet and got caught up looking for it." He reached for the book in my lap and scanned the title. "*Dangerous Days* by Mary Roberts Rhinehart. Doesn't she write mysteries? The American Agatha Christie or something?"

He didn't fool me with his diversion. He was lying. Twins couldn't lie to each other, no matter how hard they tried. If I couldn't discern the lie on his face or in his tone, my intuition prickled, and I knew the truth instantly. I reached for the book and shoved it behind my pillow.

"Are you going to tell me what you're really up to, or are we going to play games with each other?" I asked. "You've been acting strange for weeks now. Henry and I have both noticed it."

He looked down, ran a hand through his hair, and glanced up again. His blue eyes were feverishly bright, and I knew with certainty that he was hiding something. "I've been working too hard, staying out too late," he said. "I'm spending a lot of time trying to secure our footing with these people in Washington. The McLeans and their friends."

I glanced at the dark smudges beneath his eyes. "You don't need to work so hard to gain their favor. I'm sure you already have it, and if not, we can look elsewhere. I hate to see you so worn out." He wasn't only spending too many hours at the McLeans', he was going without sleep entirely.

He shook his head. "You don't understand."

"Then help me understand."

"They know everyone. If we win their trust and secure a spot as their premier jeweler, we'd be set for life. As Cartier has done in Paris and New York. Like Worth has done with his fashions in London and Paris. Don't you want that?"

I looked at my very ambitious brother, felt his fervor, and I believed him—to a point. I could tell by the set of his jaw and the way he ran his hand through his hair too often that something else beneath his ambition was driving him. I couldn't quite pinpoint what, at least not yet. But I wouldn't push him for now. He would tell me everything in time, I knew.

At last, I said, "Is this about the Hope Diamond?"

"Not exactly, no."

"That's probably a good thing."

He forced a smile that looked more like a grimace before changing the subject. "Have you received any strange letters in the mail?"

"Strange letters? What do you mean?"

"Nothing. I believe they were for Father," he added quickly. "I'm sure they're new clients."

He'd replied too smoothly, and his concern felt too slight, feigned. Again, he was lying.

"He hasn't mentioned anything to me," I said, watching his face intently.

"Well then. They must not be important," he said at last, his eyes glazing over, becoming unfocused.

"I suppose not," I replied, wondering why he'd mentioned the letters in the first place.

His face was pensive, I imagined his thoughts as turbulent and rapid as white water.

I laid my hand on his shoulder. "How about some warm milk to help you sleep?"

"How about a brandy instead."

We both laughed, and I slipped from bed, following my brother into the kitchen. My mind whirred with all he'd said and all he hadn't, and as I looked at his mussed gold hair and beautiful profile and the clear distress stamped on his features, I wondered when—and how—I'd need to rescue him from his foolishness yet again.

The chime of the grandfather clock startled me, and the remnants of the memory faded. Tears stung my eyes. I hadn't properly cried since the night Julien died, but lately I'd felt the urge more and more often. Still, I wouldn't allow myself the release the tears would bring—knew I didn't deserve it. I carried the burden of grief as both my punishment and to keep his memory close. I should have stopped him that night, been more vehement about telling the truth. I should have been there when he needed me most.

I blinked rapidly and refocused my gaze on the items Carrie had spread out across the counter.

"Do you have a mirror?" she asked.

I tried to focus on being a professional, despite the questions swirling around in my head. I pulled out a paddle-size mirror from underneath the counter. She took it, and as she tried on a set of hair combs, a brooch, and a couple of rings, she checked her reflection in the mirror.

By the time she'd finished, I was on edge. "Is there anything else I can show you?"

"I think I'll take this ruby pendant. Mother would love it. It'll go nicely with her ruby engagement ring. Perhaps it'll remind her of the happy times with Father." She fished in her handbag for her purse. Giving me another bright smile, she asked, "Would you wrap it for me by any chance, Lizzie?"

"It's Elisabeth," I said, knowing she'd only called me Lizzie because she'd heard Evalyn use the nickname a hundred times. But something about Carrie got under my skin. The Beaumont pendant she wore, her flirting with Julien the first time she met him, her otherworldly beauty. My instincts prickled every time I saw her. "I'll put it in a velvet drawstring bag if that suits."

"Doesn't Evie call you Lizzie?"

"Well, she's a friend. I don't usually go by that name."

Her blue eyes filled with false pity, and even I could see the act she put on. She clucked her tongue and said, "Evalyn is everyone's friend and no one's. She cares only about herself. Haven't you noticed?"

Evalyn had been kind to me as well as generous. In fact, she'd been generous with everyone around her. But I knew there was something that rang true in Carrie's words. Evalyn had a frivolity about her, a desperate need for excitement and thrills, and at times, a competitive cruelty that she willingly stoked between her and the others. Many in her circles were the same—including Carrie, given the way she was talking about her longtime friend to someone she scarcely knew.

Anger curled around my words. "Did you come to purchase a gift or to be rude about one of our mutual friends?"

A false, if contrite, smile touched Carrie's ruby lips. "She isn't your friend, darling. You work for her, remember? We all do in our way. And when she tires of you, she will cast you aside and move on to a new pet project. It's better you understand that now."

Her words stung. Numbly, I didn't reply and carried out the rest of the transaction, accepting her check and placing the jewelry in a bag along with our calling card. At last, I could hold my tongue no longer. "I don't understand why you recommended that Evalyn hire me if you believe I'm just another pet project that will be easily cast aside."

"I wanted to help you and your family," she said, dropping the jewelry inside her handbag. "I'd heard your brother passed away unexpectedly and that your father's company was struggling." She looked past me as if I weren't there. Or perhaps she was avoiding my eyes.

"But why? Evalyn said she'd met with two other jewelers. Why help me? Help us?" I searched her face for some semblance of truth, but her expression had shifted again, become closed, her eyes flat.

"Your brother was a kind man. It was a true tragedy that he...he passed away, so young," she said.

"You flirted with him," I blurted, unable to hold back the accusations I longed to hurl at her.

"Excuse me?"

"At the jewelry show last autumn. When you first met Julien and you invited him to Evalyn's for a house party."

She touched her hair gingerly, smoothing a curl out of her eyes. "A warm smile never hurt anyone. Besides, ask the girls. I like to flirt a little, but I'm a very married woman."

"So there was nothing between you?" I pressed.

"Come now, Lizzie. Your brother lavished every one of us with attention. You must have expected that. It was who he was."

I stared at her a moment, trying to read her, but she met my eyes without so much as a flicker of hesitation. Either she was an excellent liar, or there really wasn't anything between her and my brother.

"I hope your mother enjoys the gift," I said at last, in an attempt to smooth things over between us. I didn't need an enemy. I would still get to the bottom of things, one way or another. "Thank you for your business."

She took the package and streamed to the door. "You should be careful, Lizzie. You don't want to find yourself as the rest of us have, beholden to Evalyn and her whims. She doesn't play fair. She plays to win. She knows everyone and can make things very difficult for you."

"I'll never be beholden to anyone," I said, my tone defensive.

She smiled grimly. "If only that were true. Everyone is beholden to someone or something. You just don't know what it is yet, darling. Oh, and, Lizzie? You should be careful with Ned most of all." With a quick backward glance, she closed the door softly behind her.

She'd been watching my interactions with Ned? But she hadn't been there at any point when I'd been speaking with Ned or in the car with us. She must have talked to Evalyn about it or perhaps spoken with him? But nothing had happened between Ned and me. I wondered why Carrie would be warning me off someone with whom I'd spent so little time, especially when I was of no consequence to Ned or any of them. But as I remembered the way he'd smiled at me and his flirtatious compliments, my stomach dipped. Maybe she was onto something after all.

I suddenly felt sick as I watched Carrie strut to her car in her designer dress, hem flapping prettily around her calves, and drive away.

19

My confrontation with Carrie left me unsettled, and I found myself wishing I didn't have my appointed cleaning day at the McLeans' that afternoon. Sighing, I wrapped Evalyn's headband in paper and tied it with ribbon. I hoped she'd like the gift at least. I couldn't shake the feeling that I owed her another token, despite all that Carrie had said about her. And yet Carrie's warning echoed in my mind.

She's not your friend. You are her employee. We all are.

The others seemed perfectly willing to let Evalyn hold court and to lavish her with constant praise. Perhaps somehow, they felt beholden to her as the queen bee. But it was the last of Carrie's warnings that had left a bitter taste in my mouth.

Be careful with Ned.

I couldn't remember a time when she'd been with us in the same room for more than a moment. Perhaps some flirtation had happened between Carrie and Ned in the past, and it hadn't ended well, or maybe...Evalyn had said something about Ned offering me a ride home, about our time on the patio while we waited for her. The thought of Evalyn talking about me with Carrie made my insides swim with unease.

I arrived at Friendship promptly on time for my appointment, but to my surprise, Evalyn wasn't at home. Instead, Jerry showed me inside, set me up with her collection, and, as instructed, stood watch as I scrubbed and polished each piece and placed the precious items back in the case that would be locked away in her safe when I'd finished. Once again, Evalyn wore the Hope Diamond, and once again, it would go without servicing. Though I was disappointed not to have the chance to examine it closely again, perhaps it was for the best.

The anonymous note I'd received a few days before sprang to mind, and the disquiet I'd felt earlier returned. I didn't know who could have sent the note other than someone from Evalyn's circle, but that seemed absurd, given they'd all spent plenty of time within proximity of the Hope Diamond themselves. And yet I couldn't think of a single other person in my life who could have taken a strong enough interest in my clients, or me for that matter, to warn me about the curse. Then again, the note could have come from a perfect stranger. I wondered if any of the others had received a note, too. If only I could study Evalyn's notes, perhaps I might find some similarities to mine... I recalled what Marjorie had said about the police requesting that the McLeans keep the letters should they need them for evidence for an investigation.

"Has all been well, ma'am?" Jerry asked as I packed up my tools about an hour later.

"Well enough, I suppose, thank you." I didn't dare mention the troubling note or the visit from Carrie. While I liked Jerry and he genuinely seemed to like me, I didn't know if I could trust him. I surmised he understood the inner machinations of Evalyn's circle quite well, and he clearly enjoyed the gossip. He also seemed perfectly comfortable in the presence of those above his station. I had the feeling he would enjoy a glass of champagne with Evalyn if she invited him to join her. The rest of the staff seemed to interact with Evalyn and her friends in the most professional yet perfunctory ways and nothing more. Most important of all, I knew Jerry felt a strong sense of loyalty to Evalyn. I admired that; it was as it should be, but it also meant I needed to tread carefully.

"Where are the others?" I asked. "I thought Evalyn was going to be home today."

"There's an event on the other side of town. I don't know where precisely, ma'am, but Mrs. McLean asked me to invite you to stay for supper at seven o'clock."

I glanced down at my dress, glad I'd worn one of those I'd been gifted. There was no telling who would show at her dinner table, and to be underdressed, as I'd learned, was simply too embarrassing. But it was only five o'clock, and I couldn't imagine what I was to do while I waited for her. Amble around the house? It was best I go. I had more than enough to do waiting for me at home.

I shook my head. "I couldn't be an imposition tonight. I have a lot of work to do."

"A working woman with work to do. You are different from Mrs. McLean's other friends."

Oddly, the comment stung. I knew I was different from them, and yet hadn't I spent the last weeks trying to adapt, trying to be more like them? Jerry didn't miss my expression.

"I'm such an oaf," he said. "I've offended you." He looked over his shoulder and lowered his voice. "You aren't like them, ma'am, but that isn't a bad thing. Quite the contrary. And not to worry. Mrs. McLean should be home any moment should you decide to say hello before you're on your way? She asked me to convince you to stay if you needed a little encouragement."

I contemplated another long evening of too many drinks with

Evalyn and felt a twinge of exhaustion. Yet I also still had the gift for her, too... Perhaps I could stay a bit longer to give her the gift and head home shortly after? I could plead a headache.

"All right. I'll stay. I'll stay to say hello and give her the present I've brought for her and then be on my way."

"Very good, ma'am. Make yourself at home. Mrs. McLean would want it that way. Can I do anything for you in the meantime?"

"I'm fine, Jerry."

But after thirty minutes of sitting in the parlor, I stood and began to walk around the room, examining Evalyn's beautiful things. Eventually, I wandered into the hallway, admiring the paintings and vases there, the gilded mirror, and continued on to the study. I peered inside. The anemic light of early evening streamed through the window, casting much of the room in shadow. Books packed the large case spanning the back wall, and a beautiful cherry desk dominated the middle of the room. A stack of papers sat atop the desk.

I wondered if Evalyn kept the threatening letters in the study... Pulse quickening, I ventured inside and walked to the desk, pausing once to throw a furtive glance over my shoulder.

I didn't dare flick on the lamp. The usual guards had likely followed Evalyn and Ned or perhaps had been sent with the children somewhere, but I didn't want to risk it should I be wrong and one still lurked about. I yanked open each of the desk drawers, heart hammering in my chest. If I were caught, not only could I lose my job, but I'd be thrown off the property and potentially be forced to face the police. By now I knew the McLeans had everyone at their disposal should they wish them to be, and should an employee be accused of stealing.

I slid the middle drawer open. An assortment of envelopes and letters were jammed inside it. I covered my mouth with my hand. This was it, the pile of letters. I examined each quickly. I didn't recognize the handwriting or stationery, and nothing else leapt out at me. When I'd finished sorting through the middle drawer, I opened the bottom. It was packed with more envelopes. I couldn't believe how many Evalyn had received. To live in constant fear of someone threatening you or your children, warning you, attempting to blackmail you, had to be terrifying. I rifled through them, again not finding a connection between her letters and my own.

The sound of footsteps echoed in the hallway.

I pushed the letters inside the drawer and closed it swiftly—just as a large, lumpy form filled the doorway.

"Ma'am? Can I help you with something?"

I jumped a mile at Jerry's voice. "You frightened me!" I laughed nervously. "I confess, I grew a little bored, so I started roaming around." I blushed deeply. "I saw this desk lamp and stopped to admire the abalone inlay. It's gorgeous. Abalone can be quite fragile to work with because it's brittle, so whoever made this spent a lot of time assembling these pieces." I rambled nervously a moment about where abalone came from and how to harvest it, forcing myself to relax, to try to act natural.

"It was a gift from an Australian diplomat, I believe," he said. "You need to see it on! It's magnificent." He pulled the dangling chain that switched on the bulbs. As a pool of light poured over the abalone shell, its blue-green iridescence came to life. Traces of red and swirls of white and black appeared to move over the curved belly of the lamp. "Isn't it exquisite?"

I unclenched my hands, relieved Jerry had believed me. "It really is," I said, leaning over it as if to study it more closely. The lamp resembled a Moroccan mosaic in style but was made with a hundred pieces of abalone shell instead of tiles. I could easily imagine the hours of meticulous work that went into its construction.

As he led me back to the parlor, he asked, "May I bring you anything? Some refreshments while you wait for Mrs. McLean?"

"I'm fine, thank you, but I'd like to go for a walk in the garden if that's all right?" I needed to catch my breath and to calm my shredded nerves.

"Of course, ma'am. As you wish." He held open the French doors leading to the back garden.

As I stepped outside, my pulse slowed, and suddenly I longed to walk barefoot on the tender new grass. The weather was still glorious, despite the sun making its descent toward a blazing horizon. I always enjoyed fresh air regardless of the season, but spring held a magic all its own.

"Mind if I join you?" A voice came from behind me.

My heart skipped a beat at the now-familiar baritone of Ned McLean. He wore casual trousers and a pin-striped shirt with sleeves rolled to his forearms. His hair was windswept and his cheeks were pink, as if he'd spent time in the sun.

I hesitated. I'd wanted to avoid him, put distance between us, and eliminate the chance for any inappropriate behavior. I had no intentions toward him otherwise, but here he was, inviting me for a walk like a friend would do. What could be the harm in that?

"Come on, Lizzie," he said and held out his arm. "Let me show you where the frogs live near the pond. You can hear them singing from a mile away, especially this time of year, when the sun sets."

I silenced the warning voice in my head and took his arm, casting one last glance over my shoulder at Jerry, who I knew kept a careful eye on us.

"How have you been?" Ned asked, all smiles. "I haven't seen you in a few days."

I didn't bother to explain I'd been at Friendship with Evalyn nearly every day the past few weeks and that it was he who had been absent. Spending his time betting on horses and losing money, Evalyn had said.

"I've been busy with work," I replied.

"Sometimes I forget that you work for a living. Did you know Evie's father amassed the largest gold fortune in the country? It's too bad you can't meet him. He'd be able to connect you with the best miners for your collection. But the poor bastard passed away of cancer years ago. Evie was distraught for months, had her fill of laudanum over it. Things were a bit difficult at the time. We had a full-time nurse looking after her."

I shouldn't be surprised by his taking me into his confidence—it seemed I had that effect on people, something I'd learned since I'd met Evalyn and her friends—but it was such a personal detail that it caught me off guard. I didn't reply immediately but rather admired the elegant beauty of their yard, the fragrant lilacs and blooming dogwoods and the two ancient magnolia trees with thick, glossy leaves framed by the fiery sky as the sun began to set.

"I can imagine," I said at last. "I know what it's like to lose a loved one. It's very difficult."

"Indeed. Between you and me, her friends were a bit scandalized by her behavior. She had more than her fill of laudanum, and it made her act erratically."

"Her friends were scandalized? Those who can drink enough to drown an elephant?"

He barked out a laugh. "Well, you certainly don't mince words."

I stepped over a patch of sodden grass. "I was taught to speak my mind."

He angled his body toward mine. "I must say, that's very attractive in a woman. Not putting on airs, not trying so desperately to do and say the right thing."

His comment showed how little he knew me. I'd done nothing but put on airs since I'd met the McLeans, and it was exhausting. Besides, he couldn't be missing that sort of perfect behavior in Evalyn. She vacillated between excellent society manners and outright lewd behavior at times. Loud parties with too much champagne, playing poker and other games until dawn...

"Evalyn is no prude," I said at last.

He laughed. "That, she is not. But she does feel the need to impress everyone in Washington." He puffed on his cigar and exhaled a cloud of smoke.

I inhaled, relishing the scent of tobacco and wood, tinged with the sweetness of spring flowers. A comfortable warmth spread through me as I remembered my father smoking a cigar with a glass of red wine after a long day's work.

"You're almost smiling, Miss Elisabeth Beaumont. I'm not sure what to do with you," Ned teased.

But I knew there was an underlying jab there. I didn't smile easily, wasn't happy or light fun like the others, and he didn't know what to think of that. I suspected none of them did. I was quiet and serious, trustworthy and stalwart, and most of all studious—qualities I was beginning to realize I liked about myself, especially in juxtaposition to the people who had filled my days these past weeks.

"Cigars remind me of my father," I replied. "He's finally up and about, and I'm hoping he'll be back to work for good very soon. I'm so relieved."

"What happened to him?"

The smile dropped from my face. "Oh, perhaps you didn't know." I hesitated, summoning the strength I needed to force out the words I'd only managed to say twice before. "When Julien passed away last fall, my father... He's been unable to work since. Evalyn's patronage has really helped keep us afloat."

He drew on his cigar and exhaled a steady stream of fragrant smoke. "That sounds like Evie. She's always been attracted to a good charity case."

Was that what my father and I were? People in need of charity? The comment pricked the way some of Evalyn's had, but I managed to keep my tone light.

"It's chillier than I expected," I said. "I should have worn my coat."

"Allow me." He slipped out of his dinner jacket and wrapped it around my shoulders, his fingers brushing the skin of my neck. I shivered, whether at the cold or at his touch, I wasn't sure.

I didn't have time to examine my feelings further as Evalyn stepped out of the shade of a large tree. "Oh!" I exclaimed, surprised to catch her sneaking around outdoors.

"What are you two doing out here?" she demanded.

"Just grabbing a bit of fresh air while waiting for you to emerge from wherever it was you'd gone," Ned said lightly. "I was going to show Lizzie the frog pond, but we hadn't quite made it there yet."

Evalyn met my eyes. Her expression was anything but welcoming. "Is that so."

Feeling slightly queasy at the thought of Evalyn suspecting me for any reason, I quickly slipped out of Ned's suit coat and gave it back to him. "I'm glad you're here, Evalyn. I have something for you."

"Wonderful." She smiled tightly. "Let's go inside. It's damp out here, and my husband's jacket doesn't quite stave off the chill, does it?"

I heard the underlying suspicion in her words but pretended I didn't have a clue as to what she was referring and followed her indoors. I rescued the package from an end table in the parlor and joined her in the sitting room where she liked to stretch out on the settees.

Ned poured us each a drink from a cart the staff had already set up and said, "All right, ladies, I'll leave you to it." With that, he disappeared through the door without a backward glance.

Evalyn took a sip of her drink. "Would you like to eat? I'm starved. I've had the longest day listening to one silly speech after another, followed by a rather dull luncheon of limp cabbage and mayonnaise salad and the most bitter iced tea you've ever tasted. Really, who doesn't put sugar in their tea?" She rang the bell on the patio table next to her.

I was on the verge of accepting when I remembered I'd agreed to go to Rosalee's for dinner that night. It was already five thirty, and her home was across town. I groaned, set down my untouched glass of wine. "I'm afraid I can't stay," I said. "I've just remembered that I'm meeting someone for dinner. In fact, I'm already running late."

"Anyone I would know?" she said, a little too casually.

I thought of what Rosalee had said about not being accepted socially, and I wondered if Evalyn was a part of the reason why. Washington, DC, was a big town, full of influential people coming and going all the time, so it seemed unlikely. And what was the harm in mentioning her by name? "Her name is Rosalee Smith."

She rolled her eyes. "You know Rosalee? Isn't she the biggest bore you've ever met? How will you ever stomach an entire meal with her?" She looked at me expectantly then, as if waiting for me to criticize her, too.

"She's one of our clients," I said simply.

"Oh, say you'll stay here with me. You can always reschedule, can't you, since it's just a work thing?"

The truth was I wanted to cancel the dinner, and I was already on the verge of running late. As kind as Rosalee was, I didn't know what to say to her or how to behave, but with Evalyn, that was never a problem. She did the vast majority of the talking and the entertaining, and I could go on being my quiet, observant self.

"I don't know..."

She touched the back of my hand lightly. "Darling, Rosalee isn't...a stable woman. Or so I've heard. You don't want to ruin your reputation by spending time with her. Trust me on this."

"I should at least tell her I can't make it to dinner."

"Think nothing of it," Evalyn said. "I'll have Jerry send a telegram."

As if Jerry intuited that he was being summoned, he entered the sitting room at that very moment. "Ma'am, dinner is served if you're ready."

"Thank you, Jerry," she said, rising from her chair. "Come, eat with me instead, darling. Besides, you haven't given me my gift yet."

I hesitated. Would Rosalee be terribly disappointed? It wasn't as if I was supposed to meet her for business. I could tell her I was held up unexpectedly and reschedule our dinner for another time, couldn't I?

"I'll stay," I said at last. "And a telegram would be perfect, thank you."

"Good girl." She held out her hand and I took it, following her to the dining table.

Jerry had set out several covered dishes for us the way Evalyn liked, but she shooed him away to give us privacy.

Before we filled our plates, I held out the carefully wrapped headband. "Here's your gift."

She clapped her hands like a child. "Oh, I do love presents! What is it?"

I smiled. "You'll have to open it."

She tore through the decorative paper and opened the lid of the box. As she lifted the headband, she admired my handiwork. "It's lovely!"

"Would you like to try it on?" I said. "To make sure it fits. I can adjust the band if need be."

She slipped it on and peered into the mirror mounted on the wall across from the table, tilting her head so the gemstones caught the light. "The stones look like glitter. It's stunning! How ever in the world did you make this?"

"It took some time, but I wanted to thank you."

She turned from the mirror to face me. "Whatever for?"

"For your employment. For encouraging the others to hire me... For your friendship," I added, biting my lip.

She threw her arms around my neck and hugged me to her. "You're such a dear. Why wouldn't I do those things for you? I'd do them for anyone."

The tentative smile slipped from my face, but I returned her hug. Anyone? Perhaps it was as Carrie said. They were all there to serve her in some way, and her generosity was simply a means to bring people to her, to pin them to her side, not because she truly cared for them but because they placated some need to be at the center of things all the time.

Jerry arrived with a tray of two wineglasses and a bottle of red wine. He popped the cork, gave his mistress a small pour to taste it, and proceeded to fill our glasses.

"Now that's more like it." Evalyn dug into her plate with gusto, making quick work of roasted pork, greens with bacon and onion, and crispy potatoes. "I simply must tell you all the gossip from the event," she said when she'd finished.

I had listened to her prattle on for some time about who wore what clothing, who looked a fright, and who was flirting with who when the conversation finally turned.

"Carrie was acting strange the whole day. You know Carrie, the redhead? What do you make of her?"

I paused, unsure of what to say. She made me uneasy, and I wasn't entirely certain she'd only flirted with Julien the day I'd seen them meet.

I also got the distinct impression that Evalyn was baiting me. I weighed my response carefully and with a shrug said, "I don't know her well."

"Darling, you shouldn't shrug. It makes you look like an adolescent boy."

I reddened. "Oh, I'm sorry, I—"

She saw my expression and tsked. "I'm horrible, aren't I? You'll have to excuse me. I've had a long day. If it's your prerogative, shrug away."

"I suppose I've spent too much time around men."

"Is there such a thing?" she asked with a wicked gleam in her eye.

I blushed. "I meant my father and brother and his best friend."

"Oh, I know, silly. Now, tell me what is it that you wanted to say about Carrie. The suspense is killing me. Is it a secret?"

I wasn't going to say anything else about Carrie, but clearly Evalyn expected me to join her in gossip. I took an unusually large gulp of red wine for courage first. "Carrie stopped by my workshop yesterday."

"Her dress was ghastly, wasn't it?" Evalyn replied as if she hadn't heard what I'd said. "I've told her to stop going to that designer. He's too old. He's not keeping up with the latest styles, and she can't go around looking passé, or I won't invite her over anymore." She snickered. "Imagine, inviting her to one of my galas with diplomats and she's wearing last year's styles. I'm doing her a favor."

I really looked at Evalyn, taking in her dark brow, her eyes beginning to glaze over, and understood her in that moment. She could be petty and even cruel, and though she put on the act of being comfortable in her own skin, she clearly wasn't. Her insecurities gnawed away at her as they did for anyone who constantly pitted themselves against others. Her pettiness was a means of social survival, a way to stay at the top of the heap, and she fully expected me to act the same way, just as her other friends did.

I bit my lip, unsure of how to reply. Beaumont Jewelers wasn't yet solvent enough to walk away from such an extraordinary paying customer or from her friends. We needed them. There was also the matter of Julien. I'd learned a lot about his time with the McLeans, but I knew there was more I hadn't yet uncovered. Besides, Evalyn and her glittering world allowed me to be someone else for a while. I didn't know if I liked that someone, but I was grateful for the opportunity just the same.

She rolled her eyes. "Well? Are you going to keep me on the edge of my seat all night? Go on. What were you going to say, darling? And drink up! You're already behind me."

I was always behind her. She seemed to have a hollow leg. "Why don't I pour us a refill," I said, scrambling to think of what to say. I knew this was a test of who I was most loyal to, and Evalyn had no trouble putting me or others through the test regularly. "I'm not sure I should talk about this," I said at last.

"Haven't you heard, my earnest little friend? The truth will set you free. What could be wrong with that?"

It was how the truth would be manipulated that concerned me. And yet I plunged ahead. "Carrie stopped by the boutique and bought a gift for her mother. She also mentioned that everyone acted like your friend but are only there to serve you and get something for themselves."

At first, shock registered on her features, and then a shrewd smile carved her face. "It was good that you told me. Friends shouldn't keep secrets like this from each other, should they?" She patted my hand. "And you're proving yourself to be a good friend, Lizzie."

As a rush of pleasure washed over me, a new sensation ignited. One I did not recognize. The satisfaction of coming into Evalyn's good graces, in climbing the social ladder, and most of all, of making myself indispensable to her.

My eyes found the Hope Diamond at her neck, twinkling in the candlelight, and I knew this was my chance. “Do you think I might take a look at your necklace? I have my tools with me.”

“There’s no need to get your tools. Here.” She unclasped the necklace and placed into my outstretched hand.

I was thrilled to touch it, thrilled at its beauty and the chance to peer at it closely again. As I stared at the marvelous, infamous gem, I thought again of the note I’d received and weighed whether I should say something to Evalyn about it. Could it have been from her? Given the conversation we’d just had and given what else I’d seen go on in her circles, she seemed to enjoy toying with people’s affections. But she would have nothing to gain by driving me away, and she knew better than anyone how unsettling a threatening letter could be. It couldn’t have been her. And for now, she didn’t need to know about mine either. The truth was I didn’t trust her. Not one bit.

“It looks great, but it’s probably prudent to service it during my next appointment,” I said. “I’ll make the stone extra sparkly for you so you can really stand out.”

As I gave Evalyn her necklace, she said, eyes gleaming, “See to it that you do, Lizzie. See to it that you do.”

20

Despite my resolve to put the conversation I'd had with Evalyn from my mind, my nerves tingled each time I thought of her reaction to what I'd said about Carrie. If Evalyn confronted Carrie, that could disrupt the entire group of friends. Guilt washed over me. I didn't want to be the cause of a woman's exile, especially a woman who, for all intents and purposes, had not only encouraged Evalyn to hire me but had also purchased items from the boutique.

I peered through my jeweler's goggles at the pair of diamond barrettes my father had asked me to make. I'd been working on them since early morning, and I was ready for a break. As I put my tools away, I thought about which of the dresses I'd wear to Bea's. For the first time since I'd begun work for the McLeans, I'd been invited to join the others on a proper outing. Bea insisted we go to the pictures at the Apollo theater to see the comedy *Cheating Cheaters*, starring the glamorous Clara Kimball Young. The actress's recent divorce—after her scandalous infidelity—had fueled even larger crowds than usual to her films. I appreciated the much-needed lighter distraction, though I would do better to spend my time at home finishing the barrettes and encouraging Father to work on his new ideas. But I couldn't bring myself to decline the invitation. I was thrilled to be asked.

After the picture, we returned to Bea's house for refreshments. The rest of the circle of friends arrived shortly after, and Bea's cook prepared trays of canapés and spritzers. When she put on a Marion Harris record, several of the ladies sang along, and all were in good spirits. I was pleased to see Evalyn wearing the gold headband I'd made for her. The feather bobbed merrily as she swayed to the music.

"What is that headpiece, Evie?" a woman named Rita asked as she tapped her feet to the music. "It's beautiful."

Evalyn lightly touched the gem-studded band. "Our Lizzie made it! I just knew I'd chosen well in hiring her."

"You'll have to make one for me," Rita said. "Maybe in silver? Silver would go beautifully with my new dress."

The others joined in the fawning, and I beamed with pride. It was the first thing I'd made that had truly garnered any real attention. Evalyn looked on proudly like a mother hen over her chick. At her broad smile, a less-than-generous thought popped into my head, and yet I knew it was true. Anytime Evalyn could take credit for something that made her look good in any way, she would.

Gwen was the only one who had nothing to say about the headband, not a polite nod of encouragement or even an acknowledgment that I was there. And I found myself staring at her. She wore a long white dress with black pin stripes reminiscent of a man's suit. A white hat with a black ribbon crowned the ensemble. It was a surprising new look but not entirely flattering to a female figure with its tubular shape. Six weeks ago, I wouldn't have noticed such a thing, but with the intense education I'd had from Evalyn and her friends, the striking style was now impossible to miss. I felt a rush of gratitude once again as I looked down at the pale-blue dress Evalyn had given me. It flattered my alabaster skin and my dark eyes—another thing I wouldn't have given a second thought to before.

Gwen felt my eyes on her and turned. "Well, don't you look nice," she said, her tone light, but the lines around her mouth were pulled as tight as a bow's strings. "You're dressed like Evie again. It's very sweet that you're trying to look like her."

She was right; I looked a bit like Evalyn in features, and the dress used to be one of hers, but it was prettier than anything I'd ever owned. I pictured arriving to one of Evalyn's parties in my work trousers and my trusty brown smock, my hair loose and snarled, and I suddenly yearned for the privacy of my workshop and the comfort of my real clothes. When I wore them, they were my armor, and I didn't have to pretend to be anyone else.

I pasted a false smile on my face. "And you're wearing a really fascinating design. It reminds a bit of the swatch of fabric I left on my workbench this morning."

Judging by Evalyn's expression, she approved of my restrained yet clear jab at Gwen's dress.

Gwen's eyes narrowed. "Oh, that's right. You work for a living. That would explain why your references are...less than desirable. You don't know much about fashion."

"I suppose not. I've been too busy doing other things with my time." I wanted to lash out, be as blatantly rude as she'd been, but I didn't want to overplay my hand.

"You don't have anything to drink," Bea observed, interrupting the strained exchange. "We can't have that."

The last thing I needed was a drink, but I wouldn't be the only one to not participate or at least pretend to take part in their merriment. As Bea leaned forward to hand me a glass, I noticed her earrings, a set of pink freshwater pearls with a small gold loop that curved around the bottom of the earlobe. I stilled. Julien had made them. I glanced around the room, eyeing each of the women's jewelry. To my surprise, two of the others were also wearing Julien's pieces: Rita, a gold charm bracelet, and Sharon, an oval silver locket with vines etched into its surface.

It was strange three of the women should be wearing Julien's pieces on the same day. This was the first time I'd seen them wearing his designs since meeting them, but the coincidence of wearing them simultaneously seemed awfully convenient. I remembered how Evalyn had brushed off my comment about Carrie wearing a pendant Julien had designed; she'd assured me they'd all bought something of his at one time or another, and here was the proof. Yet it felt too coordinated, as if they were trying too hard to put my mind at ease. But why?

"Cheers," Bea said, clinking her glass against mine.

I took a sip. "Delicious."

"Isn't it? It's Perrier-Jouët, my favorite champagne."

I couldn't hold my tongue—and Bea couldn't either. "Bea, I noticed you're wearing one of my brother's designs."

She clutched her earlobes. "Oh yes, the pearls. He had such great taste."

"He did." I hesitated an instant, considering how best to needle her for information. At last, I decided to plunge right in and be forthright to see how she'd react. "It's such a coincidence that several of you are wearing his pieces today. Any particular reason?"

Bea avoided my eyes. "Are others wearing his designs? How about that." She giggled at a pitch higher than usual.

"I thought perhaps you'd all coordinated for some reason."

She indulged in a sizable gulp of champagne and said, "The truth is we wanted to show our support. For you, that is."

"Oh. That's kind of you." I kept my eyes on her until she looked away, drank another sip, and pretended the conversation to her right was fascinating.

Though I didn't know Bea well, I understood this: She wasn't one to avoid, to smooth over, to pass off a half-truth. She spoke directly and didn't back down easily from a challenge. Her change in behavior was entirely suspicious. She seemed to be hiding something, or perhaps they all were. I looked from one woman to the next, watching them as they flaunted their perfect manners and their less-than-genuine smiles. I had to admit, I felt a push-pull with this crowd. The desire to belong and the enjoyment of being swept up in the moment as if there was nothing better in the world I could be doing warred with my disgust at the way they treated each other. And for the hundredth time in a little over a month, I had to remind myself why I was there.

The remnants of another conversation drifted my way, and I turned as my name was mentioned.

"Lizzie is still single, aren't you?" Evalyn said. "Who should we set her up with, Gwennie? Now that she's one of us, we need to find her the right match. Look at her! She's positively pretty in that dress."

The last thing in the world I wanted to discuss was whether I was single or needed a man. I wished I could fade into the woodwork, be spared from this conversation.

"How about Teddy Carpenter?" Gwen said.

Carrie, who had remained silent through the exchange so far, choked on her drink. "Teddy? Teddy with the large gums and tiny teeth?"

Evalyn laughed uproariously. "Large gums? What are you talking about?"

"Isn't he the gardener?" Bea replied.

"Of course he is," Evalyn replied, and then she stuck out her own teeth like a rabbit.

Sharon, Bea, and Gwen burst into laughter. Carrie rolled her eyes and lit a cigarette.

"Oh, the gardener is perfect for Lizzie," Gwen said, her tone smug. "Is Teddy here now? I'll talk to him, see if I can set them up."

"No, it's fine," I replied quickly. "I'm not interested in seeing anyone." Henry's face flashed in my mind's eye, despite my resolve not to think about him in that way anymore.

"Come now, why not?" Evalyn said. "It doesn't have to be Teddy. I'm sure we can come up with someone better."

Carrie tapped her cigarette, and the ash dropped in a clump into the crystal tray. "At your age, it must be a little concerning that you aren't married. And for your father, too, I'd imagine."

"I've never considered marrying," I said. Though it wasn't entirely true, it certainly wasn't their business.

Gwen exchanged a knowing look with Bea, who winked at Rita, who then elbowed Evalyn. I'd have had to be blind not to notice it.

"Whyever not?" Gwen said. "Don't you like men?"

I knew her question was aimed to both make me uncomfortable and spark the others' imaginations with an image we both knew they'd find unsavory. They weren't exactly the most open-minded of women.

I rolled my eyes more for show than anything. "Of course I do. I was raised by a wonderful father, and my two best friends in the world are men." I couldn't think of three more upstanding men than Henry and my brother and, of course, my father.

"Your best friend is a man? That certainly explains a few things," Gwen shot back.

A need to defend myself arose in a hot flash, and the words tumbled from my lips before I could stop them. "I've never had to trap a man, if that's what you mean. That isn't my style."

Carrie frowned and Bea snickered. Evalyn looked positively gleeful.

I, on the other hand, felt sick. I wasn't this person—a woman who insulted others, let alone other women. Women faced enough obstacles as I knew well, and yet I couldn't seem to help myself. With every sharp word and every cutting sentence, I felt as if I were destabilizing an enemy in an attempt to regain some of their misguided respect.

"I beg your pardon!" Gwen said, crossing her arms, her cheeks aflame. She looked as if steam might shoot out of the crown of her hat.

"Would you care to elaborate, Lizzie?" Evalyn asked with a feline smile. "I'm not sure Gwen knows what you mean."

The others looked on in silence. Their expressions were a mix of pleasure and grim fascination. I felt like an animal backed into a corner, and the only way out was to use my claws. I boldly met Gwen's eye. She said nothing and, for a moment, looked as if she truly hoped I'd say nothing else, too, or she might burst into tears. As much as a part of me would have liked to retaliate further against this woman who had been openly hostile toward me since the day we'd met, I couldn't do it.

I held my untouched drink up to my lips and sipped as daintily as I could muster before setting it down. "I don't think I need to elaborate."

Gwen relaxed visibly, and the others looked disappointed. What had happened between Gwen and her husband was her own business, and though I'd told Evalyn about Carrie's slight, that was as far as I was willing to go. I wasn't in the business of airing another woman's shame for all to see.

"Girls, this party is growing a bit stale," Evalyn said. "Why don't we continue at my house? I'll have Jerry set up the poker chips. What do you say?"

"I think I'd better head home," I said.

"Nonsense. You'll come with us," Evalyn insisted.

It wasn't a request, it was an order, and though I'd grown used to her assuming I was at her beck and call, and I admittedly panicked a little when she didn't insist I join her, something inside me bristled. I'd never taken orders well from anyone, but mostly, I was eager to go home after the scene that had just played out, never mind the hours of socializing. And yet I was too weary to argue. Evalyn always had her way.

We piled into two cars and drove the short distance from Bea's to Friendship and soon found ourselves playing several rounds of poker. After, we loaded the gramophone with one record after another, singing and dancing like children. After one particularly bawdy tune, Evalyn stripped down to nothing but her silk undergarments and, of course, the Hope Diamond.

Bea laughed heartily.

"Evie!" Gwen exclaimed.

"What are you doing!" Carrie said.

"You've got the spirit of the devil in you, girl," Sharon said with a laugh.

"You said I wouldn't do it, so here I am." Evalyn swilled the last of her martini. "When have I ever gone against my word?"

I could think of several times she had but didn't say as much. I was as drunk as a sailor, even after abandoning most of the drinks they'd pushed on me. I couldn't keep up with them. I didn't recognize myself through the foggy brain the alcohol brought. Though I'd learned that was occasionally a good thing, mostly I preferred keeping my wits about me.

"There's no devil here, silly woman," Evalyn said, slurring her words. "I've got my good-luck talisman."

"You and that damned necklace," Carrie said, rolling her eyes.

"You and that damned mouth," Evalyn retorted.

And I knew the gloves were off for the evening.

"Come on, you wench," Bea said as she removed her own dress and shoes. "Catch me if you can!"

Everyone hooted with laughter, cheering them on as Evalyn chased Bea outside onto the grass. They giggled as they ran, and soon, Mike the dog joined in the fun, barking happily while he ran alongside them. As they paused to catch their breath, they fed the llama an apple and screeched like children as they took off once more, the remnants of wet grass after a freshly mowed lawn sticking to their bare feet. The rest of us watched the entertainment unfold from the safety of lounge chairs on the patio.

As evening turned to late night, we dragged ourselves back inside, and I said my goodbyes.

As I was leaving, I took one more stab at a real answer about the jewelry they'd all worn that day. Lowering my voice in a conspiratorial way, I turned to Sharon. "It's great that you all wore my brother's designs tonight. Any particular reason why?"

She hiccuped, giggled, and took another swig from her martini glass before she said, "We wore them because Evalyn told us to."

"Why?" I asked. "You don't need to go through such trouble, though it's incredibly thoughtful of you." I was buttering her up and she was clearly drunk, so I hoped to catch her in a lie—or better yet, catch her in the truth.

"It upset you, the night you saw Carrie wearing his pendant, and she didn't want—" She clapped a hand over her mouth like a child. "I'm sorry. I don't know. Ask Evalyn." She set down her glass, air kissed my cheeks, and headed outside to a waiting car.

I frowned. She was going to share something she'd clearly been told not to. As I watched Sharon's car pull away and the others gather their things to meet their own chauffeurs, Jerry sidled up beside me.

"I've called you a taxi, ma'am," he said. "I hope that's all right?"

"Thank you, Jerry." I studied his expression, the thick brow and heart-shaped mouth, the round face, and kind but watchful eyes, and decided to risk it. He might tell Evalyn that I'd questioned him, but I needed to know the answer. "There's something going on here, isn't there, Jerry? Some secret that has to do with my brother. Perhaps the Hope Diamond, too. Or maybe I'm not on the right track."

He held my gaze a moment too long, glanced over his shoulder and back again at the other women as they laughed and clambered down the steps toward their waiting vehicles. "I'm not sure what you mean, ma'am," he said finally. His eyes darted to the top of the steps leading to the front door where Evalyn stood, looking down at all of us, leaning against the column for support with a smile on her face. "But if I can be of service in any way," he added, "I'd be more than happy to help."

He knew exactly what I meant—his body language had said so—but I wouldn't push him tonight in front of the others and especially not in front of Evalyn. It was enough to know he was an ally of sorts.

"It's all right," I replied. "Thank you for calling a car for me. We'll talk another time."

He nodded, and something flickered in his eyes, affirming my suspicions. They were all hiding a secret from me, and he couldn't say what, but that was all I needed to know. I'd uncover the rest on my own.

"Have a good evening, ma'am."

I waved a good night, slid into the waiting taxi, and headed home on the other side of town.

21

I was relieved to have the following day to myself. After the many hours spent with the society ladies the day before, I couldn't stomach more talking, more drinking, more being on edge. I made a pile of fluffy eggs and toast and plenty of bacon and black coffee to chase away the residual traces of a queasy stomach. After breakfast and bathing, I felt refreshed and planned to spend the rest of the day doing what I enjoyed. Dressed and handbag in tow, I didn't bother to say anything to my father, with whom I still wasn't on speaking terms, and headed out for the morning.

Within the hour, I stared up at the impressive crown of the National Museum, framed by a bright blue sky. Sunlight poured over the front steps. Somehow I always found myself here at the museum or in the library, researching a new stone or site where they'd been excavated. My careful notes and continued education gave me a sense of accomplishment when the majority of the work I did for my father did not. Spending quiet time in my home away from home also helped me silence the questions that had plagued me for months, the most persistent among them: Why? Why him? Why my brother? Why did he have to die when he had so much life ahead of him?

I entered the building, and as the familiar, comforting scent of stone and cool air washed over me, my shoulders relaxed. I stood in the rotunda, deciding what I'd like to see first, when a woman crossing the main hall paused as if she recognized me. I realized I knew her, too, and offered a wave. It was Julia Wane, Henry's coworker and friend.

"Hello, there. Aren't you Henry's friend? Elisabeth, right?" She wore the same lab coat as before, and her hair was pinned into a bun.

"Yes, and you're Julia. Nice to see you again," I said.

She smiled. "What brings you in today?"

I flushed. "Nothing specific. The museum is a place of solace for me, I suppose. I thought I'd spend a little time marveling at the wonders of nature and science."

She smiled. "It's always nice to hear there are regular patrons who admire what we do."

"Very much," I said enthusiastically. "One day, I'd love to hear more about your work."

"As luck would have it, today is a perfect day for it. Would you care to take a look at some specimens I'm identifying?"

"That would be wonderful," I said eagerly.

She took me on a tour around an office she shared with several men and one other woman, introducing me as we went along and explaining each of the specimens the curators were identifying.

"Thelma is an illustrator," Julia explained. "She makes very careful drawings of each specimen both for identification purposes of future samples and also to accurately label each anatomical part of the reptile."

Thelma heard her name and looked up, gave us a polite smile before returning her focus to her work.

I knew from a discussion with Henry that it was common for women to work as illustrators since it was assumed their smaller hands meant they possessed strong fine motor skills. Women could also be paid significantly less than their male counterparts.

"You should meet Mary Jane Rathbun," Julia said, directing me to another wing designated for research personnel. "She's the very first woman to work at the Smithsonian as a full-time employee. She's still a curator here."

"What is her expertise area?" I asked, silently tabulating the number of women we'd passed in the halls. Each time I saw another, I felt my heart leap. It seemed the museum truly valued women working in science, at least to some degree, and that was far more than most businesses could say.

"She works with decapod crustaceans."

My brow arched. "Crabs and lobsters?"

She nodded. "And shrimp and crayfish. Mary Jane doesn't like to be disturbed often, so we'll make it quick." She knocked on the door before we stepped inside.

Mary Jane was tiny, even for a woman, at shorter than five feet tall. Her face was long and lean, her spectacles perched on her nose, and she was bent over a tray with a species of crab I'd never seen before.

"This is my new friend, Elisabeth," Julia said. "I wanted to introduce her to the legendary Mary Jane."

We exchanged pleasantries, and she showed me her current specimen. She explained a few general facts about the hundreds of species of crustaceans, and after, Julia and I left her to her work. Though her specialty was not exactly my interest, I enjoyed listening to her—I always enjoyed learning something new.

"It's too bad Henry isn't in today," Julia said. "He's been in New Mexico the past few days, acquiring some new exciting samples. You know how he is."

Envy arrowed through me. What I would give to be in New Mexico, collecting samples! What was more, I wished I could speak so candidly and easily about Henry, spend time with him without feeling as if a weight was crushing my lungs. I studied her face, searching for a sign of how she felt about Henry. There was nothing but polite and friendly interest reflected in her eyes. Relief coursed through me, and I proffered her a small smile. "I do, yes. He has all the luck, traipsing through New Mexico."

"You seem so interested in science and nature," Julia continued. "Have you ever considered applying for a position here?"

Surprised she should see into my soul so easily, I gazed at her a moment before replying. She'd voiced a dream so buried, I didn't realize I'd been secretly harboring it all this time. "I... No, I've always worked with my father. I'm a jeweler."

"Ah, so you're an artist. You prefer crafting beautiful things rather than studying them. We need more artists in the world."

"Not at all," I blurted—and realized I truly meant it. I had always preferred studying and learning to the creating, even though I could hold my own. Making jewelry didn't speak to me the way it did to my father and to Julien. "I've never considered working here because my father has always needed me, and I assumed I'd follow in his footsteps. But mineralogy is my true passion." It felt good to say it, freeing, and I practically shimmered with the relief of it.

"Well, if you ever find yourself at a loose end or in need of work, you should apply. Many of our positions for women are for volunteer work, but some are paid. Perhaps you could start there."

A lump of emotion welled in my throat. "Thank you," I said. "You don't know how much this has meant to me."

"Come back anytime," she said congenially. "If I'm too busy, my friend Helen would take you under her wing. She's a preservationist, so you'd be able to see all kinds of interesting artifacts and the process of protecting them."

I beamed—I actually beamed—for the first time in so long, I

couldn't remember the last time I had. I thanked her again before saying goodbye.

I returned home to find Father puttering around in the workshop. Feeling buoyant after the wonderful visit to the museum, I couldn't muster the strength to be angry with him any longer.

"Hi," I said, abandoning the silent treatment. "You're working?"

"It's about time, I'd say," he said, meeting my eye, and I knew then it was his way of apologizing.

"You're too talented not to use your gifts, Father. Beaumont Jewelers hasn't been the same without you." My own offered apology.

"You look happy," he replied.

Surprised by the comment, I said, "Do I? I suppose I am, a little. I'm just back from the museum."

"Ah, yes, of course. Did you visit Henry?"

"No, I met a few of the women who work there. Two curators and an illustrator. The work they're doing is amazing. I was so impressed."

"That's great, *chérie*. You've always liked it there."

"I have," I said, realizing I felt lighter. Between my father going back to work—our truce—and my perfect afternoon, I feel almost like myself again.

"These came for you." He reached for two envelopes on the workshop table.

More notes? My happy mood withered as I tucked them under my arm.

"Thank you," I said and walked upstairs to the privacy of the empty kitchen. Swallowing hard, I turned the notes over in my hands. The first was from Rosalee. As I opened it, guilt trickled through me. I'd never telephoned or called to her house after Jerry's telegram. My guilt expanded as I unfolded the small square of stationery.

Dear Elisabeth,

I must admit, I was surprised you didn't show for dinner earlier this week. I telephoned to make sure I hadn't made a mistake in our plans. Your father mentioned that you were out with the McLeans. I suppose I thought we were friends, or at least I hoped we might be. I see now I was mistaken. I apologize for wasting your time.

I wish you well.

Sincerely,
Rosalee Smith

P.S. I won't be needing the bracelet we discussed after all.

I gaped at the note. But Evalyn had assured me she'd asked Jerry to send a telegram. Clearly she hadn't, or I wouldn't have received this note. I closed my eyes, berating myself for not having had at least the courtesy to call Rosalee the next day to follow up with her. Why had I allowed Evalyn to sway me? I couldn't believe how rude I'd been, how stupid. My careless disregard for Rosalee's feelings had cost me a potential budding friendship and an important client. A client we couldn't afford to lose. Father would be furious. I tore the letter into small pieces and hid it under an empty tin can in the wastebasket.

A pit in my stomach, I turned over the second envelope. Though the letter had no return address, I instantly recognized the handwriting. It was another from the anonymous sender.

You don't seem to understand. Trouble will befall you should you remain in the company you keep. Abandon your false friends. Abandon the allure of the Hope Diamond before it's too late. Your brother didn't heed the warning, and look at him now.

I gasped. It was someone who knew my brother. Suddenly the memory of Julien asking me about a letter resurfaced again. He'd received notes, too.

Heart racing, I took the stairs in twos to the top floor and paused for a moment outside his bedroom door. I hadn't breached the sanctity of his room since his death—I couldn't bring myself to do it—but I had to know. I switched on the lamps and opened his window to let in the fresh air. A breeze whisked inside, ruffling the curtains and blowing tendrils of hair across my face. Inhaling a deep breath, I began my search.

I started with Julien's dresser, rifling through an assortment of items he'd left there in his haphazard fashion. A pair of cuff links, a hair comb, a tin of pomade, a clean and neatly folded handkerchief, a handful of coins, and a dried rose. Frowning, I picked up the brittle flower and pressed it to my nose, inhaling the scent of dust and perhaps the faintest whiff of what was once a fragrant David Austin rose. I wondered why he'd kept it. He wasn't exactly the sentimental type, especially about flowers. I mentally scrolled through the women he'd surrounded himself with from last summer and into autumn while working at the McLeans. Many were beautiful; nearly all were married. The only other explanation would be that he'd fallen for one of the hired employees. I set down the rose. It couldn't have been someone on the McLeans' staff. He'd cared too much about title and circumstance, as little as he'd liked to admit it. Of the two of us, he would be the kind of person to seek out advantage, privilege, and status. He wasn't shallow, but he understood their value in furthering his business. In this, too, I was nothing like him.

I pushed aside the clean, folded clothes in his drawers and sorted through his wardrobe. With each piece of clothing, a memory surfaced, and a ripple of pain followed. I missed him. I missed him so much, I couldn't breathe. I plunked down on his bed to take a moment to come to terms with what I was doing—with the McLeans, with Father, with my life. It was all so hard. I'd never expected things to be easy, but I'd also never really grasped how things could take a turn toward the darkest of places.

Eventually I forced myself to look through Julien's bedside table. When I found nothing, I slid my hand beneath his mattress—and felt something, a rustling of paper. My pulse quickened. Could it be?

I lifted the mattress and scooped out a handful of letters onto the floor. I bent over them, sorting through the pile, the bile rising in my throat. Unlike the many threatening letters I'd found at Evalyn's with no recognizable handwriting, address, stationery, or style, these were exactly the same as the notes of warning I'd received. The same blocky handwriting, the same cream stationery on square cards with a light silver border. Whoever had warned me had also warned Julien.

I sank onto the floor and read each of the notes, once, twice, three times. Trying to make sense of it all and where I should go from here. Someone clearly didn't want the Beaumonts involved with the McLeans, which led me to believe it had to be someone within Evalyn's acquaintance who had sent them. But why? What had happened? Julien had clearly been up to something that someone didn't like. My mind kept circling back to the conversations about a potential business proposition gone awry, to the women, too, and the way they'd talked about him. How they'd worn his jewelry, Evalyn's comments and Bea's and Carrie's. He must have been involved either in some scheme as Jerry had suggested or with a woman. I thought of what Evalyn had said about Ned's horse racing and terrible gambling habit. Had Julien been caught up there? I shook my head. It couldn't be. He worked too hard for his money. Our money. The last thing I could imagine was Julien throwing it away at the races or at poker tables. Besides, Father and I would have noticed. I'd kept the books after all.

Heart aching, I glanced around his room a final time. Everywhere around me, I felt my brother's presence. I wanted to reach out to him, to clutch at my memories and dip them in amber to preserve them forever.

There was only one person who could understand that.

In a rush of spontaneity, I dashed outside, allowing my feet to lead me until I stood in front of a house that had been as much a home to me as my own. The Coopers'. Henry always knew what to say when I was struggling with a particular piece, when I'd argued with my brother, or when anything else had gone wrong for that matter. This time, I didn't know what to say, and yet I was here.

I'd been sucked into Evalyn's complicated world, with her husband and the demands they'd all placed on me and my time. I wondered if the numerous hours I'd spent with those silly women meant I was beginning to resemble them a bit more every day, and I wasn't sure I could live with that, but to be cast out at this point felt unbearable. Henry would be appalled to see the way I'd behaved with the champagne lunches and the fluttering of eyelashes, the flirtatious way I'd smiled at Ned McLean. Still, I was here.

A light flickered on inside. For a moment, I couldn't breathe.

The chiming bell of a bicyclist sounded behind me, and I recovered quickly, turning on my heel to walk swiftly toward home again, hating myself for being a coward. For ignoring Henry's messages and flowers and invitations. I hated myself, but I still felt the irresistible pull of Evalyn and the Hope Diamond and now the letters that I knew

Julien had received, too. Now more than ever, I feared his death wasn't an accident. Something didn't feel right; it hadn't for weeks before he died. I had to find a way through this, to the other side of the madness that had gripped me since he died.

I raced home, kicking off my shoes the moment I stepped inside. As I walked toward the kitchen, I caught sight of my reflection in the mirror. I hardly recognized myself. With the new clothes and haircut, the compliments, and the many days of being a part of the most elite circle in Washington, I had been reinvented. Half in shadow, I touched my hair, my rouged lips, and watched the light spark and dance over the sapphire earrings I'd borrowed from the showcase in the shop. As I gazed at myself in the shifting light, I saw him, my brother. His beauty, his intense yet playful eyes. I touched my cheek, the hollow of my neck. He was here with me still, a part of me.

Why did he have to die?

Bitterness flooded my mouth. I steadied myself on the back of the armchair, squeezed my eyes closed, willing the pain away, forcing down the desperate sorrow clawing at my insides. I might never recover, wouldn't know how to live inside it or how to move past it. I crumpled into a heap on the floor, unable to move, to breathe, to think for what felt like an eternity.

Some time later, the sound of cars and the tram and bicycle bells, of voices in the street, bled through the open window and under the door. When a police whistle split the air somewhere in the distance, I pushed up from the floor for the second time that day, legs stiff and body cold, and locked myself away in the darkness of my bedroom.

22

I awoke from a deep, exhausted sleep after the emotional ups and downs of the night before. I was scarcely out of bed with coffee mug in hand when the telephone rang loud enough to wake the dead. I dashed into the hall and dove for the receiver.

"Hello, this is the Beaumont residence. Elisabeth speaking."

"Miss Beaumont, it's Jerry."

I frowned into my coffee cup. "Jerry? Is everything all right?"

"Yes, ma'am. I'm calling on behalf of Mrs. McLean. The McLeans are hosting a party this evening and would like for you to attend. Hors d'oeuvres begin at six o'clock, followed by dinner and dancing. It's a formal soiree, so wear your best."

I frowned. "Are you sure, Jerry? I haven't heard anything about this. Is it a spontaneous gathering?"

"No, ma'am," he said. "It's been scheduled for several weeks. Mrs. McLean says she forgot your invitation."

"Of course. Is this at Friendship?"

"Yes, ma'am."

"Thank you, Jerry. See you soon."

I couldn't help but wonder if it really was an accident. None of the women, including Evalyn, had said a word about it, and I'd spent a lot of time with them. They weren't exactly adept at keeping secrets. It was as if I were an afterthought, or perhaps Evalyn was putting me through some kind of test to see if I would still cooperate, still jump when she told me to jump.

I refreshed my coffee and padded quietly to the workshop so as not to disturb Father. Though it was nearly noon, no sound came from his room. I had plans to work on my collection one more time, to try to find some inspiration that might help me make peace with working for my father. As much as I enjoyed entertaining the idea Julia Wane had planted in my head of working at the National Museum, it wasn't feasible to volunteer and work for free as most women did, leaving my father to run the business on his own. I needed an income to help support us.

I reached for my sketchbook and thumbed through it slowly, pausing on an old newspaper clipping. Its edges curled away from the page as if the glue was worn and the paper had been smoothed down one time too many. The past few years, I'd taken to collecting articles about the very few female jewelers lucky enough to gain some semblance of notoriety and pasted them inside the front flap of my sketchbook. There were only two that had made headlines doing precisely what I thought I was supposed to do: bide my time, gain more experience, and work on my own designs until the moment came when my pieces could speak for themselves. Now, everything felt different. I was different, and I didn't know where to go from here.

Hoping for some inspiration, I skimmed the newspaper article about Charlotte Isabella Newman for the hundredth time. She had been a hero of mine; her name was well known in the jewelry business. When her boss and teacher had passed away, she'd made the company her own and stamped her designs with her own signature, "Mrs. N." It was said she employed men, too, though she was the primary designer. More importantly, she'd broken convention in every way, and I'd hoped—despite her age—to travel to her boutique on Savile Row in the Mayfair end of London one day to meet her. I'd also hoped to travel to Paris to meet Jeanne Poiret Boivin, another of the few female designers who'd made a name for themselves.

Since Julien's death, the trips we'd planned to go abroad had been postponed. My collection had been postponed. Everything else had been postponed, too.

Sighing, I opened the bottom drawer of my worktable and retrieved a small square of metal that would become the mount for a ring I'd illustrated in my notebook. I flicked on a lamp and sorted through my sketches to the design of the ring in two different scales: one sketch was to size, and the other was an enlarged version from a couple of different angles. The style of the mount was complex; a round diamond would be encircled by a halo of diamonds, and beneath the halo, I'd construct a triangular web of thin platinum strips to allow light to strike the gemstones from every possible angle. If I managed the design correctly, it would be pretty but not one of a kind.

While I enjoyed the manipulation of metal and stone, the hammering, sawing, filing, and careful polishing, it was the spark of a new idea and the feverish sketching that followed that I had enjoyed most, or so I thought. Looking back over the course of my life, my enjoyment had felt more like a proxy, as if I'd gleaned it from others who truly loved the work while I merely subscribed to their enthusiasm.

But I had to try, for my father's sake if not for mine.

I pulled on my protective eye gear and bent over the ring mount, examining my work.

Being a jeweler in my own right was something I'd strived for my whole life, without question. But what if I didn't want this life? Courting the wealthy, being a part of a world I'd never felt like I belonged to and never had. Even now with my fine new dresses, I felt like an interloper, an impostor in Evalyn's world. I had responsibilities and a life worlds apart from theirs. What was more, I could scarcely converse with them.

They spoke of charities, politicians' wives, and dignitaries and spent their days playing card games and sipping cocktails. It was hard to keep up, and though it had been something of a welcome respite from my life, I was growing more and more wary of the constant land of make-believe and showmanship and most of all their version of "friendship." I felt as if I were walking on the edge of a blade at all times.

As I glanced back at my original sketches and the ruby I'd intended for the ring, I heaved a sigh of dismay. The design would take so much work, but the bigger problem was we lacked a ruby of the right clarity and size to finish my design. I removed my eye gear and leaned over the tray of the few remaining loose gems to assess them. I'd always loved stones, regardless of size or type. Searching for them, finding them, identifying them. Learning about their chemical makeup and structures and studying them for hours under a microscope. In those moments, I knew deep down that I'd always dreamed about a different life, one I'd never given words to until I'd met Julia Wane and seen other women hard at work in the museum.

I picked up the ring mount again, assessing the multiple cutouts in the tiny square of metal. Julien had helped me cut them. I remembered that day as if it were yesterday, my frustration and my big brother—older by two minutes—coming to my rescue.

I'd redrawn the sketch many times and finally decided to start the piece.

"Everything all right?" Julien's voice came from the doorway.

I looked up from the tiny ring mount to find him dressed in the navy suit he usually reserved for meeting with customers. "Sure. Why do you ask?"

"You're frowning."

I smiled. "Yes, well, what I'm working on is quite ambitious."

"Do you need help?" He reached for a pair of protective eye goggles.

"If you would make the first cut, I can take it from there, I think." It wasn't unusual for me to sketch the designs and for my brother to finish them, but not this time. I wanted the work to be mine. Though Father had always been supportive, it was Julien who pushed me to be creative.

"This is your best work, sis." He peered at the two-dimensional rendering.

I smiled again at my favorite person in the world. "You think so?"

"I do." His tone was earnest, his blue eyes sincere. "It might be tricky soldering this piece together." I stepped aside as he took over my station, using the goldsmith's miniature saw to cut the metal into a series of uniform strips. "What do you think?"

"That's perfect," I said, sweeping the tiny metal crumbs into a marble bowl to be melted down later. No material was wasted, regardless of its size; nearly everything could be repurposed.

"I'll show you a soldering trick later when you have a minute," he said, raking a hand through his wavy blond hair. "It'll probably make this mount easier."

"When I have a minute?" I laughed. "All that's on my agenda today is ordering metals and polishing the piece Father finished yesterday. After that, I'm sweeping the store."

As the sound of Father's footsteps clunked across the kitchen floor overhead, Julien's voice, his face, his presence dissipated like smoke. And I was alone again in the workshop, and my coffee was cold. I put the ring mount back in the tray and flipped through the next few pages of my sketchbook. Some of the drawings were unfinished. Others, I'd sketched every minute detail of a piece from multiple angles. I flipped to the back where I'd outlined my collection. I'd always thought it would be something special, representative of the art nouveau movement that had been very popular with its colored enamels swirled with gold or silver, the intricate designs of dragonfly wings or beetles or butterflies, colorful cabochons of sapphires or rose quartz or amethyst, detailed and delicate, whimsical and natural. If I ever completed it, my collection would showcase a necklace, a pair of hair combs, three sets of earrings, four brooches resembling various gilded insects, and a money clip, though Father had tried to talk me out of it. I wanted to design something distinctly male for my collection as well. I'd used the Japanese cherry blossoms as my inspiration. The necklace resembled a web of thin branches with ends that curled into tiny leaves painted with green enamel and clusters of pink blossoms. A tiny diamond would be nestled in the middle of each blossom. The necklace would be a large statement piece, designed for a plunging neckline or a strapless dress.

As I traced the designs with my finger, I knew the drawings were beautiful but not unique. The art nouveau style had been popular for twenty years already and was bound to change soon. And yet I didn't know if I cared about any of it. All my inspiration, all the pressure to stand out as a true asset of Beaumont Jewelers had vanished into thin air. There were other things I wanted far more.

"What are you working on?" my father asked as he crossed the room. His hair was mussed, but his eyes were bright. He'd been spending more and more time tinkering with projects he'd abandoned, but he never seemed satisfied enough with any of them to keep at it for long. I was happy to see him interested at all.

I glanced down at the ring mount. "I'm not sure this is working anymore."

"Maybe you need a little inspiration. Perhaps a jewelry show or a tour of the shops around town. See what everyone else is selling."

"From what I saw at the bazaar, there's not much new on the horizon."

He covered my hand with his. "Maybe it's time we went to New York. It's the jewelry capital of America after all. Perhaps I can set up some meetings with some old friends. Get them to show us what they're working on."

I knew then that a trip to New York was as much—or more—for him than it would be for me. And yet the idea of leaving town for a few days sounded perfect, exciting even. I'd always wanted to see New York City and the famous diamond district, but as always, there was the matter of affordability.

"We still have a few outstanding bills," I said, "but I've built a small cushion for us. I don't know." I shook my head. "I'm not sure a trip will help me much with my designs."

"Of course it will, *chérie*. We'll visit some boutiques, research what others are working on, take in new sights. Fill up our creative wells again. I think we could both use the time away."

I studied his face, taking in the lines on his forehead, the crags around his mouth and eyes. They seemed lesser that day, softer. In recent weeks, he'd regained his appetite and had started to fill out again. "Are you sure you'd be up for that, Papa?"

His eyes softened at the name I'd called him as a child. "I think it's time we invested in our future—in your future."

I was so happy to see him becoming himself again that I didn't reflect on what he was saying. I didn't need to take time investing in a future I was beginning to realize I didn't want to be a part of, but I'd confront that hurdle another day.

"How soon would we go?" I asked.

"How about next week? Is that too soon?"

"It's perfect."

And for the first time in nearly half a year, my father wrapped his arms around me.

23

After the talk of a trip to New York and the flurry of planning that followed, I'd nearly forgotten I'd promised to go to Evalyn's that night. I dressed hurriedly, added a touch of lipstick, and made my way to Friendship. As I arrived, the melodious notes of a band in full swing floated through the house. Guests poured in behind me, and soon Evalyn's mansion looked far smaller than usual as bodies filled the cavernous rooms. The Georgian ballroom was exquisitely decorated with overflowing bouquets of roses and lilies and candlelight. A string quartet sat at the front of the room and played a beautiful piece from a composer I didn't recognize.

Everyone looked like royalty in their coattails and formal gowns. Diamonds, emeralds, and rubies sparkled in their ears or at their necks, in their hairpieces, bracelets, and even in their cuff links. I watched as women took stock of one another, deciding who looked best, who wore the most fashionable gown from the most sought-after designers.

As was my habit, I mentally cataloged the jewelry in the room. Sandra wore rose-petal pink satin with a stunning set of freshwater pearls: a double-strand necklace, teardrop earrings, and a matching pearl-studded comb that held her honey-blond hair in place. Alice wore champagne and diamonds, Bea a navy off-the-shoulder gown with a stunning ruby attached to a fine chain so thin, the gem looked as if it were floating, and then there was Carrie in royal purple with a necklace resembling a cluster of flower petals dotted with small stones of amethyst, rubies, and diamonds. Her red hair was a flame in the sea of brunettes and blonds.

I stared at Carrie, my eyes drawn to her necklace, at its handiwork—and my heart skipped a beat. I knew that necklace. It was another Beaumont piece. I shouldn't be surprised to see them now that I knew the others owned many of ours, and yet I couldn't look away.

Feeling my eyes on her, Carrie glanced my way.

Embarrassed to be caught staring, I moved swiftly to the far wall, out of the way of the flow of guests. I forced myself not to gulp down my drink, to sip slowly and focus on steadying my racing heart. No matter how often I saw her, I had not become inured to Carrie's presence. All of Evalyn's friends were attractive, but Carrie's beauty was the thing of love poems and Greek tragedies. And now that I knew Julien had flirted with her and she had flirted with him, I couldn't help but take a deeper interest.

I glanced at Evalyn as her eyes followed Carrie across the room. Evalyn's expression shifted, and some emotion passed over her features.

And it struck me.

Evalyn was jealous of Carrie, or at the very least, she felt as if she were in direct competition with her. Additionally, for some reason, Carrie behaved as if Evalyn had power over her. I watched the two as they conducted a series of air kisses on the cheek, the way they were as familiar with one another as friends should be, and yet their posture revealed so much more. Evalyn's flick of her hair, Carrie leaning away from Evalyn, their tight smiles. I could only guess at what had happened between them. Perhaps nothing. Carrie's beauty was reason enough to be jealous, especially if Ned had ever said anything about it, but I had a sense there was something more between them.

The two women separated to circulate among the guests. I forced myself to do the same, though I felt the strain once more of trying to belong when I clearly didn't.

"Hello, Lizzie. You look beautiful tonight."

I turned to find Carrie again. "I... Thank you. You do, too."

"I couldn't show up on Jet's arm looking anything but. He wouldn't stand for it." She'd tried to sound light, but her eyes told a different story.

As a waiter walked by carrying a tray of champagne, I reached for a glass and cradled it in my hand.

"May I ask you something?" I said.

"Of course," she said, taking a sip of champagne.

"I know that Julien was entertaining a business proposition with your husband and some of the other men. Do you know anything about that?"

She gently swirled the bubbly wine in her glass. "That was the rumor. Something about investing in a series of Beaumont stores. I know Jet was interested at one point."

"Really!" I said, not bothering to hide my shock. "And they were interested in investing in Julien?"

"I don't know a lot about it, but Jet did say something about a store in New York and another potentially in London. They had big plans, the two of them."

I couldn't believe Julien hadn't mentioned it. Maybe he was waiting until he'd secured the funding, or maybe something had gone wrong.

Before I could reply, a shorter gentleman with dark hair and a stocky stature placed his hand on Carrie's back and leaned to her ear. She stiffened next to him but forced a smile as she gazed into his face. When he whispered in her ear, her smile faded.

After, he nodded at me. "Good evening. I'm Jet Wellington."

Carrie's husband. A ripple of unease traveled over my skin as I took in the heavy brow framing a pair of equally dark eyes. He seemed a brooding sort, and there was no mistaking the man's sense of self-possession. His taut form appeared ready to pounce at any moment. Julien had been friends with this man?

"Elisabeth Beaumont, hello," I replied in a strained voice.

"How do you do." He nodded politely, but rather than acknowledge I was the sister of his friend and potential business partner lost so tragically, Jet Wellington turned to his wife. "I'm going to the lounge with the others. I'm sure it'll be a late night. Curtis is outside when you're ready. Don't wait up."

"I suppose that means you won't be coming home tonight. Again," Carrie said, her tone as smooth as glass. She pulled out a cigarette and lit it, blowing a delicate stream of smoke into his face.

His eyes darkened. "I'll see you in the morning," he said, tone clipped.

"You don't even have the courtesy to say good night to my friend here," she replied, clearly undaunted by his obvious irritation.

"Have a nice evening, Elisabeth," he said, suppressing his irritation. "See that my wife stays out of trouble, will you?"

"She'll do no such thing," Carrie replied, blowing a second cloud of smoke into his face.

But he hadn't heard her, or if he had, he pretended not to and strode away to join the rest of the gentlemen who had gathered at the edge of the room.

"He's a brute, isn't he?" she said.

"I..." I stopped, shook my head.

She laughed a hollow sound. "I didn't really expect you to answer that."

Eager to escape her and the awkward scene, I said, "Excuse me," and headed to the washroom to ensure my carefully—if amateurishly—applied makeup was still in place and that my hair hadn't frizzed and become a mess. I turned the corner down the long hall just as a screech split the air. I paused, wondering what could make the unearthly sound. Chattering noises followed, and I was certain then that it wasn't a person or a squeaky pipe. It was definitely an animal.

Another screech followed by more chattering filled the air. The next moment, Vinnie McLean dashed from the washroom—chasing a monkey. I blinked several times as if I'd seen an apparition. Was there truly a monkey in Evalyn's house? I shouldn't be surprised, given the llama, cows, horses, and the other animals I'd seen on the lawn. And yet I would never have expected to see a monkey inside her elegant home in a hundred years.

"Vinnie," I called after the child. "Is everything all right? Can I help with your monkey?"

He ignored me, and a pack of little boys barreled around the corner after him. As I watched their retreating backs, a laugh caught in my throat, the awkward exchange with Carrie forgotten. Children really did have a way of making anything feel lighter, less important.

"Miss Beaumont?" Jerry called as he stepped into the hallway. "Mrs. McLean would like you to join her when you're ready, ma'am."

"Of course."

I followed him to one of the many entertainment rooms where Evalyn's friends had gathered. She sat with Flo Harding, who wore a typically plain but elegant dark sheath dress that fell to her ankles.

"There you are!" Evalyn said, taking my hands in hers and giving my dress the once-over. Her words were slurred and her cheeks rosy. She'd clearly been drinking for hours already. "Oh my goodness! Look at you!" she exclaimed loudly.

Dressed in one of Evalyn's castoffs, I wore a resplendent V-neck gown in cornflower blue with a cascade of iridescent beads that appeared to drip from the waist to the hemline. At one time, it wouldn't have fit my normally curvaceous form, but I'd grown slender since the accident. Evalyn also wore a blue gown that matched the shade of her eyes—and accentuated the deep blue of the Hope around her neck—but her gown was light as air, off-the-shoulder with gathered sleeves that puffed around her elbows. A long, flowing skirt frothed around her feet. She looked like a cool whip of wind among the clouds.

"She's practically your twin!" Sharon said in a tone that fell somewhere between surprise and disgust. Her cheeks were as rosy as Evalyn's.

I glanced at the others, at the table littered with many empty glasses, and toward the back of the room at a small booth where a man tending bar appeared to be making another round. Had I been late to the party, or had they started early?

"Isn't it adorable?" Evalyn beamed, positively pleased with herself. "She'll wow the men, won't she, girls?"

"She's darling," Carrie agreed as she entered the room behind me.

Evalyn glanced at Carrie and set her glass on the table near her with too much force. A stream of liquor slopped over the rim and oozed down the side of the glass. "She isn't the only one who knows how to catch a man's eye, is she, Carrie?"

I gripped my glass tighter. Something about Evalyn's tone, her mood, left me uneasy.

For the briefest instant, alarm flickered across Carrie's face before she regained her composure. "Whatever do you mean, Evie? I'm married." She forced a dismissive laugh, but judging by the look on Evalyn's face, she wasn't fooled.

"Well, married or no, who doesn't admire a handsome man from time to time, even if he's not from our crowd?"

The color drained from Carrie's face, but she attempted to play Evalyn's game. "I'm sure you're right. We don't stop being women once we're married after all. A handsome face is a handsome face."

"Certainly. As long as things don't go too far, that is." Evalyn's eyes hardened to blue ice.

Carrie seemed to forget her manners and set her half-finished champagne on a tray. "It's been a real treat tonight, but I've been feeling under the weather all day. If you'll excuse me, I think I'll go home for a lie-down."

"As long as you're lying down alone," Evalyn shot back.

Carrie spun around to face her. "Perhaps you should look in on Ned. Everyone knows he and Warren Harding carouse with other women. It isn't exactly a secret."

Evalyn went white with rage. "And it isn't exactly a secret that you've slept with every gardener in Washington!"

Several in the circle gasped. I looked on in equal parts horror and fascination, unwilling to come between them. The rest of us—Flo, Sharon, Rita, and Bea—were too stunned to interject.

"How dare you!" Carrie said in a huff. "That's a lie and you know it."

"Evie," Bea interjected. "Lighten up, sugar. Here, give me that." She took the glass that had found its way back into Evalyn's hand and gave her a champagne flute instead. "You need to lay off the gin. It makes you ornery."

"I was only teasing," Evalyn said, her voice sliding from vinegar back to warm honey.

But Carrie wasn't so easily placated. "People cater to you only because you have money."

Evalyn laughed wickedly. "Because you're so poor? Please."

"I think it's time you left, Carrie," Flo interjected.

"You can see yourself out," Evalyn said coolly, calmly. So calmly, a chill ran down my spine. How quickly she had turned on her "dearest" friend.

"I thought you'd never ask." Carrie avoided eye contact with anyone as she threaded through the crowd, somehow still looking impossibly elegant with her head held high.

Everyone started talking at once.

Flo touched Evalyn's arm. "For heaven's sake, what was that all about?"

"Absolutely nothing," Evalyn said, mercifully changing the subject. "Let's have our palms and cards read, shall we?"

I couldn't help but gape at her rapid shift in mood.

"Is Marcia here?" Flo said.

As if Flo had summoned her, the woman I assumed was Madame Marcia was shown into the parlor. She looked every bit the fortune teller in her multicolored caftan that poured over her body in waves of fabric, ropes of beads, and her hair pinned in a loose chignon with bright-pink feathers stuffed into the twist at the crown of her head.

Evalyn greeted her with kisses on each cheek. "Marcia! Just in time. We're dying to hear what you have to say."

We made room for Marcia in our circle and cleared the table.

I was still reeling from what Carrie had shared earlier and from the hateful exchange between friends. Why should Evalyn perpetuate something so hurtful if it wasn't true? Carrie insisted she didn't sleep with every man "below her station" that headed her way, and yet her reaction to Evalyn's accusations—the way she'd gone white as a sheet—said otherwise. Had the others noticed? I glanced at each of them, but they were focused on Marcia. I, too, tried to settle in for the night, but the unease among the group was palpable in their heavy drink pours and strained smiles.

The fortune teller took her time reading tarot cards or palms, dishing out fortunes one by one. When she came to Florence Harding, she paused. "I see a house. The biggest in the land."

Evalyn gripped Flo's arm. "The White House! I knew it. Oh, Warren is going to be president one day! And you'll be the First Lady!"

"Are you sure?" Flo asked.

Marcia nodded, her feather bobbing precariously atop her head like it was coming loose from its pins. "I am. But I'm afraid he won't finish his term."

Flo paled, touched her throat, looked at the others. "That sounds ominous."

"Remember, paths may change, and with each choice you make, you may direct your fate to another course," Marcia said.

Ignoring the warning, the others chattered excitedly.

"Would you like to have your fortune read?" Marcia's large dark eyes met mine.

I shook my head. "I prefer to see how my life unfolds, one day at a time."

She nodded. "Very well."

"It's my turn!" Evalyn called gleefully. "Everyone, be quiet, please." She squirmed on the edge of her seat like a child.

Marcia shuffled her deck, offering it to Evalyn to choose ten cards. Marcia laid them out in the pattern of the Celtic cross. As she flipped them over in a specific order, she gave her interpretation of their message. She spoke of Evalyn's past and present and paused before delivering news of her future.

"What does it all mean?" Evalyn asked excitedly.

I stared at the final cards. Inverted Magician, Three of Swords, and Ten of Swords.

"You live in a false reality," Marcia said. "And one day soon, you will suffer a great heartbreak. Finally, you may lose everything you thought you'd always have."

We all gasped. Sharon looked as if she might be sick. Evalyn, on the other hand, looked more annoyed than anything.

"Bad luck," Sharon whispered.

"It's that necklace!" Bea blurted. "You have to give it up, Evie! We've been telling you that for years!"

I stared at the magnificent stone around her neck. Its color shifted as the facets caught the light. I dragged my gaze away from the Hope to Evalyn's face. She was white as cream. I couldn't believe the fortune teller had delivered two fortunes that were so negative. I imagined it couldn't be good for business, but then again, if she only delivered positive fortunes, she would lose her reputation for being accurate.

"That is all for tonight," Marcia said, hastily packing her things. She seemed perfectly aware her predictions had made one of her most ardent customers uneasy. After she'd made her quick but noisy exit, everyone seemed to release a collective breath.

"Can you believe my fortune?" Evalyn said with a tight laugh. "Bad luck. It's always bad luck that shows up in my cards, and look at me! I've had nothing but good luck!"

I studied her bright smile, remembering the conversation with Jerry about how many things had gone wrong around the McLeans and their staff, little by little, one by one. The notes Julien and I had both received as a warning, the never-ending letters of blackmail and vitriol sent to the McLeans, the way Evalyn's face had paled with the prediction that struck a chord somewhere inside her. And I found I didn't agree with her, not one bit. If she'd had tremendous good luck with the necklace, I'd never seen it, and I certainly didn't believe it now.

As everyone rushed to console her, she searched my face for some hint that I didn't believe the prediction. Why she looked to me, I wasn't sure, except perhaps she knew I wouldn't lie to her, and I was terrible at hiding my feelings. And yet in her imploring gaze, I understood what was expected of me—to assure her it was all a silly farce—whether I believed it was or not. She didn't like to be crossed, and she expected her friends to fall in line.

I pasted a smile on my face. "Don't believe a word of it, Evalyn. You really do have all the luck."

"I really do." Evalyn grinned, ear to ear.

Some hours later, in need of quiet from the tumultuous events of the evening, I stepped outside, sucking cool air into my lungs. Stars showered the night sky over the vast acres of lawn and the clusters of trees as far as the eye could see. I sighed at the kind of beauty the McLeans enjoyed regularly. It was one of the things I envied most about their lifestyle. Being closer to nature, in addition to their obvious lack of concern over money.

As I watched a pair of men cheat at a game of croquet on the lawn, I ruminated on the conversation with Carrie and all that had transpired that evening. Did my father know Julien had been discussing the idea of multiple Beaumont stores in other cities? I supposed Carrie's husband had planned to be the financial support, a business partner behind the scenes. I couldn't understand why Julien hadn't told me about any of it. That kind of expansion could have been a boon for us, and I would have supported him.

No, something else must have happened. My brother wouldn't keep things from me unless he was up to something he was embarrassed to admit. Something illegal perhaps. I couldn't imagine what else it could be.

My mind drifted to the confrontation between Carrie and Evalyn and the clear jealousy on Evalyn's face as she'd watched Carrie make her away around the party. What could Evalyn be jealous of when she had everything Carrie did and more? Her beauty? I felt as if I needed a handbook to navigate that lifestyle, the crowd, the unspoken expectations.

"There you are." An arm snaked around my waist, and something soft brushed the top of my ear. Hot breath blew gently against the exposed skin on my neck.

Startled, I turned abruptly. "I beg your pardon."

"Oh!" Ned laughed. "Good grief, Lizzie, I've mistaken you for my bride. You're gorgeous tonight!"

I hardly knew how to respond. "Ned, hi. I… Thank you."

He roared with laughter and put a half-smoked cigar to his lips. "You're so very serious, aren't you? Seems like you could use a good time. Have you had any champagne? Perhaps a whiskey?"

"I've had too much already." The drinks and lack of food had left me lightheaded.

"Never," he said, circling the bar cart stationed on the patio for guests who'd made their way outside. He held out a glass and pushed it into my hands. "Have you met our llama?"

Hesitantly, I accepted the glass. "My first time here, yes. I was astounded to see all the animals! I felt like I'd wandered into a dream."

At the mention of animals, a clatter came behind us as the French doors burst open. Mike the Great Dane galloped past us, his eyes set on some furry creature just beyond the edge of the yard. As he ran, something flashy bounced around his neck. Was that—

"Drat. She's done it again."

"Done what?" I said.

"Put that damned diamond on the dog!" Ned said, throwing the butt of the cigar on the ground.

My eyes followed the dog, trying to see which diamond he meant. "You don't mean the Hope Diamond?"

"Unfortunately, I do. She's careless with it, and it's one of the most valuable things we own, outside of our houses." A vein pulsed in his temple as he set his glass down. "I'm going to have to go after him."

I watched Mike and his light-gray flank thunder toward a copse of oak trees. Evalyn had put the Hope Diamond on her dog, more than once? Was she mad?

"Mike!" Evalyn shrieked as she wobbled toward us, teetering on her heels. She removed her shoes one at a time, tossing them onto the patio flagstones. "Why do you two look so gloomy?" She slurred her words. "It's a party. Come on, Lizzie, you're supposed to be having fun."

"I can't believe you put a necklace that cost me over one hundred thousand dollars on a dog," Ned seethed. "We're lucky our friends are honest people."

"Please, you're so full of yourself. My dad paid for that necklace and you know it. Besides, you worry too much. Lizzie makes sure the clasp is in good working order. Don't you, darling." She tugged my arm hard, almost losing her balance, and I nearly dropped my champagne.

I didn't bother pointing out that I'd only touched the Hope Diamond twice, and only once in an official capacity. She was always wearing it when I'd come to service her collection. "I'm not sure putting a necklace on a dog who is sprinting around the yard at top speed is the safest thing."

"Oh, pooh," she said. "You two are such bores."

"Call that mutt right now!" Ned said, his voice rising.

"I guess you've forgotten that I don't take orders, least of all from you," Evalyn shouted back.

"The hell you don't." He grasped her arm and half dragged her to the end of the porch.

"Unhand me!"

He let her arm drop. "You're nothing but a shallow, silly woman who cares about no one but herself. You and your diamonds. Your ridiculous friends," he shouted back. "Look at you! You're drunk out of your mind!"

Though I knew he'd likely had twice as much alcohol as Evalyn, his sudden flash of anger and the cruel calm with which he said those words suddenly left me cold, and all I wanted was to be at home in my own bed, away from these people.

"You're one to talk!" Evalyn screeched. "You can drink everyone in this house under the table. You make a fool of yourself, spending our money on horses! At this rate, we'll go bankrupt!"

"And you don't think the extravagant vacations and diamond-studded gown and the endless parties aren't wasteful?" he shouted back. "At least I often win when I gamble."

"You mostly lose! Besides, you like the parties as much as I do!"

I set down the glass of champagne that had cost more than my entire grocery bill, the tangle of their voices behind me as I made a quick exit. But the last thing I heard as I reached the patio door stopped me in my tracks.

"Are you trying to sleep with her?" Evalyn screeched. "I've watched you court every woman this side of the river. Why would she be any different!"

"You're insane! She's your friend!"

I couldn't leave fast enough. The bickering and opulence, the crowds, the desperate hope they'd find some kind of happiness. They were all so good at pretending until the veil fell away. Suddenly, I could no longer breathe.

Without a single good night, I swept past the people littering the parlor, through the packed ballroom and the few men still loitering in the study with their drinks, and quietly made my escape.

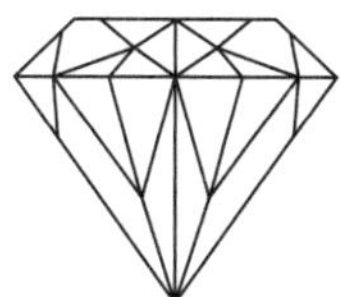

I escape the tedium and uncertainty of turnover from hand to hand, collector to collector, because Pierre Cartier values me, for a time. But soon, he attempts to sell me as the others have—to those who deem themselves more important than the rest, as money has set them apart. His attempts are fruitless. I am admired, but most fear my reputation.

Until one fine day.

A man and woman visit the boutique. They are merry, newly wed, and she will have all she desires.

"You are special customers," Pierre says to them, leading them to his office. "Let me show you my most prized pieces." He places me on a tray with other gemstones, all the while speaking to the couple in soft tones, explaining the provenance of each, cajoling them, tempting them.

The woman's eyes shine with lust, and I wonder if she will have me.

"How beautiful!" she exclaims as her husband looks on, his reserve plain.

"This is the most special stone of all," my keeper says. "It is the Hope Diamond."

"But this diamond is much bigger, its setting newer." She points instead to the pear-shaped white diamond of spectacular clarity. "Does it have a name?"

As Pierre regards the woman, he now understands. Evalyn McLean lives to impress others, and she wants the best of everything, the most, and the largest stone of all.

"Ah," Pierre says. "The pear diamond is the Star of the East. Though its origins are unknown, it is said to have been stolen from India before it traveled to Persia. I purchased it from an Ottoman sultan. It is nearly ninety-five carats in size."

Evalyn turns to her husband, who shakes his head. "We'll need to ask your father for more money."

"Don't worry. There is plenty, and he always gives me more," she says with a pointed smile. Turning to Pierre, she says, "I want the Star."

And I am forgotten again for a short time.

Pierre says goodbye to the couple with a promise to keep in touch. He has a plan, you see. In time, he lovingly creates a new setting for me, a halo of bright-white cushion diamonds that flatter my facets, and I become more beautiful than ever. But he knows my beauty is not enough, for he understands something no one else does.

It is my story that matters most.

This is how he lures her back to me, despite her laughter at such tales, despite my price. He warns her of the dark spell beyond my beauty, but Evalyn does not fear the dark, and she does not believe in bad luck. Yet when she first wears me proudly around her neck, she receives a stark and unsettling warning. She even attempts to rid herself of me briefly. Ever so briefly.

But I am hers—and she is mine—and our story is not finished yet.

24

A few days after the tense party at Evalyn's, I welcomed the escape to New York City. It was a relief to push everything aside, and I looked forward to spending time with my father. He was in good spirits, chattering more than usual on the train. As the city came into view, I felt my own mood lift. The sprawl of buildings was unimaginable, and nothing could have prepared me for the steady stream of people. By midafternoon, we had deposited our suitcase at our lodgings and were on the streets of the largest, most remarkable place I'd ever seen.

We ate street food and watched shiny new automobiles and omnibuses and bicyclists come and go. We passed rows of storefronts, the occasional park, and more taverns and restaurants than I could count. I marveled at the frenetic array of people making their way to their destinations. Like Washington, the city bustled with immigrants and workers, vendors and families, and businessmen in a hurry, though on a much larger scale. Washington, DC, suddenly felt sleepy in comparison, dull and rather pedestrian compared to the color of New York. Amid it all, I watched my father come alive. This was good for him, to be away from home and away from the memories of all that had been lost. It was good for me, too, to free myself of the cycle of parties and luncheons and working strange and late hours between social engagements where I was expected to be ready to entertain with a smile.

Father and I walked the length of the grand avenues and paid a visit to one of the few places I truly wanted to see in the city: the American Museum of Natural History. He humored me as we viewed each and every exhibit, spoke with docents, read each plaque. Most of all, I imagined what it must be like to work in such a great place, with its towering ceilings and magnificent halls and the nest of labs and offices cocooned behind private doors. It made my pulse quicken to think of it. I didn't share my thoughts with my father or the dream that had blossomed the afternoon I'd toured the museum with Julia Wane. That life wasn't an option for me, so there was little sense in feeding it.

"You've changed," Father said as we exhausted the last of the exhibits and descended the staircase in front of the museum.

"In what way?" I asked as a bus roared by us on the street.

"Your hair. Your clothes."

"Ah, yes. You noticed."

He shook his head. "I'm sorry I didn't notice it sooner."

As I looked at the grooves in my dear father's face and thought of the years they reflected, the sorrows and the joys, the last of the anger I'd felt toward him since Julien's death dissolved. I squeezed his hand. "We've both changed. I suppose that's the natural way of things, especially given what we've been through."

He nodded. "Given that, yes. But I want you to know, I see that you've grown into a confident and well-spoken woman. And you've always been intelligent, beautiful, too, but we both know there's much more to life than beauty, even if we sell it for a living."

I smiled a genuine smile at him for the first time in a long time. "I thought jewelry was more than beauty? To quote someone I know, 'The stones are nature's art, and we bring them to their highest level of beauty in jewelry that will long outlive us. They are immortal, priceless, and we merely have the good fortune of keeping them to admire for a while,'" I teased.

"Who said that?" he said, eyes full of mirth.

I linked my arm in his. "I'm starved. How about a snack to tide us over until dinner?"

We enjoyed espressos and a scoop of ice cream stuffed into a sweetened cone made from a rolled flat pastry. Later, after travel and hours of walking, Father and I slept well, despite the simple and tiny rooms we'd rented in an inn above a pub. Thankfully, it didn't appear to be a busy one, so the Irish band finished the last of their songs by ten o'clock that night. The next day, we set out to do what we'd come to do in the city.

"Ah, here at last," my father said.

We looked up at the incredible mansion at 653 Fifth Avenue in awe. Cartier's store was five stories high with a mansard roof. I'd heard the former home had been purchased with one hundred dollars and a million-dollar pearl necklace. As I stood outside the building amid a steady stream of pedestrians, for the first time, I understood why my father had left Paris to pursue his own business in Washington, DC. He couldn't possibly compete with such a well-known name in a city that considered Cartier the king of jewelry. Not in Paris and not here in New York. And yet I found my father's jewelry easily as beautiful and as innovative as Cartier's. More so in some cases.

Inside, we were greeted by a young man in a black suit and tie.

"May I help you, sir? Madam?"

"Thank you, but we'd like to take a look around on our own first," Father said.

"Should you need assistance, please don't hesitate to ask."

We walked by case after case filled with an array of jewelry, hair clips, brooches, and more. Behind each case stood a salesclerk, ready to jump at our every whim. We gazed at the artful displays, studying, assessing, and memorizing dimensions, styles, and stones. Father stopped at a case at the rear of the showcase floor and pointed at a piece he wanted to examine more closely.

"Might we see this ring?" he said.

"As you wish, sir." The salesclerk unlocked the case and set a tray of rings before us.

Father reached for the most interesting of the bunch, turning it over, eyeing its craft, and when he'd finished, he gave it to me. I studied the mount, the prongs, the lovely design.

"It's exquisite," I breathed as I gave it back to him. "Is that a red diamond?"

"Mmm," he replied. I could almost hear his mind whirring with ideas.

"Would you like to see anything else?" the clerk asked.

My father seemed startled to realize someone else was there. "Is Monsieur Cartier here today? I am a jeweler myself and an old friend. I'd like to say hello."

To my father's dismay, Cartier was not only out of store that day but out of the country at the moment. We browsed and stopped to examine several more spectacular pieces. When he was satisfied we'd seen everything, we continued our journey to three other stores, each time stopping to take notes on a particularly striking piece. We also rode the subway train downtown to Maiden Lane near Wall Street, where a row of gem merchants sold multitudes of jewelry and loose gemstones.

A light burned in my father's eyes, and I was glad we'd come, if for no other reason than to see his interest and perhaps even some excitement in his eyes. I helped him sort through piles of cabochons, examine dozens of quality diamonds, discuss the trends and patterns we saw on display. As he collected stone after stone as if to buy them, I laid my hand atop his.

"Should we buy these now, when we are just caught up on our accounts?" I asked.

"With these stones, we'll get ahead, *chérie*. I can already see what I will make." He pointed to his temple. "And I have a good idea of what you will make, too."

My smile faltered. I felt further than ever from designing a new, innovative piece. "If you're sure?" I said.

"I'm ready to work again, every day," he said quietly. "It's time."

My heart squeezed as I realized what that meant. He was moving on from Julien's death, and all would return to the way it was before: me as assistant and my wishes of little consequence in the end. I smiled weakly and embraced my dear father, keeping my thoughts to myself.

We finished the day with a meal of *moules frites* and red wine—Father's favorite—at a little French brasserie, and after, we sat in the lobby of our inn. I flipped lazily through the pages of my sketchbook, hoping an idea might spark after all I'd seen that day, but my mind was woefully blank.

"What are you thinking about?"

I looked up abruptly, surprised my father had been watching me. I cleared my throat. "Only that so much of what we saw looked the same. It was pretty but uninspired. I must say I'm surprised, given that New York is supposed to be *the place* for jewelry."

"Mm-hmm," my father said, bending over his own sketchbook. After some time, he looked up again, his eyes alight. "What happens when a particular idea or style becomes overused and saturated?"

I shrugged, knowing the question was more rhetorical than not.

"The pendulum swings," he said.

Slowly, I nodded, understanding. New ideas often came as a reaction to what was once popular, and the next designs would either be some variation of what was already popular or, for the brave creators, the exact opposite in some way.

"Art nouveau has been the popular style for well over twenty years now. I say, 'Away with the tiny details, the nature scenes, and the filmy, swirling plasticity of enamel.'" His pencil scurried across the page as he worked in swift strokes.

I sat on the sofa next to him. "Can I see?"

He'd drawn three quick sketches, still unfinished, but their direction was clear. Clean lines and shapes with hard angles rather than the soft, rounded cabochon gems and heavily intricate details of art nouveau.

"What do you think of these?" he asked, reading my face. "Precise angles. Geometric designs. Heavily metallic and shiny. Do you think women will find the hard lines appealing?"

"Let's have a look again at your sketchbook."

I studied the lines, asked him questions about clasps and gemstone placement and technical questions about design. As he spoke, I marveled at my dear father and his wonderful mind, at the innovation I was seeing play out before my very eyes. I wished I were like him, but I wasn't. I hadn't been struck by a rush of ideas or a flurry of inspiration and excitement. I felt lost, trapped in a life I didn't want anymore—or had ever wanted. Still, my father's enthusiasm was contagious, and when he'd finished explaining each of his sketches and how he might extend this new collection, we embraced each other tightly, and for the first time in months, we regarded each other with a genuine smile.

Though our trip was brief, it had been an overall success. My father was more inspired than I had ever seen him, and for a few days, I felt content in the glow of his happiness. But it didn't last as my thoughts returned to Jet and Julien's business venture, the letters I'd received, and the awkward if hostile exchanges at Evalyn's party. I still couldn't make sense of it all, and I realized how merciful it had been over the past few days to be free of her and the Washington crowd. Yet when I didn't hear from Evalyn for days, I grew restless and checked our mailbox for invitations. I waited by the telephone, too, for long spells, and I even traveled to Friendship with the intent of stopping by only to change my mind at the last minute.

I tossed in bed at night, gut churning, mind racing. Beyond my fear of being fired, I didn't know why it made me tremble to think of being cast out from Evalyn's circle. My time with the McLeans had been difficult, often embarrassing, and left me feeling inadequate far more often than I cared to admit, as if I should be grateful to have the good fortune of being in their presence. Wanting to fit into the McLeans' world was a habit I couldn't seem to shake, a drug that delivered me from the pain and monotony of my days in a world without Julien and now from my father, who expected me to return to the duties I'd held before my brother's death. I couldn't go back to that life of ledgers and the desperate need to feel good enough, talented enough, to design something innovative when it wasn't what I truly wanted. Too much had changed.

The sound of voices drifted up the stairs to my bedroom. I frowned. We had company? Given my father's reticence the past several months, I couldn't imagine who he would have invited to the house. I paused as I walked into the kitchen.

Henry, of course. He stood over the stove, reaching for the kettle.

"It's ready, Mr. Beaumont," Henry called. When he heard my footsteps, he looked up. "Liz, I didn't know you were here."

"I live here," I said, tone more acerbic than I meant it to be. When he pressed his lips together in frustration, I instantly regretted my comment. "I'm sorry. I didn't mean to say it like that."

"It's fine," he said, carrying the kettle to the table.

I watched him pour each of us a cup of hot water as Father doled out sugar cubes and strainers packed with fragrant tea leaves. We sat around the dining table making polite conversation about the weather and the news until at last, my father mumbled an excuse and left the room.

"I know you aren't keen on seeing much of me," Henry said, running a hand through his hair. "You seem awfully busy with your new *friends*." He looked at me closely, studying my face as if trying to discern what was really going on with me.

Irritated by his swift judgment and exhausted from the lack of sleep the past several nights, I didn't bother to pretend otherwise. "And? Of course I'm busy."

He shook his head. "I get the message loud and clear, Liz. You're too busy for me, too busy for any of us from your old life, so I planned to leave a message with your father instead. But you're here after all, so now you'll have to deal with me for just a few minutes more, and then I'll be out the door and gone forever, if you wish."

Stung by his anger and by the view he now carried of me—this woman he didn't recognize—I suddenly felt exhausted by it all, by everyone, by everything said and unsaid. I rubbed my eyes tiredly, anxious for him to finish and to leave. "What is it, Henry?"

"They're looking for more lab workers at the museum, in particular an assistant to help a mineralogist identify and catalog stones. Of course I thought of you instantly. It's part-time work for now, and as a woman, your pay wouldn't be a living wage, but I thought you should know."

A bolt of excitement zipped through me. The prospect of

interviewing, of being hired, of spending time doing what I now knew I really wanted to do left me feeling elated, hopeful. What if, for once, I allowed myself the very rare occurrence of following my heart?

"They're hiring inexperienced women?" I said cautiously.

"You've been collecting rocks and identifying them since you could walk. You've worked with vendors for years. And how much reading have you done about geological processes? You've made a good friend in Ken Davis, one of the best curators on the Eastern Seaboard. You're a scientist, through and through. The last thing you are is inexperienced, Elisabeth."

In spite of myself, pleasure coursed through me at the sound of my name on his lips, at the clear depiction of who I was. He was right—about all of it. I wasn't exactly inexperienced, but I hadn't had any formal schooling, no official training in a lab, outside of what my father had taught me. Still, perhaps I knew enough? Perhaps I could be brave enough to try it, no matter what.

"Are they hiring women, truly?"

He nodded. "More and more. I don't know if there are opportunities to move into a full-time paid position, but if you're also helping your father with the business, you wouldn't have time for that anyway. Assuming the interview goes well, of course. Naturally I'd put in a good word for you, and given the interactions you've now had with lizard wizard Julia Wane, I suspect she would, too." A hint of a smile touched his lips.

I allowed myself a minute to daydream about the possibility of no longer managing the shop, of leaving the sales and everything else to my father. Of escaping the constant inadequacies of my designs and the endless peddling to wealthy patrons. I pictured myself in a lab coat, striding through the sacred halls of the museum and saw the future I truly wanted.

"I don't know," I said at last, running my finger around the edge of my teacup. "I have so much to do here…and you know my father wouldn't approve."

"One day, you must follow your own path, not his," Henry said gently. "Your designs and craftsmanship are wonderful, of course, but we both know that isn't where your heart lies."

My eyes met his, and for a moment, I gazed at his dear face. No matter how much time had passed or the wedge I'd allowed to be driven between us, he truly understood me: what I wanted, who I wanted to be, to my very core. And I loved him. No matter what had happened between us or that horrible night, I would always love him. I looked away, blinking against the threatening tears.

When I didn't answer, he added, "It's your father's business. You work for him, but you don't have to."

I shook my head. "I can't do that to him, can't leave him on his own. He's already lost so much. And it's the family business. I just…I can't."

"Elisabeth?" my father called from the other room. "I need your help with the welder when you have a second. No rush. I can work on something else while you finish your visit."

"I'll be there in a minute," I shouted back.

Henry and I exchanged another long, lingering look.

He touched my forearm and withdrew his hand just as quickly. "You don't have to answer now. Just think about it."

"Thank you for coming," I said. "For telling me about this. I'll think about it."

"Of course. You know I only want you to be happy," he replied.

But with my father's voice still ringing in my ears, I already felt myself closing down, the shuttering of my emotion, and most of all, the shuttering of new possibilities that could never be.

25

The shrill ring of the telephone interrupted my thoughts. I pulled off my jeweler's magnifying glasses, set the diamond bracelet on my worktable, and took the stairs by twos to the front hall to answer the telephone.

"Lizzie, it's Ned."

My stomach clenched as it always did when I spoke with Ned. Why was he calling me? I managed a stilted, "Hello."

"I wanted to invite you to the party tonight. It'll be held at the house on McPherson Square. Dignitaries and such will be there, along with many friends. Evie would want you to be there."

Relieved I hadn't been forgotten or pushed out of the circle, I let go of a breath I didn't know I was holding. "Thank you for the invitation. I'll see you tonight."

As I hung up the telephone, I ruminated on how odd it was that Ned had invited me instead of Evalyn. Had she sent him to do her bidding, or was he the one who wanted me there? I couldn't help but think of the accusations she'd hurled at her husband at the last party I'd attended or how she'd assumed he was chasing me like he allegedly had other women.

Doubt choked my relief. Given the location and the important guests, I knew I didn't belong among those of the highest rank and honor. Nonetheless, as evening fell, I slipped into the only other formal gown I owned. It was a shocking red crepe sewn with thousands of beads, so it shimmered as I walked. I'd never worn something so clearly designed to be a showstopper.

When I arrived at the party, my stomach fluttered with nerves. I'd spent very little time at the spectacular but intimidating mansion on McPherson Square. And there was also the matter of Evalyn. I didn't know if her rage and jealousy the last time I'd seen her had been a product of her state of mind after so many cocktails, or if there had been something more that had transpired between her and Ned in the past.

As I faltered on the doorstep, Jerry whisked open the door.

He scanned the list of names and handed the sheet to the men who appeared to be the guards that evening. Given the attendees, I supposed I shouldn't be surprised.

"Miss Beaumont?" Jerry said, clearly surprised I'd come. "I don't see your name here. Are you certain Mrs. McLean sent the invitation?"

My unease flared again. "I didn't receive an invitation, but Ned called me at home. He invited me."

"I see."

"I wouldn't have come otherwise, I assure you. Should you check with him?"

"I'll speak with Mr. McLean, but in the meantime, do come in and please enjoy yourself. You look lovely."

As I started toward the ballroom, Jerry touched my arm.

"Miss Beaumont, I thought you'd like to know," he said, lowering his voice. "Mrs. McLean's lady's maid, Tillie, is out for the foreseeable future. She's lost her left eye."

"Good God," I said. "What happened?"

He quickly scanned the front hall to make sure no one was eavesdropping. "She was helping Mrs. McLean with a jammed lock on her vanity table. She decided to try her hand with pliers."

I cringed. "That's terrible."

"And the dog?" he went on. "The day after Mike ran into the trees wearing Mrs. McLean's necklace, he contracted a severe case of mange."

"Well, isn't all this frightful!"

"I wish you would be careful, ma'am," he said, tone earnest. "You're a kind person, a genuine person, and I'd hate to see you affected by the curse somehow."

"Thank you, Jerry. I'll be careful," I promised. But who could say that being careful was enough in a home where all seemed to go wrong?

He escorted me to the ballroom and stalked off to find Ned. I'd scarcely stepped over the threshold when Sharon found me.

"Look at you!" she exclaimed, Bea at her side. They kissed the air on either side of my face and scanned my outfit from head to toe. "Red is your color," Sharon said. "You've really changed, Lizzie."

For the first time in as long as I could remember, I didn't blush but merely thanked her and accepted this new truth. I *had* changed. For the first time in my life, I no longer felt lesser, as if I'd do better to hide behind Julien's radiance. His tragic death had forced me into the light. I only wished he were here to see me now.

"Let's get you some champagne," Bea said.

Rita and Gwen and a few other women I'd met but could never seem to remember joined us, and soon I was the center of their circle. Everyone gushed about my new gown, my hair, my ruby lips, and after, the conversation fractured into many conversations at once. I felt a little like the belle of the ball for the first time in my life. I wondered what Evalyn would think of her creation.

I searched the crowd for her and saw her headed in our direction. The Hope glittered darkly at her throat, and her divine canary-yellow gown sewn with dozens of yellow diamonds shimmered like a sunlit glimmer path on water. I gaped at the dozens of diamonds twinkling among the folds of her dress. My mind boggled at the cost of such a garment. Her hair waved softly around her face, and on her arm, she escorted Alice Roosevelt Longworth. Everything about Evalyn spoke of power and the message she aimed to send: I have it all and I am the queen of this town.

"Good evening, y'all," she said when she'd reached us.

"My God, Evie, what are you wearing!" Flo Harding exclaimed.

Evalyn laughed. "Oh, you know me. Always a show-off. What's a party without a party dress after all?"

Flo smiled fondly. "You look like a shooting star."

"Why, Lizzie Beaumont, what are you doing here?" Evalyn said as she took in my scarlet gown.

So it was as I'd feared. She didn't want me here after all, and Ned was wrong. I wished the floor would open and swallow me whole. "Ned invited me on your behalf. He said you requested I be here? I'm sorry, should I have followed up with you?"

"Did he now." Her eyes flashed. "Well, for future reference, yes, you should always check with me first. You know how men are. I had a very specific guest list for tonight. Very important people, if you take my meaning. I can't invite just anyone. I'm sure you understand."

"Yes, of course," I said, not missing the barb in her comment. But I wasn't going to let her snide remarks run me off. I knew this was a test of my mettle, just as she always tested her other friends. I had to hold my ground. "I'll just retire to the study or the patio and stay out of sight." The two places where the men usually gathered, and we both knew it.

"No, no, that's all right," she said, her eyes on mine. "You're already dressed and already here. You may as well stay with us."

A guest joined us, and her attention was redirected.

As they moved away, I breathed a sigh of relief. Thankful for the reprieve, I made polite conversation with the others and met a few new people. When I looked to a waiter for a glass of champagne, I found Ned gazing at me. He smiled good-naturedly and held up his drink in a sort of salute. I returned a polite smile and looked away. Evalyn had already accused him of sleeping with me at the previous party, and I didn't want to give her any reason to suspect there really was something between Ned and me. He'd been kind, friendly, complimentary but never out of line. I shifted from one foot to the other, deciding if it was a good idea to say a proper hello to Ned and to thank him for the invitation to the party or to avoid speaking with him directly.

I didn't want to be rude, so I started in his direction, but before I reached him, Evalyn slipped her hand over his arm. Their voices drifted over the hubbub in the room toward me.

"Did you see all the hens gathered around Lizzie?" Ned said, draining his glass. "She's made quite a place for herself here, hasn't she? Everyone likes her. She may usurp you as queen bee one of these days, Evie."

She swatted his arm. "As if that would ever happen."

My footsteps faltered. Me, the queen bee? Hardly. Everyone had admired my dress, but that was all. And I was surprised Ned would needle his wife in the way it would bother her most. He had to know how much it meant to her to be at the center of every crowd.

As I reached them, Ned nodded in greeting. "I'm afraid I'd better dash. The fellas are waiting for their cigars."

I didn't dare watch him go, and flushed with relief when Carrie joined us, greeting Evalyn first with a kiss on the cheek and then making her way around the circle. Evalyn and the others welcomed her as if nothing had happened between them. The slights appeared to have been entirely forgotten. In fact, the women formed a protective circle around her, and

I knew that was the stark difference between the others and me. In the end, I was not one of them. They wouldn't come to my rescue or forgive a silly spat between us. I would always need to mind myself around them, despite their relatively welcoming behavior of late. Underneath my beautiful new clothes, I was still the help, still a working woman from an ordinary family who could be cast out at any moment. Carrie, on the other hand, had already been forgiven and always would be.

After initial greetings, Evalyn invited everyone to join her in the parlor. Bea motioned to me to follow, but I was deeply aware Evalyn hadn't invited me with the others. Perhaps I was overthinking things; she had a large array of important guests after all, and I hardly fit that description. Still, I followed and managed to secure a seat next to her on the sofa. She immediately fell into a conversation with a guest to her right, ignoring me entirely. I minded my posture and smoothed the nonexistent wrinkles in the scarlet fabric of my dress. As I watched women swan across the room and gentlemen laugh boisterously in corners, I felt increasingly uneasy.

"Aren't you going to introduce me to your friend?" the woman on Evalyn's right said during a pause in their conversation.

"Hello," I said with a faint smile. "I'm Elisabeth."

Evalyn didn't make eye contact and waved her hand toward me. "Oh, this is only my jeweler, Lizzie Beaumont of Beaumont Jewelers."

Only her jeweler? Had I been demoted from friend to "the help" as Gwen had once called me? I was too stunned to realize Evalyn hadn't bothered to have the courtesy to tell me the woman's name either.

"I've heard a lot about you," the woman said. "I'm Tabitha."

"How do you do," I managed, trying to ignore the panic trickling through me. Evalyn had demoted me, relegating me to just another member of her staff. Carrie had warned me this was Evalyn's way. I hadn't wanted to believe it.

"I've heard your work is divine," Tabitha cooed. "I'll need a new necklace for the gala I'm hosting this autumn. Are you taking new clients?"

I couldn't tell if she was trying to be polite or if she'd truly heard I was skilled. I glanced at Evalyn. She avoided my eyes and looked around the room.

"Yes, I'd be delighted to show you the Beaumont collection," I said, my stomach churning.

"Let's set a date," Tabitha said, her tone eager. "By the way, your dress and hair are lovely. You look a bit like Evie. Has anyone told you that?"

"Doesn't she though?" Gwen added. "Our little Lizzie was once a caterpillar but now she's our butterfly."

"Careful, you two," Evalyn said, "I know I've done good work here, but you'll give Lizzie a big head."

I felt my cheeks go hot with as much embarrassment as irritation. A big head? Suddenly it was clear that Evalyn didn't know me at all, and it was obvious she didn't care to. In fact, I couldn't remember her asking me a single question about myself. I was nothing but a passing amusement, and her interest in me was already evaporating. She wanted to keep me at my lowly position, to keep me dependent on her. She wanted everyone beholden to her, just as Carrie had warned me she would. The power I felt dressed in Evalyn's clothes and Father's jewelry vanished. All I wanted was to be me, to look like me, to be home, away from the never-ending charade.

Sympathy flashed across Tabitha's face, and she changed the subject. "Are there any new jewelry pieces you think I'd like? Anything specific?"

I eyed the diamond necklace stacked with baguettes that came to a V a few inches below her throat and knew precisely what she'd like. "My father has been working on a new exquisite emerald necklace, bracelet, and earring set."

The truth was he had been working on the set since last summer, but he'd abandoned it. Now he was too busy poring over the sketches for his new collection.

Evalyn's head snapped in my direction. "Why did you keep that news all to yourself? I'd like to see it, too."

Of course she would. She couldn't let anyone else purchase a new item unless she had a chance to first.

"I'd be happy to show it to you." I touched Evalyn's hand, making a show of our "friendship," despite the many snubs she'd delivered that night.

She withdrew her hand. "Why don't I take a look at it tomorrow. I can stop by the boutique on my way to meet Carrie and some friends for lunch."

A lunch I wasn't invited to either. So it was true; Evalyn *was* becoming bored with me. I thought again of Carrie's warning the morning she had stopped by my workshop. I could see now she'd told me out of kindness. She'd wanted to warn me not to become part of a world as shifting as the waves and as perilous as a riptide. And yet I'd dismissed her warning out of hand. I was too desperate for work, too desperate for answers, too desperate for approval of who I was and who I wanted to be.

I swallowed the rest of my champagne, trying to quell the panic clogging my throat. "If you'll excuse me. I'm off to the ladies.'" Once in the safety of the hall and out of sight, I inhaled sharply, deciding whether to stay or to go home. But I'd come all this way, and it would be rude to leave so soon, despite Evalyn's slights.

With a deep breath, I joined the others as we filtered back to the ballroom with the larger party. Soon, I found myself receding from the crowd to stand near the window and nibble hors d'oeuvres while I sipped from my champagne glass until the wine grew too warm to drink. I was biding my time until I might slip away, unnoticed. As I edged around the exterior wall, I mingled with various guests.

When I glided toward the door to make my exit, a conversation drifted past me, and I stalled beside a waiter carrying a tray of full glasses, pretending to consider another drink.

"Her brother?" Sharon's voice. "I could see why she had a tryst with him. He was so handsome. Those blue eyes and that smile."

"He was a golden boy for sure," Bea replied. "He stood out, even among our husbands, didn't he?"

They giggled.

I snatched a fresh glass from the waiter's tray and tucked in against the wall a few feet away, waiting, listening. What golden boy? What brother? Dread pooled in the pit of my stomach.

"Jet was driving like a maniac that night, drunk out of his mind. It's not at all a surprise that he had an accident."

Jet? Carrie's husband? My breath grew shallow.

"No," Bea said, shaking her head. "Jet doesn't have it in him."

"Carrie swears he was out of town that week on business," Gwen said.

"He was definitely out of town," Bea confirmed. "Ned was with him."

Sharon's voice. "Which was how Carrie was able to meet up with her lover boy in the first place."

My stomach heaved. Did they mean Carrie and Julien? I listened intently, straining over the music and the hundreds of voices. Who else could they mean? There was the accident, the car.

"It's a shame, isn't it?" Gwen replied. "Carrie is such a flirt. It's not as if he was something special to her."

"Mmm, yes, she's always been a bored wife. Like the rest of us."

They giggled again, as if it were the funniest thing in the world to be a bored wife, planning their next tryst.

"I don't have any interest in dabbling with other men," Bea said. "One is more than enough. Most of the time, I want him out of my hair, too."

"Wouldn't it be grand if they were out of the picture entirely and we lived in one big dormitory?"

"Like college."

They prattled on, but I didn't hear the rest.

Carrie's lover. Jet was driving like a maniac.

Suddenly I couldn't play coy anymore. I inserted myself into their conversation. "Whose brother? You said Carrie had a lover."

They glanced at me in surprise. Sharon and Gwen wouldn't meet my eye.

"Rita's brother," Bea said, filling the silence. "He's a handsome devil. What are you doing there hiding behind the curtains? Come play with us."

I ignored her attempt at humor. She was lying. I could sense it in the way she wouldn't meet my eyes.

"Jet was driving drunk?" I persisted.

"Darling, he's always driving drunk," Bea said. "The lot of them are. He wrecked his car not long ago."

"We aren't exactly angels in that department either, are we?" Gwen said, and they all laughed.

My instincts flared, and I had to push them for more information. I had to know for sure that they weren't referring to Julien. "Carrie's lover was Rita's brother?"

"Carrie will be mortified if you bring that up," Bea replied. "Let's drop it. How about we dance instead?"

They all smiled at me, put a hand on my arm as if to console me like a child, and directed me across the ballroom.

I couldn't breathe, couldn't be in the presence of these people another minute. "I...I'm not feeling well," I stuttered. "Why don't you dance without me? I'll see you soon."

"Good night, Miss Lizzie," Bea replied, blowing me a kiss.

The others made their goodbyes but didn't try to stop me.

I walked to the door as if in a fever dream.

"You seem rather gloomy tonight, ma'am," Jerry said, as I reached the doorway of the ballroom.

"I don't feel quite like myself," I admitted.

"I hope you haven't come down with something," he replied. "You're shivering."

I was. I couldn't stop shaking. Carrie and Julien. Jet, the car accident. Did Jet have it in him? I squeezed my eyes closed an instant. This was all conjecture, I told myself. Not a single word of it could be proven.

"You're definitely ill. Here." Jerry put his jacket around my shoulders. "Come, I'll order the car to take you home."

"Let me just tell Evalyn."

But as I stood in the doorway and peered across the ballroom, my eyes met Evalyn's icy gaze. She didn't nod, didn't smile, didn't wave. She gave me her back, and I knew my welcome to her illustrious world was coming to an end.

26

It had been two weeks since Evalyn's formal soiree, and I'd heard nothing from her since. Though I hoped she was simply busy, I knew deep down something had shifted between us. My insides churned with anxiety day after day as I obsessively recalled the details from that night and the conversation I'd overheard about Carrie's lover and Jet's accident. I wanted to confront Carrie, to ask her about Rita's brother, to hear her say it was another lie, that even the women in her circle who called themselves friends were jealous of her and perpetuated rumors about her. I hoped I'd be afforded the chance to see Carrie again at Evalyn's one day soon.

I felt as if I stood on a precipice, my world shifting like sand with the tides, and I didn't know what came next. A part of me was relieved by the reprieve, but the other part of me longed to be included, wished I could be Evalyn's new favorite again, paraded around like a beautiful and precious doll.

I longed to call the McLeans' residence but didn't to give Evalyn space, to give myself space, too. Still, I counted the days until it was time to return to Friendship in an official capacity for my jewelry cleaning duties. When the day finally came on a steamy May morning, I wore one of my many gifted day dresses, spent extra time on my hair and makeup, and left with my tool kit in hand.

I was surprised to arrive to a quiet house.

"Mrs. McLean isn't here," Jerry said. "Do you have an appointment?"

I frowned. "Is she out for the day? I can stop by later after I finish a few of my other house calls. This is my scheduled cleaning day."

"She's left town, ma'am," Jerry replied.

"I'm sorry? She's left? Where did she go?"

"Ohio with Ned on business and then they're off to Kentucky, ma'am. For the derby."

The truth stung. Once upon a time, she'd mentioned taking me with her to the derby.

"She also asked me to give you this for repair." Jerry handed me a wrapped parcel.

I opened it, finding the headband I'd made for her. The feather was broken in three places, several of the gems had been plucked from the fabric, and the top edges of the band had begun to unravel as if it had been teased apart. Either the children had gotten ahold of it, or the headband had been intentionally damaged.

"Ma'am?" he said when I didn't answer. "I'm afraid she's left explicit instructions to keep her collection under lock and key."

"That's all right," I said, trying to hide the tremor in my voice. "I'll see her when she returns."

His eyes were contrite. "I'd be happy to leave a message for her."

It was bad enough she'd left town without mentioning it to me, but to explicitly keep me away from her collection was a message—and I could read it, loud and clear. I'd done something wrong, made some wrong step. I thought of Ned's flirtations, her accusations, but somehow I knew it was more than that, some other offense I'd made without intent.

I remembered Ned and Evalyn's exchange the night of the formal party at their home on McPherson Square.

"Did you see all the hens gathered around Lizzie?" Ned had said. *"She's made quite a place for herself here, hasn't she? Everyone appears to like her. She may usurp you as queen bee."*

Evalyn had swatted his arm. *"As if that would ever happen."*

Now there was the destroyed headband, her absence without explanation, and the way she'd dashed me off at her diplomatic party like a fleck of dust. And I understood something. Evalyn saw me as a threat, and she was pushing me out of her life.

Jerry's eyes softened when he saw my expression. "I'm sorry, ma'am. I'm sure there's some explanation."

"Of course," I said diplomatically, but I knew Evalyn wasn't one for explanations. When she'd made up her mind, she'd made up her mind, and that was the end of the story.

I left with a boulder-sized lump in my throat.

An hour later, I arrived home to find two notes tucked into our letter box. Grimacing, I opened the pale-yellow note first. It was from my mineralogist friend, Ken Davis. Happy to see his name, I raced through his letter.

Dear Elisabeth,

I've recently learned we're hiring a lab assistant in my department at the museum. I hope you will consider applying. You would make a wonderful addition to our staff.

Please call by the house should you have any questions.

Yours,
Ken

On the bottom of the card, he'd written his telephone number. I mused at Ken's kindness, but no matter what, I couldn't abandon my father. He needed me, and I knew I must let go of the silly dream of working at the museum.

I turned over the other envelope, deciding whether I wanted to open it. I knew what it would say, and I didn't need another warning, especially now. Curiosity got the better of me.

Please do as I say and stay away. It's for the best. They are not your friends. And your luck may soon run out. Your brother didn't deserve to die.

I read it and reread it, my irritation overshadowing my fear. Frustrated, I threw down the note and tore inside the house and fished the other noisome letters from my desk. One by one, I laid them out on the table to examine them. I searched for some clue as to who had sent them, only to come up empty once more. I plopped down into a chair and rubbed my eyes. After feeling sorry for myself for some time, I reached for the notes again, tracing the handwriting with my fingertip. The script was identical on each of the cards, so they were certainly from the same person, but the handwriting itself was puzzling. It wasn't curled and elegant as if written by one of the high-society ladies with expensive tutors whom I'd come to know. This handwriting was blocky and looked like it was written by an unsteady hand, someone who was uncertain of their writing abilities, in fact, which only confused me more.

Who would want to warn me? I could think of only one person in the circle who had helped me secure the job at Evalyn's and one who had cautioned me, told me Evalyn wasn't as she seemed.

Carrie Wellington.

I was done waiting for an invitation, done being threatened, done living in the dark.

In a swift and decisive motion, I stuffed the notes into my handbag and made a beeline for the door.

27

I stood on the doorstep of a large redbrick town house with black shutters and white trim. Purple irises flourished in the small garden plot out front. I knew the Georgetown house, had been there one other time before with Evalyn before racing off to a fancy restaurant for lunch. Now, as I stood on the sidewalk eyeing the motorcar parked in the street out front, its trunk popped open and the servant in livery standing over it as he worked to make several suitcases fit, I felt changed, different, and I knew the world had shifted and would never be the same again.

Hands trembling, I reached for the knocker on the door, but it opened suddenly.

"Lizzie?" Carrie's face paled as if she'd seen a ghost. "What are you doing here?" She looked over her shoulder, closed the door quietly behind her, and raced down the front steps.

"I need to talk to you about something," I said. "It's important."

"I can't right now," she said. "I'm in a rush. We're off to Kentucky. From there, I'll be traveling to our summer home in Rhode Island at the beach. I need some time away."

"And why is that?" I asked, crossing my arms over my chest, my patience wearing thin.

She smiled ruefully, touched her wavy hair with a gloved hand. "If you must know, Jet is convinced I have a new lover. He thinks if I spend time in Rhode Island, it will be good for us both. The irony is he's the one with a new lover. He plans to stay here in town while I summer up north."

"I'm not here to make small talk," I cut her off. "I'm here about the letters. Do you really think I wouldn't know they were from you?"

Carried frowned. "What letters?"

"There's no sense in playing coy. I know you sent them. The cream envelopes with silver trim?"

"I don't know what you're talking about," she insisted.

I pulled one from my handbag and read it aloud.

I read another and another, and when I stopped, I searched her face for some sign of recognition, but she seemed as puzzled by them as me.

"I don't know who wrote those," she said. "I swear. I can show you my stationery if you like."

I wanted to shout at her, to call her a liar, but the problem was I believed her. "If it wasn't you, then who? Who would send these?"

She shook her head. "I don't know. But I would never be that rude to you after all you've been through. Not after all you've lost."

"All I've lost," I repeated. "Since when does anyone care about what I've lost?" I was angry, irrational, unwilling to give her or anyone the benefit of the doubt.

"I've been nothing but kind—"

"Why did you warn me about Evalyn that day when you came to my boutique?"

She clenched her perfect jaw and pushed a lock of red hair out of her perfect face. "In case you haven't noticed, she's not the most reliable person in the world. I also did it to be your friend."

I blew out a frustrated breath. "But we hardly know each other, and we come from two different worlds."

"Your brother," she said with a shrug. "He was a wonderful person, and I've felt…such sympathy for you. It was a terrible loss."

I swallowed hard, looked down at the letters in my hand. "What about Rita's brother? Was he your lover?"

She frowned. "Rita's brother? Who told you she has a brother? She's an only child."

Heart quickening, I replayed Bea and Gwen's conversation in my head. Carrie taking a lover, Jet driving fast, the car accident. And now this, Bea's outright lie about who Carrie's lover was. Bea had been covering for someone. Perhaps they all had. They'd all worn jewelry Julien had designed and sold to them the day after I'd mentioned something to Evalyn about Carrie's pendant. I'd known then it was strange, too coincidental, and it was. They'd been instructed to throw me off the scent.

The last of the pieces slowly fell into place.

"It was him, wasn't it?" I said, capturing her gaze.

Her shoulders fell, and she blew out a breath. "Oh, Lizzie." She covered her forehead with a gloved hand, rubbed her eyes. "Julien was different from the rest." Her tone turned wistful. "He was funny and warm and so alive."

"And now he's none of those things," I said, my voice cracking.

At least she had the decency to look pained.

"You had an affair with him. I want to hear you say it," I demanded, my voice growing shrill.

She looked down, hesitated, and at last said, "It was so much more than an affair. I was prepared to leave my husband to be with Julien. I flirted with other men, but I'd never cheated on my husband before, no matter how often he'd cheated on me."

She reached for me, to console me or to hold me there, I didn't know, but I stepped out of her reach.

"Don't," I huffed, on the verge of losing my temper entirely. "Does Evalyn know?"

She nodded. "Of course. She hired you because I encouraged her to help you. Now I know she only did it to dangle a Beaumont in front of me. To remind me that she kept my secret close." Her laugh was dark, bitter. "Evalyn always has to have the upper hand. She could expose my indiscretion at any moment if she wanted to."

"I don't understand," I said. "Why would she? What would she have to gain?"

"Ned made advances toward me when we first met, and she's never forgotten it, though I had nothing to do with him in that way. That isn't my style, to steal another woman's husband."

Ned made advances toward her? It made sense given her beauty, and yet somehow it stung a little, too. "And the others?" I asked. "Do they know about my brother?"

"They know everything because she told them out of spite one afternoon."

So they'd all known the truth and had kept it from me to protect Carrie or, more importantly, to follow Evalyn's wishes.

And then another memory surfaced. A memory as vibrant and real as the sunlight overhead burst behind my eyes. A memory of that night in November that I'd never forget.

28

It had been a cool autumn night. November had come early on the back of a short rainy season followed by a parade of colorful leaves. Henry had bundled himself into a coat and cap, and I'd wrapped up in my favorite blue scarf.

"I want to show you something," Henry had said, leading us away from the sidewalk and down a short grassy hill.

Dew coated the squared toes of my ankle boots, and the damp air seeped through the meager protection of my stockings.

"Where are we going?" I asked. "Julien was nervous this morning. He said he has something to tell us."

"I know. I'm a little afraid to hear what he has to say. But this will only take a moment, and then we'll meet up with him," Henry insisted. As we crested another small hill, he pointed at a massive southern oak. "Isn't that tree magnificent? It must be three hundred years old."

The old oak seemed to peer down at the cluster of buildings nestled in the valley below it. Its branches spread wide as if competing with the undulating land that stretched out on either side of it. Golden leaves clung stubbornly to its branches, though the brisk wind jostled them playfully, carrying with it a promise of early winter.

"It's beautiful," I said. "It's amazing how quiet and distant the field feels, even with the city so close."

He grabbed my hand, tugging me forward until we stood beneath the tree's webbed branches on a carpet of colorful leaves, the smell of must and damp vegetation permeating the air.

"Elisabeth." He cupped my cheek with his hand. "I've been wanting to talk to you about something. About us."

"Us?" I felt my cheeks flame beneath his touch, but I didn't look away lest the moment dissipate and I was left there alone, wishing, dreaming, when none of it was real.

Henry smiled. "Us," he said. His beautiful face was dappled with moonlight, his breath sweet. And as he leaned toward me, my heart skipped a beat.

"Us," I breathed, tilting my face to his.

When his lips met mine, something inside me unlocked—something my body had always known, even if I hadn't been able to admit it to myself. I loved Henry Cooper. I'd loved him since we were children. I wrapped my arms around his neck and leaned into his warmth. The world melted into the night around us. We stayed together that way for what felt like time immeasurable.

Eventually, our noses grew cold, and we laughed quietly in our shared intimacy. And everything in the world felt right for a moment.

When Henry glanced at his watch, the spell was broken. "Damn, we're nearly half an hour late meeting him. We'd better go."

We locked hands, giddy with this new sensation, the new realization that we could be together, and not only as friends. We were in love.

Laughing, joyous, we dashed across the lawn, down the hill to the sidewalk. I didn't know where we'd go from here, but in that moment, I was the happiest woman alive. The kiss, that perfect night, had pushed away all the dread I'd felt about the evening ahead.

Julien had been so busy lately and acting so unusual that I was relieved when he promised to tell us everything over dinner that night. He'd chose an out-of-the-way restaurant on the edge of town. Normally I would have complained, questioned his odd choice, but I was too happy to be meeting Henry, too. Too happy to spend an evening with my favorite men in all the world.

As Henry and I raced to the bottom of the hill and down the street, turning the corner, the restaurant came into view. Julien paced the edge of the sidewalk, peering at the occasional cars that passed.

"What's he doing?" I asked.

Henry squeezed my hand. "I don't know, but I can't imagine why he'd be waiting outside for us, though...we are late. Maybe he's just impatient."

I shook my head. "No, he told me he might bring a friend, whatever that means. Perhaps he's waiting for him."

"He must be as late as we are," Henry said, peering into the dark.

Even from several paces away, I could see Julien's features in the lamplight, his acute disappointment, his longing. We'd always been able to feel each other's pain as if it were our own. That was the way of twins.

Emotion caught in my throat as I realized the friend he'd mentioned might not be a man but a woman. Someone he was courting perhaps? And she hadn't come.

"Do you think it's a woman?" I said as we walked more quickly. We were almost there.

Henry squeezed my hand. "I don't know, but given how bizarre he's been acting, I have my suspicions for sure."

"Julien!" I called, waving to him, my arm stretched overhead.

He turned at the sound of his name.

In that moment, a woman wearing a headscarf stepped out from the shadows in the parking lot—just as a car raced around the corner, swerving dangerously, driving too fast. Oblivious to the car, Julien beamed at the woman, and I knew we'd guessed right. He had a new girlfriend, and he wanted us to meet her. But why hadn't he introduced us sooner, and why had he been acting so strangely about it all?

And then time collapsed and all moved as if in slow motion.

The sound of a roaring engine. The driver narrowly missing a fire hydrant. The squealing of tires as they hit a puddle and skidded.

In less than an instant—a hundredth of a second—Julien's face changed to one of surprise. His eyes went wide.

Henry's voice echoed in my memory. Shouting my brother's name.

The car sped away as my mind grappled with the scene before me, trying to understand what I was seeing. Julien was on the ground. Had the car hit him? What was happening? The woman bent over him a moment and then fled, the wind tearing away the headscarf that covered her hair. Her red hair.

Screams drowned out every thought, the sound of sirens in the distance, until at last, Henry took me in his arms, and I realized then they were my screams. I screamed and shook and lay in the street, calling his name like a siren, covering his body with mine.

My beloved, ebullient, ambitious, perfectly imperfect brother was dead.

29

I gasped as the memory pulsed in the air around me.

"You were there!" I said, voice at a fever pitch. "It was you he wanted me to meet!" At last, I knew the truth, and it was worse than I could have imagined. Jet Wellington, one of the most powerful bankers in the country, hadn't liked the fact that his wife was falling for another man, and Jet had either killed Julien or hired someone else to do the job. I gaped at her in horror, eyes welling with tears.

Carrie reached for my hands, and I stumbled backward a step.

She looked as if she might be sick. "That night was a horrible accident. My husband had just come home from the betting tables at the Oyster Club. He'd been drinking, probably had smoked opium, too. I don't know, but he was a mess. He'd wanted to scare Julien off, send a message. Lizzie, you must believe me. Jet wouldn't hurt him intentionally. He said our chauffeur pushed him out of the driver's seat, that it was our driver who'd had an accident. But I'm not...I'm not certain of anything. I don't know." She shook her head. "I only remember the headlights that night, seeing Julien's wide eyes, you and your young man bent over his crumpled body. The way I'd run from him. From it all." She closed her eyes, releasing a stream of tears.

I shook my head, stepped backward, my breath coming in great heavy gasps.

Lies. It was all a lie.

She was covering for her husband, and we both knew it. He'd been the one driving that night. He'd been the one who'd had the accident, not her chauffeur, not some hired hit man. But it could never be proven. Jet Wellington and his network of powerful allies wouldn't allow him to pay the consequences for taking the life of a lowly jeweler who was sleeping with his wife. Men of their caliber deserved better.

"Shut up!" I screamed, covering my ears with my hands, trying to block the terrible memory. Trying to cork the pain oozing from every inch of my body. "I can't. Please stop talking!"

"You must believe me when I say that night was a mistake," she pleaded. "A terrible tragedy. And I will never forgive myself for not running away with Julien the first time he asked me to. I live in this big empty house with a man who sees me as something else he owns. I'm…I'm so alone."

"You're alone? *You're* alone! I don't care if you're lonely. I lost the most important person in the world because of your greed. What is it with you people? You have this…this insatiable need to have it all, at any cost!"

"Please try to understand." She reached for me. "Jet married me to access his trust fund. He doesn't love me. We barely spend time in the same room together, let alone in the same bed." Her eyes filled, and her voice wavered as she went on. "I know that what Julien and I had was unconventional, but I don't believe loving someone is wrong, no matter what the circumstances are. Things aren't that simple. They never are."

"They are simple," I said, now shaking violently. "When you love someone and you aren't available to be with them, you let them go. This is your fault!"

A trail of tears streaked her powdered cheeks. "I'm devastated I've lost him."

"No," I said through clenched teeth. "You don't get to be devastated. You hardly knew him. He was nothing but a glimpse of a better life to you. To me, he was my best friend, my brother, and you took him from me."

I didn't want to hear any more—couldn't bear it. I stumbled into the bright light of midday, away from Carrie and her perfect Georgetown house and her perfect car, desperate to outrun the sorrow flooding my senses.

If only Henry and I had ignored our impulses, not skipped away over the grass into that moonlit field for a moment of selfish passion, we would have been on time. We would have seen the car speeding toward him and skidding on wet pavement. We could have pulled Julien away from the curb. We could have saved my brother's life.

If only.

Now my beloved brother was a whisper on the wind, a shadow hovering at the edges of my vision, and yet the part of me connected to him, even still, felt so alive I could hardly contain it, contain him, be both of us separately and myself all at once.

I walked blindly toward nothing and no one until my ragged breathing ebbed and my feet chafed against my shoes and the only thought that remained was how I longed to relive that night, to be there for him when it mattered.

But I wasn't and I couldn't, and nothing could change the fact that he was gone.

30

After my confrontation with Carrie, I floated through the house from one room to the other, despair and anger warring inside me. I was glad Carrie would be out of town for months. I didn't want to think about her or be faced with the trouble of avoiding her. And yet I couldn't banish what she'd said about her husband from my mind. Was he the one responsible for Julien's death, or was it the chauffeur? Did it matter? The tires had hit a wet patch in the road and skidded uncontrollably. I'd seen it myself that night. I'd seen it behind my eyes a thousand times, every moment of every day. Carrie believed Julien's death was an accident, and though I wasn't inclined to believe anything she said, I knew, at least in part, she was right. Julien's death was a horrible tragedy but an accident either way, whether I wanted to admit it or not.

I also understood why Julien hadn't wanted to tell me about Carrie. I wouldn't agree he should spend time with a married woman, and given his track record, I wouldn't have believed he would commit to her. For Carrie to leave her husband would have made a mess of both of their lives. She would be cast out of her social circles, and he would have put the Beaumont reputation in danger. Never mind the harm he'd caused to his many new friendships with Jet and Ned and the other husbands.

Julien's dream of expanding the business was a bust—they'd never support a man making off with one of their friends' wives.

When I'd thoroughly wrung myself out, obsessively reviewing the details, the conversations, the way Evalyn's friends had acted, and the horrible events of that night, I flopped down on the sofa out of sheer exhaustion.

I'd scarcely closed my eyes when the telephone rang.

I sat up, frowning. It was half past nine. Who could be calling at this hour? I could think of only one person who would be selfish enough to ignore the time. Who would demand her wish be fulfilled as soon as she had one. Suddenly hopeful I hadn't been entirely shunned, I lunged for the telephone.

"Lizzie? Hi, it's Bea. I'm sorry it's so late."

"Oh," I said, not bothering to hide the disappointment in my voice. "Bea, hello. Is everything all right?"

"Unfortunately, no. It isn't." She paused, and I could make out the faint sound of her sniffling.

"What's happened?" I said, gripping the receiver.

"It's Evie's son, Vinnie. He's"—her voice cracked—"he's been in an accident. Hit by a car. He's...he's just passed, the poor child."

I gasped. The child, named after Evalyn's older brother—who had also been killed in a car accident—was dead of the same cause.

As was Julien, a voice whispered in my head.

Bile surged up my throat. The curse. The Hope Diamond.

Bad luck will befall you.

And it had come for Evalyn again. I shook my head. No, it couldn't be. My God, that sweet little boy so full of life, gone too young.

My heart ached as I remembered our conversation the day I showed little Vinnie how to use the jeweler's tools, and again, seeing him sword fight with Ned on the lawn. The handful of other instances

I'd seen the child, he'd brightened every room he stepped into, just as his mother often did. I couldn't believe he was gone. Grief swelled until I felt I'd drown. My throat was raw with it. Vinnie, dead at nine years old. It was unimaginable.

When I didn't reply, Bea filled in the silence. "I'm not sure when the funeral service will be, but I wanted you to know. We're all stunned, of course. And Evie is… Well, I've been here all evening and need to go home, but I hate to leave her alone, and the others haven't made it home from the races yet. She's hysterical, Lizzie. Could you come over for a little while? The doctor has given her something to sleep, but she hasn't nodded off yet. I didn't know who else to call."

I gripped the phone. "Yes, of course. I'm on my way."

"I'm afraid Mrs. McLean isn't seeing any guests," Jerry said after he'd greeted me. His eyes were red, his shoulders slumped.

Guest. I'd been relegated to a guest when once I'd been called her friend. A pang hit me as I realized my suspicions had been correct all along. I was entertainment for a woman who was lost, who lacked meaning in her life. She'd always had too much of everything and everyone, and yet I'd been a fool for her whims. I'd lost myself somewhere amid the parties and luncheons and too many cocktails. Despite the hateful comments and the way she'd toyed with others, I'd considered Evalyn a friend.

"Bea called me," I said. "She asked that I look after Evalyn for a while." But perhaps it was better that I left. It was clear Evalyn didn't want me here anymore.

Bea breezed into the front hall. "I'm so glad you're here." As Jerry stepped aside, she yanked my arm and pulled me to her. "She's been unhinged. Wailing uncontrollably, screaming at Ned, at the staff. Ned is roaming the grounds somewhere… I finally got her to take something to help her sleep."

Bea's face was swollen, her hair mussed, and she smelled of whiskey. She'd clearly been crying, too. I returned her embrace.

"I'm so sorry," I said. "I can't believe it. He was so young. Such a darling little boy."

"To lose a child… I could never imagine it until today." She wiped at her eyes. "That poor boy."

"You're a good friend to her," I said.

Confusion passed over her features. "Of course. I've known Evie for ten years. And losing one of your babies is the worst thing a mother can imagine. I couldn't let her go through that alone."

My throat was tight as I thought of the worst thing I could imagine happening and how I'd gone through it almost entirely alone. "She's lucky to have you," I said.

"I'm exhausted. I've been here most of the evening, and I need a break," she said. "I gave her a double dose of Veronal to sleep. Perhaps check on her in a couple of hours? Keep her company should she wake?"

I nodded. "I will."

As Bea left, I wondered what Evalyn would say when she found me there at her side in her most vulnerable moment. Perhaps I should leave her a note and return home? If she really had taken a powerful dose of Veronal, it could be hours and hours before she stirred.

At last, I decided to stay, to rest on the sofa until she awakened. Only, I couldn't rest. I tossed and turned until I pushed up from the sofa and wandered into the parlor. I looked around for a place to sit, for a book or a deck of cards, for something to occupy my hands and most of all my mind. Nausea roiled in my belly each time I thought of little Vinnie, imagined his young body crumpled and bloody, the way

Julien's had been. I squeezed my eyes closed, pushing away the image. The poor child. He was a sweet, convivial little boy.

Jerry appeared in the doorway. "Can I bring you anything, ma'am? A drink perhaps? Something to eat?"

"A drink would be nice. Whatever you have that's easy. Thank you."

"Yes, ma'am."

He returned with not one but two whiskeys and held one out to me. The other he retained for himself. "I felt today's events called for one."

I nodded. We sipped from our glasses in companionable silence for several long moments until at last, I said, "How did it happen?"

"He was hit by a car, ma'am. It was more of a hard nudge than anything, because the car was barely moving when Vinnie ran into the street. Apparently he got up from the pavement a little dazed and continued on his way at first. The McLeans were alerted about the incident and were already on their way home to look in on him. In fact, Mrs. McLean had had some premonition that her son wasn't well. Vinnie passed away a few hours later. The doctor said he was bleeding internally." He took a deep drink from his glass.

"Did it happen in Kentucky?"

"No, ma'am. Mr. and Mrs. McLean left the children at home with their nannies while they were away in Ohio. They were scheduled to leave for the races tomorrow."

"Of course, I see," I said, though I didn't see. My father had never left Julien and me while he was on vacation. And he certainly wouldn't have left us to a nanny, but that was the difference between the wealthy and those who worked for a living. We formed closer attachments, real bonds, and nurtured our relationships as a matter of course. Or perhaps out of necessity because we simply didn't have the opportunity to make a different choice. Either way, I couldn't imagine having so much distance from my father.

"I was surprised to see you'd come, ma'am," Jerry said, swilling the last of his whiskey.

"Why is that? I am Evalyn's friend after all." I cringed inwardly at my unintentional harsh tone. It wasn't his fault that she had distanced herself from me of late. "I'm sorry. I didn't mean to be rude. I'm just... tired. Concerned."

He offered a conciliatory smile. "What I meant to say is that I thought you might wish to steer clear of the household given the events and...the things we've discussed before about the diamond."

"The bad luck, you mean."

"Yes, ma'am. As you can see, it affects all who spend time here, in her presence and in the presence of the diamond. I'd hate to see bad luck befall you. Again."

Bad luck befall me...again.

An echo of recognition struck me, and I gasped. "Jerry? Did you send those notes to my house? The warnings?"

The color drained from his face, but he didn't reply.

"It was you!" I set down my glass. "They frightened me! At first anyway. The last note made me angry. Why didn't you just tell me you were concerned?"

"I didn't think you'd listen, ma'am. And after everything that happened here at the house and with your brother and now with little Vinnie... I'm sorry. I didn't mean to scare you. It's none of my business, but you were so kind. So different from the others. I was trying...I was trying to be—"

"You were trying to be a friend."

"Yes, ma'am. You've always treated me like a person. I wanted to pay you a kindness in return."

I laid a hand on his broad shoulder. "Thank you, but next time, just say so. There's no need for spooky notes. I accused Carrie of sending them."

His round face scrunched into a frown. "Oh goodness, I didn't expect that. I apologize."

"It's fine, really." After another companionable pause, I held up my glass. "Might I have another? I could use it."

"Right away, ma'am, but I'll sit this one out. I have some work to get back to."

"Of course. And, Jerry?" He turned back to me. "Thanks for being a friend. I didn't know how much I needed one."

He nodded. "Anytime, ma'am."

After he refilled my glass, he scuttled off in the direction of the kitchen while I sat in this grand parlor in this grand house alone. I couldn't stop thinking about the similarities in the deaths, the stream of misfortunes, and what on earth I was still doing there. I was putting myself firmly into harm's way, too. And yet it was all so absurd. Life was filled with heartbreak and difficulties, and no one was immune. No one walked through life unscathed, and everyone suffered a hardship of some kind, with or without a curse. To be alive was to feel, and to feel was to suffer.

Eventually, I drifted off to sleep—until a door slammed shut, rattling the windowpanes. I bolted upright, looked around in confusion for an instant before I remembered where I was.

Ned stalked across the room. His usually neat hair looked tossed as if by the wind, his tie was askew, and the right edge of his shirt was untucked. He reeked of whiskey.

"Ned," I said. I couldn't force out the insufficient condolences, the meaningless "I'm sorries." They wouldn't bring back his son, and they wouldn't make him feel better. Instead, I said, "If there is anything I can do to make you more comfortable, to take your mind off things, to help around the house—anything at all. I'm here. Evalyn is asleep."

He poured himself a large glass of whiskey, set down his drink, and grasped my hands, holding them so tightly his knuckles whitened. "Thank you." He released me and ran a hand through his hair, making it stick up in clumps. "You can have a drink with me."

We drank a whiskey and then two, while he told me stories about little Vinnie. At one point, he paused, and I knew he was crying. Emboldened by the whiskey, I laid my hand atop his for a brief instant. When he met my eye, I withdrew it quickly.

"I'll just look in on Evalyn," I said. "I'll be back in a moment."

I stood on wobbly legs and realized then how much I'd had to drink and how little I'd eaten that day. Clutching the railing, I took the stairs to Evalyn's bedroom, where she lay sprawled on the bed in an awkward pose. Her limbs were thrown across the covers. I pulled a blanket over her as I had my father for many months and tucked it in around her. I stared down at her, wishing her pain away. I knew something of that pain, of loss, even if it wasn't my child. That was a special kind of hell I hoped never to experience. Her face was streaked with black trails of makeup, and the skin beneath her eyes looked bruised. In this position, she was as ordinary as I was, as ordinary as anyone.

My eyes fell to her neck. She wasn't wearing the Hope? This was the only time I'd seen her without it, other than the night she'd put it on her dog. I wondered what she'd done with it. Perhaps the clasp had broken or come undone? I felt around her covers gently, groping for the rough edges of the necklace. I peered under the bed, looked through her vanity and the array of haphazard hair combs and tubes of makeup. I glanced around the room and spied it on the floor in the corner of the room, as if she'd clawed the thing from her neck and thrown it, and perhaps she had. Perhaps she'd desperately wanted to rid herself of the charm that wasn't so lucky after all.

I stared at it, couldn't look away. Should I... Could I...

Hands shaking, I carefully picked up the necklace. Cradling it gently, I tilted the Hope to catch the light, but the room was mostly in shadow, and the generous blue of the gemstone appeared almost black. My pulse thumped loudly in my ears as I stepped into the hallway where a lamp was ablaze beneath a large oval mirror on the wall.

Did I dare?

I gazed at myself in the mirror until my eyes became unfocused, my mouth a red slash, my form an indistinct outline. And I couldn't help myself. Mesmerized, I slipped the most infamous diamond in the world around my neck and fastened the clasp.

I don't know what I'd expected. A sudden sensation to ripple through me or some premonitory revelation to flash in my mind? Instead, I felt only the weight of the stunning necklace and its cool metal framework against the tender skin of my neck. I swayed as if in a trance, watching the light reflect off its facets, searching for the flash of red in its depths that made it so unique. I squinted, blurring my vision as I imagined those who had worn it before me through the centuries. Kings, actresses, sultans, and the wealthiest among the wealthy, and now, there was little me. *Foolish me.*

My gaze refocused abruptly.

Reflected in the mirror behind me stood a figure. Ned. I turned quickly, my mouth open to say something, but the words died on my tongue.

"I gave that to Evie as a wedding gift," he said quietly. He touched the diamond with his forefinger, traced its outline, and let his finger drift over each of the cushion diamonds along the chain until his fingertip brushed my collarbone.

"I'm sorry. I shouldn't be wearing this." I fumbled with the clasp. "I was looking in on Evalyn, and she wasn't wearing it. It looked like she'd thrown it in the corner… I don't know what I was thinking."

"You were tempted by its beauty. Just as I am tempted by yours."

My hands fell to my sides. Somewhere inside me, I knew pretty words didn't and shouldn't mean much—that Ned was out of his mind at the moment, and I'd had so much whiskey, I was hardly myself—and yet I felt myself drawn to his words and the brush of his finger on my skin.

"I'm ordinary, not beautiful," I insisted. "I always have been, but I'm fine with that. It's something I accepted many years ago."

"You don't see yourself as you are, Lizzie."

Words I'd heard before, from a man I loved. My heart squeezed as I stared back at Ned, thinking of one man, missing one man, loving one man, and it wasn't him.

In that moment, Ned tugged me toward him and pressed his lips against mine. He tasted of whiskey and cigarettes and the kind of longing I recognized in myself that I'd buried for so long. Only that longing wasn't for him. It wasn't for this. *What am I doing?*

I pulled away. "Ned," I said. "This isn't right—"

"Lizzie? What are you doing! Ned?" Evalyn shrieked, her voice so shrill it was otherworldly. Her eyes were crazed, her hair a mess. "My diamond," she gasped. "Why are you wearing it! You! You thief!"

"I'm sorry," I said, fumbling with the clasp. "It isn't what you think. I was here to look in on you, to see if you needed anything, and I found the necklace on the floor—"

"You found your way to my husband, too!"

"Calm down, Evie," Ned said, his words slurred from the whiskey. "Nothing happened, I swear."

"You were kissing her!" she screamed. "I knew it! And you! First you pretend to be all meek and sullen, and then you start dressing like me and taking over my friends, and now you try to steal my husband and my necklace! The night of the party, when you two were cozy, walking the grass in the moonlight, your giggles at my expense," she shouted. "I knew you were after my husband."

"Evalyn, that isn't true. I swear it." I tried to take off the cursed necklace, but my hands shook too violently.

"Let me," Ned said.

"Don't touch her!" Evalyn said, shoving Ned out of the way. She clawed at my neck.

I yelped in pain as she wrenched at the Hope Diamond, finally unclasping it and taking it from me. "I'm so sorry, Evalyn. It's not what it looks like. I swear, I—"

"You are not me. You are not his wife!" she screamed.

My own fury began to mount. She had some nerve, behaving as if I were the enemy when she had toyed with me from the beginning. "I know about Carrie and Julien, and so did you!" I said. "Why would you hire me, bring me into your home, and befriend me when all this time, the lot of you were hiding the truth?"

She sneered. "I agreed to hire you because Carrie felt so guilty about Julien that she begged me to. Said your business desperately needed help. I did it for her. And frankly, I enjoyed watching her squirm in your presence. She could hardly stand it. Serves her right after all those men fell at her feet like she was some kind of goddess."

Her jealousy oozed from every word, and I felt sick.

"Evie, you're out of your mind," Ned said.

Ned was right; she was out of her mind. We all were in that moment.

"I'm so sorry about Vinnie," I said, trying to calm her.

"Don't say his name! Get out! Now! I never want to see you again!" She shoved me, hard.

Surprised, I stumbled forward, landing on my hands and knees.

"Calm down, Evie," Ned said, gripping her arms and trying to hold her in place.

She screamed and struggled against him like a feral cat, shoving at him, swearing, as tears streaked down her face.

I took the stairs as fast as I could manage and ran through the house, unseeing, toward the door. I stepped outside into the night, the pressure in my chest building until I could scarcely breathe.

I touched my throat where the Hope had once been, where I had felt at once emboldened and strangled by its power. I didn't want to be here, didn't want to be her. I didn't want any of it or this life. I wanted to be myself, without pretenses and extravagances or jewelry worth more than a human life. I wanted my simple life back. The one filled with hope and laughter and, most of all, him, my brother.

A sob escaped my lips, and at long last, a deluge of hot tears began. And I walked alone, under the cover of night, toward home.

31

I couldn't remember how I found my way home that night. I remembered only the pain that had become too large to contain and the rain. The rain had coated my skin, slicked my hair to my face, pelted my cheeks like a punishment. I couldn't believe I'd let Ned kiss me. Worse still, I'd worn the Hope Diamond. I reached for the diamond at my neck over and over again as I thought of it, my fingers grasping at nothing. Relief flooded through me each time. I didn't want to see the stone again or to speak of it.

I reported all I'd learned about Jet Wellington and the chauffeur the night of the accident to the police. An investigation ensued, but nothing came of it. There was no evidence, and the Wellingtons had access to the best lawyers in Washington. But it did what I hoped it would do. It damaged their reputation, and Jet's business prospects suffered, for a time.

For the first time since Julien's death, I allowed the cruel capriciousness of the accident to envelop me so entirely, I lost sense of time and space. I wept great, shuddering sobs for hours, days, weeks until I was weak from the kind of pain that fills one to the brim, that makes it hard to face another moment of living and breathing. I'd been a ghost for months, a wisp of wind, a hollowed-out tree trying so hard not to feel anything. I'd thought Evalyn and her world would somehow make me feel less empty, less alone, but the truth was they had made things worse. I'd been living a life not my own and forsaken everything that was good and real and true about myself. Evalyn had taken Julien's place as the figure behind whom I'd hidden. I understood that now.

My father looked in on me as I grieved rather than the other way around. He lovingly nursed me back to the light. He said little, but I saw my pain reflected in his eyes and a kind of strength, too, and I reached for it, for him. We comforted each other, and little by little, I came back to life again.

As I recovered, so did Father. We went for long walks and talked about him. Julien might not be in the bedroom across the hall any longer, but he would always be one of the best parts of me. He'd live inside my memories and the part of me that only a twin could feel, that only a twin could know and understand. But I was at last beginning to embrace the small gift his absence afforded me: I was forced to know myself. To think about what I wanted outside of my dear brother. I was forced to examine my own heart and dreams and desires without seeking approval or instruction or even help from the person I'd leaned on too heavily, whose shadow I'd refused to step out of until now. I'd never known who Elisabeth Beaumont truly was, and I was discovering that I liked her. I didn't need the Evalyn McLeans of the world to make me feel worthwhile again.

One autumn day six months after the awful encounter with Evalyn and Ned, I slipped into one of my old familiar dresses that wasn't of the latest fashion, taking comfort in the soft, worn fabric. After, I bagged up everything Evalyn had given me to donate to a women's charity. I would buy my own clothes in time, those that suited my tastes and, above all, my comfort. Stomach rumbling, I headed downstairs for a late breakfast. My father joined me in the sunny kitchen in which I'd spent so many of my days laughing and listening to stories told around the table. That day, it didn't ache to be there amid the memories. It was a balm to my rawness, my uneven edges, and my tender new view of the world.

Father made us toast with jam and poured us each a cup of coffee. "Are you going to work on your collection today?"

I took my time chewing a bite and sipped my coffee before answering him. "I'm not going to finish it, Father." My voice was soft but steady, strong.

The briefest flash of sadness lit his eyes, and then it was gone as quickly as it came. He sighed and nodded. "I thought you might come to that conclusion one day."

"You did?"

"You did everything I asked and more, but your heart was never in it."

I was struck by his words and the fact that he'd known all along that I wasn't a jeweler, would never be, despite my competent skills. My eyes fell to the dark brew in my cup. "I can't do it," I said. "I can't peddle jewelry to those people. I'm not like Julien. He was charming and friendly, and everyone he met loved him. They wanted to buy from him. All those dreams he had about expanding the business… They aren't mine." I braced for a spike of pain and was surprised instead by the relief saying his name aloud brought.

"Your designs are wonderful, *chérie*," my father replied, trying one last time to convince me to stay, to work at his side.

"They're good, but they aren't great. You are the true talent, Papa. I am merely the office assistant and a great admirer of craftsmanship, nothing more. We both know that is true, however much we wished it weren't. I have tried to live your dream, but it isn't the right one for me."

He turned his cup round and round. "What will you do?"

I let out a breath, relieved he hadn't fought me or tried to persuade me to stay. "I'm going to apply for a position in the labs at the National Museum, through the Smithsonian Institution. They're looking for an assistant to the mineralogists. At least they were a few months ago. I'm hoping they still are, and if not, I'll apply to be an illustrator until there is another opening."

He reached for my hands, a smile brimming at his lips. "My daughter, a scientist! Imagine what she will learn and do and see."

I felt my eyes fill with tears for the hundredth time in as many days, but this time, they were tears of relief, tears of joy. "Thank you, Papa." I stood and kissed him on the forehead. "Now, I need to go. There is something I must do."

I traveled westbound toward the National Mall. Taking my time, I strolled along the verdant lawn, the Washington Monument rising high in the distance. At over five-hundred-fifty feet, the obelisk was the tallest building in the world for a few years, until the French erected the Eiffel Tower. Still, the monument spearing the Washington skyline was a marvel of engineering dedicated to America's first president and a symbol of democracy, and yet I'd never cared to visit it. There were far more interesting places, at least to me. I turned up the path leading to the National Museum, jittery with nerves.

I paused, allowing a memory to sweep me away for an instant to a summer afternoon after a picnic with my brother and Henry when we'd walked along the banks of the Potomac. I'd worn a pair of Julien's trousers rolled at the bottom and cinched tightly at the waist with a belt. We'd laughed as we told jokes and collected rocks. Henry and Julien had skipped the flat rocks across the top of the water. They'd teased me about my heavy collection, weighing down my pockets, and it had felt like we'd be in our blissful bubble of laughter and lazy days forever.

"Look at this one!" I said, finding a small piece of quartz with an irregular shape.

"You're as brainy as a scientist." Julien had thought he was teasing me, but I'd taken it as a compliment.

"You really think so?"

"All that note-taking that you do. And you spend more time with the magnifying glass than with any of us." He'd splashed me then, and I'd chased him, eventually smearing his face with mud. The three of us had devolved into a full-scale water and mud fight. By the time we'd made it home, we looked as if we'd been in a war.

Henry had given me a book about mineralogy that year for my birthday. The memory gave me courage as I looked up once more at the impressive museum facade. I inhaled a calming breath and walked through the door.

Julia Wane greeted me in the main hall with an encouraging smile. "I'm glad you've come. I wasn't sure how things would go with your father."

"He's happy for me," I said, all enthusiasm. "Should I get the job, he's going to hire someone to help him in the shop."

"That's wonderful," she said. "And you're going to get the job."

I bit my lip. "We'll see."

"Come, let me show you to the office where you'll be interviewing."

An hour later as I answered each question, identified numerous stones, and explained my passion for geological processes, the mineralogist took careful notes. When we'd finished, he shook my hand with a smile.

"It was truly a pleasure speaking with you, Elisabeth. I need to consult with the others, but I won't keep you in suspense. You're by far our best candidate. Give us a call on Monday morning, and we'll get you started with what's next."

As I descended the steps into the chill of a beautiful autumn day, my heart full, I knew exactly with whom I wanted to share the good news.

32

I walked the wide street beneath the chestnut trees, sunlight filtering through the golden leaves. As I entered the cemetery gates, the scent of damp decay mingled with woodsmoke. Under my arm, I carried a bouquet of yellow roses and a small pouch. When I reached his resting place, I crouched over his headstone and brushed away the crumpled leaves that covered his name. Removing my glove, I traced the grooves of the lettering. The granite was cold beneath my fingertips.

JULIEN BEAUMONT,

BELOVED SON AND BROTHER,

OUR DIAMOND IN THE ROUGH.

JUNE 7, 1890–NOVEMBER 23, 1918

I told him about Father and the shop, about confronting Carrie and making peace with her on my own, and also about the museum job. It had been a year to the day since he'd gone, and though I still couldn't believe it at times, I'd come to accept it.

"I miss you," I whispered at last, and as I said it, an image of him from our childhood filled my mind, of the sunlight glowing behind him, his bright smile, the warm look in his clear blue eyes as he threw his arm across my shoulders, and I knew in that instant he would never leave me. That he would be as proud of me as I was, as Father was, too. He wouldn't want me to stay frozen, without hope or direction, unable to follow the path that called to me. He'd want me to thrive.

I laid the roses on the slab of stone and removed the drawstring pouch from my handbag. After I opened it, I shook it slowly over the headstone. Diamond dust glittered as it fell. I kissed my fingertips and touched his name again, brushed an errant leaf from my skirt, and stood.

I wound through the cemetery, my heart a bit lighter. I would never stop missing my brother, never stop wondering what our lives could have been like together, the four of us, never stop lamenting what might have been. But I knew as long as I carried his memories inside me, I'd never be alone.

I took the tram to my neighborhood, my heart bursting with hope. As I walked the short block to the Coopers' home, I thought of Evalyn's face that night as I had left. Her crazed eyes, her grief, her hair standing on end as she chased me from the house, and I felt a deep current of empathy. To lose someone you loved more than yourself, in her case a child, could cripple you forever. I hoped it didn't. I hoped she would see her way through the grief one day and go back to throwing her magnificent parties. I couldn't imagine an Evalyn without fountains of champagne and outrageous games and extravagances no ordinary person would believe real.

I never returned to Friendship, never collected the last of the money owed to me, never again laid eyes on the Hope Diamond. Not only was I ashamed of what had transpired between Ned and me—something I'd never wanted—and the way it had destroyed the last shreds of the short-lived friendship with Evalyn, but I'd betrayed myself. Betrayed my heart. I didn't know what I was thinking those frenetic, absorbing, destructive three months, but I knew now, and that was all that mattered.

When I arrived at the Coopers' doorstep, I paused a moment to stare at the brass knocker in the center of the bright blue door. Would he be happy to see me? Would he see me at all? I'd avoided him for so long... Perhaps he had moved on, wanted nothing to do with the Beaumonts since I had abandoned him in addition to everything else. I only hoped Henry could once again see me—the girl and now the woman he had once loved and not the shell of a person I had been the last year—and forgive me.

His mother answered the door. She wore a housecoat, and her cheeks were flushed.

"Elisabeth, dear, are you all right? I'm afraid Mr. Cooper is ill, or I would have answered the door sooner."

"I'm sorry to hear Mr. Cooper is ill."

"It's nothing serious," she said dismissively. "You know how men are when they have a little sniffle. You'd think they've gone and contracted the plague." She chuckled at her own joke.

"Is Henry at home?" I asked, emotion welling in me like a swollen tide after a storm. I needed to see him, needed to explain.

"I'm afraid not, but I'll tell him you stopped by."

I felt my face drop, my shoulders sag. "Tell him I really need to speak with him, please?"

"Would you like to wait for him? He should be home within the hour."

I pictured myself in their comfortable living room on the flowered sofa, waiting, watching the grandfather clock tick, making small talk with Mrs. Cooper, and I shook my head. "It's fine. If he could telephone me or stop by the house when he arrives? That would be great."

"Of course, dear. I'd kiss you on the cheek, but better not so I don't pass off the cold."

"I hope Mr. Cooper recovers quickly. Goodbye, Mrs. Cooper."

She closed the door and, dejected, I turned toward home.

But I'd only passed three houses when a familiar lanky form came into view, a familiar head of auburn hair, a familiar stride that I had memorized.

Henry.

I strode toward him, picking up speed with each step. He picked up his pace in turn until we raced at each other and then stopped abruptly, only inches apart.

"What's happened?" he demanded, breathless.

"I'm through with it. I'm never going back there."

Confusion filled his eyes. "Where? Home? The workshop?"

I shook my head. "To the McLeans' or the others, for that matter. It's over. I've told my father I don't want to want to be a jeweler or a salesman anymore. I've applied for a job at the museum."

A cautious smile crossed his face. "That's wonderful. Congratulations."

"I've been a fool, Henry." I looked at him hopelessly, longing nearly choking me. I had to say it, to tell him how I felt. "I wish... I didn't know how to..."

But he knew already. He'd always known.

"Shh," he said, gently pressing a finger to my lips. "You haven't been a fool. You've been heartbroken, my love. We both have been. But you're here now."

My love.

He cupped my cheek a moment, gazing intently at me, and let his hand slide down my neck to my shoulder. I scarcely moved, unsure of how to respond. This beautiful man, whom I'd known nearly as long as I'd had a conscious thought in my head, loved me, wanted me at his side. I imagined what that meant, where we'd go from here. I imagined his lips on mine, the way they had been that one terrible, fateful night. Now the accident and what had happened between us that night was a thing of the past, my indecision and guilt a specter I had snuffed out at last, and suddenly I felt as if I were soaring above us, over the city, into the clouds looking down at a world of possibility.

I launched into his arms and buried my face in his neck, inhaling his scent. When I looked up at him, searching his dear face, joy brimmed in his gray eyes. He leaned over me, and his lips brushed mine. We stayed locked together until a motor car honked raucously as it drove by.

We drew apart, laughing. It felt good to laugh—I'd nearly forgotten how.

As he took my hand in his, I said, "Will you have lunch with me?"

"My love, I thought you'd never ask."

I smiled and we walked toward our favorite café, watching the sun pour over the rooftops, the pedestrians strolling by, and cars streaming around the bustle of Logan Circle before continuing on their way, as we continued on ours, together.

EPILOGUE

Though I never set foot in the house on McPherson Square or at Friendship again, I couldn't help but follow Evalyn and her friends in the papers through the years. They continued to live flamboyant lives filled with important people and nothing important at all. I'd heard it through the grapevine when Evalyn and Ned were divorced. Given the number of women he'd been with and the amount of alcohol he'd consumed, it was no surprise. And yet I'd felt a certain sadness for them, for all that was lost.

One chilly spring morning, I opened the papers, and there she was again, in the headlines.

"What are you reading?" Henry asked, bending over me to kiss my forehead. "Your face is scrunched."

"She's gone."

His eyebrows knit together in the way I'd grown to love. "Who?"

"Evalyn McLean. She passed away, of pneumonia."

"Oh, I'm sorry to hear that."

"Me too."

I couldn't imagine such a vivacious woman frail and on death's door. I'd seen her from a distance a few years back. She was driving and had pulled to a stop at a traffic light. She still wore her tightly curly hair in a tamed waving bob, but it was threaded with gray. She was wearing a hat, a large fur around her shoulders, and her gloved hands gripped the steering wheel. Her face was drawn and her eyes were directed ahead, far away, as if she were searching for something beyond the horizon. Her simple beauty was eroded by time and loss and disappointment, but the tilt of her chin somehow told me she was as vibrant as ever. Something about her endless vitality made me happy, made me feel young again.

I'd waved but she hadn't seen me, even as I'd stood on my tiptoes at the edge of the sidewalk, straining to catch her attention—straining to catch a glimpse of the Hope. When the traffic light had changed to green and the car had inched forward, I'd seen it. A glint, a flash of flint-blue at her neck before she'd sped away. As if spooked by the sight of a ghost, I'd rushed home. Evalyn, it seemed, still stubbornly believed her talisman brought her good luck, even if every sign pointed elsewhere.

I scanned the rest of the article. She'd passed away at sixty years old, predeceased by not one but two of her children, her parents, and her ex-husband. Ned had died in an asylum. Most of the McLeans' estate had been lost with their spending habits, and to pay the remainder of their debts, there was to be an auction of Evalyn's jewels, including the Hope Diamond.

I gasped. "They're going to auction the Hope Diamond!"

We exchanged a look. And I knew, without uttering a word, that Henry understood what I had to do.

The day of the auction, I put on my Sunday best and made my way to the auction house. The place was crowded with exactly the kind of people I'd expected: those from the elite circles I'd so gladly walked away from many years before, except these were a whole new set. The world had shifted, moved on, and there was a new stream of important people filling the vacancies of the rich and powerful just as eagerly. One face I did recognize. A jeweler fast becoming one of the most renowned in the country and around the world: Harry Winston.

The auctioneer called the crowd to order. "Next up, the lot of Evalyn Walsh McLean's jewelry, including the famed Star of the East and, of course, the Hope Diamond."

The crowd hushed.

The auctioneer rattled off the statistics about the incredible collection and decreed if there were no takers for the lot in its entirety, each piece would be auctioned off in due course.

"Sir." A gentleman raised his paddle. "Could you tell us more about the Hope Diamond?"

"Certainly."

The auctioneer returned to the Hope to describe its dimensions and its history, the audience rapt by his every word. While I listened, I found myself asking the question that had haunted me those years ago when I'd first stepped into Evalyn's world. Was the curse real? After the many misfortunes that befell Evalyn, her staff, and her friends, the deaths of her children and her husband, and, of course, Julien's death as well, I knew what I believed. I believed in possibilities.

At last, the auctioneer came to the part for which we'd all been waiting.

"It is said this rare blue diamond is cursed. Many believe it brings bad luck to all who own it and potentially all those who hold it, wear it, or"—he paused for effect—"even to those who merely look upon it."

The crowd gasped again.

I pictured Evalyn's face and her would-be delight in such a spectacle surrounding her beloved necklace and smiled.

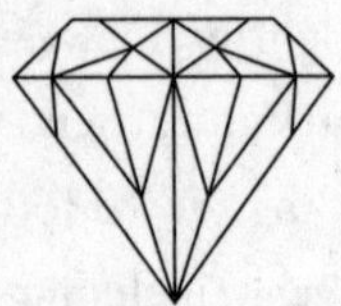

Evalyn flaunts my beauty for I am cherished. She wears me every day, and at night, guards protect me while I wait in a cold metal box, locked away until the sun rises and the day begins again. She claims she does not believe my story, but misfortunes surround her until she loses not one but two children. She, too, loses a husband. Like the keepers before her, she is frivolous, values little, and her estate declines until there is little left.

Her days flow away quickly, and when illness prevails, Evalyn is gone.

I am quickly seized again, kept locked away until one day I am retrieved and put on display before a crowd.

I dazzle them into reverent silence.

A man with a gavel announces my worth and sings a song of prices, but there is only one man who may keep me, for a time, like the others. I am awarded to Harry Winston, and Evalyn's debts are paid.

I tour the world with other gems of note, enchanting all who look upon my beauty. Mr. Winston tempts collectors and princes and the world's most revered to add me to their collection, but no one can afford me, and no one can afford the hidden cost I carry. My reputation, my story.

At last, I am sent to a grand building with a dome roof, its halls graced with natural wonders. And it is here where I reside, in the Hall of Gems, where anyone may delight in my beauty. But not all are pleased. Soon, letters pour in from all over the country, beseeching the Smithsonian Institution to release me, to sell me to a new keeper. For they do not want their country cursed or misfortune to befall anyone who gazes upon me.

Yet their pleas go unanswered, and for now, I remain.

I bide my time among the most unique stones in the world, and I wait. I wait for what comes next.

Perhaps you will see me, winking from my perch as I rotate beneath a bright white light, my facets glittering, capturing your imagination. But beware. Legends are a mix of lies and truths, and I am legendary. I may carry the darkness they claim. I may not.

Only you can decide.

AUTHOR'S NOTE

My fascination with the Hope Diamond began in middle school when my love for nature and science emerged for the first time in a real way. In part, I thank my teacher Mrs. Anderson at Franklin Elementary School in Tennessee for that. She was an incredibly kind, passionate, and intelligent woman who not only delighted in my love of rocks and trees and the planets but pushed me to achieve for myself and no one else. It's my dad, though, who taught me about the geography that makes up our world and the rocks therein. During that time, my collection of rocks grew—I still have many perfect and imperfectly beautiful specimens from those days and from my many adventures since—and I began to read about them, too. When not exploring, I was always reading. (Not much has changed!) It was in the pages of our hefty encyclopedia that I first discovered the Hope Diamond. Like many other legends I'd cherished reading and dreaming about, I knew I had to see the diamond in person one day. I'm happy to say I've had the chance. I've even had a few moments alone with it. One day during off-season on a terribly rainy day, I dashed inside the museum as it opened and found the magnificent Hope twirling beneath the bright gallery lights in all its glory. We may have even shared a secret.

FACT VERSUS FICTION

The legend of the Hope Diamond has inspired many stories and articles, especially those conveying falsehoods about its provenance and the winding path it traveled before it became part of a permanent collection at the National Museum of Natural History. In *The Hope Keeper*, I twine the legend with the facts, though I depart from the facts in only a very few instances where incorporating snippets of the legend added a bit of lovely intrigue. Should you be interested in reading more about the diamond's history, I urge you to check out the Smithsonian's website. They have an entire page dedicated to the Hope Diamond, deciphering fact from fiction, and more about Evalyn Walsh McLean as well as the gemstone's other owners. Additional research books that I enjoyed include *Hope Diamond: The Legendary History of a Cursed Gem* by Richard Kurin, *Jewels: A Secret History* by Victoria Finlay, and Evalyn's memoir co-written with Boyden Sparkes, *Father Struck It Rich.*

As in the novel, Evalyn Walsh McLean was well known in the political arena and among other influential circles. She was a good-time girl, as they say, always looking for the party, a thrill seeker, and a legendary spendthrift. She sent out thousands of invitations to her exuberant soirees and spent the kind of money on each event that would make your eyes water. Eventually her superfluous spending caught up with her, and in her later years, she was forced to part with many of her fine things, including the Hope Diamond, which she pawned several times only to repurchase it again. The diamond was truly her claim to fame, and there was nothing she loved more than being the center of attention.

Evalyn's love of attention led her to become the subject of many tabloids and the target not only for threatening letters but for swindlers. In fact, she was the center of a scheme in which a former FBI agent who was wanted for murder claimed he'd made a deal with the Lindbergh baby's kidnappers. He told Evalyn he needed an advance on the $100,000 for the bribe. Ever generous and concerned for the baby, Evalyn advanced the rogue the money only to discover he'd fled. In the end, she helped lead the police to him, resulting in his arrest and imprisonment. There was never a dull moment in the McLean household.

Despite Evalyn's enormous privilege, her emotional life wasn't an easy one. Along with her son Vinnie, she lost another of her children, her daughter named after her, young Evie, at the age of twenty-four. Evie overdosed on sleeping pills, and it was deemed an accident. Evalyn's husband, Ned, was another story entirely. Their marriage ended in an extremely contentious divorce that made headlines. Ned was a ne'er-do-well and a suspicious man who fully believed in bad luck, a trait not uncommon to gamblers. He sent Evalyn telegrams in code and hired a host of guards to follow their every move as well as detectives to handle the nefarious threats and letters they received almost daily for years. He practiced his own set of rules to encourage good luck for his nearly constant horse-racing bets. A womanizer struggling with various forms of addiction and increasingly erratic behavior, he was forced by the trustees of the *Washington Post* to sell the paper. Ultimately, he was court-ordered to be committed to an asylum where he died of a heart attack triggered by his alcoholism.

After Evalyn's death of pneumonia at the age of sixty, Harry Winston purchased her entire jewelry collection at auction and toured internationally with the Hope Diamond. Several years later, he donated the infamous necklace to the National Museum of Natural History in Washington, DC, where it joined a stunning collection of some of the world's rarest and most beautiful jewelry, rocks, and minerals in the popular Hall of Gems. The Star of the East, the magnificent pear-shaped diamond also mentioned in the book, disappeared sometime during the 1980s from Winston's collection and has never resurfaced.

Other characters who were true to life in the novel include Alice Roosevelt Longworth, Florence Harding, and Madame Marcia the fortune teller, who did predict President Harding's election and premature death. President Warren Harding died of a heart attack while in office, likely due to strain after discovering many of his support staff and other cronies were engaged in illegal activities. Mary Jane Rathbun, the crustacean scientist we meet briefly at the museum, was something of a real-life heroine. She worked from a young age and made such an impression gathering live specimens on the East Coast that she was hired as the first full-time paid female employee at the National Museum of Natural History. She was appointed second assistant curator of marine invertebrates in 1894.

The rest of the cast, including Elisabeth Beaumont and Carrie Wellington, are my own creation.

THE SMITHSONIAN INSTITUTION AND ITS WOMEN

The first library of the Smithsonian Institution was established in 1846, but the extensive system we know today was not established until 1968. Currently, the archives collections number nearly three million volumes, including fifty thousand rare books and manuscripts. Since its opening, women have been working as lab technicians, curators, assistants, illustrators, educators, preservationists, and in many other roles at the Smithsonian Institution. Unfortunately, much of their work went uncredited for decades, and more often than not, they were considered volunteers and did not earn a paycheck. This changed slowly over time as female contributions to society became more apparent and women's rights expanded. The Smithsonian Institution has never had a female at its head, and women have rarely been appointed to higher managerial levels throughout much of its more than 180-year history. Still, talented women have assumed important roles since the 1850s.

To say I enjoyed researching and writing this book is an understatement, as challenging as it was. As challenging as writing a work of fiction always is. Perhaps you, too, will visit the notorious and glorious Hope Diamond in person one day and fall in love with it as I have.

READ ON FOR A LOOK AT

QUEENS OF LONDON

BY HEATHER WEBB

Available now from Sourcebooks Landmark

1

Alice wiped her knife clean. Specks of blood dotted the snow-white handkerchief even after what she'd thought had been a good washing the previous night. The man who'd met the end of her blade was strong, but she'd nicked him well enough that he'd turned heel and run, the tosser. Another street brawl, another lout who thought he could disrespect one of her girls, and she'd shown him a lesson all right. She stowed her razor in the hidden pocket of her dress and headed to the kitchen for tea and a bite to start the day. Her mum was still in bed as usual, with her latest illness and weak lungs. Her brother loudly skulked around his bedroom, and her sisters were God-knew-where, but Dad was bent over his plate at the table. The only wretched member of the wretched Diamonds that Alice loved to hate and hated to love. Still, he was family.

Family first, above all else.

Alice had recited those words at her dad's insistence her whole life. If the family didn't rely on each other, they'd all be on the street, he'd say as he collected the earnings they'd made from emptying pockets, clearing out shelves, and swindling the gullible. And they nearly had been on the streets year after year, as he frittered away their income and landed himself in jail for picking fights with the wrong people.

Despite it all, Alice had never questioned her dad's motto. The family's proclivity for crime meant they must stick together, like it or not, and mostly, she didn't like it. She vastly preferred the family she'd made for herself: a certain group of friends—certain *associates*—who followed orders and watched her back rather than beat it with their fists the way her dad had most of her life. Her girls were the Forty Elephants, and she was their appointed queen. Commander. Woman in chief. Anyway, if they tried the malarkey that her dad got away with, she'd give them what for, and they knew it.

"What's the mark?" her dad asked, drowning his breakfast tea in milk. His hair was slicked back with almond oil, and a spray of salt-and-pepper whiskers swept over his jawline. His eyes were red-rimmed from too much gin the night before.

"You know I don't talk," Alice replied, taking a bit of buttered toast that had already started to go cold. She didn't share details with anyone but those involved in the scheme. It limited the chance for double-crossing.

She brushed the crumbs from her wool dress and set her dish in the sink.

"Watch it, girl," he replied. "You're getting a big 'ead. That's when mistakes 'appen."

She was glad the codger couldn't see her expression. These days, her jobs brought in far more quid than his did. More importantly, her jobs meant posh dance clubs, free-flowing gin and Irish whiskey, the fastest roadster on the streets, and beautiful clothes. For a short time, her winnings gave her freedom from the squalid life in which she was raised, elevated her above the muck and mire of London's darkest corners south of the Thames in the Elephant and Castle neighborhood. For every bolt of silk she cashed in, she transcended the grimy violence of her day-to-day and became someone different, someone with endless possibilities. At least until the money ran out—and the money always ran out. She wasn't the type who believed in saving just to take it to the grave.

Her brother pushed past her much faster than most could on a peg leg. He'd lost his leg in the Great War, shot clean off. Served him right, some would say. He'd been a bully his whole life and mostly a good-for-nothing stirring up trouble with the McDonald brothers, leaders of the Elephant and Castle gang. At war, his time came due. Tommy had always looked after her, though she was the eldest of eight and he, nearly three years younger. They'd been inseparable for a time. Wasn't much she wouldn't do for him or him for her.

Her brother placed a piece of bread in the turnover toaster, cranking the knob on the metal contraption that pushed the bread over a heating element until both sides were evenly cooked. When finished, he scraped a knife laden with butter across the surface and downed the nearly burned toast in a couple of bites. "You going out?"

"Nothing you need to concern yourself with," Alice replied. "But I'll see you later. At the pub."

"All right then."

All her brother needed to know right now was that she had a job. It was Friday, a day when the stores were swarmed with shoppers—and her girls' best day of the week to do their own *shopping*. Alice knew better than to hit a store in the early days of the week, when the shop-girls were bored and paired up with customers two-to-one.

Before she could leave, her dad grabbed her elbow. "You've had some wins, but you're headed for trouble with that attitude, you 'ear me?" He squeezed, his fingers digging into her flesh until she cried out. He may not be able to beat her senseless anymore—she was a grown woman, taller than most men, with large fists and a mind three times as quick—but he still had the ability to wound her.

"You underestimate me." She wrenched from his grasp. "And people see through you. That's how you always get caught."

He lunged for her, but she sidestepped his outstretched hand and headed for the door. "Don't wait up," she called over her shoulder. She snatched a brolly on the way out in case of rain.

He shouted expletives as Alice slammed the front door behind her.

A big head, my ass, she thought. He didn't know the meaning of humility except to dish it out to others. He'd never shown her mercy, not even as a little girl; he hadn't shown it to any of them. She and her siblings had collected impressive bruises over the years to prove it. Even the Lord Mayor of London had permanent scars on his face after a meeting with her combustible dad.

Outside, the scent of rain lingered in the air, and a bank of clouds hung low and so thick that not a single shard of sunlight pierced them. Good thing she'd come prepared. She walked purposefully to her car, not losing pace as a rat scurried across her path before disappearing beneath a stack of abandoned crates. She'd grown up with them scampering through her flat—the nasty creatures were practically her siblings. She'd suffered their sharp teeth far too many times. Truth be told, she was lucky she still had all her fingers.

She opened the door to her shiny black Chrysler and slid into the driver's seat. She smiled as the smell of new leather rushed her senses. Nothing beat the smell of money. She drove across the borough, parked her car in the street, and strode to a shuttered munitions factory. These days, the old factory served as a meeting place for the Forty Elephants. It was quiet, abandoned, and not a place the coppers spent much time patrolling, though she and the girls had fended off squatters a little too often. Still, it was a decent location, despite the grit and grime that blanketeted every nook and cranny.

She wound through the musty dark around broken machinery that had begun to rust from the perpetual damp air that seeped through the building's cracks and shattered windows. When she reached the back office, the Forty Elephants were already gathering, seating themselves around the table.

They were waiting for her, as they should be.

Alice took her role as leader of the oldest and strongest all-women crime syndicate very seriously. The Forty Elephants had been around since before Queen Victoria's days, though they'd never been properly organized until Mary Carr had come along as the first queen. When Mary passed away, Alice had taken over, made the gang stronger, larger, and taught them both the art of the con and how to use a knife when the circumstances called for it. The circumstances almost always called for it.

Maggie, one of Alice's best girls and closest friends, gave a short wave as Alice entered the office. Baby-faced Maggie looked youthful with her round face and blond curls and the fact that she barely reached five feet in height. Her appearance fooled people; Alice had never met another woman as good with a blade as Maggie was. Her friend also had the foulest temper in London. On occasion, her hot head got them into trouble, especially when she'd been drinking, and drinking was Maggie's favorite pastime.

"Hiya, girls," Alice said. "Are we ready for a big day?"

The Forties whistled and clapped.

"That's what I like to hear. Enthusiasm," she said. "If all goes well today, we should bring in enough for new frocks and a nice night out."

Her words were met with more cheering.

Before listing the jobs of who would do what that afternoon, Alice quickly scanned the room, making sure everyone was present. Maggie and Scully, June, Marie, and Lily Rose. Sherry and Bertha and the other fifteen girls were also present. One face was markedly absent: Ruth.

She'd been out a lot lately, either sick or with injuries. With Ruth in and out, Marie's recent flightiness, and Lily Rose's obsession with the new boyfriend who kept trying to lure her out of the gang, Alice thought it might be time to remind them all how lucky they were to be counted among her esteemed band of hoisters.

"It's time we had a little chat about loyalty."

All eyes were trained on her, expectant.

"Who helps you put food on the table?" Alice asked.

"The Forty Elephants," several said in unison.

"Who has your back when your sweetheart leaves you in the cold?"

"The Forty Elephants!" Their enthusiasm grew.

"When you're in trouble or you need someone to do your dirty work?"

"The Forty Elephants!"

"That's right, ladies," Alice said. "Loyalty. And if you don't know who you pledge your loyalty to, you don't belong here. You turn your back on us, we turn our back on you—and leave you with a lasting mark you'll never forget."

The women whistled and pounded on the table.

Alice silenced them with one wave of her hand. "Your loyalty to us and to me must be absolute, or we all go down. Your mistakes become ours. We work together as one, you hear me?"

More cheering.

She paused to let her words sink in. She didn't like doling out punishment to her own. In truth, it always left her a bit sick to the stomach, but it had to be done. Being a leader wasn't an easy thing, and the rules—and consequences—that she enforced were always for the good of their vetted cocoon of thieves. Gangland wasn't safe without a system, without rules. And her rules were simple. First, sell all items that were hoisted; showing up in last week's frock was the perfect way to get nicked by a copper. Second, wear their Sunday best to a job to throw the clerks off their scent. Looking like a washerwoman was a sure sign they didn't have the cash to buy posh clothes in posh stores. Third, never ever take up with a man outside their ring of associates without Alice's seal of approval. Finally, one of Alice's personal rules and a code she'd always lived by: help any woman in serious need, as long as it didn't put the other Forties at risk.

Still, loyalty mattered most of all.

The office door flew open and banged closed, and a flustered Ruth dashed inside. "Sorry I'm late." She slipped into a seat gingerly, as if it pained her to move.

"Look who's late again." Lily Rose rolled her eyes.

"What was it this time?" Alice asked, though she already knew the answer. Ruth was boarding with her wanker of a boyfriend these days, and they were seeing a lot less of her. "Don't tell me it's bloody Mike again." Alice looked more closely at her then. "Jesus, that shiner from him?"

Ruth looked down at her hands in her lap. "Mike came home from the gin house pissed as usual, after God knows how many pours. Angry as a lion, too." She sniffed, wouldn't meet anyone's eye.

"Let's have a look." Alice bent over Ruth, gently lifting her chin to examine her left eye. It was swollen shut and big as an orange.

"I think he's broken a couple of ribs, too," Ruth said, wincing.

Alice shook her head. "He's going to keep at it, you know. When are you going to leave him?"

"My brother is single," June offered.

"Your brother looks like he was dragged behind the back of a wagon," Maggie piped up.

"Too true," June agreed.

The titter of laughter eased the tension.

Ruth shrugged. "I–I don't know. I love him."

"Well, he clearly loves you, too," Alice snapped. She'd like to say she didn't understand it, why Ruth stuck around while he beat her senseless, but she did. Her own father had taught her what a man's love looked like: all fists and words that cut twice as deeply.

"I don't know what to do," Ruth said, tears streaking from her healthy eye down her cheek. "If I try to leave him, he may try to kill me."

Alice's anger gathered like a storm cloud. Her girls deserved better than this, but she couldn't very well force Ruth to leave Mike. Alice could hire an Elephant and Castle man to protect Ruth for a little while. Problem was Mike was one of the gang, too, so that wouldn't be the best option.

"I seem to do things wrong all the time, so he punishes me," Ruth continued. "I guess I'm too dense to learn how to please him."

"You aren't dense, Ruth, and for Christ's sake, you don't need to be punished," she said. "You've done nothing wrong."

"At least I yelled back," Ruth replied, sniffing.

"As was your right."

"What time is it? I can't stay long." Ruth's eyes filled with fear. "If he wakes and I'm not there, he'll be spitting mad." She looked like a small, frightened bird.

Alice bit her tongue. She didn't know when Ruth had become less herself, had shrunk so small that she'd become this shell of a person, especially since she had all the backup she needed with the Forty Elephants. But nothing Alice could say would dissuade Ruth, and with the woman's broken ribs and black eye, she was bloody useless for the shopping they were going to do in a few hours anyway.

"Fine," Alice said. "But you're on the next job."

Ruth nodded and shuffled carefully across the room to the door.

After she'd gone, Alice assigned the girls their posts for the day's shopping trip. When they'd all left, she stayed behind a moment, thinking, feeling some semblance of guilt, an emotion she scarcely recognized let alone experienced. Ruth was a grown woman. She made her own choices, and yet Alice couldn't help feeling like she was somehow responsible for the woman's safety. She was the queen of the Forties after all, and her girls' business was her business. They counted on her. She offered them a better life than the worst of the slums where they'd come from, a life of good times and finer things.

But for the first time, Alice wondered if what she was offering them was enough and, more importantly, if she was doing her job as leader of England's most notorious female gang. As she walked to her car, unease slid over her skin like the encroaching fog.

READ ON FOR A LOOK AT

THE NEXT SHIP HOME

BY HEATHER WEBB

Available now from Sourcebooks Landmark

1

Crossing the Atlantic in winter wasn't the best choice, but it was the only one. For days, the steamship had cowered beneath a glaring sky and tossed on rough seas as if the large vessel weighed little. Francesca gripped the railing to steady herself. Winds tore at her clothing and punished her bare cheeks, reminding her how small she was, how insignificant her life. It was worth it, to brave the elements for as long as she could stand them. Being out of doors meant clean, bright air to banish the disease from her lungs and scrub away the rank odors clinging to her clothes.

Too many of the six hundred passengers belowdecks had become sick. She tried not to focus on the desperate ones, clutching their meager belongings and praying Hail Marys in strained whispers. She wasn't like them, she told herself, even while her body betrayed her and she trembled more each day as they sailed farther from Napoli. Yet despite the unknown that lay ahead, she would rather die than turn back. As the ship slammed against wave after unruly wave, she thought she might die after all, drift to the bottom of a fathomless dark sea.

She couldn't believe she'd done it—left Sicilia, her home, and all she'd ever known. It had taken every ounce of her courage, but she and Maria had managed to break free. Dear, fragile Maria. Swallowing hard,

Francesca looked out at the vast tumult of water and pushed a terrible thought far from her mind. Maria would recover. She had to. Francesca refused to imagine life without her sister.

She tucked her hands under her arms for warmth. Everywhere she looked, her gaze met gray, a slippery color that shimmered silver and foamed with whitecaps or gathered into charcoal clouds. Already she longed for the wide expanse of sea surrounding her island home in a perfect blue-green embrace, the rainbow of purples and oranges that streaked the sunset sky, the craggy landscape, the scent of citrus and sunshine. She wrapped her arms around her middle, holding herself as if she might break apart. Reminiscing about what she once cherished was foolish. Somehow, she had to find things to like about New York.

Freedom from him, if nothing else.

She would never again meet the fists of her drunken papa. At the memory of his bulging eyes and the way his face flowered purple, she rubbed the bruise on her arm that had not quite healed. She would no longer spend her days stealing so he might buy another bottle of Amaro Averna or some other liquor. Paolo Ricci could do it himself. He could tumble from his fishing boat into the sea for all she cared.

A shiver ran over her skin and rattled her teeth. Like it or not, it was time to go belowdecks. As she weaved through the brave souls who paid no heed to the wind despite the cost to warmth, she wondered briefly if any first- or second-class passengers had defied the cold on the upper-class decks overhead. The ship was tiered and divided into three platforms; the two above her were smaller and set back so a curious lady or gentleman might lean over the railing and peer down at steerage. As if they were a circus of exotic animals.

Francesca descended the ladder into the bowels of the ship. The air thickened into a haze of stink and rot, and the clamor of hundreds of voices floated through the cramped corridors until she arrived at the large room designated for women only. She passed row upon row of metal cots stacked atop each other, filled with strangers. Some women lounged on the floor in their threadbare dresses and boots with heels worn to the quick. Their eyes were haunted, their wan figures gaunt with hunger. One woman scratched at an open sore; another smelled of urine and sweat and squatted against the wall of the ship with a rosary in hand, pausing briefly in her prayer to swipe at a rat with greasy fur, driven by hunger, the same as her. The same as they all were.

Francesca tried not to linger on their faces and moved through the room to her sister, who lay prostrate on her cot, and reached for her hand.

"You're so cold," Maria said through cracked lips, clutching her sister's hand. "You'll catch your death, Cesca. Promise me you'll be careful."

Heart in her throat, Francesca swept her sister's matted curls from her face. Death was not a word she wanted to entertain. The terror they'd harbored since they'd sneaked away from their home in the middle of the night, that overwhelmed her each time she considered the unknown before them, was bad enough. Death had no place here.

"Nothing can catch me now. We're too close."

Maria smiled and a glimpse of her cheerful nature shone in her dark eyes. "That hard head serves you at last."

Francesca forced a smile, desperate to hide the concern from her face. Maria had always been frail, easily ill and quickly bruised, yet still she glowed with some internal light. Often, Francesca imagined her as a fairy, an angelic creature not of this earth. She laid a hand on Maria's brow. Her skin burned with fever, and sweat soaked through her gown. Maria had fallen ill on the first leg of their voyage from Palermo to Napoli and had worsened each day since. Francesca had worried the captain wouldn't allow them to board, but she and Maria had passed the inspection rapidly—after Francesca paid an unspoken price in a back room on a narrow cot. But they were on their way, and that was what mattered now.

"Another few days, Maria," she whispered. After five days at sea, New York Harbor must be close. Once they arrived, they would need to find a doctor to tend to the fever immediately.

Maria moaned and turned on her side, her shoulder nearly scraping the underside of the woman's cot suspended above hers. "I'm so thirsty."

Francesca was thirsty, too. Their water rations had scarcely been sufficient, or their food for that matter. What did the crew care about a pack of hungry, dirty foreigners? They saw so many, week after week. Desperation was nothing new to them.

Francesca turned over her water canister in her hands. No one would part with their rations; she'd asked passengers in steerage all day yesterday and had finally given up. Poverty didn't move them or the story of her very ill sister. Each had their own story of woe. And it was out of the question to approach second- or third-class passengers. A guard stood at each of the doors connected to the upper levels to keep the wanderers out.

Unless... An idea sparked suddenly in the back of her mind.

"I'm going to find more water." She pulled the blanket around Maria's shoulders. "Don't try to get up again. You need to rest."

Francesca rummaged through their small travel case for the only nice things she owned. She pulled on her mother's finest dress, fastened on a pair of earbobs, slipped a set of combs into her hair, and kissed the medallion of the Virgin Mary around her neck. The medallion she had stolen two years ago.

For months, she had admired the shiny golden trinket as it winked from the hollow at the base of Sister Alberta's neck. It was the first time

Francesca had felt the sharp edge of envy. A rush of shame soon followed. She loved the nun like family, and Francesca knew it was a sin to want what wasn't hers. One day when Sister sent her to fetch a book, Francesca found the necklace gleaming in a bright ray of sunlight that streaked across Sister's dressing table. She'd held it a moment, stroking the outline of the Virgin Mother with her thumb, wishing she'd had the medallion's protection. She'd been unable to resist it and slipped it inside the folds of her dress. It wasn't until the following day that she wondered why Sister had sent her to look for a book that wasn't there. Perhaps it had been a test—a test Francesca had failed.

Francesca's chest tightened as she thought of the nun. Sister Alberta was a Catholic in exile, though she'd never explained why, and had lived two lanes away from Francesca and Maria in their little village. The nun had befriended them when their mother disappeared, taught Francesca to cook and both sisters to read and even speak a little English. Sister had loved them.

"You putting on airs for someone?" said Adriana, an Italian woman from Roma. She wore thick rouge, and though she was traveling in steerage, her dress looked finer than those of the other women with its lace trim and shiny beading. It was also vivid purple. All the better to attract male attention.

"I need more water." Francesca's gaze flicked to her sister and back to the woman she was certain traded lire for sex. Not that Francesca minded. She wasn't bothered by other people's choices, especially when it came to survival. God must understand need when he saw it, if he was truly a benevolent God.

Adriana crossed her arms beneath her bosom. "Plan on flirting with the captain for it?"

Francesca snapped the compact closed. "I'm going to the upper decks, see if someone will spare some."

Or perhaps she would just take their water. She was good at that, taking things.

"Better work it harder, *amore,* if you want to fit in with that lot." A woman with no front teeth rose from her bed and dug through a handbag tucked beneath her pillow. "Here. Have some of this." She held out an elegant bottle of perfume.

Francesca felt a rush of gratitude. She reached for the bottle and dabbed her neck and wrists.

"I've got some rouge, too." Adriana produced a small tub. "You'll have better luck with the guards this way."

Another cabin mate watched them quietly, pushed up from her bunk, and took something out of a bag she'd been using as a pillow. "It was my *nonna*'s." She clutched a cashmere shawl to her chest. It didn't look new, but it had been well cared for and could still pass for acceptable among the upper class, at least Francesca hoped. "The gray will be pretty with your eyes," the woman continued. "Please, be careful with it."

Francesca hardly knew them, yet they lent their most precious belongings to help her. An unspoken sense of unity hung in the air. Tired of suffering, they'd all left their homes behind and hoped for better times ahead.

"I...I don't know how to thank you all," she stammered as a swell of emotion clogged her throat.

"Show those *puttanas* they aren't better than us," Adriana said, winking.

At that, Francesca smiled.

She blew her cabin mates a kiss to whistles and cheers. Holding her head high, she threaded through the narrow hallway, wound through a room filled with barrels and clusters of steamer trunks, and passed a huddled group of passengers playing card games. She approached the ladder leading to the second-class deck quickly, before she could change her mind, and ascended it.

And there, at the end of the next passageway, a crewman stood guard.

When he spotted her, he stepped to the right and crossed his arms, blocking the entrance.

She clasped her hands together like a lady should, stretched her five-foot, three-inch frame to full height, and, ignoring the thundering in her ears, marched toward the guard.

He stood stiffly in a navy uniform, the name "Forrester" stitched across his breast pocket in yellow thread. "I can't let you through, miss. There's no steerage allowed here."

Her stomach tightened, but she forced a smile. "Excuse me, Mr. Forrester, I am second class. I have friend in steerage. I visit her but now I return."

The wiry seaman peered at her, his gaze traveling over her worn shoes and dress.

Nervously, she dug her thumbnail into the flesh of her index finger, willing herself to remain calm.

"Second class, you say?" His eyes rested on her rouged lips.

"Yes. Excuse me," she said, her tone clipped as if she were insulted.

He stared at her for a long, uncomfortable minute. At last, he angled his body away from her, leaving just enough room so her body would brush against his in an intimate way.

She pushed past him, ignoring his groping hands, his breath on her cheek. Too relieved to be annoyed by his behavior, Francesca darted quickly down the narrow corridor. At the first door, she peered through a small oval window. The room was crowded with luggage. She continued forward, pausing at each window, becoming more anxious as she went. When she came upon the dining saloon, she found the door locked and the room empty. Though the evening meal wouldn't be served for another couple of hours, she'd hoped the room might be open for late-afternoon tea or libations. It must be the first class who were offered such luxuries. She huffed out an irritated breath and continued down the narrow corridor.

Ahead, she saw a young woman wearing a pale-blue frock with a fashionable bustle and a wide-brimmed hat trimmed with ribbons. She was prettily dressed, her frock likely one of a series that she rotated every other week, something Francesca aspired to have one day soon. As she neared the woman, the scent of roses drifted around them and filled the cramped space. Francesca met the woman's eye briefly and nodded, even as she stared back at Francesca like she were diseased.

Ignoring the uncomfortable exchange, Francesca continued to the end of the corridor to the last room before the cabins began. It was a storage room filled with barrels and shelves of foodstuffs. It, too, was locked.

She leaned against the door. Of course it was locked. They wanted to prevent thieves from pilfering goods—thieves like her. Sister Alberta's lectures about letting God provide rang in her ears. Yet had Francesca let God provide, she would have starved to death on more than one occasion. Had she let Him provide shelter and comfort, she would have suffered broken bones at her father's hand for many more years. God gave her plenty of free will, and with it, she chose to provide for herself. Only she wasn't doing that so well either.

She fought back tears. Maria needed water desperately. Could Francesca risk it, try first class? It would probably turn out the same, but she had to try. Fists clenched, she pushed back from the door. She weaved around several male passengers and a woman in a striped dress, pausing to ask them for water, but they first looked annoyed and then ignored her. When she reached the first-class deck, another steward stood watch at the top of the landing.

"You there!" He pointed at her. "You aren't allowed here."

Concentrating, she searched for the words Sister Alberta had taught her.

I need, You need, He needs, We need...

"I need..." she began tentatively. "You need Forrester." She shook her head. "Forrester needs you. The captain is angry."

The guard squinted. "What for?"

"The captain is angry," she repeated, willing her pulse to slow. "You go now."

"Nice try, miss, but I ain't leaving my post. Now be on your way."

"I—"

The door behind him swung open, and a shrill voice cut the air. "Boy! I need your help at once!" A middle-aged woman draped in furs glared at him with expectation.

The guard's scowl gave way to one of feigned interest. "How can I help you, madam?"

"The linens on my table are filthy, and I want them changed immediately. That poor excuse for a waitstaff is ignoring me entirely, and I won't have it."

"I'm sure they'll be with you soon, madam."

"You would have me stand in the middle of the room while others are being tended to until someone *decides* to help me?" she shrieked.

"Of course not, madam," he said quickly, realizing his mistake.

As he darted after her, Francesca's knees went weak with relief. With haste, she followed them at a short distance to the dining saloon, but as the wealthy came into view in their elegant silks and jewels, her footsteps faltered. If the fashionable women she'd seen in second class had been intimidating, these women felt otherworldly as they sparkled in diamonds and bright red and blue stones, smiling and floating around the room with unimaginable grace.

What was she doing here? In that instant, she realized how completely ridiculous she appeared in her borrowed shawl and rouge, her modest earbobs and combs. She could never pass for first class. Not ever.

But as Maria's dear face flashed in her mind's eye and Sister Alberta's voice echoed in her ears, Francesca remembered what she must do. How far she'd already come.

"Time to be brave, Cesca." She whispered Sister Alberta's words the day they had departed Sicilia.

Ignoring the bold stare of a lady dressed in cornflower-blue silk, Francesca followed the others inside the dining saloon.

Rows of tables dressed in elegant linens fanned around a center point in the room where a grove of potted trees made the space more welcoming with their lush greens. Above, the ceiling formed a dome of glass panels edged with shiny bronze. Francesca imagined sunrays streaming through the milky glass on nicer days, spilling over the crystal goblets and water carafes, and making them sparkle like diamonds. The dining room couldn't be more different from the dark hole crammed with unwashed bodies where she spent her days.

The startling contrast between what her life was and what it could be had she been born in a different world held her there, transfixed.

READING GROUP GUIDE

1. Why do you think the author included scenes from the Hope Diamond's perspective? What do they add to the narrative?

2. Do you believe in curses? What would you do if you thought you'd been cursed?

3. How is Elisabeth different from Evalyn's crowd? Compare their manners, mores, lifestyles, etc.

4. Peer pressure is a dominant theme in the novel. How does Evalyn use her power and influence to draw Elisabeth in, and how does Elisabeth change due to that influence (whether she wants to or not)?

5. Consider Elisabeth's relationship with her father. How does he put pressure on her, and how does he support her?

6. At first, Elisabeth keeps her relations with the McLeans a secret from her father. Do you believe this was the correct decision? When do you believe it is right to keep a secret, and when should

you be outright and honest?

7. From what you can discern about Julien's character, describe Elisabeth's relationship with her brother.

8. Do you believe Elisabeth handles her grief about her brother in a healthy way? How is her grief affected by her guilt?

9. What makes Elisabeth realize the life of a jeweler isn't for her? Why is it difficult for her to change her career path? Have you ever wanted to make a big change like that in your life? If so, what challenges did you face?

10. How does Elisabeth change throughout the course of the novel? How does her relationship with her father, her friends, and Henry also change?

11. What challenges did women face in the workplace in the early 1900s? In what ways are these challenges similar to what women face today? In what ways do they differ?

12. Have you ever visited the National Museum of Natural History in Washington, DC? Do you have a favorite museum you like to visit?

13. Would you consider yourself someone who prefers studying and learning over creating or vice versa? Do you believe these are two separate fields, or can they be combined?

A CONVERSATION WITH THE AUTHOR

What was the inspiration for this novel?

I've been fascinated with the Hope Diamond since I was a kid. Something about its size and beauty and, of course the biggest draw of all, the idea of a curse roped me in! As my rock collection and master's degree in geography can attest, I've been a lover of the natural world and the stones that are both the ground beneath our feet and an instrument of beauty my whole life. When I started thinking about a book about the Hope Diamond, I kicked around a few different ideas. I even wrote a hundred pages of a different idea entirely and decided it wasn't the best direction. That idea withered away after sitting in a file for a few years, and then I was in Washington, DC, for other research and stopped by the National Museum of Natural History and there she was, that vivid, stunning diamond glittering in all her glory. A new idea came to me within days after seeing it again.

What is your writing process like?

It really depends on the book. If the book focuses on a particular event in history, I start with plot and setting and, from there, develop a fictional character that would be the most challenged within the context of that story. If I'm writing biographical fiction (like *Strangers in the Night*), I begin with the character and really delve into the details of their lives and expand into layering the themes from there. As for setting, I often think of the world in which my characters live as a character as well, one that lives and breathes and feels very immersive. I really enjoy digging into that aspect of writing.

Once I have an idea in mind, I do what I like to call "front-loading" my research. I stock up on loads of great resource materials and create both a historical outline and a character map for my main characters. From there, I write a synopsis of the story and then get writing! Somewhere in the writing process, I do my best to travel to any relevant locations in the novel. It really helps me build a sensory world for my readers when I can experience a place.

What went into the decision behind writing from the Hope Diamond's perspective? How did you approach that?

I didn't set out to add the Hope Diamond's perspective when I began the pre-writing and plotting. In fact, I thought I might write the book as a dual timeline. The dual timeline wasn't quite working though, as it was weighing the story down and slowing the pace too much. After I cut the past timeline, I started playing around with other literary devices. I honestly don't know when the diamond's point of view really struck me, but I thought, why don't I see how it feels? I loved it immediately. It was so fun writing from the perspective of an infamous, yet inanimate, object, and it brought with it the added bonus of more bits of the diamond's legend and history.

Do you have a favorite character from the novel? A favorite scene?

Oh, my favorite character has to be Elisabeth! She's brilliant but aching and lost, and her grief is so overwhelming... I think we can all relate to her on some level. On the other hand, I also love Evalyn! I like a character that's complex, far from perfect, and fascinating, often a bit wild, even if they aren't particularly likable, and Evalyn is all these things.

What would you like readers to take away from Elisabeth's story?

I'd like for them to be intrigued by the Hope Diamond and its history, to want to visit it one day at the museum. Perhaps, too, they might become interested in learning more about women working at the Smithsonian Institution, the many fascinating gemstones and minerals with which our wide and incredible planet is built, and also the fine craft of jewelry making as an art form. I'd also like for readers to consider the way grief shapes who we are and how it can hold us back but also present opportunities for growth if we let it.

Acknowledgments

As always, I'm ever grateful for my star agent, Michelle Brower, who is my shepherd through the challenges of the publishing world. I'd like to offer a hearty thanks to my wonderful editor, Shana Drehs, and also Liv Turner, for helping me create the story I wanted to tell. I'd also like to extend my gratitude to the copy editors, publicity team, and marketing team, especially Molly Waxman, for delivering a beautiful package to my readers. Thank you, thank you, thank you for making my books possible.

To my critique partners and dear friends Kris Waldherr, Julianne Douglas, Kerry Schafer, and Eliza Knight, you make me a better writer and a better person. I adore you all. And as always, my dear family and friends, your belief in me and support of my stories mean more than you'll ever know.

To my readers, reviewers, and the many wonderful librarians and booksellers who champion my books, thank you from the bottom of my heart. You are my people.

ABOUT THE AUTHOR

Heather Webb is the *USA Today* and international bestselling author of historical fiction, including her most recent: *Queens of London, The Next Ship Home,* and *Christmas with the Queen.* In 2015, *Rodin's Lover* was a Goodreads Top Pick, and in 2018, *Last Christmas in Paris* won the Women's Fiction Writers Association STAR Award. *Meet Me in Monaco* was selected as a finalist for the 2020 Goldsboro RNA Award in the UK, as well as the 2019 Digital Book World's Fiction prize. *Three Words for Goodbye* was a *Prima* Magazine's 2022 Book of the Year. To date, Heather's books have been translated into twenty languages. She lives in New England with her family and two mischievous cats.

QUEENS OF LONDON

Maybe women *can* have it all, as long as they're willing to steal it

1925. London. When Alice Diamond, a.k.a. Diamond Annie, is elected the Queen of the Forty Elephants, she's determined to take the all-girl gang to new heights. She's ambitious, tough as nails, and a brilliant mastermind, with a plan to create a dynasty the likes of which no one has ever seen. Alice demands absolute loyalty from her "family"—it's how she's always kept the cops in line. Too bad she's now the target for one of Britain's first female policewomen.

Officer Lilian Wyles isn't merely one of the first female detectives at Scotland Yard; she's one of the best detectives on the force. Even so, she'll have to win a big score to prove herself, to break free from the "women's work" she's been assigned. When she hears about the large-scale heist in the works to fund Alice's new dynasty, she realizes she has the chance she's been looking for—and the added bonus of putting Diamond Annie out of business permanently.

A tale of dark glamour and sisterhood, *Queens of London* is a look at Britain's first female crime syndicate, the ever-shifting meaning of justice, and the way women claim their power by any means necessary, from *USA Today* bestselling author Heather Webb.

"Gritty at times and tender at others, Queens of London *unmasks the most lawless—and likable—gang of women you've never heard of."*

—Sarah Penner, *New York Times* bestselling author of *The Lost Apothecary*

THE NEXT SHIP HOME

Ellis Island, 1902

Ellis Island, 1902: Two women band together to hold America to its promise: "Give me your tired, your poor. . .your huddled masses yearning to breathe free. . ."

A young Italian woman arrives on the shores of America, her sights set on a better life. That same day, a young American woman reports to her first day of work at the immigration center. But Ellis Island isn't a refuge for Francesca or Alma, not when ships depart every day with those who are refused entry to the country and when corruption ripples through every corridor. While Francesca resorts to desperate measures to ensure she will make it off the island, Alma fights for her dream of becoming a translator, even as women are denied the chance.

As the two women face the misdeeds of a system known to manipulate and abuse immigrants searching for new hope in America, they form an unlikely friendship—and share a terrible secret—altering their fates and the lives of the immigrants who come after them.

This is a novel of the dark secrets of Ellis Island, when entry to "the land of the free" promised a better life but often delivered something drastically different, and when immigrant strength and female friendship found ways to triumph even on the darkest days.

"An unflinching look at the immigrant experience, an unlikely and unique friendship, and a resonant story of female empowerment."

—Pam Jenoff, *New York Times* bestselling author of *The Woman with the Blue Star*

For more Heather Webb, visit: sourcebooks.com